The Towpath

A Time Travel Suspense Thriller

The Towpath

A Time Travel Suspense Thriller

Jonathan David Walter

ROUNDFIRE
BOOKS

London, UK
Washington, DC, USA

CollectiveInk

First published by Roundfire Books, 2024
Roundfire Books is an imprint of Collective Ink Ltd.,
Unit 11, Shepperton House, 89 Shepperton Road, London, N1 3DF
office@collectiveink.com
www.collectiveink.com
www.roundfire-books.com

For distributor details and how to order please visit the 'Ordering' section on our website.

Text copyright: Jonathan David Walter 2023

ISBN: 978 1 80341 634 2
978 1 80341 642 7 (ebook)
Library of Congress Control Number: 2023944022

A CIP catalogue record for this book is available from the British Library.

Design: Lapiz Digital Services

UK: Printed and bound by CPI Group (UK) Ltd, Croydon, CR0 4YY
Printed in North America by CPI GPS partners

We operate a distinctive and ethical publishing philosophy in all areas of our business, from our global network of authors to production and worldwide distribution.

To my wife, Rebecca, for supporting her crazy husband's pursuit of his dream.

To my sons, Nathan and Wesley, for inspiring that dream.

Time flies over us, but leaves its shadow behind.
— **Nathaniel Hawthorne**

Chapter 1

The Losing Side

Former Land of the Erielhonan, Date Unknown

The Redeemer didn't belong, and the horse knew it. The animal shied at her approach, its dark eyes rolling. The Redeemer stepped to the horse's hindquarters, bent, and ran the bowie knife's serrated edge across the tendons of its rear left leg. With a whinny, the horse threw its head back and tugged at the restraining rope.

The Redeemer didn't have time for remorse or hesitation, not with the lantern already tied around the animal's neck, the flame capering about within. The vessel would be here soon, the summer storm over Lake Erie on its heels. She cut the rope with the knife, stepped aside, and slapped the horse's hindquarters with the flat of the blade. It hobbled down the beach.

She glanced into the deepening dark, willing her eyes to adjust. The boat emerging from around the rocky outcropping was barely visible, a dark shape caught in the gloom like a splinter. She couldn't gauge its distance without the moon and stars for illumination. But that didn't matter. The lack of light was to her advantage, not theirs. They'd see the bobbing lantern light slowly moving through the dark.

Eventually, the profile of the vessel became narrower, its prow coming about to face the inlet. The jouncing light was drawing them in.

That's it. Keep coming. That's not a horse with a lantern you see, that's another vessel. You have room to come closer to shore.

Putting her knife between her teeth, she dropped to all fours and crawled up the embankment toward the swaying trees. Arriving in the scrub grass at the tree line, she sank to her haunches. It was getting closer, perhaps two-thousand feet offshore. Given the speed of its approach, there'd be no going back now. She waited.

Noises interrupted the rhythm of the crashing waves. Shouts. Men. *Distressed* men. Their vessel grounded on the shoals.

She turned to the trees and whistled. Moments later, soft footfalls. Some came with spears, others with war clubs, others with bows and arrows. None with remorse. Some followed in pairs, portaging canoes with paddles, to go get what was *hers*.

More wheezing and rustling in the brush, and then they were standing before her, seventeen wolves poised for their soon-to-be prey. She surveyed their dark shapes, which she knew were bare-chested and painted. Hardened by many battles. Faces handsome and angular, like the flint arrows they bore. Faces from different nations: Seneca, Oneida, Cayuga, Onondaga. And then, of course, the Mohawk, represented by a single man: the man who'd come to them silent and nameless; the man who was the most ruthless of them all. They were one legion united in blood, and they now awaited her command.

She clapped twice, and the one called Searching Sky came forward. Joining her on the ground, he began to construct a small campfire. By and by, a wisp of smoke coiled skyward. Soon, flames wavered in the strengthening wind. Staying crouched before the firelight, she began slow, deliberate hand gestures to communicate her intentions. She signaled, *"no survivors"* and *"take whatever you want, should Geha allow it."*

She knew they would follow her anywhere, even if her uncanny knowledge of the white man's whereabouts continued to mystify and even terrify them. She'd laid a well-lit path to vengeance, and they'd reaped untold riches along the way.

Tonight's mission would be repayment for those debts, and it might even be her last time with them. That place deep within the nearby river valley would be waiting. Her way back to her true time and place. And if all went as expected tonight, there'd be nothing left to keep her here. A treasure unlike any other awaited on that vessel, and it was a tool for her redemption, not theirs.

I'm coming, Hannah.

From what the chieftain had confirmed at knifepoint, her quarry would be a medallion, about the size of a sand dollar. It might even be in the possession of a demon, an impostor and deceiver, who'd likely be hiding with it in the bowels of the ship. Barricaded. Protected. Such was their way. But not hers.

Raising her right hand, she signaled *"This circle,"* before jabbing a thumb at her chest *"is mine."*

She then stepped back, brought her knife up, and passed the blade over her bald scalp.

Her men raced past her, spears and war clubs raised. She turned to the vessel. The sailors aboard were now at the deck and sweeping the water with their lanterns. Others were furiously pulling a rope hand over hand, at the end of which dangled a small cutter containing a handful of other men, glints of metal showing in the lantern light. They were holding shovels.

Go ahead and dig. Get off the boat. The only things you'll be digging are your own graves.

The Redeemer's men were knee-deep in the surf and guiding their canoes from either side like pallbearers. They piled in with practiced efficiency and were soon cutting through the choppy waves, each canoe a hewn spear.

The last one out would be hers. She strode into the surf, ignoring the cold black water sucking at her deerskin leggings. The remaining men climbed in with her, weapons in hand, well aware by now she didn't need or want any weapon besides her knife. They'd long given up offering her spears and clubs, and no longer insisted she carry fire. For they knew that she already carried fire inside her.

I'm coming, Hannah. Mommy's coming.

They used their paddles to push off the shallow rocks and were soon racing out to meet the big ship. Minutes later, a rumor of tall billowy sails showing in lantern light. Then, screams. The sailors who'd thought they could dig their way out were now face down and bobbing with the waves under the jostling light—which just grew brighter.

She looked up. The jib sail was crawling with flames. She couldn't have it go up in flames—not yet. The impending storm's rains were not a given. It might just give the little inlet a glancing blow, but not enough to squelch the fire.

Her canoe drew parallel to the starboard side of the ship. She leaped up to the gunwale, her armpits taking the brunt of the impact. She hung there for a moment and exploded upward. She was on the deck. Eyes darting, knife twirling in her right hand, she stayed low, creeping along the gunwale. Her objective would be aft, below deck.

Protected.

A burning mass crashed into the main boom to her left. She stumbled against the gunwale. She got to her feet and saw the object on the deck. It was one of her men, the one called Long River. He was motionless, his charred skin hissing and popping.

Something else loomed over her. Her knife came up. He was outlined in the firelight like some devil, a devil that had just tossed her man like a small child. His tan, leathery face was curled into a sneer, deep-set lines pulling together. She moved past the face. It couldn't kill her. The machete in his left hand could.

She pivoted into a fighter's stance: right leg forward, left leg back. On the balls of her feet. Knees slightly bent. Her knife in her right hand, loose in her grip. Face muscles relaxed, impassive.

A small smile played across the big man's sunburnt lips. "Gros putain."

She feinted with her knife to draw his eyes up and then dropped into a squat and rotated her hips, striking out with her right leg. The big man was swept off his feet. He landed with a thud, the machete clanging to the deck. A few cast-iron pots rolled loose from a splintered crate and surrounded his head.

She grabbed the machete, tossed it overboard, and glanced over her shoulder. No one at her rear. She leaped forward, knife raised. The man's huge hand shot up, but her knees found the sensitive spot just below his sternum. The hand recoiled. He wailed. She dug her knees deeper into his stomach and brought her knife over her head in a two-handed grip.

The force that slammed into the base of her skull stunned her. She fell off him. She hadn't seen him grab one of the pots. She lay dazed, dimly registering the man lifting himself from the deck, laboring and wheezing.

She felt a chill at the small of her back. She reached beneath her. *Her knife.* She was lying atop the flat of the blade.

The man walked over, heavy boots clunking across the hard wood, the pot handle lost in his hand. He raised the makeshift weapon over his head, chest heaving.

Now.

She gripped the knife's hilt and rolled right just as the pot came slamming down onto the deck. The man's momentum sent him pitching forward, off balance.

Driving the knife into his exposed chest, she then dragged it downward, opening him from sternum to groin. He gasped. She yanked the knife free and was up and moving before his viscera could slap to the deck.

A sailor was crawling on his elbows, a glistening dark wake trailing him. Her nameless Mohawk man was striding up behind him, his war club held loose at his side. He planted a foot between the other man's shoulder blades.

His eyes found hers. He smiled.

She smiled back.

He took the club in both hands and wheeled it up and over his head, its smooth wooden ball catching the firelight. He swung down. The man's head burst like a pumpkin.

The guttural screams and grunts were dying down now, giving rise to the sounds of thrashing waves. The storm would be upon them soon, tossing this shallowest of Great Lakes into a fury. A voice bounded up and down like a whimpering dog, gurgled, and then was silenced. The ship—or what was left of it—belonged to her ... almost.

She pressed her fingers to the back of her head. Tender to the touch but nothing compared to what she'd endured before. Her hand absently traveled to the front of her neck and grazed that deep ruin.

I'm coming, Hannah. Mommy's coming.

She twirled her knife between two fingers and stepped past broken crates and downed rigging until she arrived at a stairwell descending into darkness. She began to ease herself down the steps in the way her men had shown her: measured stealth. She lowered her right toe from the top step to the second, gently transferring her weight from the ball of her foot to her heel. She then lowered her left toe—

CRACK. The third step exploded beneath her, splintered wood rocketing in all directions. She stumbled backward up the first two steps and fell to the deck, which was beginning to heave and dip. She sat up. A last man. There was always a last man. And he was waiting in the passageway with a pistol. She ran through her options. Rushing him would be suicide. She'd be shot before she was halfway down.

The boat shuddered and tilted. She stumbled past the stairwell, and flung her arms around the mainmast. The fire was now overhead, leaping from sail to sail. It wouldn't be long before it engulfed the entire vessel and all opportunity with it. She turned, scanned the deck, and saw the large man's motionless body. She tried to imagine dragging him across the deck and dropping him down the stairs as a decoy. It was no good. She was strong, but by the time she wrestled him into position, the boat and all of its contents might be gone, and possibly her with it. But the idea in itself wasn't bad.

Her eyes settled on the charred remains of Long River, who lay just beyond the foremast, his upper body still crawling with embers. She studied him a moment, small in stature, but stealthy and a good hunter. But his hunting days were over. She ate up the deck in a few long strides, gripped his ankles, and dragged him across the ever-tilting boat.

Quivering lightning threw harsh shadows across the deck and lit the foaming waves beyond. Her remaining men were returning in their canoes as instructed. Their part was done.

She arrived at the stairwell and positioned Long River facedown at the threshold. The sky to the west flickered. A low rumble rattled the ship. The pots where the big man lay clanged together and rolled apart. She grabbed Long River by his hips and maneuvered him into a half-standing position over the threshold. His last mission. She shoved his hips, and gravity took hold. He went thudding down the stairs on his backside.

CRACK. A bright flash. Long River's body contorted. She leaped down the ruined staircase two steps at a time. She was in the darkened passageway next to Long River's pitching body. Her knife was loose, active, *ready.* She hesitated. The muzzle flash had made it difficult for her to see in the dark. But that would work both ways. Unless the man had closed his eyes when firing, he'd need some time too.

She crouched low and flattened herself against the bulkhead, out of the firelight spilling in from above. A mixture of dank rot, smoke and gun powder filled her nose. She squeezed her eyes shut, willing absolute darkness. Then, she eased them open and looked down the passageway. A red rectangular outline floated in the darkness. It was a closed doorway, lit from beyond. But it was partially obscured by a darkened figure, from which a thin trail of smoke extended forward like a ghostly finger. The figure was quiet but not silent.

Her ears prickled at the rustling of fabric and clinking of metal. He was reloading. She squared herself in the passageway and took aim. Thunder boomed just as she flicked her wrist and hurled the knife. A concussive force shook everything, including her insides. She didn't hear the knife strike him, but a moment later, there were a series of thuds along the right bulkhead. Then a slow *hiss*. The silhouette was sliding to the floor.

Another blow rattled whatever objects were in the cabin beyond. The waves were battering the hull now. A series of taps ran across the deck above and then began to pelt it in earnest. The rain was here. She crept down the passageway. A prolonged flicker held the passageway alight, tossing long shadows against the bulkheads—and him. He was slumped against the right bulkhead, his white tunic darkened at its chest. But the knife wasn't in his chest. It was lying next to his left hand, the blade wet with blood. The son of a bitch had pulled it from his chest.

But none of that mattered now. She leaned over him, his dark skin mysterious in the gloom, his eyes open wide and vacant. The life inside them had fallen through a trapdoor, gone without a sound. Eyes like—

The passageway went dark again. The world around her tilted. The man slammed face-first against the opposing bulkhead and flopped to the floor. The passageway rocked back to the right. The vessel was groaning and pitching. A grating sound issued beneath her, and something came loose. The boat was drifting, free of the shoals and listing to port.

I'm coming, Hannah. Mommy's coming.

She picked up her knife and approached the door.

The door wouldn't open. The Redeemer pushed harder, but whatever was on the other side wouldn't yield. Stepping back, she slammed her left shoulder into the door, giving it all her weight. She repeated, until whatever rested beyond it began to grind across the floor.

Battered shelves topped with wicker crates came into view through the crack. Some were overturned, their contents emptied onto the floor, which creaked and groaned as she muscled forth the unseen monolith. Under a single swinging lantern, she saw coins, jewels, bronze plates, little statuettes, and other valuable looking things she couldn't name. But nothing that looked like her quarry. She wedged herself into the room and glanced about, chest heaving. The object barring entry was nothing more than a squat bureau. There was an odd hush in this place despite the chaos outside. But it wasn't just that it was quiet. Something about this place felt *slow*, as if she were in a dream.

She panned her gaze right and paused. In the far-right corner, perched upon a bench covered with crushed red velvet fabric, sat a girl. She couldn't have been more than seventeen. Her legs were tucked protectively underneath the skirts of her riding habit. Her entire lower half was lost in the garments, as if they were intended for an older, more robust woman.

The Redeemer studied the mouse of a girl, who studied her back. The girl's full lips were slightly parted, her nose delicate and upturned, her eyes lined with thick lashes. A lock of hair had spilled loose from the small white cap she wore, and she blew it aside.

"Are you here for it?" the girl said, her English accent rich, and from the sound of it, high class. But fake all the same.

"Yes," the Redeemer said, her seldom-used voice feeling arid and high.

"I wasn't expecting a ... woman," the girl said.

"Cut the bullshit."

The girl blinked and shook her head. "I don't understand."

"Cut the bullshit."

The girl regarded her for a long time, unfazed by the chaos outside, as if it merited no attention at all. When she spoke again, her voice was in a southern drawl. "Suppose it's a relief to be myself again." She exhaled, shifted on the bench, and ran an eye over the woman standing before her. "You're unlike any lady I've ever seen, and only savages boast shorn heads."

"Where is it?"

The girl ignored the question, her inquisitive eyes falling to the Redeemer's moccasins and deerskin leggings. "Never thought I'd see a white woman try to align with them. You can't win. Hope you know that. You're on the losing side of history. No changing it."

"Not the losing."

Dawning realization passed over the girl's features. "You're straight up nuts. You've spent too much time back here. Haven't come up for air in a long time, have you? I tell you, it's like surfacing after going diving. If you're gone too long and too far, you're gonna get the bends. Especially if you come back too quick. But that's what you're fixing to do, ain't it? I suppose it don't matter. Reckon we're both dead anyway."

The room shook as if in response to her words. The girl was lurched forward, and she grasped the shelf running the length of the wall above her. The lantern swung and twisted uncertainly on its ceiling hook as if unsure of where to put the dark.

The Redeemer staggered and placed steadying palms on the tilting floor where the plunder was skittering past her to port. The waves would start pummeling the deck above if they hadn't already. She righted herself. The girl did too, sitting up and feeling it necessary to smooth her skirts.

"Give it to me," the Redeemer said.

The girl's eyes were resigned, the curiosity gone. She barked a laugh, but there was no mirth in it. "Actually, relieved you're taking it. But you'll still be marked. If you make it off this boat and get back to whenever it is you're from, that is. And you

gotta make it work, or else they won't trust you. Nothing will."
She cocked her head. "When are you from?"

The Redeemer didn't answer.

"You're after someone. Who?"

The Redeemer pointed her knife at the girl. "Now."

The girl eased her hands from her lap and began to fidget open her top button, her fingers trembling. But her eyes didn't leave the Redeemer's. She reached down into her jacket. A braided rope necklace coiled up in front of her chin as she pulled it out, her small hand curled around whatever was attached to it. She lowered it and looked down at what lay nestled in her palm.

The Redeemer stepped forward.

The girl extended her palm outward.

The Redeemer froze mid-step. What glared back at her caught the lantern light and nearly blinded her. She shielded her eyes until the light had shifted enough for her to make out what it was. Its shimmering crystals threw brilliant reflections all about the cabin. She licked her lips and became aware that she'd been holding her breath.

"They never knew I had it," the girl whispered, her eyes still on it. Her voice seemed to come from somewhere else. "Has its own life force I reckon. And here they thought I was the precious cargo. Picked me up over in Green Bay. Fixing to ransom me back to the Brits. Little did they know."

The Redeemer was only half-listening. She floated forward, her left hand outstretched, the knife all but forgotten in her right hand.

The girl leaned back but then seemed to think better of it. She tucked her chin and lifted the necklace up and over her head.

The object dangling in front of the Redeemer's face shone like the sun. It called to her—not with words, but with thoughts. Something about *mine*. There were other thoughts too, but she couldn't understand them.

Mine? Is that what it's telling me? It's mine now?

She stepped in front of the lantern's light, dousing the object into shadow. She paused. Her left hand woke up, as if freed from temporary paralysis.

She blinked. "How do I use it?"

The girl squinted at her. "You dunno?"

"Tell me."

The girl started to open her mouth.

The violent wave that slammed into the ship lifted the Redeemer off her feet. Her last clear memory was the ceiling scrolling past. Then the world was flying at her. It was a world of black water and smoldering flame. Gone, the girl and the medallion. Gone, any hope for saving Hannah.

Chapter 2

Junk Night
Portage Falls, Ohio, June 21, 2021

The wheels didn't match. The brakes were too soft. The intersection where the top tube met the seat post bulged like a cyst filled with puss. But Aaron Porter didn't see his bike's imperfections. No, what leaned against his grandparents' garage, its red frame aglow in the fading light like the electric coils of his grandmother's stovetop, was a magnificent creation—*his* creation. Letters in peeling white paint across her top tube announced her name: SHELBY.

The name was an ode to his late grandfather's love of the Shelby muscle car, which was built with the best parts of other cars to create something altogether new and special. And his bicycle was just that: an amalgamation of parts harvested from other bicycles over the course of dozens of junk night crusades.

Tonight would be another such crusade. He pulled Shelby and her attached Schwinn trailer from the garage and climbed onto a saddle he'd taken a year ago from a rusted-over mountain bike designed for a woman. But the saddle had been fine, and its shorter and wider dimensions were more comfortable for his ample backside.

He looked over the low-slung rooftops of Sand Run Estates. To the west, a bank of purple-black clouds spanned the horizon. Zipping his parka, he pushed off and coasted down the driveway, the trailer rattling behind. He slowed at the driveway's apron and glanced up and down Juneville Drive. Nothing but garbage cans with the occasional bag sprinkled in. He clacked his canvas Skechers onto Shelby's pedals and mustered up his momentum. Shelby was slow to pick up speed but was coasting at a nice clip by the time he neared the Maplewood Drive intersection.

He squeezed her handlebar brakes well before the stop sign. The brakes were already soft, and with her trailer hitched up, Shelby was like a train that needed plenty of forewarning to come to a complete stop. Slowing at the intersection, he planted one foot on the asphalt and glanced up and down Maplewood before looking across the intersection, up Juneville.

Nothing interesting or abnormal. No glints of metal or unexpected shapes. He looked right, down Maplewood, toward the park at the end of the street, which was nicknamed *The Courts*, despite not having a court of any kind thanks to the Homeowner Association's funding drying up several years ago.

A sudden movement made him jolt upright. A trio of mangy tabby cats darted past him side-by-side up the middle of the street. A moment later, they were around the corner and gone from sight.

Odd. Cats don't usually run in packs like that.

He turned back to The Courts. More movement. This time, it was a person, and they were hurrying toward The Courts' entrance. The figure's back was turned to him, and they wore a large overcoat, despite the balmy weather. Even at a few blocks away, he thought the slouched posture and shuffling gait looked familiar.

Mr Ipser. Had to be.

The old man was probably rushing to The Courts to ensure nothing valuable got left there now that the light was fading under the approaching storm. Ever the dutiful steward, Mr Ipser wasn't going to let a little thunderstorm stop him from caring for *his* lot, which wasn't really his lot given he lived four houses from it. But someone had to care for it, and so he did.

It was too generous to call the two-acre spit of land at the Cuyahoga Valley's eastern rim a *park*. Accessible by a footpath lined with six-foot-tall hedges on either side, The Courts was instead the perfect escape for teens to conduct all sorts of debauchery: drug-related, sexual, or otherwise. A visitor to The Courts on a weekend morning could be treated to any number of visual pleasantries, used vape pens, empty beer cans, soiled condoms, to name but a few. Aaron had always wondered if Mr Ipser cleaned up those items when tending to the park's mangy grass, because they always went away after a couple of days.

It wasn't until Aaron was twelve that Gram would even allow him to go to The Courts with his older brother, Owen, and his friends. There were two rules about The Courts. The first rule was to stay away from the Sand Run Caves, a network of natural sandstone grottos set into the eastern cliffside of the Cuyahoga Valley National Park's gorge about a mile southwest of the neighborhood. One could easily get to the caves using the switchback trail that descended from the southwest corner of The Courts before it linked up with the Ohio & Erie Canal Towpath Trail, an all-purpose footpath extending the length of the national park. The treacherous cliffside trails near the caves were to blame for many deaths—mostly drunken or high teenagers—and that section of park had been closed to the public for a decade. But Gram knew that no signage or gate could stop the rebellious youth from exploring.

The switchback factored into rule number two: any trips the boys took into the heavily forested valley had to be together or in a group, and in such cases, they were to only use the well-groomed and gentle switchback, which of course took forever to descend. If Gram were to be believed, a descent into the valley using any other method would result in certain death. But just this past spring, Aaron had found a more efficient way when his garbage pickings were slim and he knew that Gram wouldn't be expecting him home anytime soon. That night, he'd come upon a small footpath accessible from the northwest corner of The Courts and descended it as far as he'd dared, finding that it also intersected with the Towpath.

The Towpath

But The Courts wasn't just a name without a namesake or a conduit to a wild and sprawling national park. It was a place of bright and smoldering memories, and none of them ran hotter than the one that still stung his heart. What his stepfather had said to him that day at The Courts had changed things. It was then he knew that his stepfather wasn't just some stand-in provider Mom had married when he was three-years-old. Not just some rare specimen in lily-white Portage Falls with his dark skin and African features. Not just some impassive soldier programmed to take and give orders as a result of his years of service to his country.

No, that day he'd become something else: Dad. And what his new Dad had said to him was something his six-year-old brain couldn't process at the time. It was too big for him and so he'd cried instead. It was a memory he still kept submerged now at fourteen, something he couldn't allow to surface for risk of crying again.

A gentle breeze was now tugging at the hood of his parka. The sweet, unmistakable scent of wet ozone wafting up his nose. The prickle of thunder hanging in the air like a promise. His pulse quickened. The anticipation of a storm had always excited him. Maybe it was because of how small it made him feel—how small it made everything feel. He knew there were dominant forces in this world, and they were greater than the arbitrary conflict that had ripped Dad from his life. Beyond the manufactured poison that entered his grieving mother's veins, turning her into a husk of her former self. There was comfort in knowing there was a higher power, an unseen hand that gave motion to all.

Now, it was on his doorstep. Loving storms as he did, it was different when you were out in them, hauling your pickings around in a bicycle trailer. The plastic zip-up cover on the trailer was enough to protect kiddos from dust and spraying pebbles, but it was far from waterproof. He didn't want to find out how inadequate it was, so he pushed off in the direction of The Courts.

A low rumble sounded, but it was distant. Everything was distant now, as if receding from the street. The squat ranches and bungalows were begging off to allow the junk-covered tree lawns to take center stage. Some instinct overcame him as he crossed the Bernard Drive intersection. He looked down Bernard to see a collection of large, irregular objects sitting in front of what he thought was the Flores' home. He debated turning down the street but decided against it. It would interrupt the pattern he realized he'd just chosen, and he needed to be efficient tonight. If all went well, he'd have time to check out whatever it was on his way back home.

He continued past Bernard and turned left down Sunset Drive, the last cross street before the Maplewood cul-de-sac—and The Courts' entrance. He took it to its southeastern cul-de-sac before doubling back the way he'd come, crossing Maplewood to the northwestern cul-de-sac. There, in front of the last house on the left, he spotted a stain-glassed lampshade. The shade had a thin crack running down its right side. But that was okay. It looked mostly intact and couldn't be construed as bar swag, which would earn him another lecture from Gram. He placed it in the trailer and moved on.

Turning left on Maplewood, he hung a quick right up the next street. Nothing much here besides a rolled-up area rug, a threadbare armchair with springs poking from its back, and the top of a birdbath.

He doubled back, coasting toward the intersection of Maplewood. It was here the first raindrop tapped the crown of his head. He tugged the parka's hood up and over his head and was soon surrounded by an echo chamber. His shoulders and back relaxed, as did his pace. A low rumble sounded overhead as if in response to his lethargy. Lightning flickered and guttered out a moment later.

He sped up and hung a right, the lampshade rolling about in the trailer. Moments later, he found himself again at the Bernard intersection. He thought about what he saw on Bernard. But *saw* wasn't it, was it? Sure, he saw that there were large items set out on the curb. But the sense that had compelled him to pause and look had been more like a deep intuition. He wasn't one to delay his own gratification—his round belly, fortified by Hot Pockets, Cheddar Cheese Combos, and Oreos, was a resounding testament to that. But some *thing* had told him to leave the cul-de-sac at the end of Bernard for last. Whatever the feeling, he'd delayed long enough. He turned and made a beeline for the Flores' house.

As he began his premature process of applying Shelby's brakes, the first things to catch his eye were the hulking forms covered in plastic. Another low rumble, and this time the lightning quickly followed, the forms inside the clear plastic coverings flickering into view.

Furniture. A loveseat under one covering and a coffee table under another.

He flicked on Shelby's handlebar-mounted LED light and swiveled her toward another mass of objects which covered half the tree lawn to the right of the driveway. He squinted through the now steady rain, his eyes roaming over several items: a floor lamp, a frayed wicker basket, and a large oval mirror. He might have considered taking the mirror had it not been spiderwebbed with cracks. He swiveled Shelby's handlebars to the right and the light picked up more of the same: dated furniture, relics from another time that had no place in a modern home, the likes of which even the most opportunistic garbage picker wouldn't claim, no less profit from.

Something still nagged at him. That sensation, that *thing*, that had compelled him to look down the street earlier. He knew there was more. *Why?*

A crack of thunder. The night lit up. His phone vibrated in his pocket. He didn't have to check the caller ID to see who it was. Gram would be getting worried.

Hang on, Gram, just another minute.

Something had illuminated near Shelby's front tire, just outside her cone of light. Yet it shone brilliantly. A moment later, he found the source—and it was a problem. The glimmer of light had come from *inside* a box. He wasn't shy about swiping objects left out in plain sight, but probing into other people's boxes and containers was too intrusive, too personal, too desperate—even if it was garbage. It was no different from rummaging through someone's garbage can in search of their credit card statements. No less desperate than a dumpster dive behind a McDonald's. No, Aaron Porter had garbage-picking standards and drew the line at all things enclosed, things that shouldn't be seen by anyone before meeting their maker inside the garbage truck's crusher. He'd maintained that dogged standard to date and didn't intend on violating it tonight.

But, still...

He adjusted the angle of the light and aimed it down onto the cardboard box, the swooping Amazon arrow logo showing on one of its top flaps.

Top flaps look open. No, Aaron, time to go. Nothing to see here. Just turn Shelby around and go home. A steaming Hot Pocket smothered in queso dip and bacon bits awaits you. You can wash it all down with your usual two-liter of Dr Pepper.

He got off the bike. He took a tentative step and stole a glance at the Flores' home. There hadn't been any lights on when he'd approached and there weren't any on now. He looked right, then left, and then over his shoulder. Just warm light spilling out from living room windows across the street.

Another flicker, and another glimpse of something shiny inside the box. He squatted over it, the steady rain pelting the box's surface, making its opened flaps chatter like a mouth. The box had a curated feel to it. Its position looked intentional. Or was he imagining it? He reached up to Shelby's handlebars and maneuvered the light, twisting it down to focus deeper into the box.

More glimmering. He placed his hands on either side of the box like someone preparing to lift an organic specimen. He thought if he were to lift the box, its contents might split the now sodden cardboard and spill to the ground. Instead, he gave it a gentle shake. It was heavy, and loose things clanged about in there.

He eased open one flap, then the other. What caught the light made him reel back, his breath catching. It was as if someone had stuffed the sun inside the box. He squinted into the glare. The water beading on the surface of the objects within only amplified their brilliance. He reached up to the handlebars and turned off the light.

His eyes readjusting, he exhaled and thumbed away water droplets from his cheeks. Except it wasn't rain. Couldn't be, not with his parka hood slung up and his head bent against the rain. His Adam's apple was jogging up and down in his throat. He was crying. *Why?* He looked away from the box to compose himself.

Quiet your mind.

He closed his eyes, and Dad's words came back to him, "Remember, Aaron, *Sapere Verdere*. See it. Be patient, son."

He focused on his breathing. Dad was at his elbow now, his husky voice lowered to a whisper: *"Quiet your mind. It's what I tell my men. You're not too young to learn this skill too. Gather yourself, and then try again. But don't just look. See, I tell them, like the great Leonardo Da Vinci himself used to say: Sapere Verdere, know how to see. Should that man be wearing a long coat in this weather? Why's that woman nervous? Why's she avoiding the eyes of others? Why's that child lingering nearby, alone? Is he stalling for time? If so, what's he waiting for? See with your brain first, son, not with your eyes. They'll deceive you."*

He at last opened his eyes. He started with the obvious. What lay inside the box was a bunch of coins: quarters, nickels, dimes, and perhaps hundreds of pennies. But it wasn't the heap of coins that got his attention, it was the two large objects partially buried in them. From what he could see from their exposed edges, they were no less mesmerizing in the dark. Each object seemed to possess its own light source, glowing somehow, which he thought was impossible for metal. Or gold?

He reached down and grabbed the more visible of the two objects, the coins parting like a clamoring sea. The storm was gone and with it any concern of Gram. The world felt slower somehow, dreamlike.

There was something old about this object. And it was heavy. He grazed its tapered edges with his forefinger. Sharper than expected, abnormal, and rough to the touch, unlike the clean machine-cut edges of modern coins. This felt handmade.

He rotated it and ran his thumb across its bumpy and unmarked backside and turned it face up again. The object was saucer-like, about the diameter of a hockey puck, with a jagged hole the size of a shoelace eyelet just a few centimeters from its edge—which he guessed was its top. He studied its face, willing himself to *see* its details, which were many. A raised spiral pattern occupied the entire face of the … medallion.

Yes, a medallion.

The pattern was interrupted occasionally by sunken glass chips. He looked closer at the design, which appeared to move, the shrinking spiral maintaining its proportion as it encircled a black inset oval. The word he was looking for popped into his head: logarithmic.

His friend from his former life on Ross Avenue—and enduring crush—Libby Jaite, or "lobster-eyed Libby" as Simon Kent called her on account of her lazy eye, had given her eighth-grade science presentation on common patterns found in nature. She'd gushed about how logarithmic spirals existed everywhere: from nautilus shells, to the heads of flowers, to the shapes of galaxies themselves. As far as Aaron was concerned, Libby could have recited a recipe from the back of a box of cake mix and he still would have listened with rapt attention. Her breathless description about how the spiral maintained its sacred proportions no matter how big or small it got gained a foothold in his brain, as did everything else she had said.

He looked closer at the black oval, which was like staring into an abyss. That abyss stared right back. His mouth started to water as he held the medallion closer and gazed deeper into its central eye.

The eye pulled at him. Desired something of him. *Needed* him. He licked his lips. An unsettling certainty raced forth from some dark and faraway place, a place without a name, a place where time stood shapeless and still. How he knew this, he had no idea. A voice without words spoke into his mind then, bypassing his ears altogether. It began to whisper a single phrase over and over again.

"Mine boy who rides Shelby."

Chapter 3

Carving Shadows

Near Wayne National Forest, Southern Ohio, June 24, 2021

Hidden inside the crook of a massive dead oak, the Redeemer watched the straggler shamble through the ravine below. Challenging as it was for her to take any animal these days— they could sense her presence from a mile away—she could still snag the occasional fawn or injured adult deer. In this case, it was an injured adult, whose stuttering gait may have resulted from a wolf or coyote attack. It was no matter to the Redeemer, who wasn't in it for the sport, she was in it for the food. And this prize would provide several days of good eating.

The deer came into range with its left flank in full view. The Redeemer drew back on the long-range bow and released the arrow. The animal shuddered and fell over. It was dead in minutes.

She used her knife to carve off its lower legs and gut its innards where it lay. Some parts of the viscera would make a good eating for other critters, and who knew, perhaps they'd come to ignore their fears of her if she kept them well fed— doubtful, but worth a try. She loaded the carcass on a tarp-covered sled. A sturdy nylon rope from the sled was connected by a heavy carabiner clip to a weightlifter's belt around her waist. Now, she towed the deer with as much ease as one could expect, her sled contraption allowing her to face the direction she was heading while having her hands free.

By and by, the forest became thinner and hotter, the humid June air finding the low places and cooking them in earnest. But the sparser vegetation meant she was getting close. The wheezing of the low underbrush was no less deafening here as it parted for her sled, broadcasting her location to anything with ears, which could've been her last mistake had she traveled this forest four hundred years ago. In a way, she'd been just as reckless then.

Her mind wandered back to those severe men she'd left behind. Those with dark eyes, of stealth and cunning, at one with forest and sky and water, with the skill to approach prey from fifteen feet without being heard. That is, until she'd come along. She the demon, the witch, the one whose company had rendered useless their endemic skill. Had she not been so deft at predicting the whereabouts of the white men — and killing them — things may have gone differently for her.

She summited the last rise, and a dilapidated bier came into view: her cabin. Now with more space, she unhooked the chain from her waist, paid it to its full length, and pulled the sled up and onto the homestretch, the ruddy path she'd worn in the underbrush from hundreds of trips into the forest's southeastern reaches, where all creeks spilled into the Ohio River, where many sources of food could be found — if she was lucky.

A sky purple and dim found her in front of her cabin. At four hundred square feet, the structure was in desperate need of a match to relieve its misery. The cedar-shingled roof drooped inward, sagging over the tiny porch. The rotted foundation was more like an organized pile of splinters, formerly giving harbor to countless insects and rodents. But not anymore. A reek of mold, mildew, and animal carcass: *home*.

Like most of her possessions, the cabin was gained by the loss of a life — its former inhabitant, who was now buried in a shallow grave a half mile away. A meandering turn of events but favorable all the same, unlike the boat mission, which had been too much, too close. That place and time to which she'd traveled to make things right had become haunted and hopeless. A dead end. She'd considered her options afterward. Stay nearby and hope for a break, or move on and make a living in her true time. Reflect and regroup.

In the end, she'd moved on, but she could never go back to the way things were, or the person she'd been before her life had turned toward sublime brutality. Not after all she'd learned and experienced. She'd changed, and it was for the better. She now swam against life's current. The Earth knew it. Its most primal inhabitants knew it. She knew it, but she didn't care.

Tonight, she'd again proven that neither curse nor conjuration could pluck her from the big engine. That fucking engine—modern civilization—turning on axes like some massive drilling machine, boring through nature and time, casting off the dreams of the worthy like pulp. Her dreams might be ground up with them someday, but not before she seized the controls of the machine and ran it over the edge. For with her she carried the elixir of death. Her redemption for those who belonged. And she would see that they joined her when the big engine fell.

The light was almost gone. She entered through the rickety front door and past a bed that was nearly too small for her. Just beyond the bed, a water-stained desk and a wood-burning stove. She reached into a dark corner beyond the stove, found the handle of her oversized chest cooler that was filled with dried ice and wheeled it out and onto the little porch where the deer lay in the sled.

Over the next hour, the curtain of night fully descended, she sat beside a gas lantern and cleaned the animal. She rinsed the carcass with a hose she'd attached to an elevated rain barrel and used her knife to skin and quarter it, stuffing anything edible into small plastic bags before stacking them into the cooler.

She was tired. She stood and wheeled the cooler inside as exhaustion began to rise into her cheeks and settle behind her left eye. That wretched place where her sight had been blunted. Eyelids drooping, she pressed her lips to her knife's steel and lay the blade flat beneath her pillow. She'd sharpen it tomorrow.

She looked into the corner opposite the stove. Her caged roommate was becoming more sluggish, his eyes glazing. The substance was working and the symptoms would begin soon. At sunup, she'd move him outside a good distance away, for she wasn't sure how contagious he might become. She hoped that by now she'd built up some immunity, but it wasn't a bet she was willing to make. The substance was working, and that was enough for her. More testing would be needed, but that would happen in time. These promising thoughts eased through her as she settled onto the old mattress, which groaned and squeaked under her angular body. She was asleep in minutes.

***

She dreamed of darkness, a starless sky over a black sea. No hint of a horizon or any useful bearing. The sea churned and frothed beneath where she was suspended in air like an offering to a drowned god. She gazed out over inky waves cresting with faint whitecaps. After a time, a soft glow tugged at the corner of her eye. The light was warm and inviting—but sad, somehow. There was a profound loneliness somewhere nearby, and it was beckoning her. To her left.

She turned to the light, but it remained just at her periphery. She continued turning until finally a vast field of flames came into view. Like her, the flames were hovering above the rolling waves. They were whispering, their voices childlike. After a time, they grew in number and size, as if they'd been alerted to her presence. They approached, tentative and curious. They surrounded her now.

How'd that happen so fast?

They closed in on her, getting louder. Closer now. Orbiting her head. Shouting. She couldn't understand what they were saying. But they were … lonely. So lonely. They danced all about her head, capered in front of her mouth, poised to race down her throat and into her heart, which was pounding in her chest. They screamed, spiraling all around her, these miniature galaxies of light.

Please. I don't understand!

She squeezed her eyes shut.

Please.

She waited, breathed, and waited some more, her heartbeat thrumming in her temples but slowing. The noise quieted too, the soft sloshing of the waves now the only sound. She inhaled briny air, exhaled, and eased her eyes open.

A single flame remained, smaller than those that had just swarmed her. Guttering with a gentle glow, it was leaning toward her. It was weak, tired, and infantile. It was—

"Mommy?"

Her throat grew thick. In a cracking whisper, she said, "Baby? Hannah? Is that you?"

"Mommy, I'm scared. Where am I?" The flame brightened and licked the air as if in panic. "I can't find you! Where are you?"

"I'm here baby. Mommy's here."

She approached the little flame, which swelled and flared in response. She reached with unseen fingers, her invisible legs heavy. But she wasn't going to be denied.

"I'm coming, sweetheart."

The flame that was Hannah became trident-shaped, tiny arms flanking a wispy head. It was reaching like a toddler who'd fallen and now desired their mother's comfort. The flame grew as she approached. Her legs protested, but in time, she arrived and cupped the precious little fire with trembling hands now visible in the light.

Her baby swelled inside her palms. She was warm to the touch but not hot. The Redeemer began to sing to her baby in the way she had when she'd first cradled her at Saint Thomas Hospital, exhausted, but smitten by the precious life that breathed and sighed on her breasts.

You are my sunshine...

The same song she sang to her then fifteen-year-old when she'd found her lifeless in her bedroom, her blue eyes staring up into nothingness, never to see again. Her own tears dripping into her daughter's opened eyes. Those lifeless eyes appearing to cry.

My only sunshine...

She felt no sense of time as she rocked and swayed with her baby. She sang again and again until her voice began to falter. Her little girl was with her again, the precocious three-year-old who made her read *Love You Forever* over and over, refusing to fall asleep.

You make me happy when skies are gray...

The six-year-old who wanted her peanut butter and jelly sandwiches quartered instead of halved, which would make her scream, *"Now I have four sandwiches, Mommy!"*

You'll never know dear, how much I love you...

The shy fourteen-year-old who belted out *Let It Go* into her hairbrush as she pranced around the safe confines of their tiny kitchen. The teen who'd be petrified if her classmates ever found out.

Please don't take my sunshine away...

The fifteen-year-old who became cold and sad, harassed by unseen cowards, jaded and mistrustful of anyone, including her own mother. The girl who cut herself, who medicated, who—

Hannah guttered, "Mommy, what's happening?"

"I-I'm here, baby. Don't you leave me now, sweetheart. Mommy's not letting you go again."

Silence.

"Hannah? Baby? Stay with me, hon."

"It's okay, Mommy. I know you'll find me soon."

"How? How can I find you? Tell me. I've tried and tried."

"You will. He's found it."

"*Who*, sweetie? Who's found it? What did he find?"

"Mine boy who rides Shelby."

Hannah flickered and wavered in a wind now more obstinate. But the little flame didn't gutter out or scatter into embers. It instead liquefied and began to melt in the Redeemer's palms. It ran into the creases of her fingers. She thrust one cupped hand under the other to keep the liquid from spilling into the darkness, but it was no good. Like mercury, it sought the gaps between her fingers and slithered through them, falling in resplendent streams into the water. She could only watch.

Then, the streams slowed their descent in midair. They began to intermingle, coalescing into a single spherical shape. It flattened against the night before resuming into the waves. Her pulse quickened.

The medallion.

The details of its face took shape: the spiral motif, the crystals, the *eye*. Then it was below the water's surface. Her body became lighter, and she could move more freely again. She dove headfirst into the water. Cutting its surface, she could see the shimmering shape fading fast as it plunged into the depths. Wreckage surrounded her again, splintered and charred. Bodies beneath the orange blanket of fire above, tangled in chewed-up sails and rigging.

She was inside now, this groaning coffin that would hasten her to Hell at the bottom of the lake. Bubbles pushing past her, she plunged through its torn open bowels, her lungs screaming from a lack of oxygen. It was there, floating like a golden balloon, still tethered to the girl in pink—its cord caught about her outstretched arm. Her eyes were wide as her delicate hands clawed at nothing. Her legs pinned by the overturned bureau. The Redeemer went down with her.

Just a little further.

She scooped with her arms and kicked with her legs, the weight of twenty feet of water dulling her ears, ready to crush her head. She extended a hand.

Closer.

Her heart hammered. Her head like a bomb about to go off.

I can get it.

Then she was being pulled away by powerful arms.

No!

They were pulling her up now, through the large hole in the wreckage. She tried to wriggle free. They were too strong. Up she went with her Mohawk man, too weak to fight. The golden disk now a blur of light rushing away. Down it went with the boat into darkness.

She awoke with a start, gasping, sweating. She sat up, the bed creaking in alarm at her sudden movement. She swung her legs over the side of the bed, bent, then buried her face into her palms, chest hitching. But she didn't cry, wouldn't cry—there were no tears left.

But Hannah had said something. While there'd been other dreams like this one ever since the boat, her baby in the flames, the medallion always just out of reach, this time had been different.

Mine boy who rides Shelby.

What did it mean? The phrase was like the one she'd heard in her thoughts when the girl had shown her the medallion. But it made no sense. *My* boy who rides Shelby? What is Shelby? And what did it have to do with her seeing Hannah soon? Whatever the reason, something had changed.

She looked over at the old wooden shelf opposite the foot of the bed. The hazardous materials canisters topping the shelf stared back at her. She got to her feet and strode to her mini-laboratory and crouched next to the cage. The raccoon was still alive, but the bleeding would begin soon. She had to get him outside. This sixth experiment had been the most successful. She'd found the right amount—not too much of the substance to make the creature die instantly, but not too little either, for to study her final subject, it couldn't be permitted too much time. Now, she'd have to find a bigger specimen to test the same relative dosage, a creature of about two-hundred pounds, about the size of a man.

If what Hannah had told her in this latest dream was true, then she might be able to kill two birds with one stone. She sat back down on the mattress and pulled her knife out from beneath her pillow. Her eyes again finding the canisters, she twirled the knife absently between her fingers, the muscles and tendons of her wrist moving like the inner workings of a clock, the spinning blade its macabre hour hand.

Chapter 4

The Old Neighborhood
Portage Falls, Ohio, June 26, 2021

The midmorning sun spilled through the towering oaks of his old neighborhood, laying down puddles of light for Shelby to coast over. His old street conjured the 1970s with its rows of identical brick ranches stretching from east to west. He crested a low rise and found himself in a satisfying cruise. To his left, Mr Wolf was stepping back from his oscillating sprinkler, apparently having just realigned it to better cover his tree lawn, which was already a lush green. The sprinkler greeted Aaron with a deep *salaam* before rearing to repeat the formality to the rest of the man's impeccable lawn. Aaron gave a lazy half-wave, but Mr Wolf's eyes were locked on the directional output of his finely tuned watering operation.

He pressed on. Movement—to his right. He slowed. It was *her*. But it was too late. He couldn't stop Shelby in time to turn around and pretend he'd forgotten something. No, he'd look like an idiot if he did that. His thoughts hurried in his head. Why was she home on a Saturday morning? Shouldn't she be fishing, hunting, hiking, or all of the above?

Libby was facing him now, bent to the bed of her dad's camouflaged Chevy Silverado, rifling under a similarly camouflaged tarp, a few strands of wispy blonde hair falling loose from her ponytail, framing those high and freckled cheek bones.

Beautiful.

She looked up, her good eye finding him.

His cheeks turned to ovens, and the pavement scrolling under Shelby's wheels suddenly became more interesting. Out of the corner of his eye, he could sense her pausing.

Does she really hate me?

Her lazy eye wasn't that noticeable. But Simon Kent had ensured the entire world noticed it, doubling over in laughter the day Libby had arrived at school in the sixth grade wearing an eyepatch. In gym class later that same day, he'd *arrghed* like a pirate and hobbled around as if he wore a peg leg after she'd emerged red-faced from the girl's locker room.

Aaron hadn't laughed and would never forget the way Libby's bottom lip had quivered before she lowered her head and bolted out into the hallway. The gym teacher, Mr Harper, had stared daggers at Simon before dashing after Libby, his belly shaking from exertion.

Simon was lucky he hadn't gotten suspended for that charade. Aaron had refused to speak to him afterward but had eventually caved when Simon approached him at his locker later that week, on the verge of tears, and begging Aaron — his only *true friend* — to forgive him. Aaron still wondered how things might have gone had Simon expressed as much remorse to Libby. He hadn't, and to this day, Libby didn't just hold a grudge against Simon — she'd cooled to Aaron too.

Guilt by association.

He could feel the heat of Libby's stare diminish behind him as he coasted downhill toward the intersection of Hillcrest Avenue. He paused at the intersection and gasped. She could no longer see him, could no longer see his embarrassment. His crush on Libby was like having a sick hole inside that could never be filled, a raging cauldron that licked at his stomach whenever she was near, rising to heat his face and wet his forehead.

He felt like such an idiot around her, and now was no different. Around Libby he was self-conscious about everything, the placement of his hands, the way he walked, the way he stood, whether or not he should meet her eye — for if he did, she might somehow detect his obsession.

After each interaction with Libby, he would evaluate everything. It would consume him well into the night and hold his eyes open. And it would happen again tonight, he knew. Then his thoughts would inevitably wander to those hazel eyes, those coltish freckles, that wispy hair. He'd muse over her looks that conjured beauty from another time, a time of wild fields, stables, and farm houses; of old log fences, stone wells, and shimmering stars. As if within those straw-colored locks, he could be transported altogether and wish never to return. He'd think of that delicate place where her neck met her collar bone, where he so desperately wanted to put his lips. He'd imagine how he'd come up from behind her and take her in his arms, brush aside her hair, and kiss her pale neck. And just hold her there. They'd watch the world pass by without a care. For there was nothing else. Then, they'd get lost in that world together.

His whole body was trembling, his knuckles whitening from his death grip on Shelby's handlebars. He let go, put his hands on his hips, and exhaled. After a time, his breath slowing, he put foot to pedal, but didn't push forward. There was that little brick ranch, the second to the last home on the left.

Just turn Aaron. There's nothing left.

He ran his gaze over the home's faded brick exterior, the lawn's knee-high grass—punctuated by weeds and dandelions which would give Mr Wolf a coronary—and the red yard sign declaring: FOR SALE.

Still for sale. Of course, it is.

His memories were more vivid lately, and he absently reached up underneath his T-shirt and ran his thumb over the textured surface of the medallion, which hung about his chest with the help of a cord necklace he'd found in one of Gram's kitchen drawers. He hadn't told anyone about the two medallions—the other of which lay hidden atop a section of exposed ceiling joist in his attic. Not even Owen knew about them.

He thought about Simon. But the prospect of telling Simon put a knot in his stomach. As he tried to imagine Simon's reaction, another feeling, strange and alien, began to stir inside him. It was as if he didn't want Simon insulting it. He turned the weird emotion over in his head, unable to approximate it to anything he'd ever felt. It was as if it had been implanted inside him. He caressed the medallion once more.

I won't let him hurt you.

He let go of the medallion and pulled his gaze from his past.

***

Aaron had only to descend two carpeted steps before the unmistakable scent of the Kents' man cave assaulted his nose. It was an eclectic mixture of sweat, mustiness, and pipe smoke. Mr Kent had been fighting the good fight in his efforts to keep pipe smoking alive, and the entirety of the Kent's basement was a resounding testament to his commitment. The sweet scent of flavored tobacco penetrated everything: carpet, furniture, and even the Kent boys' clothing, which Aaron knew would be heaped on the floor in the adjoining laundry room. The scent wasn't unpleasant, though, and it made him feel as if he were being teleported to another time whenever he entered his best friend's basement.

He strode into the man cave, its bygone-era quality going beyond just smell. The faux wood wall paneling, Mr Kent's vintage record player, and the avocado-green refrigerator — which rattled like a sick person — helped complete the time warp. It had been a week since he'd last visited, but he didn't have to look around to know that the other signature relics would be in their rightful places, as if frozen in time.

One such relic was slumped in the center of the room. Colors long faded, the suffering plaid-patterned couch faced a 60-inch flat screen TV mounted on the wall nearest the stairs. Nestled in its sagging middle cushion, wearing flannel pajama bottoms and an oversized *Fortnite* T-shirt, sat a small teenager. Simon was in his usual posture, hunched over the edge of the cushion and cradling a game controller in his soft hands. His thumbs were hammering the buttons. His dark brown hair was in its usual state of dishevelment, as if he'd just woken up.

Diminutive as he was, Simon wasn't exactly thin and had Aaron's influence to thank for that. Simon darted his flint-like eyes over to where Aaron stood in the entryway and then back to the TV.

"Nice of you to finally show up."

"Y'know, it's like three-point-something miles for me to ride here. I don't see you biking to *my* house."

"That's not *your* house."

Aaron rolled his eyes and stepped over a discarded Mountain Dew can.

Simon paused the game, tossed aside his controller, bent, and began to rifle through empty snack wrappers near his bare feet. His hands closed around a fresh bag of Cheetos, and he tossed it at Aaron with a little more force than usual.

"You're welcome."

"Thanks," Aaron muttered, tearing open the bag and popping a Cheeto into his mouth.

Simon turned back to the TV. "Dr Pepper's in the fridge."

"Maybe later," Aaron said, navigating the minefield of wrappers to the couch.

Simon slid over just far enough for Aaron to sit, and the couch immediately groaned as he settled onto it. Simon pulled out his iPhone—the latest model—and began tapping on its virtual keyboard. He saved whatever he was doing, tossed the phone aside like another snack wrapper, and resumed his game.

"How's the blog going?" Aaron asked, already knowing the answer.

No reply.

"You're gonna have to face the fact that people only watch video now. They won't read. You gotta get over that fear. The camera won't bite you."

Simon shook his head. "Simon Says will stand on its—"

"You *really* renamed it *Simon Says*?" Aaron sighed. "C'mon man. You'll *never* get any traffic. Simon Says is way too overloaded—it'll never appear in the search results."

"I ain't fuckin' changin' it. The right people will find it."

Aaron considered the last time he reviewed Simon's handiwork online—which always gave negative reviews for *every* game—and he came away belly laughing instead of educated by Simon's detailed breakdown of the latest *Grand Theft Auto*. At first, he'd been surprised to see that the blog entry had generated twenty-two comments. But on closer inspection, the comments were limited to just two users: someone who called themselves *Dickslapper8,* and *Simonsays69*—Simon's very own digital persona.

Aaron wasn't as current with the latest Internet lingo and trends as most other teens, but he knew a troll when he saw one, and Dickslapper8 fit the bill. Whoever it was—Aaron envisioned a middle-aged man in his mother's basement—knew how to press Simon's buttons, and Simonsays69 fell for it every time. In reading the comments, he'd never seen such creative uses of the words vagina, cock, scrotum, and dildo.

Simon abruptly leaned back, having apparently reached some desired checkpoint in the game. "Almost done with this game, which sucks. Then I'm moving on to the new *Call of Duty,* which will prolly suck too."

Sensing that Simon was as present as he would likely get, Aaron hesitated and then said, "Saw Libby on my way here."

Simon shot him a look before returning to the task at hand, which was maneuvering a gun-toting soldier through some war-torn environment. "Oh, yeah, and what did my best friend have to say about me this time?"

"Y'know, it's not all about you," Aaron said, trying to keep his voice even. "Hard to believe, I know."

Simon grunted in reply.

"She actually didn't say anything. Neither did I. It was super awkward."

Simon sighed. "Dude, that was like, forever ago. She needs to get over it."

"Well, I don't expect you to be best friends with her, but … whatever." Aaron exhaled and then decided to change the subject. After a moment's thought, he asked, "Hey, what was Gabe's routine this morning?"

Simon paused the game, a smile already forming on his lips. He leaned forward, the couch creaking. "I heard shouting this morning," he said, "so, I got up, walked over to the bathroom, opened the door, and there he was, screaming, *You Fuck!* at himself in the mirror over and over again…until he threw up."

Aaron almost spit out a Cheeto as he burst into laughter. Simon chuckled at his own creation too. When the laughter died down, Simon looked at him expectantly like a toddler awaiting the next page of a picture book.

Aaron composed himself and furrowed his brow. "Well, I didn't get a chance to hear shouting this morning. No, for me, it was music blaring in my ears at five in the morning. I woke up, and there he was next to my bed, shadow-boxing to *Eye of the Tiger* and wearing nothing but a Princess Leia wig."

Simon was no longer sitting on the couch. He was rolling on the floor and holding his belly in convulsive laughter, empty snack wrappers crinkling beneath him. Aaron couldn't help but snort his own laughter. He'd come up with funnier, more creative stories about Owen before, but even haphazard efforts like this one worked surprisingly well for his hard-to-please friend, who also had an overachieving older brother. After a time they calmed, and Simon plopped back onto the couch, just getting warmed up. "W-well," he said between hitching giggles, "that's nothin' compared to what I saw Gabe doing this morning. I walked into the bathroom, and there he was, on the toile—"

"You what?"

A blur raced into the room, decked out in highlighter yellow Adidas soccer gear. Simon was swept off the couch and onto the floor. And this time, it wasn't by his own doing. He was struggling in the headlock his older brother had him in. Gabe's usual megawatt smile was on full display as he scrubbed his knuckles against Simon's already disheveled hair. Simon's soft hands pulled at his brother's sinewy forearm to no avail.

"Stop, you ass! Quit it!"

"What did you catch me doing?" Gabe asked, more amusement in his voice than anger. "I'm all ears!"

"Nothing! Just stop! Christ! Stop!"

Gabe released Simon, who was panting from the sudden physical exertion. Uncoiling his lithe body from the floor, Gabe stood, dusted crumbs from his uniform, and brushed aside a lock of shoulder-length hair from his dark eyes. He grinned at Aaron and presented his fist. "What up, A-dog!"

Aaron smiled back, set aside his bag of Cheetos, and leaned in to accept the fist bump.

"Hey, a little birdie told me that your bro beat the crap out of Littlefield! Bout time."

Aaron tried to think of something interesting or witty to say under the brilliant spotlight of Gabe's attention, but could only muster, "Yeah, it was pretty crazy."

"Man, I wish I coulda seen that shit," Simon said. "Fuckin' hate that prick."

Gabe, too absorbed to chastise his brother for his foul language, said, "Yeah, your bro is a scary dude, man. What'd ya think woulda happened had Dean and Reid not pulled him off?"

Aaron hadn't considered this. To Aaron, Owen was Owen, and as impulsive and violent as he could sometimes be, he was also empathetic, kind, and loyal to a fault. But what would have happened? He honestly didn't know, because there'd always been someone around to intervene when Owen's anger boiled over. He just shook his head.

Gabe pursed his lips and said, "Wonder if those two will ever be cool again."

Aaron hoped that Owen's relationship with Connor Littlefield would finally end, but he somehow knew otherwise. It was an odd sense of clarity.

Simon, who was allergic to pregnant pauses, reached for his phone and started tapping on its screen.

Gabe stretched his arms and checked the time on his Fitbit wristband. "Alright, fellas, gotta get to practice. Oh, hey— Aaron, tell your bro...tell him I said, way to go." And then, more to himself, muttered, "Can't stand that prick." Then he was on his way up the steps, taking two at a time. The storm door cracked shut a moment later.

Aaron settled back onto the couch, and for the next fifteen minutes listened to Simon swear under his breath as he *evaluated* another game.

His vibrating phone startled him. He pulled it from his pocket and looked at the caller ID: Owen. Calling, of course, not texting. Owen had neither the time nor the patience to thumb-out a text message. But at that, Owen didn't call unless there was a good reason.

He answered the call, "Hey, what's up?"

"Where are you?" There was urgency in Owen's voice.

"Simon's."

"Shit. You're all the way over there?"

"Yeah, left this morning. Told Gram I'd be here. She knows."

A brief pause, and then Owen said, sheepishly, "Oh, okay—I, uh, was over at Carrie's last night."

Aaron knew that Owen's usual ruse was to have Gram believe he was staying the night at Reid Marlowe's house instead of his girlfriend's.

"It's fine," Aaron said. "Gram thought you were still at Reid's when I left this morning."

An audible sigh. "Okay, cool, cool."

Another pause, and Aaron could sense Owen was about to get to the point of his call.

"Hey, how d'ya feel about an adventure tonight?" There was energy in his voice.

Aaron glanced at Simon, who was pounding away on his controller. It felt as if he'd just gotten to the Kent's house, but then again... "Well, what time?" he asked. "I'll need time to ride back home."

"Don't worry 'bout that. We'll pick you up."

He was about to ask who *we* was, when Owen asked, "Staying there for dinner?"

"No, told Gram I'd be home by dinner."

Simon, who was listening despite his preoccupation, muttered, "You'll eat here. You always do."

"Guess I'm eating here. I'll let Gram know."

Owen fell silent and Aaron could sense his mind working.

Finally, Owen said, "Okay, that'll work. Trust me, it'll be fun. You won't wanna miss it."

"Well, what—"

"Just be ready by seven."

The connection was cut.

"Owen?" Simon asked, not about to risk looking away from his game.

"Yep."

Aaron thought again about getting picked up. Picked up by who? And what about Shelby? "Hey, mind if I leave Shelby here?" he asked. "Can I put her in the garage?"

"*It,*" Simon corrected. He then shrugged. "I don't give a shit. My old man's outta town, so he won't care if you put it in there. Hell, my mom won't even notice. Go for it."

***

Tires squealed. A subwoofer thumped. The masculine sounds of the Audi's V6 engine assaulted the evening's calm as Aaron stood waiting alone on the Kents' front porch. Simon had refused to pull himself away from his video game, and so here Aaron stood with his hands stuffed in his pockets. His heart might as well have been stuffed in there too. He'd known who was going to be picking him up even before this obnoxious soundtrack filled the air: *Connor.*

The thumping and revving sounds were now at the corner of Cornell and Hillcrest. Drops of sweat fell from his armpits into his already dampening T-shirt. His right knee jittering as the black Audi swung into the driveway and lurched to a stop. The booming bass fell a few octaves as Owen threw open the passenger-side door and trotted up to Aaron in his black Portage Falls Panthers football shorts and T-shirt.

A voice barked from the driver's seat, "Make room for Portly!"

Owen fired an annoyed look over his shoulder and turned back to Aaron. His eyes were pleading. "Before you say anything, it's cool. We had it out. This is ... his way of making things cool again. Trust me. You wanna go with us."

Aaron looked past Owen and into the car. Connor, whose nose was covered with some kind of brace, was in the driver's seat and jawing with Reid Marlowe and Dean Cavanaugh, who were seated in the back. Dean was moaning his usual troll-like laughter.

Aaron returned his attention to Owen. "Well, what's the surprise?"

"If I told you, you might not go. But it's the chance of a lifetime. *Trust me.*"

Aaron winced. "What's that supposed to mean—I might not go? Why can't you tell me?"

"Believe me. I know you. What we're going to do is ... not exactly legal, but it's something you'll regret not doing if you don't get in." He gestured to the car.

Dean had gotten out and was now slouched against the trunk. "Hey, Portly, you're sitting, bitch! I'm not gonna sit like that all the way to Cleveland." He erupted into meathead laughter.

Aaron looked at Owen. "Cleveland?"

Owen sighed. "You're not gonna go, are you?" He glanced around as if to check for eavesdroppers and drew closer. "You know how Connor's dad is part owner of the salt mines under Lake Erie?"

Aaron nodded.

"You know the mines that go like thousands of feet deep?"

Aaron nodded again, growing impatient.

"Well, Connor's parents are outta town. He swiped his dad's access badge this morning. We can get in. Said he overheard his dad say that mining has stopped since there was some kind of legal issue with the state or something like that." His mouth curled into a sly smile. "So, get this, nobody's been down there for days. Connor says it's safe, though, and they'll still be pumping oxygen down there. It's cool. We got a case of beer and plenty of flashlights. It's dark as hell down there, but we'll be fine." His eyes turned pleading again. "C'mon, man, you gotta go! Connor actually mentioned we should invite you. He feels bad about calling you … you know, last week."

Aaron wasn't buying that for a second. But he had to admit that a chance to go down into the fabled Blake-Littlefield salt mines wasn't something that came along often. It wasn't as if it was open for public tours. His pulse quickened as he imagined what he might see down there, his thoughts drifting back to when he was six or so, when Dad had told him and Owen all about the mines as they'd been fishing for perch on Lake Erie—a rare opportunity between Dad's deployments. It was another one of his favorite memories of Dad.

"Remember, boys. There's always something below the surface," he'd said as they'd drifted on a head boat near Whiskey Island, sinkers dragging across the bottom but not catching anything. Aaron had been indulging in his second Dr Pepper. "They've got these massive crushers down there that smash up big chunks of salt. Huge conveyors send the salt to the mine entrance, and then up some high-powered elevators. Those big mountains you see over on Whiskey Island? That's history being dumped out right there, granule by granule, right before your eyes. Never thought there was a mine under this big body of water, did you?"

Aaron's armpits were now slick.

I could go down there.

He looked at the idling car, then back at his brother. "You know I don't like him," he said. "I'll never forget what he said about Mom and keeps saying about me."

"I know, I know," Owen said. "But dudes say stuff like that to each other."

Aaron's face grew hot. "Like calling me fatfuck?"

The hopeful look on Owen's face faltered. "Yeah, yeah, I know. It was a douchebag thing to say, and I destroyed his nose for it. Look, I get it if you don't wanna go. Just didn't want you to miss out."

Aaron's hyperdrive memory raced back to Owen's beating of Connor. His brother was his protector. As long as Owen was around, he'd be safe. His shoulders relaxed, and he stood a little straighter. After a moment's thought, he asked, "Am I allowed to have a beer?"

Owen's features softened, and he favored his little brother with an uninhibited smile. "As many as you want, as long as Dean's List doesn't shotgun 'em all first."

Chapter 5

The Salt Mines

The clang of the metal gate sent a jolt through his shoulders. Then, the doors were whirring shut, sealing his fate inside a cramped elevator about to descend two-thousand feet into the Earth.

In truth, Aaron's fate had been sealed the moment he'd found himself sandwiched between Reid and Dean in the back of the Audi. Fortunately, Connor's leaden foot had gotten them to downtown Cleveland in less than thirty minutes, before Dean's bawling laughter and the booming bass had become completely intolerable. He'd breathed easier as the car pulled onto the access road leading to the hulking salt mountains of Whiskey Island, which were situated at the mouth of the Cuyahoga River where it emptied into Lake Erie.

Now, as the rickety elevator lowered into darkness—Connor said it would take about three minutes—the reality of what lay beneath settled over him like the weight of the lake itself. Beneath the gigantic body of water was an ancient seabed, providing millions of tons of salt to Northeast Ohioans and beyond. A place of total darkness. A place of impossible depth. A place where oxygen was in short supply without the aid of modern technology. Goose bumps crawled up his arms. He closed his eyes, reached up and under his shirt, and ran his thumb across the medallion's surface. Soon, his breathing relaxed.

The elevator thudded to a stop. The outer gate screeched open and the doors whirred apart. They stood peering out into a dark and cavernous space. Aaron expected the air to be damp and musty, but it was instead dry and arid. A single sodium light fixture, suspended some twenty feet above them, cast a lonely puddle of light onto an earthen floor. The light revealed a massive concrete wall beyond, stretching from floor to ceiling, a steel door at its center with red letters that said: TURN HANDLE SLOWLY.

Connor strode out in front of them toting a large duffel bag. Before they'd entered the elevator at the surface, Connor had gone into the workers' garment area and grabbed several hard hats affixed with headlamps. Reid, observing a cluster of portable oxygen packs nearby, had asked Connor if they'd need them underground.

Unlike his nose, Connor's bravado was still intact, and he'd dismissed this precaution. "Trust me," he'd said, "there will be plenty of oxygen down there. They've never had an incident. My ol' man told me hardly anyone wears their emergency oxygen packs down there anyway, since they have a shitload of alarms that'll go off if the oxygen level drops so much as a fraction of a percentage. We'll be fine. Plus, like I overheard my ol' man say, they got camera people coming tomorrow to take photos. Insurance shit or something like that. That's another reason they won't dare turn off the oxygen, the ventilation system, or the power. Think about it, they can't afford *not* to have it habitable down there."

They were now gathered under the overhead light. "You'll need these," Connor said, reaching into the bag and pulling out the hard hats. Owen and Reid took theirs and trotted off to explore the alien world. Dean grabbed his, fiddled with the headlamp and put it on before resuming his protective grip on the handle of his oversized chest cooler. When Connor at last fished out Aaron's hard hat, he extended it but then pulled it back before Aaron could take it, a smirk forming on his lips.

"Ready for this, Portly?" he said, the smirk turning into a smile that didn't reach his blackened eyes. He watched Aaron, as if daring him to reply.

Aaron didn't.

After a lengthy pause, he thrust the hard hat at Aaron.

Aaron played hot potato with it before letting it clang to the floor.

"Way to go, butterfingers. Better not have broken it."

Aaron bent, dusted it off, found a switch near the lamp and flicked it on. It still worked.

"You're lucky it still works, Portly."

Connor turned and marched toward the steel door. "Follow me, ladies. Gotta get through a couple airlocks before the fun begins." He pulled the door handle slowly as instructed and it groaned open. Dean followed Connor through the opening like an obedient collie and Reid wasn't far behind. Owen hung back and sidled up next to Aaron. "Hey, you cool? There's no shame in going up and hanging at the surface."

Aaron licked his lips. "Nah, I'm good." But as the elevator door closed behind them, taking with it all its light, he could hear the tremor in his own voice.

"Okay. Just stick with me."

They followed the others into the airlock, which was fifty square feet of claustrophobia. The air was thicker in here, and another lonely overhead light revealed bubbling veins of yellow foam insulation—looking hard as rock—in the seams where the room's pockmarked concrete walls met floor and ceiling.

Airtight.

A digital readout near the opposing steel door declared the air quality outside the airlock suitable, with the oxygen level at twenty-one percent and the temperature a comfortable seventy-one degrees.

"See, we're golden," assured Connor.

Reid said, "Hang on a sec. They gotta have cameras crawling all over this place, right?"

Connor was already shaking his head. "Yeah, they got cameras, but they're not storing the data anywhere. You saw the control room up there. There's no one there to monitor the operation. I doubt anyone is monitoring it remotely, and it's fucking expensive to store all that data. My ol' man is way too cheap to foot that bill, especially with nothing happening down here over the next couple days."

Reid wasn't convinced. "Isn't swiping your dad's badge gonna add some kind of data point into the system?"

Connor rolled his eyes. "Dude, seriously, if you're that scared, I don't know why you even came this far. We already used his badge, so we might as well go all the way. Anyone else need training wheels?" He glared at Reid and Owen, but only gave a cursory glance toward Dean, who'd do anything he asked. He didn't bother looking at Aaron. He then adjusted his hard hat and turned to the steel door, his headlamp playing over the door's gunmetal gray surface. More bold red text implored them to open this door slowly too.

"All you gotta do is follow me through the door and then a couple more doors after that. Then we're in, easier than Dean's List's mom."

"Hey, what the he—" Dean started, but Connor talked over him.

"From there, we'll grab a couple golf carts, and it'll be Mario Kart all the way out—'bout two miles out under the lake."

When the last airlock door clanged shut behind them, they found themselves in a dark tunnel. Aaron swung his gaze from left to right, seeing but not fully registering the small dust particles swimming in front of his headlamp. A corridor of bored-out earth stretched into darkness before them. Electrical wires traced an earthen ceiling patterned with grooves. There were no lonely light fixtures here to keep them company, just their own headlamps, cones of light swallowed by darkness before they could reach ten feet.

But as Aaron crunched over stray granules of salt, his eyes adjusted, registering an elevated conveyor belt running along the left side of the tunnel. It looked worn with age and use. Piles of detritus lay to the right: discarded chunks of salt mixed with dirt. Tire tracks led off into the dark, giving symmetry to the grooved ceiling above. Tire tracks from—

A high-pitched *BEEP* reverberated across the corridor. *From behind.* He turned and squinted into a pair of bright lights racing toward him from some place to the right of the airlock bulkhead. Another pair of lights followed close behind. The staccato popping of the gas-powered engines grew as Dean and Connor pulled up in a pair of golf carts.

Connor shouted over the chuffing engines: "We should be good with two. Me, Owen, and Dean's List in this one. Reid, Portly, and the cooler in the other."

As Owen and Dean climbed into the first cart with him, Connor turned his attention to Aaron. "Portly, your job is to hold that cooler in place behind you. Don't fuck it up."

Dean was about to protest at being separated from his beer, but Connor stepped on the gas before he could utter a word and the cart lurched forward. Dean cursed something inaudible and swung his massive frame onto the cart's small backseat, which faced backward.

A weight settled into Aaron's stomach as he watched the cart—and Owen—accelerate into darkness. He turned to see Reid watching him with a concerned look on his face.

"Dude, you cool with this?" he asked.

Aaron nodded, bent to the cooler, and took a handle. Together, they hoisted the cooler up and onto the shallow backseat. He climbed into the passenger's seat, and Reid got into the driver's seat, his gangly legs bumping against Aaron's.

"Think you got it?"

Aaron nodded, placing his palm on the cooler's lid to keep it from toppling. He thought of Shelby. She and her trailer would have been perfect for this two-mile journey.

"Well, alrighty then," Reid said, "let's do this." He put his foot down on the pedal, and they lurched forward, the cart's modest light beams and their headlamps no match for the impenetrable dark.

***

"Christ, it's not a race," Reid said as they zipped down the tunnel in pursuit of the others, who had at least a two-minute head start.

Aaron glanced at Reid, his long ponytail whipping about from beneath his hard hat. He was the only friend of Owen's who didn't look down on him and call him fat ass or Portly, or exclude him out of malice. Reid wasn't calculated like Connor or boorish like Dean. Of Owen's friends, Reid made Aaron the most comfortable, and he decided he ought to be grateful to have Reid as his partner for this plunge into the unknown. His stomach settling, his feet began to absently knead the cart's plastic floorboard. He was riding Shelby again, her pedals like phantom limbs, her tires kicking up dusty plumes on the Ohio & Erie Canal Towpath. Except his garbage-picking companion was back at Simon's, unable to usher him into this forbidden world. His muse, his trusty sidekick, his partner in crime, who he figured could take him as fast as this golf cart.

Then, a small square of light, suspended in the dark like a cellar window. Something about it felt familiar. His pulse quickened as they approached it. Details of the lit box came into focus, like the intricacies of a diorama scene: tiny orbs of light at the top and heaps of what looked like teaspoons of sugar at the bottom. Saliva welled in the back of his mouth and the knot returned in his stomach. The skin on his upper chest where the medallion rested began to itch. He reached up and under his shirt, scratching his skin beneath the medallion. But it was no good. There'd be no relieving it.

I can't do this. We shouldn't be here.

Then some instinct took command of his thumb, bringing it to the medallion. He began to trace the medallion's surface, grazing the raised glass chips, feeling the textured swirl. The unbearable itch was replaced by a desire to put the medallion in his mouth, the same feeling he'd had when he'd stared into its dark eye that night in the rain.

"You okay, man?" Reid asked.

Aaron broke from his trance and looked over at Reid to find him glancing at him sidelong.

He nodded. "Yeah, guess I just experienced déjà vu or something."

Reid turned back to the light ahead, which was approaching fast. "That shit happens to me *all* the time," he said. "Sue always tells me that time doesn't work the way we think it does. Something about it not being perfectly sequential—she's usually baked out of her mind when she gets all philosophical like that. But who knows? Maybe you've been here in another life or somewhere like it."

It took Aaron a moment to recall that Sue was Reid's mother. But he didn't have time to ponder this any further. A winter wonderland enveloped them.

"The main lode, ladies!" Connor shouted as they entered a cathedral-sized space. He slowed his cart, and Reid did the same, their engines sputtering and then jolting to a stop.

Aaron gaped at the colossal room. The ceiling had to be at least fifty feet high. Industrial-sized light fixtures hung from the grooved ceiling like dainty pendants, casting light upon a world of bone-white snowdrifts. Except it wasn't snow. It was *salt*—loads of it. Huge tire tracks stood out in relief, leading down the center of the chamber before vanishing into a smaller opening at its far end. Piles of salt nearly twenty feet high caked the right wall. The salt drifts buffering the left wall were perhaps half as high, allowing for the same elevated conveyor belt that had accompanied them down the long tunnel to pass through this space as well. The cables suspending the conveyor from the ceiling were pale and encrusted, looking like secretions from some mammoth creature that had calcified mid-drip. Aaron ran his gaze along the conveyor, watching it pass beneath a high catwalk that ran perpendicular to the walls some two-hundred feet away. Just beyond the catwalk was a latticework of metal railings and stairs, which straddled the smaller opening where the conveyor ultimately vanished.

Connor put words to the imagery, "Way down there, past all that metal shit, is where they crush up the salt. My ol' man wouldn't take me back there, but there's supposedly some huge crushing machines that chomp up large salt rocks and boulders to make them finer. Then it's put on the conveyor and sent all the way back to where we came from."

"What's through those tunnels?" Owen asked, gesturing toward a series of smaller openings along the right wall just beyond the salt mountains.

"Offshoot veins," Connor said. "Workers drive front-end loaders down those tunnels, blast out more salt with charges, and bring it all back here. Place just keeps expanding, like a fucking ant farm."

Under Lake Erie, thought Aaron, shivering despite the comfortable seventy-degree temperature.

When finally he pulled his attention from his otherworldly surroundings, he found he was the only one still sitting in a cart. Connor and Reid were already crunching through the center of the lode where the salt drifts parted like a white sea, apparently a game trail for the massive trucks and loaders.

Reid knelt, grabbed a fist-full of rock salt, and attempted to massage it into a workable snowball, but it fell apart instantly. Owen coiled into a sprinter's stance, exploded forward, and raced up one of the salt embankments. He planted one foot to gain purchase but caused a small avalanche and came skidding down on his ass. Connor howled at the sight. Reid chuckled.

Dean might have burst into his trollish laughter, but was instead gulping a can of Natural Light, his head thrown back. He lowered the can, crunched it in his bear-sized hand, and tossed it to the ground. He bent to the cooler for another.

"Hey, dumbass," Connor said, "you can't leave that here. It's why I brought these." He reached into his duffel, pulled out a large trash bag, and shook it open.

Connor motioned for Dean to toss the can in. "Listen, *nothing* gets left down here. Doubt they'll notice a few shoe prints in the salt with all the tracks everywhere, but they'll sure as hell notice cans of Natty Light." Setting the bag in the back of one of the carts, he pulled a can of chewing tobacco from his front pocket. "Owen, you in?"

Owen, who was dusting salt from his shorts, said, "Nah, I'm good." He then gave an impish smile and jabbed a finger at Aaron. "But that guy needs a beer!"

They all made sounds of raucous agreement—all except for Dean, who'd have gladly shotgunned the entire case of beer. Before Aaron knew what was happening, Reid was pressing an opened beer can into his hand. In truth, he was looking forward to it. An adventure. Danger. Getting up to no good. Plus, Owen was with him. What was there to worry about? His eyes lingered on the aluminum can, its cold condensation soothing his palm like a wicked pact. He drank.

Chapter 6

Falling Dark

Three beers later and the room began to vibrate. Gently at first, but becoming more pronounced as Aaron shuffled forward in the snow, which was salt, then was snow again. His grin was plastered on his face. He'd never felt such euphoria, warmth, *love*. He focused and refocused on the faces floating around him. He loved them all, including Connor, who'd given him a high-five and was now clumsily draping an arm over his shoulder as the five of them shuffled in a disorganized circle singing *Sweet Caroline*.

Aaron's bungled thoughts couldn't replay his previous actions in clear sequence, least of all what had ignited this bizarre group sing-along. It wouldn't be until much later that he'd recall plopping down near the base of a salt embankment and making salt angels. An untamable instinct had commanded him to belt out the Neil Diamond classic, which was one of Gram's favorite songs. It would have been easy to chalk it up to too much booze—at fourteen, it wasn't as if his body was conditioned for that sort of thing—but this had felt like something else. As he'd worked his hefty arms and legs into frenzied semicircles, displacing small braids of salt into the classic angelic pattern, the song had erupted out of him. And he wasn't just singing it. He was screaming it.

Dean had collapsed next to him and was soon howling the lyrics and making his own clumsy salt angels. Then Reid, Owen, and even Connor had joined in to create a basketball team of snow angels beneath the blurring overhead lights. Connor's dire warning to leave nothing behind all but forgotten as their hardhats lay strewn about.

Now, they stood together, rocking side to side, howling the lyrics again and again—that is, until Owen stumbled backward from the group and plopped onto his ass. Aaron watched his brother's unfocused eyes turn up in horror as the beer can flew from his hand, somersaulted in the air, and emptied all over his T-shirt.

Connor burst into laughter. Dean bawled. Aaron laughed a little despite himself, but his laughter died when Owen shot to his feet, his face screwing up with rage.

Aaron tried to force his dulled mind to think of some way to defuse things, and something Gram often liked to say came back to him. Trying to speak around a slow and clumsy tongue, he said, "Owwwen, weeer not laughin' atchu. Weeer jus laughin' witchuuuu."

Reid and Dean made noises of agreement, but Connor wasn't having it. "Whatever," he sneered, "that was funny as hell! The athletic, Mr Everything-Owen-Porter just fell drunk on his ass! Ha! Look at 'em! Shit-faced! We need to capture this." He whipped out his iPhone and mimed taking a photo.

Before anyone could react, Owen stepped forward, slapped the phone away, and slammed his palm into Connor's chest.

"Want me to break your nose again, prick?" he growled through gritted teeth.

Connor staggered to the floor.

Aaron tried to make his mouth work again but nothing came out. Then bile was rushing up his throat and into the back of his mouth—fast. Before he could take a breath and will it back down into his stomach, a geyser erupted from his mouth and nose.

It was over a moment later, and through eyes that felt on the verge of bursting, he glimpsed Owen slowly backpedaling as he stared down in disbelief at his puke-coated shirt.

The others had fallen silent, including Connor, who'd gotten up and was dusting himself off. Aaron lowered his gaze to the thin line of spittle dangling to his cargo shorts. He spat it out. *Silence.* He slowly looked up at his brother, and then Owen did the last thing Aaron expected.

Owen gave a sheepish grin and clapped his hands. "Aaron!" he shouted. "My drunk-ass bro! Whoo-hooo!"

The rest of them hooted and hollered as Owen wriggled out of his shirt, balled it, and wiped his shorts and sneakers.

"Hey, Aaron," Reid said, "we need to get you another beer. You lost all yours!"

The others burst into hysterics all over again. All but one person. Aaron spat again and glanced over at Connor, who wasn't laughing or even smiling. Aaron then looked at Reid, who was chuckling, but also watching Connor sidelong. Aaron was about to suggest that maybe he and Owen head up to the surface—it was getting late anyway—but Reid cut in before he could.

"Hey, we still got plenty of gas in these carts, right? I mean, this place is enormous. Would be a shame if we didn't at least explore some of it. What d'ya say, gents? Change of scenery?"

They all directed their attention to Connor, their unofficial steward.

Connor's dark expression was replaced by one of mischief. "Yeah, let's explore," he said. "I know just the place to go."

***

Connor, now riding with Dean and Reid, chose the farthest offshoot vein to the right and sped down it. Owen put the pedal to the floor and fell in right behind him, the carts' rumbling engines amplifying as the space enclosed around them. The perfect darkness was back, swallowing all the light from their headlights and the lamps of their hardhats, which Reid had fortunately reminded them to grab before they'd set out.

Through massive intersections, they drove, vein colliding with vein, the passing openings looking like yawning mouths. It had been Aaron's suggestion that he ride with Owen—the thought having gained clarity after he'd voided his alcohol-filled gut—and he'd nudged Owen as they'd headed to the carts when they were back in the main lode.

"I think you oughta let things cool down a bit," he'd said. "Why don't we ride together?"

Owen had just stared at Aaron as if he'd grown a third eye. He looked over at Dean and Connor, who were climbing into the first golf cart, and Aaron could see from his confounded expression that the thought had never occurred to him.

What do you mean cool down? What did I do?

In the end, reason had prevailed, and he'd agreed to go with Aaron.

Now, Connor began to slow as they approached another intersection and Owen responded in kind. At the mouth of the intersecting vein to the left rested a hulking metal monstrosity encrusted with course rock salt. Its bucket had been removed, as had its tires, giving the front-end loader the appearance of a beached whale lying on its belly, its parts cruelly harvested.

"They just leave shit down here since it's so damned big," Connor said. "My ol' man told me they'll send it all down in pieces, put it together, and that's that. Once it's down here, it stays down here."

As Owen pressed the gas pedal to continue past the intersection, Aaron was so focused on the scrapped vehicle that he gave little notice to the bright orange sign posted to his right, standing at the mouth of the vein they were now about to drive down.

***

They came to an elbow in the labyrinth, the vein curving sharply to the right. At the elbow, a large vehicle stretched its long salt-covered boom into a square hole in the wall about six feet high and just as wide. The vehicle was roughly the size of a large pickup truck and had a long conveyor belt extending from its rear. Thick power cables originated from some unknown place in the dark and wormed their way up and inside a metal housing along the vehicle's left flank. A green digital readout was still illuminated near its conveyor. It was showing hectic diagnostic symbols. A shallow puddle of brown water surrounded the vehicle like a moat.

"Check it out," Connor said, "looks like they were just drilling down here."

Reid whistled. "Yeah, and it looks like you weren't kidding about them getting the hell outta here."

Climbing from his cart, Reid strode past the glare of the headlights and over to the drilling vehicle. He pointed at the little digital display. "Looks operational. Wonder if we can do some drilling!"

"Nah, wouldn't mess with it," Connor said. "I think this is where the shit storm began—where they were told to stop. My ol' man said they were working one minute and then were told to leave everything as-is the next."

"What woulda happened?" asked Owen, who was now standing next to Reid and Connor.

Connor turned a cool eye to him. "Shit if I know."

For the first time, Owen had a look of concern. "Fellas, maybe we just bag it and—"

"Check it out," Connor interrupted. He was gesturing toward the dark section of vein opposite the driller. A light breeze was drifting toward them from the dark. Just visible in the gloom were a pair of massive Goodyear tires—each as tall as a man. "Hey, Dean's List, point the cart's lights at it."

Dean climbed into the cart and swung it around so its headlights were trained on the tires. They belonged to a massive vehicle, its elongated shape more exaggerated than any loader Aaron had ever seen. Its steel bucket alone was the size of a small car and its rear engine housing looked distorted given how far back it stretched beyond its rear tires, which were coated in bone-white powder. The rust-colored loader had the appearance of a grotesque insect.

We really are in a giant ant farm.

"They must have been undercutting down that way," Connor said. "It's what they do before drilling."

He then pivoted and looked over his minions. His gaze settled on Owen. "Who has the balls to start her up and drive her down that tunnel?"

Aaron wanted to say, "Why don't you? You seem to know everything already," but instead fell into a bout of hiccups.

Owen shouldered past him and Reid.

"I won't just drive it," he said, "I'll *dig* with it!"

Aaron shook his head and tried to shout for his brother to stop, but his attempts at words were drowned out by his now rapid-firing hiccups. The knot in his stomach was tightening again. Then he was on one knee at the side of the cart. He was wheezing now, only dimly aware of his shirtless brother trotting up to the loader with Dean tottering and hollering after him.

His vision was blurring by the time Owen was twisting the door handle and swinging it open. He couldn't muster a word, and if he could, no one would hear him, for they were too fixated on Owen to notice. Then he vomited. This time, nothing came out of his barren stomach, and his dry-heaving intensified until he was on all fours. All sound faded into the distance, including the deep clang and rumble of the monstrous engine coming to life.

Owen, they're going to capture you.

This dim thought was as odd as it was somehow logical.

They'll turn you.

The loader's headlights were creating harsh white puddles in his periphery. The light was swinging away from him then, moving toward the path that led to that nameless thing dwelling in darkness, that thing that had called to him the night he'd gazed into the medallion's eye.

Mine boy who rides Shelby.

Owen was going to meet it. The sound of the rumbling engine retreated into darkness. Dread fell heavy into his stomach as the loader's tires crunched over unseen debris. The Earth began to shake. Then the ceiling was falling.

Chapter 7

Mistake on the Lake

Near Wayne National Forest, Southern Ohio, June 30, 2021

The Redeemer was in darkness again, plagued by the same vision that had haunted her ever since the lake incident. But not quite the same. This time the hungry flames overtook her, crawling up her fingers and singeing them to the bone. Then they were all over her arms, neck, and face—an onrush of orange, yellow, and red. She was screaming.

There was no medallion slipping through her fingers this time. No diving headlong into the murky depths of the lake only to be ripped away by her Mohawk man's powerful arms. Her little girl's voice repeated "Mine boy who rides Shelby" again and again as the Redeemer wore a helmet of flame. She tried to reply, but nothing came out, her thoughts instead screaming *Who? Where? Tell me!*

The voice became silent then, the roaring of the flames the only remaining sound. But even that sound began to ebb, and with it, the intensity of the heat. *No.* She couldn't wake up now. Not yet. This was different. Oxygen returned to fill her nose, casting a thin veil over the dreamscape. She was leaving again.

No. Tell me.

Silence.

As her eyelids fluttered at the edge of sleep and wakefulness, the voice returned to her in a whisper, as if carried on a cautious wind.

Hannah's voice uttered four words before guttering out like the tiny flame she was, "Mistake on the lake."

The Redeemer's eyes shot open.

Mistake on the lake.

The voice had been faint, but those words had been unmistakable. Gooseflesh coated her arms and legs. She was on her dingy mattress again, staring at a rotted ceiling that was still captive in predawn shadow. She'd come so close to obtaining the medallion that night on the lake but had failed. Is that what Hannah meant?

Mistake on the lake.

She pored over the possibilities. The event that night was an obvious conclusion, but what did it have to do with *Mine boy who rides Shelby*? What did that mean and who was the boy? Who was Shelby? She wondered if it could've been the name of the horse she'd taken from the white men the night before the raid. But there were other horses she'd taken before that, and they were proportionate in number to the men she'd killed. In other words, many.

Mistake on the lake.

Could there have been another *mistake*? Something nagged at her, just at her elbow. She sat up, groped under her pillow, and snatched up her knife. She twirled it for a long time, the blade glimmering in the waning moonlight.

Mistake on the lake. Mine boy who rides Shelby.

Minutes later, she thought she knew. But was it enough to go on? Enough to send her back to the place where the ache was still so tender? Yes, she decided, it was. The vision had told her where to go. Her men would've obeyed it without question. But she'd need the contrivances of modern man to act—an uncomfortable compromise. She needed wheels, and she had to do some research to narrow things down.

She rocketed to her feet and began to dress. Her tests had gone well and her last subject—a large buck—had been close enough to the size of her final subject. There was a fracking operation a few miles northeast from her cabin, not far from State Route 78. There would be plenty of vehicles there.

***

Two hours later, the pickup truck's gas gauge showing close to empty, she found herself coasting down an exit ramp near Cambridge, Ohio, just north of I-70 and west of I-77. It was high time to ditch the truck as its owner would've reported it missing by now. She skirted the edges of town, avoiding major intersections and parking lots until she came across a metro park entrance.

Pulling the truck onto the narrow driveway, she coasted down a road in dire need of repaving until she arrived at a small parking lot near a trailhead. No other cars were about. She parked. A carjacker might have been concerned about leaving behind fingerprints, but this was of no concern to her. The police couldn't track ghosts.

Thirty minutes later, she was walking through the center of town. She jaywalked across the Eighth Street and Steubenville Avenue intersection toward a stately building dressed in dark red brick and white molding, its windows high and arching, the Guernsey County Public Library. Taking two steps at a time, she shouldered her way through the front door and past the front desk.

The odor of aged paper attacked her sensitive nose, which wrinkled in response. What she was looking for would be easy to spot, just find the dimwits staring at the glowing screens. In less than a minute, she did.

She went to sit at the nearest available computer station. A sheet of paper had been taped over the monitor with bold black text stating NOT WORKING.

She clenched and unclenched her fist where her knife should be. To her right, a pimple-faced teen sat hunchbacked at his computer station. He wore a hoodie despite the eighty-degree weather outside and had large headphones covering his ears. She watched him, an idea forming. She'd forgotten that login credentials were needed to access the library's computers. She could just use his.

She tapped him on the shoulder.

The boy jerked in his chair. When he turned and saw her, his mouth fell open, and he darted his eyes from side to side, as if in search of the culprits pulling a prank on him. The Redeemer stared back at him.

She cleared her throat to use a voice that hadn't uttered a word to a modern human in years. "Can I use your computer," she said, the sound of her voice escaping like a cold wind from a cellar that had been shuttered for centuries. "Just for a couple minutes?"

The teen sat frozen, the color now gone from his face.

She waited.

After a long moment, the teen slowly nodded. Leaning across the carrel desk, he unplugged his headphones, snatched up his book bag, and rose from his chair on unsteady legs.

"Thank you," she said, "I won't be long." But even as she said this, she knew the teen wouldn't linger to reclaim the computer. She lowered into the chair, ignoring the curious stares from other zombies who'd become more aware of the reality around them. Leaving her glasses on, she turned her attention to the web browser window still open on the monitor's screen, the headline on the website the teen had been visiting breathlessly announcing "Surviving BlizzCon 2021."

She snorted and didn't care who heard. *Surviving.* While it had been years since she'd used a computer, muscle memory returned and she navigated the browser to Google.com. She sat back and drummed her fingers on the desk's surface.

Mistake on the lake. Mine boy who rides Shelby.

Reaching for the keyboard, she typed MINE, BOY, CLEVELAND. She was about to hit Enter, but then sat back, giving her query more thought. A moment later, her search amended with the word ACCIDENT, she hit Enter.

The search results loaded, returning a list of headlines. The top result read *"Toddler killed, mom in hospital after being hit by truck in Cleveland."* She scanned the next headline, which reported a fifty-seven-year-old man killed in an East Cleveland crash. She scanned the next headline, and then the next. The monitor's low resolution only allowing seven results to appear on screen at once, she rolled the mouse's wheel with a forefinger to scroll down—and stopped.

There would be no further scrolling. She didn't breathe, she didn't blink. The eighth headline down stated "One Teen Dead, One Missing in Freak Accident at Blake-Littlefield Salt Mine," *Cleveland.com.*

The headline was followed by a date stamp of June 29, 2021, and a brief teaser paragraph. She clicked the hyperlinked headline, not bothering to read the teaser.

The Cleveland.com website loaded, and the article came into view. She inhaled, leaned forward, and read:

Cleveland, Ohio—The Cuyahoga County Medical Examiner has identified the victim in the fatal mine accident that happened late Saturday night.

Dean Cavanaugh, 16, was preparing for his junior year at Portage Falls High School. The honors student was expected to be a key starter on the Portage Falls football team this fall. Cavanaugh was killed instantly when the ceiling of the southeastern-most vein in the mine complex collapsed on him.

Police have also reported Owen Porter, 16, missing. Also a junior-to-be at Portage Falls High School, Porter (6', 180 lbs) is a highly decorated player on the Portage Falls football team and was listed in All-Ohio Second Team as a sophomore. He was also in the running for the Cleveland Plain Dealer's Offensive Player of the Year last year.

Three other teenagers were involved. Cleveland police released this additional information:

- 16-year-old Reid Marlowe was treated at MetroHealth Medical Center for minor injuries and was released.
- 14-year-old Aaron Porter was treated at MetroHealth Medical Center for minor injuries and was released.
- 16-year-old Connor Littlefield, who happens to be the son of mine owner Kevin Littlefield, was not injured.

Police say the five teenagers entered the Blake-Littlefield salt mine at approximately 8:30 p.m. on Saturday night. It is still unclear as to how the teens gained entry to the mine, which is located 1,900 feet under Lake Erie. At 11:07 p.m., an apparent earthquake of a 2.6 magnitude was detected by remote monitoring sensors near Whiskey Island. While authorities are still determining if the boys could have possibly triggered the event, mine officials have stated that production was abruptly halted on Friday, June 25, when it was determined workers' safety was in jeopardy due to an increased rate of "convergence" — which is the reduction of opening between the floor and ceiling — at the far southeast end of the complex.

In a statement released on the afternoon of June 28, Blake-Littlefield spokesman Kenneth Chow explained the abrupt pullout:

"During a routine drilling procedure at the far southeast end of the mine, we detected an acute rate of convergence and believed that the layer of shale above the mine may have been depressed by an unknown aquifer. It hadn't been previously detected by our equipment — which I assure you is highly sophisticated and undergoes rigorous evaluation to ensure it meets ATSM international standards. We self-reported the concern to the Ohio Department of Natural Resources out of fear we might negatively impact the integrity of the native geology if we proceeded. Upon further discussion with state officials, we agreed that it was best to immediately suspend production and surface our workers out of growing concern for their safety, and for the preservation of the environment."

When asked how the five teenagers, one of whom is the son of the mine owner, could have gained access to the mine — which features sophisticated closed-circuit TV cameras and tightly monitored access control—Chow was less forthcoming.

"We're working closely with local law enforcement officials to determine how this could've happened."

According to Chow, electronic explosives are usually detonated at night, but were not expected to be live at the time of the incident. Police have asked for patience as they determine the teens' possible role in the collapse, which partially blocked the tunnel where the accident occurred, causing the aquifer to empty into the tunnel. While authorities have stopped short of calling off a search for Owen Porter, the instability of the vein—which is now submerged in three feet of water—will make it difficult for investigators to search for his body. Chow did note that workers had been instructed to avoid starting any vehicles near the unstable vein, fearing that even a modest vibration from a running engine could trigger a collapse. Alcohol is believed to have been a factor in the break-in. Police say that Cavanaugh had a high concentration of alcohol in his system.

Monday evening, the Portage Falls community pulled together to remember Dean Cavanaugh and offer support to the other teens involved in the accident. In a statement released on the afternoon of June 28, Portage Falls school officials expressed their sorrow about the tragic incident and informed the community about the availability of grief counselors in its wake.

"Providing support for our school family is an important priority in our district," the statement reads, "to assist students and staff in coping with this horrible event, counselors and high school personnel will be on hand to provide support, this evening, June 28, beginning at 5 p.m. Counselors and school personnel will also be available tomorrow, June 29, from 8 a.m. until 5 p.m. at Portage Falls High School."

The Porter family in particular has experienced its fair share of tragedies. Sergeant First Class Martin Porter, stepfather of Owen and Aaron, was presumed killed in action in 2014. Just 35 at the time of his presumed death, Martin was a member of an armed special operations team that had come under heavy attack in Iraq. The fatal encounter claimed all members of his team. All but Porter's body were recovered and brought back to the United States. While presumed dead, his disappearance is still classified as Missing in Action (MIA). Amanda Porter, 43, wife of Martin and mother of Owen and Aaron, no longer lives with the boys, who are under legal care of their grandmother, Mildred O'Malley, 68.

"These boys have been through so much," said Rosa Delucci, whose son Tony is a friend of Owen Porter. "No child ... no child should ever go through..." Mrs Delucci trailed off before putting a hand to her mouth and breaking into tears.

The Redeemer read it again. And again. She thought of the boys' names.

Cavanaugh.

Might be a problem since he's dead. She didn't know the Cavanaughs but might need to circle back on that lead.

Porter.

She knew the name but didn't know the family. With one of the brothers missing and probably dead, that could be problematic too.

Marlowe.

She knew of a *Richard* Marlowe. Did he have a kid? Another unknown, another possible lead.

Littlefield.

Her pulse quickened. The offspring of Kevin Littlefield— that fuck. If son was anything like father, he needed to woo his friends with daddy's connections, money, or any combination of the two.

Money.

She sat forward, the rear right leg of the chair scraping the carpet. A few zombies poked their heads from over the top of their monitors at the sound of this real-world stimuli but she was only dimly aware of them now.

Money. Mine boy who rides Shelby. Shelby ... rides Shelby.

She drummed her finger on her lower lip.

Could it be, drives Shelby? Like the Ford Mustang Shelby?

If anyone was pretentious enough to let his kid drive an expensive muscle car, it was Littlefield. The kid might have even stolen it from Daddy. She turned the idea over in her head and decided it fit. A plausible lead. She bent and grabbed her knapsack, the liquid contents of the canisters swishing about. Rising to her feet, she slung the bag over her shoulder and strode out of the library and into the whitewash of the late afternoon.

Connor Littlefield who drives a Shelby, you've got something of MINE.

Chapter 8

Gone

Portage Falls, Ohio, July 21, 2021

Not Mine.

Aaron stood in the doorway of his brother's bedroom, which occupied at least a third of the upstairs living space. The room contained the only second-floor bathroom, a cozy little half bath, its ceiling set aslant with the contours of the bungalow's roof. But Aaron couldn't use the bathroom he and his brother used to share.

More than three weeks had crawled by since the accident, the accident he'd felt coming yet had done nothing to stop. The accident that had stripped away all he had left: his only brother, his protector, his hero. *Owen.* He couldn't cross the room to the bathroom even though his bladder insisted that he did. Why couldn't his body understand that the world now ceased to have any meaning? That it was devoid of all hope?

Not mine.

He couldn't walk past the hamper still brimming with Owen's spent athletic shirts and shorts. He couldn't walk past the dresser topped with Cleveland Indians bobbleheads. He couldn't walk past the framed photo showing a grinning Owen standing dwarfed next to living-NBA-legend and fellow Akron-area native Lebron James, who was the guest speaker at one of Owen's awards banquets.

Not mine.

He couldn't walk into the little bathroom where he'd encounter the toiletries on the little porcelain sink: the Old Spice Sport deodorant stick, the Nautica cologne, the Barbasol shaving cream.

Not mine.

For he knew if he were to enter the bedroom he might not make it out. His legs would go weak, and he'd crumple where he stood. He'd stagger into Owen's unmade bed and bury his face into those musky sheets, folding the pillow over his nose and mouth, breathing in the last remaining scents of his brother, willing himself to suffocate, giving himself over to the cold gray of his brother's death.

Despite his body never being found, Owen *was* dead. Everyone went away. His biological father was a mystery. Dad never came back from the war. Grandpa passed away. Mom— wherever she was—might as well be dead. She sure as hell hadn't attended the vigil. Now, Owen. *Gone.*

Not mine.

He lingered in the doorway for what seemed an eternity until somehow, summoning his will, he was able to turn away. But his eyes were slower to move from all that was left of his brother as he clicked the door shut. He shuffled down the hallway toward the staircase. He'd use the downstairs bathroom … again.

Chapter 9

The Player

Time and Location Unknown

Connor Littlefield's cares, which were few, were now far behind. But something wasn't right. He shouldn't be feeling carefree, should he?

I should be scared.

His fog-filled brain struggled to stitch together his whereabouts before this sweet numbness. It seemed he was just at the *Rockin' on the River* festival at the Portage Falls Riverfront Square, the only place to be during the summer weekends, a bazaar of live music, fair food, beer, and plenty of ass.

The band had been some kind of Beatles cover band ... or was it Led Zeppelin? He hadn't cared as his focus had been elsewhere. Carrie Mattingly, Owen Porter's newly single ex-girlfriend, had been gazing at her shoes while Casey Sill and Lindsay Bailey were cocooning her, whispering in her ears with exaggerated concern etched across their heavily made-up faces. Rumor had it they were trying to get Carrie out of the house; get her to let her hair down and forget the tragedy—if just for one night. They'd succeeded in getting her out, but the cocoon she'd built around *herself* must have been portable. The girl clearly didn't want to be out, no less at a noisy drunken festival.

I'll fix that, Connor had thought at the time. *After all, I've lost my best friend too.*

He'd use her grief and be a shoulder to cry on. Before she knew it, he'd be in her pants, and she'd want it. She always had.

But what had happened? Why can't I remember?

His groggy mind fought through some more of the fog. Tony Delucci had been with him. Tony had just returned, double-fisting a pair of translucent solo cups brimming with Bud Light. His fake ID had worked like a charm yet again, and Connor had been all too happy to use the impressionable Tony and his magic hall pass. Despite what had happened at the mine less than a month ago, he'd convinced Tony to blow off some steam with him, which meant trying to complete the trifecta: get high, get drunk, and get laid.

After the accident, the questions he'd gotten from the police and the accusing looks from his parents had been temporary inconveniences. He'd known how to play the game and the waterworks came without much effort. He'd slipped into his wide-eyed teen persona, the kid who just wanted to impress his friends in his own misguided way and show them how proud he was to be the son of a father who'd *made it*. The ruse would've worked on his gullible parents without the tears, but why leave it to chance? Dad had yanked him into an embrace, his velvety businessman voice affirming undying allegiance between father and son.

"Hey, bud, your old man has the best attorney money can buy," his father had whispered, his aftershave nauseating up close. "You remember Garrett Flynn, right? Well, he's on it. You'll be off the hook. The environmental bastards will look like idiots for making us pull outta there when Flynn is done with them. Hell, the Marlowes will be kissing our asses since they'll be off the hook too. And don't you worry about the Cavanaughs and the Porters. They won't be able to sue. Flynn'll see to that. You watch."

Flynn had worked his magic, making sure all fingers were pointed at the state of Ohio's natural resources jerk-offs for fucking up standard shutdown protocol. And Connor had been all too happy to get things back to normal.

A scraping sound issued somewhere near him, high and cold. He didn't want to hear the scraping sound, which was harsh, sobering, and interrupted his musings like the raking of fingernails over a chalkboard. His dim memory of the riverfront wavered. Then it was back again.

He'd been planning his approach to Carrie, conjuring ways to pierce the female cocoon, rehearsing cocky but witty things to say. But he'd been hesitant. He'd never used his reliable charm and wit on a girl whose boyfriend had gone missing and was probably dead.

That's when he'd sensed someone looking at him. He'd become adept at catching surreptitious glances from girls who pretended they weren't interested in him. But they all were. Girls were just better at hiding it than guys. Connor Littlefield was even better at detecting it. That instinct was the only thing that could've snared his focus from Carrie.

He looked toward the tall brick clock tower looming over the Portage Falls Riverfront Square. At the base of the tower, maybe a hundred feet away, stood a tall, strange-looking woman sucking on a lollypop. She was an island unto herself. His mind labored to picture her. Her platinum blonde hair was pulled back in a French braid, not unlike the white-haired princess hair from that animated Disney movie.

Was it Frozen?

The hair framed a long oval face, which was almost entirely obscured by a pair of bug-like aviator glasses that gleamed in the dusky light. Given it *was* dusk, this should have tipped him off that there was something off about this woman. But he'd been too distracted as he'd run an eye down her. She stood on a pair of Rollerblades, which amplified her already considerable height.

A grown woman on Rollerblades? And she's sucking a lollypop? How old is this woman?

The tall woman must have known he was returning her gaze because she plucked the lollypop from her mouth and smiled, revealing a set of straight bright white teeth.

Too bright, too straight.

Connor, unaccustomed to blushing, dropped his eyes. When he chanced another look, the woman still appeared to be gazing at him behind those bug-like glasses despite the throng of festival-goers milling in and out of her line of sight.

Her smile widened further, and what she did next caused the cocksure Connor to avert his eyes and blush all over again. She eased out her long tongue—still bright red from the sucker—and waggled it obscenely.

Blood raced to fill his cheeks. And despite the oddness of it all, blood was racing somewhere else too.

He paused, remembering Tony and Carrie. He glanced to his left to see Tony chumming it up with Derrick Cassell just a few feet away. He decided he'd stop being a little pussy boy. He'd be a man. This older woman wanted some of Connor Littlefield. Buoyancy returned to his jostled nerves. He'd meet her gaze and give her the ol' Connor Littlefield nod, the nod that said, "*Yeah, I know you're checking me out.*" But when he turned to look back at her, she was gone.

Straightening up, he scanned the throng without trying to appear too obvious. Was she approaching? Did she skate away? Tony had become lost in the sea of festival-goers and was out of sight. It was as if this woman had lured Connor out into a forbidden stretch of open water, separating him from his lifeboat. He pivoted to his right, and then to his left, nearly completing a one-eighty before his eyes caught on that same face with those oversized glasses, the red appendage that had slithered out just moments prior now hidden behind that same pink smile.

She'd come up from behind him and was now leaning against a brownstone building in an alleyway twenty or so feet from where he stood like an idiot. Her chosen location was a quiet cove amid the turbulent waves, and it was only for him to find. In her long fingers she cradled two plastic beer cups. She saluted him with one cup and raised the other to her lips and took a long pull. The skates lay in a heap near her feet, which were shod in white ankle socks. The droll sight of this woman standing in her socks on shadowy cobblestone pavement between buildings might have made him laugh if it hadn't been so weird, so confident, so … brazen.

She then lowered the cup and cocked her head, her French braid falling over one shoulder, the sliver of one eyebrow appearing above the rim of her glasses. Then the corners of her mouth eased down to a pout, as if she were disappointed he wasn't coming into her quiet cove to accept his beer.

He put one foot in front of the other and walked to her.

The woman's blinding white teeth gleamed again as he closed the distance. She extended the beer, and he accepted it with a hand he hoped didn't look as shaky as it felt. Her nails were long and pink; everything about her was long, including her sculpted legs, which were covered by fishnet leggings beneath cut-off jean shorts.

"Thanks," he said, lowering his voice to a baritone.

"I'm Mary," she said, in a voice that couldn't be more opposite from a baritone and didn't fit her appearance.

The voice didn't seem to fit *any* appearance. It was high, thin, and somehow alien. But this thought evaporated as he took full measure of her up close. Her breasts bulged against her pink *Life is Good* T-shirt. Unlike a lot of girls his age, this older woman pulled her shoulders back to amplify her chest, unapologetically, no ambiguity in her intent.

"What's your name?" she asked.

"Connor," he said with a slight tremor in his voice and cursed at himself inwardly for sounding like such a pussy.

The woman's smile grew, but she didn't say anything.

He was about to speak, about to say something cocky and witty, but his thoughts were jumbled.

The woman didn't seem to notice and instead nodded in the direction of the clock tower.

He followed her gaze.

"Wouldn't it be nice if we could turn back the clock?"

What?

He turned back to find her staring at him again behind those insectile glasses. He hesitated and then nodded.

Satisfied, she again looked in the direction of the tower and sighed.

"Because if I were twenty years younger, then maybe you'd fuck me."

If he'd been drinking his beer at the time, he might have spat it onto the cobblestone.

She must have registered his disbelief, because she smiled again, favoring him with those white teeth, which looked crooked in her mouth now that he saw them up close.

"Ever fuck an older woman?" she asked, her smile now devilish.

In that moment he noticed for the first time just how pale her face was, as if it had been coated in white powder.

"Y-yeah," he said. He'd nailed Lisa Davenport—who was a year older than him—down at The Courts last summer, but that had been with the aid of one of his special tablets. The encounter was a messy one he wanted to forget, and the looks he'd gotten from Lisa and her friends in the weeks that followed made him temporarily suspend use of his special formula ... but just temporarily. He thrust the cup to his mouth and took a swig.

"Oh, so I'm not too far out of your range?" She drew closer, her breasts pressing against his upper arm. She wrapped an arm around his shoulders and gave his opposing arm a playful squeeze. She then let her fingers trace down his bicep to his forearm and then to his hand, engulfing it in those long fingers. The touch was supposed to be sexual, supposed to arouse him. So why was it so ... off?

She then leaned closer and put her lips to his ear. "Ever fuck an older woman in the back of your car?"

Her fingers were no longer engulfing his hand. They were cupping something else, squeezing gently. Her nose was in his ear, her breath heavy. Something about her breath made him think of death. But still, he was growing hard at her touch.

"Finish your beer," she whispered.

Connor tipped his head back and finished his beer.

Chapter 10

Experiments

"Connor," said a high voice.

The festival was a wavering memory now, growing ever paler. Clawing for what memory remained, Connor grasped one last image, which floated into view like a fading tendril of smoke. It began to play like a movie clip, albeit in slow motion. Because *he* had been in slow motion and ... numb.

He'd been walking the tall woman to his car, eager to show off his Audi, eager to watch her fold those long fish-netted legs into the passenger seat. Maybe she'd blow him as they drove off to some secluded place—he hadn't decided where yet. But something had changed in *her*. Yes, it had happened as they'd approached the car.

"You don't drive a Shelby?" she asked.

The question was odd, and by then his legs had begun to feel weak, and he had to brace himself against the driver's side door. The woman had stared back at him from over the top of the car.

"Are you okay, Connor?" she asked, without a trace of concern in her voice. She opened the passenger door and dropped the skates onto the leather seat.

More scraping now.

"Connor."

He ignored the voice. He was still back at his car, in the Key Bank parking lot near the festival. There, his eyes had grown heavy just before he'd slipped into the crease made by the slightly ajar driver's side door, which then swung full open and smacked the SUV in the adjacent parking spot. He was a snared fish in a trap, too weak and too numb to pull free.

"Wake up, Connor."

No. Can't. The numbness was still a warm blanket.

"Connor, do you know where you are?"

He could feel his eyelids beginning to flutter, a warm glow winking in and out. The rude scraping here was unavoidable. Had to get away.

"Wake up, Connor."

No. He squeezed his eyes shut, but it did no good. He was in a place of pain. His eyelids peeled open to reveal a brightness that was harsh and cruel. An orange glow came into focus, becoming smaller and more concentrated, moving. A shadow squatted beyond the wavering light, androgynous like a department store mannequin: long, lean, and bald.

"There you are. Nice of you to join me again."

It was her, but not *her.* He squinted at the figure and regretted it, a rumor of pain at his right temple growing sharp, making his head feel as if it were being penetrated by a twisting screwdriver.

"What, don't recognize me?"

The slow and methodical scraping continued. He strained to focus on the figure despite the screwdriver boring into his skull. Gone was the platinum hair, the glasses, the pink T-shirt. This woman—this thing—was bald and sinewy. No full breasts, just modest bumps beneath a tank top. No fishnets, just bare legs crawling with scars in the firelight.

He took in the rest of her, the taut torso, the leathery and similarly ravaged arms, the sculpted shoulders. Then his eyes caught on the horror of her neck, the puckered scar that arched upward like another smile, toothless and boiled over.

Finally, there was her face. The white foundation had been wiped almost entirely clean, just a few smudges remaining near her hard jawline. Her eyes were almost as disturbing as the grin-like scar slashing her neck. The left eye was a milky saucer, but it was the dark right eye that made him avert his own eyes.

It was emotionless, impassive, and penetrating; an eye that missed nothing and gave nothing. It was an eye of death, and he was caught under its cold scrutiny.

Caught.

His arms and legs had been hog-tied behind his back. He couldn't see what she'd used to bind him. He could only look in one direction on this hard-packed earthen floor: toward the small fire, toward *her*.

The scraping sound ceased and was replaced by that icy voice. "Those Rohypnol pills you had in your pocket could get you into a lot of trouble, Connor. How many girls have you drugged and raped?"

His head still pounded, but now the left side of his neck and face screamed. He'd been laying on his left side for who-knows-how-long, and the tendons in his neck had been stretched to their limits.

"W-what?" he croaked, his throat feeling as if it had been stuffed with a wad of sandpaper. "Where am I?"

The woman continued her rhythmic scraping, her right shoulder and upper arm gently flexing with each pass of the ... what? Knife? Because that's what it sounded like. He couldn't glimpse what she was doing from his low vantage point opposite the flames.

Flames — wouldn't that draw attention?

Wherever he was, it was dank with fungus, or moss, or some other kind of rotting vegetation. Rotten, like her breath.

"Mary, where am I?" he repeated in a slower, calmer voice. He'd learned from his dad that using a person's name could build trust and decided now was as good a time as any to employ the technique.

She paused a moment and resumed scraping. "My kitchen," she said, without looking up.

He winced as he tried to turn his head to take measure of his surroundings. The flames were creating angry shadows on an irregular stone ceiling that sloped to some indeterminate place in the back of the room. In the back of the *cave*? That would explain the mustiness. He strained to turn his head further, but his neck screamed in protest. Obeying the pain, he lowered his head to the floor. But he'd caught a glimpse of something else: *stars*. His pulse quickened. While the time was unknowable, this cave was shallow.

Good sign.

"Mary, how'd you get me here?"

She didn't look up. "I've dragged a two-hundred-pound adult buck three miles through dense forest on a child's sled. You were nothing."

He swallowed and realized he'd never been so thirsty. "Why are you doing this?" he managed.

The scraping stopped. The woman raised a gleaming blade at least eight inches long in front of her lifeless eyes.

Connor forgot about the pain in his head, the strain in his neck, the numbness of his limbs, the thirst. "Oh g-god. I'm sorry! I didn't hurt anyone, I swear—please!" His voice was small, weak, pathetic.

"Do you know how many men I've killed with this blade, Connor?" She rotated the knife in the firelight, that dark eye studying its every contour.

"Please! I'm sorry!"

The dead eye settled back onto him. "You remind me of many things, Connor. Do you know that my daughter killed herself? She took pills and went to sleep because pieces of shit like you—cowards—harassed her."

He was going to hyperventilate. A warm sensation was blossoming in the crotch of his shorts. "I'm s-sorry. Please! I'm sorry about your daughter! I didn't hurt anyone! Please!"

She gave a humorless chuckle. "Didn't *hurt* anyone? Know what else you remind me of? Your piece of shit father."

What? She knows my dad?

A wavering thread of hope to grasp.

She knows my dad.

The words tumbled from his mouth. "My dad can help! He's got lots of money. I-I can call him!"

"Your dad is what's wrong with this world. He'll soon be consigned to the ash heap just like everyone else."

She resumed her scraping, and he could sense she was moving off the topic of his dad.

"Mary, I swear, I can make him understand!"

She paused and spun the blade between two fingers, as if testing its balance, her expression neutral and focused. "There's one thing you can do for me, Connor."

"Yes! Anything! I can help—I promise!"

She rose, the hilt of the blade swinging back into her palm. She rounded the small fire and squatted before him. Her face was horrible. "Where is it?"

He inhaled. "What? The ... pills? Is that what you're looking for?"

"No, Connor, seeing that those are what I used to drug *you*, I think I've already found them."

His mind raced back to the alleyway at the festival. Her hands had been all over him.

So stupid.

She could have plucked the repurposed container of dissolvable vitamins from his pocket at any time, putting one or more of the roofies in his beer while distracting him. Maybe when she'd directed his attention toward the clock tower?

When she was stroking me?

She was studying him with that impassive eye. "You really must be slower than I thought, especially for someone cunning enough to break into a salt mine. I must say I'm really disappointed."

He was at a loss. "I have weed," he ventured. "It's back at my parents' house."

She shifted on her haunches, this show of impatience making his breath catch again. He couldn't take it.

"Please! Tell me!"

"The medallion, Connor. Where's the *medallion*?" She set down the knife and raised both hands, forming a circle with her fingers.

"Medallion? I-I don't know what you're talking about."

"I promise, if you tell me, I'll let you use your phone."

She nodded toward the back of the cave. Next to three canisters, their metal surfaces glimmering in the firelight, lay a clear plastic bag containing his iPhone.

Connor searched his brain frantically. There was nothing he could grasp. He closed his eyes and shook his head. She was going to kill him. "Please," he said. "I don't know. I swear to you, I don't know anything about any medallion."

The right side of his face erupted, causing what little saliva he had in his mouth to launch into the fire.

"I was hoping I wouldn't have to resort to violence, Connor," the now distant voice said, which was calm and measured despite the blow.

Tears stung his eyes. He whimpered an unfamiliar sound that he thought would come from someone else—someone small and weak. He ran his tongue over his upper gums and tasted blood. An upper tooth jiggled loose from the pressure. Warm blood coating his tongue, he spat and the tooth flew into the fire.

"See, now you're missing a tooth too. We finally have something in common."

He glanced up through tears to see her smiling with her own missing teeth, her mouth like an old wooden fence with missing pickets.

"But you still have some catching up to do to be like me. Should I relieve you of more teeth, or are you ready to answer me?"

"I thwear. I thon't know!" he cried out, the new gap in his teeth drawing the focus of his tongue.

"I'm a patient person, Connor. I've had to be to get to this point. But you're standing in my way, and I'll be goddamned if I'm going to let a spoiled, spineless coward like you derail me." She sighed. "Let's try another approach, shall we?"

Connor didn't know what to say. Whatever the approach was, it wouldn't be good. He hadn't been able to give her anything, and he didn't think he could. She was going to kill him.

"Which of your friends drives—*drove*—a Shelby? You clearly don't. Is it Reid Marlowe? Dean Cavanaugh? Either of the Porters? Tell me, and I'll keep my word and you can use your phone."

"Y-you mean like the Mustang-looking car?"

"Yes, Connor, that's what I mean."

Who drives a Shelby?

The woman leaned forward and began rotating the blade. It moved faster, and faster, and faster, as if in rhythm with his hurrying heart.

"Think Connor. Who drives a Shelby?"

He closed his eyes.

Shelby, Shelby, Shelby … who drives a Shelby…?

The friends she'd listed were with him the night of the mine fiasco. Why she was targeting any of them, he had no idea. His mind ticked through each of them. Couldn't be Reid, or his parents. Reid had gotten his license this past spring but hadn't gotten a car yet. His dad drove a Toyota Camry, and his mom drove some kind of minivan—Connor didn't know what kind since he'd never had a reason to care. Reid's little slut sister was too young to drive.

Not Reid.

Dean's parents *could* afford to buy him a car, but they hadn't pulled the trigger yet and neither his mother nor his father drove anything approaching a Shelby. Dean was an only child, so that left out any siblings.

Not Dean.

That left Owen. Owen couldn't even afford a bicycle, let alone a ... his mind caught on something. *Bicycle.* Owen didn't have a bike, but Portly did. Connor had forgotten all about that fat ass tagging along with them to the mine. *Yes!* Owen's weird fat brother had given his bike a name, hadn't he? *Shelby.* It was something a three-year-old might do. Hell, Portly had even scrawled the stupid name on the worthless red scrap of metal, hadn't he? This crazy bitch had it all wrong. It wasn't a car she was looking for. His heart soared.

"I know!" he blurted.

She leaned forward. "Do tell."

"You're not looking for a car! You're looking for a bike!"

The woman paused and cocked her head like a creature hearing the soft footfalls of prey. "A bike?" she repeated. Her eyes remained impassive, but the rotating blade was slowing.

He sensed she was deciding whether she could believe him, so he plowed ahead, nodding vigorously, "Yeah, Portly—I mean, Aaron Porter—named his bicycle Shelby."

The woman let the blade's hilt go limp in her hand, dangling it between two fingers. Her horrible eyes were roving restlessly as if in search of some hidden truth or corroboration. She hadn't expected a bike. He'd given her something, hadn't he? Something valuable.

Now, maybe I can get the fuck outta here.

His chest heaving in relief, he pressed on, "I can tell you where he lives, if that helps."

The woman rocketed to her feet before he could process what was happening.

"Oh, god!" he screamed, tucking his chin to his chest, closing his eyes, preparing for the knife, the cut, death. "Please! I helped!"

She put a foot to his back and forced him chest-down to the ground. A wind whipped across his back where his wrists and ankles were bound. A sudden release of tension. A moment later, he was spreading and clenching his fingers in relief.

"Congratulations, Connor. You're very lucky I keep my promises. As I said, you can use your phone now."

She strode over to the clear plastic bag, snatched it up, and tossed it over to him. It hit him square in the palms, and he fumbled and dropped it. But the plastic bag was a good sign. She didn't want her fingerprints on his phone, which meant she was going to let him go.

"Go ahead and call or text for help," she said. "I'll sit with you a while to make sure help is on its way before I leave you. You were very helpful, Connor."

With clumsy fingers, he pried open the thick Ziplock freezer bag and pulled out his iPhone.

Why not just let me go?

But at that, he held his phone to his face and waited for the Face ID to recognize him. The screen remained dark. And shouldn't he be seeing his background photo by now? He tapped on the blank screen and waited to see a prompt for his six-digit passcode. Still nothing. He turned the phone over. It was his—at least, the navy-blue protective case looked like his. He looked up at the woman, who wasn't looking at him, she was *studying* him.

"What's going on? Is it dead?"

"It's not your phone, Connor. The protective case *is* yours though."

"What? You said I could use my phone!"

"I did say that, didn't I? But let me tell you something, Connor. You're serving a higher purpose now. You're going to help forge a better tomorrow. You want to make the world a better place, don't you?"

"Lady, I have no fucking clue what you're talking about!" He tried to stand but realized he couldn't. His ankles were still bound.

"You may not know this, Connor, but you're getting a taste of my own special batch of moonshine. I've been perfecting it over the past three years in good ol' hooch country, no less. In fact, you're the first ever human taste-tester."

"What are you talking about, you crazy bitch?"

"I'm talking about the future, Connor. Not just your future, everyone's future."

"What? What the fuck does that have to do with my phone?"

"You see, our mobile touchscreens contain layers of capacitive material: conductive metals and wire grids that harness electrical currents beneath the glass. Every time you touch your screen you're essentially shocking yourself because your skin also holds an electrical charge. But the exchange isn't enough to do any real damage. It's this combination of glass, electricity, and capacitive material that gets its attention."

"Its attention? What kind of crazy are you, you bitch?"

The woman continued absently, as if talking to herself, "The pool, deep within the Earth. The substance looks like glass when it isn't disturbed. The nearby crystals, the charged air inside. Eerily similar."

"You make no fucking sense."

"I make perfect sense. I'm describing what's about to happen to you, Connor. You've been helpful, so it's the least I can do. In the end, it's all about testing. Getting the right amount. I tested trace amounts at first, watching how it interacted with touchscreen devices I'd taken from other people who no longer needed them—people like you, Connor. And sure enough, it was as attracted to capacitive screens as a fly is to shit. It immediately coats the glass and assimilates it into something new. But the user will never know it, because it just looks like glass and their device still works as normal. I'd validated this myself by the way, interacting with an infected phone and then returning to the complex before the symptoms got too bad.

"S-symptoms?"

She didn't answer. She reached down and grabbed the long-sleeved T-shirt she'd been wearing at the festival, wrapped it around her mouth, and knotted it behind her head. She then grabbed a pair of clear plastic glasses from somewhere on the other side of the fire and put them on. Stepping back several feet, she sank to her haunches and cocked her head. She watched him.

He was about to speak, but something began to tickle the pit of his stomach. Before long it was a vise, and it was tightening. A tremor ran through his entire body, ending at his fingertips, which could no longer grip the phone. It thunked to the ground. Saliva welled in the back of his mouth, the vise tightening more as acrid bile pushed its way into his esophagus. Bile, and the flavor of something else … blood. Sweat dripped into his eyes. He rolled onto his back, and his chest began to hitch in rapid-fire bursts.

"Take comfort, Connor. You're getting a heavy dose." Her thin voice was muffled and gentle now, almost maternal. "I won't be able to do this for everyone, so consider yourself lucky. It'll be over for you very soon. For everyone else, let's just say the symptoms will come on more slowly, masking themselves as the flu. But then the bleeding will start. Perhaps it'll be diagnosed as dysentery since everyone will shit blood at first. Then the vomiting will begin, and no one will be able to eat or keep any food down. Authorities will struggle to find the cause. But they'll come up with nothing. That's because it's unlike anything modern man has ever seen — it infects you in a way never before imagined. There are no living terrestrial carriers of this disease, animal or otherwise. Many will get their chance to go viral with just a few taps of their smartphone. Best of all, it is transmissible between proximate screens. One contaminated screen becomes two, and so..."

Connor's mind was angry static. No thought could find a home in there. He could dimly feel his heels kicking a staccato beat on the ground despite the ankle bindings. His fingers clawing the dirt. The boiling acid building in his gut forced its way through his intestines and into his shorts. The relief was immediate, but temporary, as more acid was quick to fill his voided bowels. His lips parted, and the boiling mass in his stomach took it as an invitation to race up and through his throat. He couldn't turn his head as the volcano erupted from his mouth. This time, there were no teeth flying out with it; there were chunks of something else. It was warm, and it was slapping down onto his face

The distant voice said: "That's your stomach lining, Connor. Your body is being turned inside out." The voice then paused and added, "The storm will be here soon, so I need to run. Some old friends await. You've helped me a great deal, Connor. Rest assured, I'll be back to collect your body."

Chapter 11

Demons and Denials

Portage Falls, Ohio, July 24, 2021

Aaron welcomed the cool dark of his little dormer bedroom, its window air conditioning unit on full blast. The darkness was a reprieve from the visual reminders, the Portage Falls football T-shirts and shorts stacked near the foot of the basement stairs, the weight plates leaning implacably against the barbell bench in the basement, the oversized container of whey protein standing sentinel atop of the fridge. Evidence of his brother was everywhere, but at least the darkness protected him from seeing it.

Gram had been all too happy to leave everything as-is, convinced that Owen was coming home since he was, in fact, still *missing*. Her insistence to anyone who dared suggest that her grandson wouldn't come strolling through the door at any given moment had caused everyone around her to walk on eggshells, including those few remaining extended family members who'd visited over the past month. Including Aaron. The memorial service, as awful as it was, was made more awkward by Gram's assertion to all mourners that the event was just a formality and that she was simply indulging those who felt a misguided need for closure. Plus, it was a waste of money, drawing from the savings she'd reserved for her own funeral. They would all laugh about it later when Owen returned. They'd all see.

Aaron's mind drifted back to the previous day, when he'd reached trembling hands above the fridge to grab Owen's container of protein. He'd been hesitant at first but had steeled himself, he couldn't take seeing it anymore. Owen's bedroom and the little half bath upstairs were different. Aaron could avoid them, but he couldn't avoid the kitchen, his ever-expanding waistline advertising as much. He hadn't so much as lowered the container when a firm hand closed around his wrist. It was cold and possessed a seemingly supernatural strength. He gasped.

"What are you doing with that? Owen *needs* his protein! Lord knows he doesn't get enough!" Gram's deep-set eyes were narrowed, the crow's feet bracketing them—which usually emanated warmth—were like cold dark places. Her nostrils flared. Everything about the woman had turned sharp and cold over the past several weeks. Her hair more frayed and brittle, her cheeks more sunken, her already thin lips nonexistent. But those lips had been opened wide, revealing clenched teeth as she tightened her grip on his arm.

"You put that back right this instant! Right this instant! You hear me?"

Aaron stood still. He tried to signal his arms to move, to reach to the top of the fridge and deposit the container, but the message got lost somewhere between his head and his neck. It didn't help that Gram was still squeezing his wrist with her surprising strength.

She shook it. "Do you *hear* me! Put it back!"

Aaron could feel his lips tremble. His eyes fell to the linoleum and began to trace its geometric patterns. A moment later, with hands shakier than before, he lifted the container to the top of the fridge and set it down.

Gram released her death grip.

He turned to face her, a hot tear running down his cheek. He blinked away another tear and willed himself to meet his grandmother's gaze. She was the only real family he had left.

The old woman melted. All fight seemed to drain from her tired body. She collapsed into his chest and began to sob. "Oh, Aaron. My sweet Aaron. I'm so sorry. I-I-can't keep doing this." She pulled back and placed a gentle hand on his cheek, an apparent attempt to quell his flowing tears. Her tears fell freely now. "You don't deserve this. You're such a brave boy, my Aaron. I'm so sorry. I know how hard it is for you to see Owen's things. I didn't mean to…" She trailed off and sniffled. She pressed close to him again, her strength returning, a different kind of strength. His head lulled against her wiry hair as her voice came to him in an urgent hush. "We'll get through this. We always do. He'll come back to us. I know he will." She stepped back, swiped at her eyes and glanced toward the window above the kitchen sink. She remained that way for a long time.

"Your mother called today," she said finally, without taking her eyes off the window.

Aaron thought he'd lost his ability to feel any bit of surprise, but this news was unexpected. He hadn't talked to Mom in over a year, and the last time he had, she'd stolen forty-five dollars from his Yoda piggy bank.

"She wants to come over," Gram said. "Mind you, she didn't so much as have a trace of guilt in her voice for missing your brother's … vigil."

Aaron nodded. It was his turn to stare out the window. After a while, he said, "I don't want to see her." The finality of this statement felt jarring coming from his own mouth, but it was a relief to say it. He looked at Gram to gauge her reaction.

Her nod was immediate and supportive. "And I don't expect you to. I think it's best you're not here when she comes."

Aaron nodded again, relieved; the tension he'd felt just minutes before now falling from his shoulders, his neck, his hands. He realized just how tired he was. "Okay," he said, "when is she coming?"

Gram sighed. "Well, she *claims* she's taking the RTA from East Akron first thing Monday morning. Says she'll be here by eight or so. You know, Aaron, she still won't tell me what happened to her apartment or the money the Army gave her and you boys." She shook her head. "Thinks I was born yesterday."

The Gram he knew was back in full force, her fist balled on her hip. She tossed her other hand in exasperation. "I have no idea where she's living, or *who* she's living with." She shook her head again, turned back to the window and planted her palms on the countertop.

Aaron seized the opportunity. "Can I stay at the Kents tomorrow night? That way, I'm gone first thing Monday morning."

Gram's shoulders tensed for a moment but then eased up. Continuing her study out the window, she gave a weak nod. "Yes. Yes, I think that would be good." She turned to him. "But no shenanigans, you hear? I *do* like the Kents, but that Simon ... you know I don't like his mouth, right?" She turned back to the window. "The way he addresses adults is just, Jesus, Mary and Joseph, I don't know how his parents find that kind of behavior acceptable. Just like Eddie-Haskell-Littlefield's parents, who I still blame for everything. Those poor Cavanaughs, I just don't get it, Aaron. I just don't."

Aaron noted that she didn't include her own family in that statement.

"Now, his older brother is just a wonderful boy. Always so polite. Your grandfather really liked that Gabe Kent. And you know how he felt about most teenagers." She turned back to him. "I'm fine with it as long as Mrs Kent is."

Back to the present moment, Aaron shifted in bed, his thoughts now turning to the coming day. Spending time at the Kents' house was a welcome glimmer of light. He had to go to the bathroom but didn't want to go through the trouble of rolling out of his warm cocoon and trudging down the creaky wooden stairs and risk waking Gram. She needed her sleep. He'd hold it a little while longer. Such was the peace of the small hours before dawn, which could slog by as slow as they pleased. The daylight would come soon enough to beat down the door of darkness, seize him by the back of the neck, and force him to again confront the reality of his missing brother. His protector. *Gone.* He couldn't help himself now, didn't want to relive the event, but his mind betrayed him.

That night.

That night when Owen was swallowed by darkness. That night when the world fell.

The events had been a blur, and a part of him still wondered if his brain had intentionally rendered them that way out of self-preservation. Or perhaps it was the medallion's doing. Maybe it had sickened him to better insulate him from the horrific details that would follow: Dean being crushed by the falling ceiling, the roar of chaos and rushing water that had swallowed Owen and pushed its way billowing out from the collapsing vein like some vengeful spirit that had been awakened.

Then it was Reid, shouting for him to climb into the golf cart. As they careened down the miles-long tunnel, he numbly listened to Reid's hurrying words from where he sat swaying in the passenger's seat.

"Oh my god, oh my god, oh my god. Shit!" he repeated to himself.

Aaron almost tottered out of the speeding cart.

Reid flung out a hand to steady him. "Dude, Dean's List is dead!" he cried, fighting a new wave of panic. "Shit, man, oh *shit*! And Owen ... oh Christ, he's gone, man! He's gone! Ohhhh *shit*!"

He released Aaron's arm and grabbed a fistful of his hair— then free of its ponytail—and tugged it as if doing so might somehow pull the event from his mind. "Oh my god, oh my god, oh my god. Shit!"

Connor was far ahead of them in the other cart. But somehow, they got to the elevator before Connor could take it up without them, which Aaron had no doubt Connor would have done. Then there were vague images of spinning police cruiser lights followed by the harsh whiteout of the ambulance's interior. The arrival at the hospital was dreamlike, and a part of him was grateful for that.

His bladder unrelenting now, he rolled to his side and sat up. Putting cold feet on a cold floor, he walked out of his room to greet a morning that would be even colder.

Chapter 12

The Vision

Desperate fingers of daylight reached through the basement's slotted windows like a child feeling for a lost toy in the dark. A crevasse, a cave. Such was a place in which Aaron now found himself.

"Dr Pepper?" he asked.

His eyes fixed on *Call of Duty*, his fingers moving in a flurry over the controller, Simon said, "Do I look like I can drink that shit right now?"

Aaron rolled his eyes, opened the fridge and set the unopened Dr Pepper can on the wired shelf alongside dozens just like it. "Guess I really am keeping Dr Pepper in business down here," he said.

"Well, my mom didn't get the memo that it wouldn't be a month until you … came over again," Simon said, his tone uncharacteristically careful.

In truth, what Aaron had looked forward to most about spending time with Simon was that he *wasn't* careful with his words. Over the past month, Aaron had heard enough of *You're in our prayers*, *Our thoughts are with you*, and the laziest of all, *Thoughts and prayers*. Most people who'd attended his brother's memorial—many of whom he hadn't known—made sure to use some variation of those magical incantations while screwing up their faces into what they thought must have looked like textbook portraits of grief and concern. But in the end, neither their thoughts nor their prayers could bring his brother back. After all, they hadn't returned his missing father, resurrected his deceased grandfather, or even slowed his mother's dance with the needle.

When he'd arrived at the Kents' a little after four, he'd parked Shelby in her usual spot next to the garage and tried to make a quiet entrance through the back door and down the basement stairs. But Mrs Kent had intercepted him before the storm door could slap shut, engulfing him in a tangle of hair, tears, and cloying perfume. To her credit, she'd said nothing of thoughts or prayers when she stood back to appraise him.

"It's so good to see you, hon. My boys are so excited to have their other brother—my third *son*—over."

Aaron guessed that some kids might be offended by another woman claiming the sacred title of *Mother*, but his heart swelled nonetheless. Mrs Kent could be his mom any day. Even better, her next words had offered something tangible, actionable, *good*.

"I just spoke with Mil—your *Gram*—and she said it's okay if you spend more than just one night here. Sorry I didn't catch you before you left your house, but we can fix that. We'll swing by your house some time tomorrow evening and get more clothes. The boys will love it—*I* will love it. They've been at each other's throats without you, Aaron."

She then put her hands on her hips and raised her delicate voice as high as she could. "And, I've been telling Simon that he needs to get out of the house. Now, I know how much *you* enjoy riding your bike and being outdoors, Aaron, so he's *agreed* to go bike riding with you first thing in the morning. Isn't that right, hon?"

A moment passed before a grumble floated up from the basement.

Mrs Kent leaned closer to Aaron and whispered, "And between you and me, Simon's got quite the spare tire going."

Aaron chuckled, but the laugh died when his eyes fell to his own bulging belly.

***

99

When ten o'clock came Aaron didn't bother stifling a yawn, the lack of fresh air over the past several hours making his eyes feel like stale balls in his head. He unrolled the sleeping bag Mrs Kent had given him and spread it out on the floor next to the couch, one of the few spots of carpet not covered by game cases or snack wrappers.

But he'd been okay to let the day fizzle. Simon would need his pound of flesh before subjecting himself to the rigors of physical activity the following morning. Aaron figured he could use these stagnant hours as ammo for when Simon would surely complain tomorrow. He'd already decided that he'd make Simon ride the Towpath Trail with him and maybe they'd even stop by the Beaver Marsh for good measure.

Maybe I should tell him I want to go bird watching, too?

Smiling to himself, Aaron slipped into the sleeping bag and rose to one elbow. "You'd better get some sleep," he said. "We're getting up early. I'm not waiting for the trail to get crowded. Best time to be down there is well before nine. And, *Acuweather* says rain by noon."

Simon tore his attention from his game. "My ass. I said I'd go for a bike ride, not torture myself."

But after some huffing and grumbling he saved progress on his game and scooped up his phone. He began to tap in a fury.

"Capturing some good comebacks for Dickslapper8?" Aaron asked.

Without looking up, Simon lifted a hand from his phone and extended a middle finger. A moment later, entry finished, he pocketed his phone—which Aaron knew he slept with at all times—and turned off the TV. He grabbed his rolled-up sleeping bag and brought it over to where Aaron lay. Plopping it onto the floor, he unrolled it without bothering to find a pillow since sleeping—like wearing clean clothing—was a minor annoyance that had to be dealt with.

"You gonna get the light?" Aaron asked, more amused than annoyed.

"Shit." Simon struggled to his feet and huffed over to the light switch. Shutting off the lights, he lit his way back using his phone's flashlight app and let out an expansive sigh when he collapsed next to Aaron. "The shit I do for you," he muttered. A few minutes later, after some rustling around in his sleeping bag, he was snoring.

Aaron stared off into darkness. He was tired but not tired. The minutes passed, and eventually, the medallion began to assert its weight on him. He closed his eyes, willing his mind to focus on something else, anything else. He needed to sleep. But still, it beckoned. *Why?*

Libby was his usual nocturnal muse, but her freckled cheeks and wispy hair couldn't distract him from what he knew he wanted to do—which was insane. He licked his lips, saliva building in the back of his mouth. It was like awaiting the need to vomit, that agonizing line between wanting to rid his body of sickness but not wanting the jarring act to actually take place, one that could burst the blood vessels in his eyes. His fingers bracketed the medallion now, its outer edges smoother than he remembered. And somehow, the entire medallion felt smaller in his grip.

Do it now.

A gentle tremor rippled through his hand and up his arm. It wasn't clear if it was from the medallion's doing or his.

Do it now.

Before his mind could protest, his hand operated on its own accord, bringing the medallion to his mouth. His opposing hand wriggled free of the sleeping bag and rose up and tugged wider the neck opening of his T-shirt. His head retreated into his shirt like a turtle's head into its shell.

Do it now.

He turned the medallion over so that its topology would be pointing down onto his tongue. And with his best friend sleeping less than two feet from him, he slipped the ancient object into his mouth.

At first, there was nothing save the taste of metal. Placing a dingy quarter in his mouth would have tasted no different. But its size, while still large, wasn't just manageable, it was … comfortable. The object settled on his tongue, matching its contours, its precise surface area.

Then a sharp pain erupted, like a dozen needles stabbing his tongue. The tips of the small glass chips ripped into his flesh. Except they were no longer small. They were growing. Sinking. Expanding. *Probing*. They hooked deep into his tongue that should have been writhing, but wasn't. It was frozen, anesthetized. *He* was frozen, his entire body numb while this thing gripped his tongue like a leech.

Static overtook his thoughts, burying them beneath a buzzing storm of black and white, which was growing ever denser, ever darker.

A droning noise rolled in the dark places behind his eyes, building until it was a deafening roar. It screamed into him. He couldn't cover his ears. Couldn't summon his arms, his hands, his fingers. His body was motionless, but his heart wasn't. It was hammering as if preparing to leap from his chest. Somewhere deep inside him, buried beneath layers of bone-rattling reverberation and growing darkness, he knew he was holding his breath.

***

Then, total darkness. The roar retreated and dissipated until it was nothing more than an electric hum between his ears. He opened his eyes to a nightscape. Inhaling, he took in briny and humid air. There was a gentle lapping sound.

Water.

He was no longer in the Kents' basement. His eyes adjusting, the darkness took shape. A vast carpet rolled beneath him, the water's surface chopped with whitecaps. He floated bodiless in this place.

He looked skyward. If there was a moon, it was shrouded by unseen clouds. No stars were about. But there *was* a light source ... to the left. He turned to see a glimmering orange finger of light reaching into the expanse, dipping and rising with the waves, tapering to the invisible horizon.

He turned further, the light's intensity increasing. A raging inferno floated into view, hovering just above the waves. He squinted into this sudden brightness, the details of the fireball taking shape. It wasn't a single flame, but dozens—no *hundreds*— of smaller flames, all of which were different sizes, shapes, and intensities, clustered about in a loose formation. Some were blinding white while others were dimmer shades of oranges and yellows. He reached out to feel their heat, expecting to see his own hands, but he saw nothing, and he felt nothing.

Then, whispers. They were floating toward him. He couldn't make out their words. Some were louder and more urgent than others—especially the white ones. He watched the space beneath them where the water rose and fell, a distance of which couldn't have been more than a few feet. The flames fell silent as the water rose up, as if waiting in apprehension. When the waves dipped without touching them, their chorus was set abuzz all over again.

He watched the dimmer lights now. They were guttering, looking on the verge of extinguishing, water or no water. Something about the quiet little lights tore at a place deep inside him. They were children—of this he was certain.

The bright lights seemed to be aware of him now, getting bigger as they approached. He ignored those lights and focused on the dimmer lights. They had names. One little orange flame was named Ian. Another one just like it was called Tabitha. A little one near the back of the cluster was Hannah.

Hannah. Why is that name familiar?

Before he could ponder it further, the white flames encircled him, growing louder.

I shouldn't be here.

He found he could turn again, and so he did, floating through a gap in the ring of flames. There was something else he needed to see. It was old, and it didn't want to be seen.

Sapere Verdere.

He scanned this dark place with his bodiless eyes. After a time, a long horizontal shape came into view, sitting low on the opposite horizon. It was darker than the surrounding night, as if carved from deep shadow, the top of it irregular, jagged.

Land.

Before he was aware of it, he was floating toward the land formation, the noise of the flames retreating behind him. Silhouettes of swaying treetops stood in relief beneath a glimmering sky. A bright beacon lit the world in this direction. It was the moon. The stars were on fire. He lifted his eyes to the purple-black tapestry—which was richer than any night sky he'd ever seen—and back down again to the approaching land. The contours of the shoreline were familiar, as was the cleft between the two spits of land now visible in the moonlight. He continued over what he now knew was Lake Erie, heading toward an inlet he realized was the mouth of the Cuyahoga River. Where was Cleveland? Where were the lights? The buildings? But something *was* there, and it was down that watery road, further inland. Something that didn't want to be found.

Sapere Verdere.

He glided over the mouth of the raging river where it emptied into the lake. He traced the meandering Cuyahoga like a sports car hugging the curves of a lonely coastal highway, the choppy water reflecting ribbons of pale moonlight. Thinking he might be able to see his own shadow flying, he glanced down but there was nothing to see but untamed river and forest. The topology of this place was barbaric and overrun with fragrant vegetation. The river was wider than he remembered. And where were the dams? Shouldn't he have glimpsed bridges by now? What about the Towpath Trail, and the Cuyahoga Valley Scenic Railroad line, which ran north and south? Neither feature strayed far from the river at any point.

A thin trail of smoke rose along the eastern bank. Before he could decide on his approach, he was floating headlong over the towering sycamores and cottonwoods lining the river. Toward *it*. Acrid smoke was now in his eyes, and he shut them and held his breath as he drifted right of the column.

Once past the smoke, he floated up another thirty or so feet to get a sense of the scene below. Directly beneath him was a clay-packed spit of land in the shape of a keyhole, formed by the Cuyahoga's sharp bend to the West and a small oxbow lake's bend to the East. The patch of land was no more than a couple hundred feet square. Thin land bridges connected the patch to the surrounding forest at its northern and southern ends. A large clearing lay at its center—the source of the smoke.

He drifted down in a lazy loop around the smoke column to the source: a campfire. Then he saw figures, sitting in a loose semicircle around the blaze, casting lanky shadows. There were at least a dozen of them, all sitting cross-legged near the fire while one figure lay stretched out on the ground a few feet away, covered by a blanket or shawl. Red firelight gleamed upon the hairless scalps. One of the figures held to his mouth a long instrument, his cheeks contracting and expanding in rapid fits.

Aaron lowered to ten feet. Five feet. To the ground.

He was near the farthest man to the left. He'd been wrong to think that the scalps of these men were red because of the firelight's glare. This man's entire head was *painted* red. A tall narrow strip started at the center of his forehead, rising to the crown of his head before curving to its base, with bristles dyed a brighter red than the skull paint. The mohawk's bristles couldn't have been hair—they were too sharp and coarse, reminding Aaron of porcupine quills.

He studied the man. Shimmering ribbons of firelight reflected in his dark eyes like embers over coals. The Mohawk Man flitted those eyes to another man sitting next to him, who was now offering him the long wooden pipe. The Mohawk Man accepted it and wrapped his lips around the pipe and puffed his cheeks in and out, inhaling whatever substance was packed in the pipe. He exhaled dark smoke, causing the feathers dangling from his ears to sway in circles.

Aaron took in the rest of the men, all of whom were barechested like the Mohawk Man, but with differing body and facial art. It struck Aaron that none of them had spoken a single word since he'd arrived.

A man with a silver hoop curving down from between his nostrils was running a knife along the length of a severed tree branch in long protracted strokes. The man's carving looked to be an absentminded occupation, as if he was just passing the time, as if they were *all* just passing the time, waiting for something or someone.

Drifting back from the Mohawk Man, Aaron went past a small armory of weapons near the trunk of an oak tree. A trio of quivers were slumped against the trunk, brimming with feather-fletched arrows. He rose from the encampment and the sleeping figure came back into view. He'd forgotten about the sleeper. The person's bald head was free of quills or even paint. But Aaron couldn't see their face, which was nuzzled into the blanket. Their skin was lighter than the others, and their broad upper back and shoulders stretched the blanket to its limits.

Then Aaron was drifting over the figure, banking in a tight circle down to where the figure's face was tucked into the blanket's folds. Aaron's body, wherever it was, jerked despite itself. The head had been shaved, but the shelved brow, the auburn eyebrows, and the deep-set eyes—while closed—were unmistakable.

Oh my god.

His heart thundered inside his eyes.

Oh my god.

He tried to speak, tried to utter the name, but his lips wouldn't part. His eyes just remained fixated on the sleeping figure before him, unable to reconcile the sight: his brother. When a sound *did* make it out of his mouth, it sounded like a distant moan. "Owwwwen? Owwwwen?" He tried to speak again, and this time his words took better shape, "Owen! OWEN! It's Aaron!"

Owen's eyelids fluttered.

"Owen!"

He wanted to shake his brother by the shoulder, jostle him awake, let him know he was with him. Except he had no hands. There was nothing with which to reach. He drew closer to his brother's ear. "Owen, it's Aaron! It's me!"

Owen's eyes rolled beneath his eyelids but did not open.

What have they done to him? How is he even here?

Then Aaron sensed a presence. Wherever his body was, it reacted, the hairs on the back of his neck standing up, a chill tracing his spine. He didn't want to look away from his brother. But his eyes betrayed him. He looked up to see a figure standing over Owen. It was the Mohawk Man. He was dangling the pipe between two fingers, his weight resting casually on one leg, his head cocked like that of a curious dog. Aaron hadn't heard the man's approach.

He held his breath.

He can't see me. I can't even see myself.

The man must have heard Owen stirring. Aaron let out a thin, unsatisfying breath through his nose, his lungs expanding to their bare minimum.

There's no way he knows I'm here. I can't even see myself.

But what the man did next made Aaron's breath catch again. He smiled, those dark eyes glistening with mirth. They weren't trained on Owen. They were trained on him. The man's smile grew into an indulgent grin.

Something about that smile triggered a new emotion in Aaron. Not fear. Not resigned defeat.

Anger.

He was being mocked by this man who stood over his only brother. He no longer cared if the man could hear him. Didn't care if he was putting himself in danger. He'd seen too much, had lost too much, and had grieved too much.

Speaking through clenched teeth, he growled, "That's my *brother*. You can't have him."

The Mohawk Man took his time bringing the pipe to his mouth. He inhaled and abruptly sunk to his haunches. The movement was swift, graceful even. His cheeks bulging, the man lifted his chin, and when he opened his mouth, Aaron's sense of space and time was lost in boiling smoke.

This world, inhabited by his brother, was disintegrating. Whatever world Owen had found, or had traveled to despite the mine disaster, was all lost in the gray. The Mohawk Man's ever-widening grin and the smoke were the last things Aaron saw before it was all torn away.

He lurched upright and spat out the medallion, which fell to his chest like a spent cartridge. Tumbling onto all fours, he broke into a fit of dry coughing, his ribcage aching as he hacked into his sleeping bag. He had to rid his lungs of the smoke. His arms useless whips, he rested all his weight on his forehead, his burning chest expanding and contracting.

There is no smoke.

When his coughing slowed, his breathing settling, his other senses made their grudging return to the present, and he realized he was back in Simon's basement.

A rustling, then a voice husky with sleep said, "Porter, what the hell? You alright?"

Aaron rotated on his head to find his upside-down friend in the dark. "Yeah, I'm okay," he said in a voice small and hoarse. "Sorry. Bad dream."

Simon was already rolling to his other side.

Aaron rested on his head a while longer, focusing on his breathing, reliving what he saw. His rational mind insisted it was a dream, but the burning in his nostrils suggested otherwise. How was that possible? He collapsed onto the sleeping bag and turned onto his back. He didn't bother covering himself—he was feverish, and there'd be no sleeping tonight. Vision or no vision, he'd been surprised by his anger directed toward a man who was probably dangerous.

But another emotion coursed through him now as he studied the ceiling's popcorn texture in the moonlight.

Hope.

The outburst had come from an unexpected windfall of hope. A sudden light in the shadows. His brother, wherever he was, *whenever* he was, was *alive*. There was still a chance. Somehow, the medallion he'd placed into his mouth had shown him there was still a chance.

Chapter 13

Ghosts in the Valley

By a half past seven the following morning they were dressed and standing in the garage. Groaning and cursing, Simon shifted around boxes and crates until his unused mountain bike came into full view: a pristine Giant ARX.

Aaron watched his friend wheel the bicycle into the crisp morning air and gingerly mount it as if it might rear beneath him like a wild horse. Once astride, Simon slung a knapsack onto his back containing all the essentials, bags of Cheetos, tubes of Pringles, sleeves of Oreos, and for good measure, cans of Mountain Dew and Dr Pepper.

Aaron had spent no less than ten minutes convincing Simon he wouldn't need his iPad for the bike ride, and Simon had finally relented when Aaron declared in solidarity that he'd leave behind his iPhone. In truth, Aaron had no interest in his phone. He couldn't escape what had happened the previous night, how the medallion had opened something inside him and had taken him somewhere else, some *time* else, to find Owen. It was no dream—the smell of pipe smoke still clung to his inner nostrils. He'd been there. That man had seen him.

He took up Shelby's handlebars and slung a heavy leg over her top tube. His mind had run a marathon last night, and his sluggish body was all too happy to agree. The medallion now hung heavy and cold beneath his T-shirt, as if robbed of its energy too. But there was something that wasn't heavy this morning: his heart. His *hope*. Owen was alive, and from what Aaron had glimpsed, unharmed.

As he pushed off down the driveway, he thought of that place, that small spit of land between the oxbow lake and the sharp curve of the river. He'd never been there but figured he knew where it was. Had to be north of the Beaver Marsh. Maybe there was something there to find? Some clue about how to get to that place, that *time*, where his brother was being held? The only problem, it had to be at least two miles north of the marsh. Persuading Simon to ride that far would be an exercise in futility. Not that he could tell Simon anything about this weird desire. He'd need an excuse for going that far north. And if Simon resisted—for he surely would—what then? Aaron decided that if it came to that, he would ditch Simon—*for Owen*.

These thoughts consumed him as they pulled onto Cornell. He noticed a tall, white-haired woman on inline skates turning down Hillcrest before disappearing from sight—which was odd, because most white-haired people Aaron knew were elderly and she wasn't built like an elderly person. He pushed the thought away and focused on the day ahead. Regardless of what he might be forced to do today, he knew it would be a good day. He took in the vibrant morning. The pale blue sky was brighter than he'd seen it in weeks.

***

The bluegill writhed and flapped as Libby Jaite reeled it in from the murky pond. But now, with the hook plucked from its mouth, all the creature's fight had been plucked out with it. It lay motionless save for its rapidly expanding and contracting gills.

The fish was in a foreign land now, lying on a cold flat stone. It couldn't have known it was doomed before it closed its mouth on the worm.

She studied the fish's dorsal fin, which rose from its nape like a mohawk, its scaled skin glimmering green and blue under the morning sun, and its black, unblinking eye, which betrayed no emotion. At just fourteen, Libby had caught at least a hundred bluegill. But with each catch, she found that no two fish looked alike. There were always minor differences, the colors of the scales, the sizes and shapes of the fins, the fullness of the bodies. And her only catch this morning—which was on the smaller side—was now suffocating in the thin oxygenated air.

Just a moment longer.

But there was never simply a moment longer, was there? Time was the silent killer that devoured all. It felt no sympathy as it ate the hours, minutes, and seconds. Then, it moved onto your dreams, hopes, and desires.

Mom had loved this pond. It was too small to warrant its own name, but that was to its advantage. The vast Cuyahoga Valley was dotted with numerous lakes, ponds, and streams, but good luck finding any solitude at any of the top fishing spots. Mom had introduced her to not only this pond, but also the small outcropping of flat rocks that jutted out into it, accessible by a meandering footpath through a forest of reeds. It was *their* place, so much so, they created a small bench using a pair of squat logs and a long slat of plywood. On the makeshift bench, they'd used a fishing knife to inscribe: JAITE POINT.

Mom would often comment on the energy of this place, a place that Grandpa had introduced to her when she was just a little girl. But there was something more, something unsaid. Libby knew there was something on Mom's mind whenever they were down here, whether they were sitting in silence with their fishing lines submerged, or baiting their hooks and rigging their lines. Something had always lurked behind her lucid eyes, like a rumor of some protected memory. But Mom could never quite muster the words even though Libby knew she desperately wanted to say them and would trail off when she'd meet Libby's questioning gaze, as if having decided better of it.

Libby didn't need to be convinced of this place's energy. It possessed its own sort of power, existing just beyond what the five senses could perceive. On more than one occasion, she'd swiveled on the bench, expecting to see someone behind her. But there would be no one, just the reeds swaying in the breeze. Whenever she'd think of what it was that had startled her in the first place—enough to make her turn and check her rear— she couldn't pinpoint the cause. It was as if she were being watched.

Her last visit with Mom now came back to her as she watched the suffocating fish. Libby hadn't known it would be her last visit. By then, the cancer had already metastasized, spreading to Mom's lymph nodes. Mom's voice had been ragged with exhaustion, her skin ashen, her eyes sunken. But she had been smiling, nonetheless.

"You know," she'd said, "that place really is special. I know you've felt it. And Libs ... I want you to know something. I ... saw something down there once. Might have been, let's see ... thirty years ago? Was just a teenager at the time. But I was sitting in our spot, which looks a lot like it does today. Time hasn't had its way with Jaite Point in the same way it has with me." She barked a laugh, sending a jolt through Libby's shoulders. She then fell into a fit of coughing. A nurse rushed in, but Mom waved her off with a feeble hand. When she composed herself, she continued in a wavering voice, "But I saw something, Libs. *Someone* down there, someone who didn't belong—"

The coughing erupted again, and the nurse wouldn't be dismissed twice. She darted over to Mom, adjusted her bed to a seated position, and put an oxygen mask over Mom's face. She shot a glance back at Libby and shook her head. Mom had had enough for one day.

Had enough.

It was the last time she saw her mother alive. She could now feel her lower lip tremble at this memory. But she wouldn't cry. She knew Mom would always be with her, especially in this tucked away place. And Mom had been right all along. There *was* an energy here, and that energy was *her*.

She grabbed the bluegill, its gills now palpitating like a failing heart, and lowered it gently into the pond. Springing to her feet, she dusted off her worn Levis and paused, watching the minor disruption in the otherwise serene water. The fish's blue-green scales could be seen beneath the rippling surface, catching a few rays of the morning sun. And then the fish was gone, darting down to its murky home.

Where it belonged.

"Congrats," Libby said to the fish and to whoever or whatever was listening. "You now have a moment longer."

***

"How much longer? My ass is killing me."

Aaron looked over his shoulder, not bothering to conceal his annoyance. "You gotta be kidding me. We just got down here."

Simon frowned. "Can we at least take a break? I'm trying here." And then under his breath, he muttered, "The shit I do for you."

Aaron felt the heat rise into his cheeks. He imagined slamming on his breaks, letting the ungrateful foul mouth ram into him and go flying head-over-heels into the brush. Because Simon, of all people, didn't know what it was like to lose someone. No, the only loss Simon had ever experienced in his sheltered basement-dwelling life was the death of his hamster, Spazzy McGee.

But instead, Aaron exhaled and stared off into the passing trees. Simon accepted *him* for who he was and he knew he should do the same. They'd only ridden a mile up the Towpath since picking it up at the park entrance off Timi Trail—which was closer to Simon's house than The Courts' switchback—but he knew he shouldn't expect too much from Simon.

"I'm way fatter than you," he said, finally. "You shouldn't be asking *me* for a break. But fine, how about we take a break at the Beaver Marsh? We should try to get there before it gets too crowded anyway."

Simon grunted, but didn't protest.

Aaron glanced up through the foliage. The sky had thinned to a brooding gray. It would rain soon, and they just might have the place to themselves anyway. For the most part, they had. But something felt off, and he'd noticed it just a few minutes into the ride. The underbrush on either side of the trail was *alive*, seeming to rustle and sway on its own accord. It made the hairs on his neck stand up. It didn't make sense. The prevailing winds blew from west to east, but the breeze didn't feel strong enough to account for this bustling activity. If it were from the wind, then shouldn't his baggy T-shirt be billowing and flapping? His hair blowing?

Even odder: they'd spotted two large families of deer galloping north along a ridge. It was as if they were running from something. Simon had even sighted a beaver waddling near the edge of the trail before disappearing into the brush, something Aaron had never seen in his dozens of previous rides on the Towpath. Tree limbs had bowed and snapped back from leaping squirrels, and birds shot through the canopy like whistling darts. All of the commotion seemed to be moving north.

The direction we're going.

Then the forest had grown quiet, as if it was waiting for something, and the medallion began to assert itself again. The itch was returning where it hung about his chest.

They'd only encountered one other human. The large dark-skinned man had been jogging north up the trail. He wore a sleeveless T-shirt, showing off tribal-looking tattoos on his arms. Aaron felt light-headed for a moment as they approached the man from behind and then passed him, the sight of the tattoos resurfacing the vision of the men from the previous night. And there had been something else, something familiar about the man.

Simon now squirmed on his seat, his bike wobbling as he dug into his cargo shorts' pocket. He brought his glowing iPhone's screen to his face.

"Watch it," Aaron said, reflexively squeezing Shelby's handle brakes. "You're gonna wreck."

"Oh, relax," Simon called back without taking his eyes off the screen. "Gabe just texted me. Looks like Littlefield didn't make it home last night. His parents are calling around everywhere looking for him."

For all Aaron cared, Connor could never come home. His daddy and his army of attorneys had neatly swept up the mess from the mine. A nuisance to be swatted away, even if it had killed Dean and ... done what exactly to Owen? Transported him?

Simon shrugged and pocketed his phone. "Maybe someone finally killed that assclown."

They rode on. The forest was striking now beneath the gray canvas, the Towpath a fissure cut into an emerald. To the right, the trail was beginning to sidle up to the abandoned Ohio & Erie Canal. To the left, the Cuyahoga River snaked ever closer to the trail, the two conduits of water creating a thin causeway.

"Thank god," Simon said.

Aaron looked ahead and saw it too: a bright patch, just a couple hundred yards away. They were approaching the Beaver Marsh, its open light piercing the gloom like a knife.

Chapter 14

The Beaver Marsh

Libby stepped up and onto the Towpath. She checked her watch: a half past eight, plenty of time to stop by the Beaver Marsh and do some sketching. She'd left her fishing pole and tackle box back near Jaite Point, tucking them inside the hollow of a downed oak tree, where no one could find them unless they possessed a sixth sense. It was easier that way. From her house up on Ross Avenue, she could make the four-mile trek down to the pond and back without having to carry too much or cram extra supplies into her backpack, which already contained her sketchbook, a set of always-sharpened colored pencils, a small pocket compass, a pair of compact Nikon binoculars, a can of pepper spray, and a laminated map of the Cuyahoga Valley.

Mom had always loved reminding Libby that physical maps never ran out of batteries or needed software updates. Dad insisted on the compass so his little girl could always find her way back home after her solitary hiking and fishing trips. Dad, after all, shared Mom's lack of faith in modern contrivances. Libby supposed she'd been infected by this mentality, too, and the number of times she'd forgotten to bring her phone with her into the valley outnumbered the times she'd remembered it. And today was yet another tally mark in the *forgotten* column.

She would be at the north end of the Beaver Marsh clearing in under ten minutes. Now would be the perfect time to snag a coveted spot on the observation deck before it got too crowded or hot. But with a glance up at an overcast sky that was growing ever darker, she figured there wouldn't be too many people out today anyway. Save for the crazy ones.

***

Aaron's forehead grew hot at the sight of her. Libby Jaite was emerging from the shade at the north end of the clearing, her head turned toward the western reaches of the Beaver Marsh, taking in the spotted lilies, the reeds, the beauty. A gentle breeze off the water had pulled loose a few golden strands from her ponytail, spilling them over her eyes. She wore a faded black graphic T-shirt that hung to mid-thigh of her faded jeans, which were ripped at their knees. Her hiking boots were caked with fresh mud, leaving behind dark shadows on the floorboards as she approached. Slung over one shoulder was the blue strap of a backpack. In her right hand, a slender notebook.

"You've gotta be kidding me," Simon said, slowing his bike. "See, this is why I hate this place."

Aaron was ready to say, "Take it easy. She won't bite" — which might have been more of a reassurance for him than it would have been for Simon — except nothing came out. Because she was turning her attention from the marsh to look at them.

He dropped his eyes to the planks and watched them pass under Shelby's wobbling tires. Warring emotions fell into the pit of his stomach where they began a vicious fight, knotting each other up. If he honored Simon's wishes and turned and left, then it would be obvious he was avoiding her. He'd forever be the spineless coward who'd given in to the whims of his prickly friend. If he continued forward, he could choose to ignore her, but then Simon might force an awkward scene by making some callous comment about her eye. Aaron would then stand by red-faced as the two of them traded verbal barbs — just as spineless. Then again, Libby might be the one to initiate it. He knew she wouldn't back down from Simon.

Then, there was the third and most terrifying option of all. He could ride up to her, smile, and say, "Hi," Simon be damned. He could take command of the situation for once, not allow it to be another thing that just *happened* to him. He could be the confident orchestrator. He considered the option. The thought of it should have made his stomach flip, but for some odd reason it didn't.

Approaching Libby was an act usually consigned to some late-night fantasy. But today was different. The air was charged with something, some force that defied word or sense. It was quiet here too. He didn't hear any chirping birds or splashing frogs. He only heard her footfalls, those boots clunking over this physical contrivance, this bridge. This object that held her weight, her graceful form, her aspect. *Her.* That same object holding him.

He needed to approach her now. Whether the need was triggered by that unseen charge, the medallion, or some other force—perhaps that same force that had made the surrounding forest restless earlier—he didn't know. Yet he relaxed. Her gravity and the power she held over him now seemed arbitrary. There was something bigger at hand, and his usual feelings were trite by comparison, especially compared to what he'd experienced over the past month, and *nothing* compared to what he'd experienced last night. That thought dredged up yet another thought.

What would Owen do in my position, right now?

The answer was obvious. Owen would have already ridden up to her without a moment's hesitation.

I can obey my instincts too.

He had no idea what he'd say to her, but he didn't give his mind an opportunity to protest. He pedaled forward.

***

Libby's heart sank. The beauty of this place had just been defiled, sapped, kicked down the road like an old tin can. There he was, *Simon Kent*, riding her way. His dour gaze like some smoldering iron. That bully, that blight for which she had no hope of escape.

119

No, any hope she'd had for that had died when the prick hadn't been expelled for what he'd done to her that day, that attack three years ago that had made her flee the gymnasium sobbing. His impulsive cruelty was downright shocking. Most people had to work hard to say something confrontational or insulting. That's because it didn't come naturally. It took effort. But most people weren't Simon Kent, who had to work hard *not* to belittle and insult people.

And now here she stood, rooted to this walkway on what should have been a perfect morning for taking in the beauty and serenity of this place. Seeing it, capturing it. Its buzzing activity, its birds and their colors showing brilliantly beneath this gray canvas. Except, where were the birds? Now that she thought of it, why was it so quiet? Just minutes ago, the forest had been astir, a cacophony sweeping past her like a wave as she walked south. But this thought didn't have time to fully bake, because here he was approaching on his bicycle with Aaron Porter.

Aaron ... oh, Aaron. Why? Why are you with him?

She just stood there, unsure of what to do next. She could turn and walk away—the most sensible option—but being on foot meant she couldn't get away fast enough. Or—

Her breath caught. Here came Aaron Porter, separating himself from that prick. She swallowed. This was a rarity for him. He'd surprised her once before, and it had been a moment she'd never forget. It was her first day back at school after Mom had passed—a miserable day—and he'd approached her before boarding his bus to go home. He'd tripped over his words, looked at his shoes at least ten times, and blushed a dozen shades of red. But in spite of all his obvious pain, he managed to tell her how sorry he was about her mother, and that he would be around if she ever needed to talk about it.

Now the butterflies in her stomach began to beat their wings in a fury. What would she say to him? She'd heard the news about Owen. Everyone had. Aaron knew suffering. In fact, he'd lived a lifetime of it already. And he'd just lost his only brother, what, four weeks ago?

Yet here he is … now, smiling at me. Smiling?

Her quiet and thoughtful former friend from Ross Avenue, who, for some unspeakable reason, hung out with Simon Kent, was smiling and approaching her after years of barely meeting her gaze. Simon on the other hand had stopped pedaling and was standing like an angry statue halfway between the south end of the clearing and the observation deck.

She straightened and resumed walking toward the observation deck. Toward *him*.

***

"Hey there," Aaron said, slowing to a stop.

The usual Aaron would've agonized about what to say for at least ten minutes, would've no doubt stared at her like a paralyzed mute. But he was now abuzz with this electricity. Not knowing its cause, he plunged ahead while it still coursed through him.

"What are ya up to?" he asked.

Libby didn't meet his eyes at first. There was a pink rash rising in her cheeks, and she swiped a loose strand of hair from her forehead and tucked it behind her ear. The movement sent a barb of heat through his chest.

She shifted her weight to one leg, and despite her baggy T-shirt, Aaron became more aware of the feminine curve of her hips.

"Just checking out the sights," she said, her voice cool and clipped.

His mouth reacted, not allowing his thoughts to hold it hostage. "Same here. Just down here for a bike ride." He gestured toward Simon. "And I'm making grumpy over there come with me."

Libby stood a little straighter and cocked her head. She leaned past him to better see Simon.

Aaron turned to follow her gaze. Simon was sitting half-astride his bike, his arms folded across his chest, his eyes dark pits ready to swallow Libby.

And me, thought Aaron.

"Ooooh, he looks so pissed," she said, before settling onto both feet and looking at Aaron with her good eye. "Better not talk to me too long, Aaron. He might start shitting fire."

A pig-like snort escaped Aaron's mouth and it startled him.

Libby threw her head back and laughed. Her eyes were alive, her straight white teeth on full display.

Before Aaron knew it, he was laughing too.

"What the hell's so funny?"

Aaron turned to see that Simon was a few feet away now, his eyes narrowed. Aaron wanted to say something innocent and disarming, but Libby answered for him.

"You're what's funny."

Simon's jaw dropped, and then he clamped it shut. His accusing eyes cut to Aaron's.

Aaron found words. "You, ah, just looked like you were about to shoot fire bolts from your eyes over there, that's all."

Simon didn't look impressed. Aaron prepared himself for Simon's whiplike tongue, but instead, Simon sighed and glanced out over the Beaver Marsh. "Can we just go now?" he asked. "This place sucks."

Aaron wasn't ready to leave. Not now, not with this feeling, and not with her being here. He improvised. "Okay. You hungry though? We haven't touched the snacks."

His expression still dark, Simon grunted and unslung his bag from his shoulders, unzipped it, and pulled out a squat can of Pringles. He popped it open, pinched a small stack between his fingers, and stuffed the stack into his mouth. He handed the can to Aaron, not bothering to look at Libby.

"Nah, I'm good," Aaron said, sneaking a glance at Libby, who was watching Simon, her arms knotted over her chest.

A slight tremor rolled through Aaron's stomach then, and it had nothing to do with hunger or the tension between his two companions. There was a clacking sound—to the south—and it was getting louder.

"You know, maybe Aaron wants to stay out a bit longer. I think you could grant him that after..." Libby was saying, but Aaron was only now dimly aware of her words. That other sound was growing, getting closer. The itch in his chest was now insistent. He turned to the sound. Whatever it was, it was coming their way, and it wasn't good.

"Well, I wouldn't be such a dick if..."

He barely registered Simon's voice. The prevailing sound was this odd cadence, a series of *clacks* followed by gentle *whooshes*. Getting closer.

He watched the shadowed forest at the south end of the clearing, where he and Simon had emerged only five minutes prior. What came from those shadows next made his legs buckle.

Chapter 15

The Woman on Skates

The first thing he noticed about the figure was the platinum hair, which was braided in a ponytail and framed a long face. Large sunglasses obscured most of that face from a distance, save for the bright pink lips. And there was something between those lips...

A lollypop?

She was on Rollerblades, but he knew she wasn't going to just skate past them and continue down the path. It was no coincidence he'd seen her near Simon's house.

"Dude, you okay?"

He felt a harsh poke on his shoulder. He turned to face Simon.

"Holy shit, dude. You don't look so good."

"You alright, Aaron?" Libby asked.

Aaron blinked, as if emerging from a trance. The world stabilized a little now that he was facing them, away from the approaching woman.

Simon stood back and frowned. "Whoa. Hello, freak show."

Libby's attention was now on the woman too. Without looking away from her, she whispered, "Aaron, do you know her or something?"

Aaron didn't answer. He was backing away from them, ignoring their concerned expressions. He knew he needed to step off the bridge's main path and onto the observation deck, which he now wished had steps. How he knew to do this, he didn't know. But by positioning himself here, he'd force her to slow to negotiate a sharp turn. Maybe she'd fall. He watched her approach sidelong. Twenty feet away now. Ten feet. Five.

The woman plunged the heel of one skate. In an easy arc, she sling-shotted around Simon, Libby, the bikes. She came to an abrupt halt just a few feet from where Aaron stood with his back against the railing.

The woman wasn't frowning but smiling. She clacked forward. She was tall to begin with, but the skates added at least another four inches of height. Her whitish hair was without a doubt some kind of wig, reminding him of the princess from that Disney movie, *Frozen,* which was fitting, because he was frozen — his reflection in the round mirrors on her face a portrait of fear.

Something was off about her mouth, and it had nothing to do with the sucker. Her brilliant white teeth were set at an unnatural angle with her lips, reminding him of a sheet of paper that hadn't been properly fed into a printer. She wore a purple bandanna around her neck with a white motif scrawled across it. Something about the pattern was primal, tribal, old.

Her smile held as she studied him. She then pulled the sucker from her mouth and tossed it into the marsh.

He jerked at the sudden movement, but she didn't seem to notice.

"It was getting old," she said in a thin high voice. Her breath smelled of cherry and something else, rotten and decayed, like leaves in a damp cellar. The sucker hadn't quite masked it.

"Nice wig," came a voice around a mouthful of potato chips.

The woman turned and looked at Simon as if he were some insect she could stomp at any moment.

Aaron blinked and tried to regain some sense of control.

See with your mind. Sapere Vedere.

He focused on the rest of her, and it didn't take him long to find the bulge at her right hip, her shirt riding up slightly to reveal a leather sheath.

When she turned back to him, the smile was gone. "I believe you have something that belongs to me."

Aaron looked at Libby and Simon. Libby's good eye was narrowed, studying him. She was interested in his reply. Simon was watching him too.

The medallion. She was here for it. He knew it. But it was part of *him*. His connection to Owen. Giving it away would sever that connection. He felt he'd known this before ever putting it in his mouth.

"Hey, lady," Libby said, "I *highly* doubt he has something of yours. Aaron would never hurt a fly, much less steal."

The woman turned to look at Libby and then turned back, as if Libby was some minor annoyance that warranted no further attention.

"You know what I'm looking for, Aaron Porter, who lives with his grandmother up on Juneville Drive. I bet you have it with you right now."

He inhaled and drew back.

"Oh, yes, Mr Porter. I know all about you. I know about what happened in the mine. I know about your brother, Owen, who went missing after that unfortunate accident."

"Um, *freak show*," Simon said, "I don't know what the hell you want from my friend, but I suggest you stop stalking him or I'm calling the cops. Shit, maybe I'll take your picture and post it online for everyone to see."

"I wouldn't do that if I were you," she said. "I know where *you* live, too, Simon Kent. I've been following you since you left your house up on Cornell."

"What?"

"Oh, yes," she said. "It wasn't hard to find Mr Porter after overhearing his grandmother speaking with his mother on her front porch this morning. She let it slip that he's staying at your place. How kind of you to take him in."

She turned back to Aaron. "But I must say, your mother isn't looking too hot, Mr Porter. Must have a very nasty fentanyl habit. But not my problem."

Aaron didn't know what to say. She knew where he lived. Knew about Gram. Knew about Mom. Hell, knew about Owen. *Knew about the medallion.*

Then movement, reflecting in the woman's glasses. It was behind him—to his right. The woman didn't seem to notice the movement as she drew closer, apparently done with idle chitchat. The smell of decay growing stronger.

She whispered in his ear, "I don't have time for coyness. I'll be forced to hurt you or *worse,* if you don't give it to me."

Before Aaron could react, her hand was in the right pocket of his shorts. "If you have it, I'm going to find it," she whispered, her rotten breath in his ear as she rooted in his other pocket. As she reached to his rear pockets, her shoulder brushed against his chest.

She paused and stepped back. "Oh, I see." She brought a hand up to his chest, her long fingers like tentacles, probing the medallion's contours from over his T-shirt.

A scream cut the air, and it wasn't his.

"She's hurting my friend! Help!"

The woman pulled back from their private conversation. She couldn't ignore this disturbance.

Aaron let out a ragged breath and flung a hand to his chest to find that the medallion was still there. He looked over to see Libby standing in the middle of the bridge, pointing in his direction with one hand, and frantically waving with the other. She was beckoning the figure who was trudging toward them. Aaron whirled and saw the figure, his lumbering gait familiar. It was the large man they'd passed earlier.

The woman rolled back from Aaron and turned to face the approaching man.

The man slowed to a trot. His sweaty brow was furrowed, his dark eyes narrowed beneath thick eyebrows. Aaron could tell that the man was deciding whether he should intervene, or if this was some kind of elaborate teen prank. He flitted his gaze from face to face, the movement looking practiced.

Then his eyes found Aaron's, and Aaron knew where he'd seen this man. He'd been one of the cops who'd arrived at the house that last day on Ross—when Mom had overdosed and lost her family forever. When it had all unraveled. Aaron could picture the man as he was then, the dark blue officer uniform, the Glock on one hip, the radio on the other.

The big man now slowed to a walk, and he reached up and plucked the earbuds from his ears and let them dangle from the neck opening of his damp T-shirt. His chest heaving, he placed his hands on his hips. And as he crossed the remaining few feet, he fell into a swinging gait, his shoulders drawn back, his chest out, that walk of an officer approaching a stopped vehicle on the side of the road.

He fixed his attention on Libby. "What's the problem here?" His voice was deep and commanding.

"That lady's hurting our friend! She's stalking him!"

The man turned, cocked his head, and looked at the odd woman. He appraised her for what seemed an eternity.

The man then turned to study Aaron, but Aaron didn't see recognition on the man's face. Finally, the man looked back at the woman.

"What's your name, ma'am?"

Aaron watched the woman, who stood mirroring the man's posture, her hands on her hips, her head cocked.

Calculating.

The man crossed his big tattooed arms over his chest. "Well, name?"

"This is none of your concern," she said. "I suggest you get back to your run."

The man rocked back and forth on his heels and theatrically darted his eyes to the sky as if weighing this option. He dropped his gaze to the woman. "No can do. These kids have just *made* it my concern. You're talking to a senior patrol officer for the Portage Falls PD, and I can make your life *very* difficult if you don't cooperate. I'm never off duty. Now, I'll repeat. *Name.*"

"The Redeemer."

The man stood still. He then squinted and shook his head. "Do you think I'm a damned moron? I suggest for your sake, you make my life easier. Now, your *real* name?"

Aaron's pulse was speeding with a mixture of fear and hope. Then he thought of the woman's right hip. He watched her. She was turned slightly in profile. Her right hip facing him. Her fingers twitching just above that sheath.

She's going to do it.

She spat her dentures onto the deck.

Aaron numbly watched them bounce across the floorboards. He looked back up at her.

Her mouth was now a grotesque smile, a set of crooked yellow teeth with large gaps between them.

"Name's Mary Campbell."

In one fluid motion, she flung her hand to her hip, shot out her arm, and flicked her wrist. Aaron was confused by the movement. Her right hand was extended. Open. Palm up. There was nothing in that hand. Her shirt was pulled up, revealing the leather sheath against her pale skin. The *empty* leather sheath.

Libby screamed again.

Chapter 16

Flight into the Forest

Aaron looked over at the man. He was staggering backward toward the railing on the opposite side of the bridge. His eyes wide. His mouth agape. It was a mouth that couldn't speak and would never speak again. Not with the knife buried to its hilt just below his Adam's apple.

Aaron could only watch as the man pitched against the rail. Writhing. Contorting. His eyes pleading.

"Holy shit! Oh, Christ!"

Simon's voice was distant. Aaron swayed on his feet, his head feeling as if it were tethered to his body by a loose string. It now drifted to face the woman, who was rolling up to the dying man.

"We gotta get outta here!" Libby was shouting. "Leave your bag, Simon! Leave it! Get on your bike—now!"

Then Libby's firm hand closed around Aaron's wrist. It was pulling him forward, away from the railing and toward the intersection where the bridge met the deck, where Shelby leaned against a rail post.

"Aaron, we gotta go!"

He followed Libby in numb obedience, unable to stop watching the woman, who'd now drawn near the man. She grabbed the knife's hilt and gave it a vicious yank. A red fountain erupted.

The sight of blood sent a jolt through Aaron. His eyes regained their focus.

"Jump on!" Libby shrieked. "Let's go. Let's go!"

Libby was straddling Shelby's top tube. She was freeing the seat for him.

He climbed onto the seat and wrapped his arms around her waist. Her backpack pressing into his face, she stood and pushed all her weight down onto the pedals, grunting: "C-mon, c-mon. Damnit!"

The bike wasn't moving. Sobering, Aaron extended a leg, planted a heel on the rail, and pushed off. A moment later, Shelby had the momentum she needed, and they pulled away from the observation deck.

They rattled north across the span, his legs dangling awkwardly, the tips of his Skechers skidding over the planks. He glanced back. The woman was lifting the large man by his lower legs, his twitching body propped atop the eastern railing, the wooden beam swaying under his weight. With a shove, he went plummeting into the marsh. The resulting splash should have made the crowns of trees near and far explode with darting birds. Except there were none.

Shelby wobbled as Libby continued standing and pushing all her weight onto the pedals. Aaron held his gaze firmly on the woman, watching her casually wipe off the blade. She then turned to face them. She dipped her hips. She exploded forward.

He turned to Libby and found his voice just as they thumped off the bridge and onto the limestone gravel of the Towpath.

"She's coming! Go, go, go!"

"Going as fast as I can!"

His back arching past the point of discomfort, he strained to look back again. She was gliding after them on those skates, her rangy body occupying the trail's entire width, her legs splaying from side to side like those of a spider crawling its web to devour a fly. Gaining ground fast. He leaned and looked past Libby to see Simon ahead on his bike, his legs flying up and down like pistons, going as fast as he could.

Not fast enough.

They weren't going fast enough either.

He shouted into Libby's bouncing ass, "Gonna slip my feet under yours! Raise your right foot a little!"

She did, and he slipped his right foot under one mud-caked boot.

"Now the left!"

She lifted her left foot just enough for him to wedge his other foot under it. Then, as she pressed down on the right pedal, he did the same, and the foliage on either side of the trail began to pass with greater speed.

"We gotta pull alongside Simon!" Libby shouted. "He isn't going fast enough!"

Aaron didn't answer, instead looked back again. The woman was bigger, no more than ten feet away now. She'd picked up her pace too. As the world tumbled past, he watched with a mixture of horror and fascination as the white wig blew off her head, revealing a bald scalp shadowed with stubble. The pale foundation on her forehead ceasing at an almost nonexistent hairline. He looked at her right hand. The knife was there.

"Move to you right!" Libby yelled to Simon as they came alongside him. "Aaron, grab his bike! We need to combine our speed!"

Aaron turned his attention to Simon, whose hair was matted to his forehead. His mouth hanging open and scooping the air. He reached out and grabbed the seat post of Simon's bike.

"Simon, try to match our rhythm!" Libby shouted.

Simon glanced sidelong to take in their movement. Soon, he was mimicking them, the two bikes hurtling side-by-side up the Towpath.

Aaron looked back again. She'd kept up and was holding steady at a distance of ten or so feet. There was no sign of fatigue in her. The same couldn't be said for Libby, who was heaving. The three of them couldn't maintain this pace. The trail was too flat. He didn't think the woman would tire anytime soon. A thought struck him.

Tire.

Their mountain bike tires could handle rough terrain, but the woman's small skate wheels couldn't. They'd be useless. The Cuyahoga Valley National Park was crawling with hiking and bridle trails. There had to be *something* coming up they could use.

They raced on, Aaron alternating between checking their rear — no change in the woman's position — and glancing ahead to either side of the trail. Still nothing.

"Libby, keep an eye out for —"

A whistle sounded in the distance, far ahead and to the west. It was the Cuyahoga Valley Scenic Railroad.

Then a gust rippled the back of Aaron's T-shirt. He lurched, turned, and immediately pressed himself into Libby.

The woman was now within a few feet of Shelby's back tire. She was twirling the knife in her right hand like a baton.

He glanced down. Ribbons of his T-shirt were flapping behind him. He didn't feel anything. Panic rose in his chest. Was he so pumped full of adrenaline that his body had gone numb? Had she slashed his back open?

"Aaron, talk to me!"

Without taking his eyes off the woman, he screamed, "Go, Libby! *Go!*"

Libby shifted in his grasp. She looked back. Her scream caught in her throat.

The woman laughed. She was toying with them, enjoying this sport. Her smile grew as she tossed the knife from her right hand to her left and then back again.

Then, in a blur, she swept the blade across Shelby's back tire. Shelby shuddered and then righted herself.

Libby's scream made it out of her mouth now.

Aaron had no way of knowing if the slash had been enough to cut the hard rubber, but he'd know soon enough.

The woman continued laughing. She knew they couldn't outrace her. This was a game. Something awoke inside Aaron then. It was hot and sharp, reminding him of what he'd felt last night. He again saw the Mohawk Man's derisive smile, that look that said *There's nothing you can do about it.*

He removed his hand from Simon's bike—it was doing no good there anyway—and balled it into a fist. He waited. Her enjoyment was going to cost her. He'd make it cost her. When she swept her blade again, he'd catch her arm on the backside of its arc and would punch or shove with all his strength.

His jaw set, he kept his eyes on the woman.

She then cocked her head, the smile on her thin lips growing. *She's expecting me to lash out.*

She fell back a foot or two, rising from her speed skater's stance to coast upright. Water was now beading on her glasses. He didn't feel the rain, all his attention was on the large knife, which she was casually twirling between two fingers. *Too casually.*

Keeping his eyes on the woman, he let go of Libby's waist, reached around her, and nudged her hands from the handlebars. He needed access to the brakes. He turned to Libby.

"Sit on my lap," he said, straining to keep his voice even, praying she even heard him. "Be ready to push on the handlebars with all your strength. Gonna have to brake hard. Can't outrun her."

Libby did hear him. She eased her hands off the grips and slid them to the center chrome section of the handlebars. She lowered herself onto him.

"On three?" she asked.

"On three."

They braced themselves.

"One. Two. Thr—"

Together, they forced their legs rigid. Aaron squeezed the brake levers with his fingers while simultaneously pressing his palms against the handlebars with all of his strength to counteract the momentum. He leaned back on Shelby's seat, hoping his and Libby's combined weight—along with Shelby's poor braking ability—would be enough to keep the bike from flipping.

Time seemed to slow then, Shelby's front tire gyrating as if it would rattle off her frame, her back tire chain-sawing the ground, kicking up plumes of dust. Libby came off Aaron's lap a good six inches before plummeting onto his crotch.

A force slammed into Shelby's back tire. Then, into *him,* glancing the back of his left shoulder. Then the woman was soaring past them. The dust-coated wheels of her skates pointing skyward. Her right leg outstretched at an awkward angle. The knife airborne. She hit the ground and tumbled into a bed of clover along the trail's edge. The knife clanged to the path just a few feet from where they stood straddling the bike.

He immediately groped at the pain shooting through his shoulder.

"You okay?" gasped Libby.

He reached under his shirt, felt his lower back, and brought his hand out in front of him. No blood. He reached to the front of his shirt and felt the comforting contours of the medallion.

"Yeah, think so."

"Get moving!" Simon shouted.

Aaron looked up to see Simon glancing back at them from where he stood half-astride his bike some twenty feet ahead. He was watching the woman. Aaron followed his gaze. The woman was struggling to her hands and knees, her arm angry with red scrapes.

Libby placed her foot over his where it still rested on the right pedal and he pressed his left foot to the ground and pushed off. A sharp pain erupted in his shoulder at the sudden movement, but they got the momentum they needed.

This time, he kept his hands on the handlebars. As they pulled away from the woman, he caught another glimpse of the knife where it lay, just ahead of them and to the left—within reach. He had an urge to slow and bend and grab it but could sense the woman getting up. He pulled his left foot out from under Libby's and drove it into the ground near the knife's hilt. It made contact. The knife went spinning sideways into the underbrush.

They sped up the Towpath.

"There's another path!" called Simon, who was still ten feet ahead of them.

"Turn down it!" cried Libby.

Simon did, and Aaron and Libby turned shortly thereafter, thumping onto the clay and stone trail, a tremor rising through Shelby's seat post.

Aaron looked down at Shelby's rear tire. The rubber tube was flattening where it met the ground. His and Libby's combined weight would soon be resting on the rim.

"Shelby's back tire is shot!"

Libby looked back. "Great! Any more good news?"

"We're going downhill."

They descended the trail, the dense patch of forest offering no rumor of distance. The land was buckling around them, the trail cutting a deep trace into the hillside and giving rise to steep embankments on either side.

Ahead, Aaron could see the trail bend north and then south like a switchback. He looked behind him, which was now up.

Nothing … yet.

The rain was now pelting them in earnest, and his ass bounced as they clattered over hard ruts and rocks. Libby's backside, now perched on the nose of the seat, pressed further into his crotch with each bounce, a development that would have sent his hormones raging into overdrive in any other situation. He pulled his left foot free of Libby's and extended his leg over a narrow gully, using his foot to brace against an embankment to better negotiate the tight turn. A whistle cracked the air. He remembered the train. If his memory held true, it would be chugging south from its northern rail yard this time of day.

If they were heading down the escarpment, then they'd be heading toward the river. Heading toward *the tracks*. He looked northwest through a gap in the foliage and glimpsed the silver coach cars with their red and yellow stripes. The train *was* heading south.

"Simon, we gotta pick up the pace!" he said. "We gotta beat the train—can't stop."

"Christ, I'm going as fast as I can!"

He looked over his shoulder again, expecting to see the woman through the trees, a tall silhouette stalking down the hillside. Nothing but darkened forest.

They sped up. Ruts and rocks be damned. The train whistle sounded again. He glanced past Libby to see the trail flattening between a gloomy grove of spruces. They passed through the grove, slowed, and made a sharp left turn. A patch of light stretched before them now. At the bottom of the clearing were the tracks.

The whistle bellowed again. They were almost right on top of it. The train was fast approaching the intersection of the path and track.

"We won't make it!" Libby said.

"Our only choice is to beat it! Keep our speed. Shelby's tire's done, but we'll use our downhill momentum to get to Brandywine."

"You nuts, Porter?"

Libby squirmed. "You're serious?"

"We can't stop! If we don't want to be on foot, then we need to haul ass."

"We're staying on our fucking bikes, Porter."

"Then we need to beat the train!"

The black engine came into view through the thinning trees, maybe a few hundred feet away.

He wedged his feet under Libby's and began pedaling.

"This is nuts!" Libby screamed, but began pumping her legs too.

Thirty feet from the track.

The coaches came into view.

Twenty feet.

He gritted his teeth. Libby clamped her hands over his on the handlebars.

Fifteen.

He darted his eyes north, toward the black diesel. It was fifty feet away. Approaching fast. But they were approaching the tracks faster. They were going to make it!

Ten.

"Aaron!" Libby screamed.

He looked past her just in time to see Simon's bike inverted in midair. Simon was floating above it. A moment later, Shelby's front tire slammed into Simon's bike and was upended. Libby was no longer sitting on Shelby. The muddy soles of her boots rose in front of his face as she sailed headlong over the handlebars. He was next to be separated from the bike. The sky tumbling. The ground rising to meet him.

The train roared past ten feet in front of them.

Chapter 17

Raindrops and Arrows

Aaron found himself squinting up at them. Simon's left ear was bleeding, and there were leaves tangled in his hair, but he was standing upright. His usual look of annoyance fully intact on his face. Libby's hair had been darkened by the rain, but she didn't seem to have a scratch on her.

"How are the two of you standing?"

"You're way fatter than us," Simon said. "And, as they say, the bigger they are, the har—"

"Shut up, Simon," Libby said. "Aaron, can you stand? We have to move."

He rolled onto all fours, leaves and twigs spilling from his back. He struggled to his feet and rubbed the mud from his knees, which were scraped, but not bleeding too badly. He was standing no more than two feet from a pricker bush that might have carved him up had he fallen any further off the trail. His back now aching along with his left shoulder, he felt for the medallion. Still there. He shot an angry glance at Simon.

"I'm serious. What the hell happened? We were gonna beat the train."

Libby stepped back to appraise Simon too.

Simon glanced at each of them and exhaled. "I dunno. Didn't think we'd make it, so I hit the brakes—a little too hard. Didn't even see where my bike ended up." He gestured toward some indistinguishable spot in the bushes.

He fired an angry glance of his own at Aaron. "But who the fuck tries to beat a train? And maybe I should be asking *you* why that crazy bitch is after something *you* have. Because, let's see, last I checked, we were running for our lives and are now at the bottom of this hill because of you!"

Aaron fought to contain his anger, wanted to tell Simon that their bikes wouldn't have gone off into the underbrush—and now likely mangled—had Simon continued over the tracks.

Instead, he looked away and shook his head. The woman was out there, and they couldn't linger. But he knew he'd have to tell them the truth soon. Explain the medallion. Explain everything. He rubbed his shoulder and looked at Simon. "Trust me. You'll know everything once we get somewhere safe. It's a long story. And, *no*—I didn't steal anything. Now, can we get moving?" Without waiting for an answer, he walked up and down the trail, scanning the underbrush, looking for hints of red. Nothing.

"Oh, Christ."

He turned to see Simon frantically patting down his pockets.

"Christ. Think I lost my phone. Oh shit. Not good, not good."

"Take it easy," Libby said. "We all fell in the same general direction." She gestured to where Aaron stood parting fronds and branches next to a large maple. "Your bikes can't be far from where Aaron is right now. Just find your bikes."

"Okay Einstein, but a bike is one thing. A tiny phone is a whole other thing."

"Then maybe you shouldn't have chickened out and wrecked your damn bike, Simon."

"Oh, fuck y—"

"Shut up!" Aaron shouted. "We don't have time."

Not seeing anything, Aaron turned back to the trail, guessing Shelby had to be closer toward the—

Something whistled past his forehead. He turned to follow its path. The arrow was in the nearby tree trunk, its feathered fletching thrumming like a fishtail.

They looked at each other, wide-eyed. Their bikes and Simon's phone would have to remain hidden where they lay. Together, they leaped into the underbrush.

***

Aaron barreled through a latticework of branches. To his right, Libby was slipping through narrow gaps in the bushes. To his left, Simon was crashing through a dense thicket.

They pushed due south, parallel to the tracks. Aaron swam through a row of sedge, praying an arrow wouldn't slam into his back and burst through his chest. But the woman hadn't been carrying a bow of any kind.

Then they were sprinting through the woods uninhibited. The brush opening to needle-covered causeways through stands of tall evergreens. The open space was both good and bad. They could run faster here but were more visible.

"Follow me!" Libby called over her shoulder. She then gasped and lurched back.

Aaron pulled up, and his feet slipped on the wet duff— nearly out from under him.

"What is it?" he asked, fighting to maintain his footing.

She was pointing at a large hemlock a few feet away.

He looked. This time, the arrow had come from the east. It was swaying in the tree's trunk, which may have been Libby's torso had she kept running south.

The urge came to him then. Drop the medallion on the forest floor. Give the woman what she wanted. What *they* wanted. Because there *were* others. But if he did that, then what of Owen? The medallion had forged his only link to him. He couldn't sever it. Not now. Not until he understood more. They had to run. His other thought had been to get to the small village of Brandywine, and that's what they needed to do.

"Cross the tracks," he said.

"What?" said Libby. "We have to head back to Portage Falls!"

"They won't let us go south."

"They?"

Aaron turned to see Simon wheezing and staggering forward, having fallen too far behind to be aware of what had just happened. Then his eyes fell upon the arrow.

"Oh, you gotta be shitting me!"

A blur whistled past Aaron's face.

"This way! Go!"

They sprinted for the tracks, changing their direction at the insistence of an arrow like panicked bison, charging toward an open expanse where they could be cut down.

As they scrabbled up the graveled slope and over the rail ties, two more arrows fell aslant into the narrow clearing on the opposite side of the tracks—south of their position and well clear.

They burst into the foliage on the opposite side of the track.

"Keep heading that way!" Aaron called out.

Libby looked back to see him pointing in the direction of Brandywine and frowned. She slowed between stands of thickets, allowing Aaron to catch up. "Isn't Azure Lake that way? We can't get around it to get to Brandywine unless we head way north! We'll be blocked by the river if we keep going due west!"

"Yeah," Aaron said, wheezing, "but there's a narrow strip of land between the river and lake and we can follow the river north."

Libby looked doubtful.

"Guys!"

Simon broke into the clearing, staggered, and put his hands on his knees.

"Can't ... keep ... up."

Aaron looked at Libby who only looked back at him. He didn't hesitate. He walked over to Simon, dipped beneath him and leaned him over his shoulder. He stood and gasped as Simon's weight settled onto him, sending a fresh shudder of pain through his other shoulder, which still ached.

They walked, heading due west as fast as they could manage, the dense brush giving way to deep furrows in the terrain, looking as if some giant had pressed its fingers upon the Earth to lay claim to it.

Then they were descending a narrow trace, the land leveling to a floodplain. At the bottom of the descent, Libby paused to allow them to close the distance.

The words tumbled from her mouth, "Aaron, I hope you're right about that strip of land. I don't think there are any other options. There aren't any bridges nearby."

Bridge. Aaron tried to think if there was anything manmade closer by in this stretch of forest. Any structures. Any place to take refuge.

Then he had it. There was a pier, jutting into the water from Azure Lake's southwestern bank. And that pier was on the same property as the Kendall House, which was a stone's throw away from the lake *and* the river. Plus, the house was accessible by road. He'd never actually visited the turn-of-the-century farmhouse, but had seen pictures of it and could recall reading an article on the *Cleveland Plain Dealer's* website about how the house had been restored by the Cuyahoga Valley National Park Conservancy with the help of some wealthy and anonymous donor, who now supposedly lived there. Maybe they could help.

He quickly explained his idea to Libby while gingerly stepping over a fallen tree trunk, Simon groaning from being jostled. "Plus," he said, "it's much closer than Brandywine and I don't think I can carry him that far."

"Yeah, I agree," Simon grunted. "Let's end this shit. Get somewhere inside."

Libby didn't answer right away, her eyes flitting in all directions, scanning the forest. "I've never been there," she said, finally. "But I don't have a better idea."

***

Ten minutes passed without incident or arrow, but something else now pummeled them from above. The sky had fully opened. The wind had also picked up, blowing in from the west, the trees leaning into one another in succession as if whispering a game of telephone. Simon swore something unintelligible. Libby glanced back to see him squirming on Aaron's shoulder. His back was getting battered by the rain.

"Can he walk again?" she asked, not trying to keep the disdain from her voice, wanting to replace "he" with "it."

Apparently agreeing he'd had enough of the rain on his back, Simon slid from Aaron's shoulder with the look of a cat who'd been tossed in a swimming pool. Then again, he'd had that look his entire life.

Libby unslung her bag, reached in it, and grabbed her compass. She popped it open. The bright green arrow swung over the white numerals and tick marks before wobbling into place between the N and the W. They were heading in the right direction. She looked west to see a trembling stretch of pale light through the trees. It was mist over the Cuyahoga, and it now dawned on her just how far the river pulled away from the Towpath and the eastern slopes in this reach of forest.

"Keep going this way," she said. "Can't be far."

An unsettling thought struck her as she closed her compass and pocketed it, and it had to do with the compass's arrow. The arrows from their invisible assailants had felt somehow calculated. In judging how closely they'd come to hitting her and Aaron, it seemed they both ought to be dead by now. She carried an eye across the swaying trees, but there was nothing to see in any direction. Nothing to hear over the rising wind.

She thought of the land strip between the river and Azure Lake. It would be a logical pinch point to cut them down at close range and remove their bodies. With arrows there'd also be no report of gunfire. She shuddered at the thought of their dead bodies being dragged across the forest floor, never to be seen again. Dispatched, like the officer who'd been dumped into the marsh like some dead animal.

She picked up her pace. If the two of them couldn't keep up, then what? Could she just leave them behind and hope they'd make it to the house? She glanced back at Aaron's earnest red face as he trudged beside his unworthy friend.

No, can't leave him behind.

By and by, rutted ground gave way to marsh, her footfalls now causing gentle splashes. She turned slightly south to skirt the swamp and was soon pushing through a dense stand of reeds. The boys followed without a word. Ten minutes later, they spilled out onto a well-manicured lawn the size of a meadow. The house's white siding and black shutters peaked through the wispy leaves of a nearby willow. Her heart leaping, she fell into a trot. As she emerged on the other side of the tree, she noticed a soft glow coming from an upstairs window.

Chapter 18

The Kendall House

Libby was running across the lawn to the house. Aaron lagged far behind, a cramp in his side as he trudged over the freshly mown grass. Simon dawdled even further back.

Aaron rounded the house to its front, and a gravel parking lot came into view. The lot was small, with a black Jeep Compass parked in the spot nearest a flagstone walkway, which led up to a small concrete stoop. Libby was scaling the stoop to the home's front door, which was thankfully covered by a columned overhang. Warm light glowed from beyond the large curtained windows on either side of the porch. The two-story colonial home was almost *all* windows.

Libby turned and gave him a look that said, "Here goes nothing."

Aaron turned and took a moment to look over the sprawling front yard, which was bisected by a narrow driveway leading out to a rural road.

The road might be another option if this doesn't work out.

Then again, the dense forest on either side of the road would offer plenty of hiding spots for someone armed with a bow, arrows, and an intent to kill. And, they still had to be at least five minutes from Brandywine by car, which might as well be an hour on foot.

His thoughts were interrupted by Libby's furious pounding on the door. She stopped, waited a moment and then banged again.

Movement caught his eye. The curtain in the window nearest them was swaying. Libby noticed the movement too. She grabbed the door's casing to steady herself and leaned out in front of the window.

"Please, we're in trouble! We need your help!"

Aaron squeezed in next to her just a few inches from the door. Staring at the small peephole set at eye level, he added, "We just need to use your phone, that's all!"

Silence. Another minute passed. He exchanged a look with Libby, who pursed her lips and shook her head.

"What the hell?" Simon said, the exhaustion that had kept his mouth in check for the past half an hour apparently at an end. "This coward won't let us in! I say we just get outta—"

A heavy *clink*, followed by a series of rattles and more clinks. A moment later, the door eased open, a brass chain stretching taut over a man's pale face. Intelligent blue eyes peered back at them through round wire-rimmed glasses. His forehead wrinkled in concern. Aaron decided it was a kind face. But the voice from the man was fast and strident.

"I've been called many things," he said, "but *coward* isn't one of them." He closed the door.

Aaron turned and shot an angry glance at Simon, who only shrugged, as if his mouth were an untamable weapon that acted upon its own set of laws.

Then, more rattling, and the door swung open. The man stood to one side with an outstretched arm, welcoming them into the old house.

***

Simon was the last to trudge into the foyer. The man stepped around him and closed the door. He turned a heavy dead-bolt lock near the brass knob and reached up to the top of the door and slid a heavy-duty bolt lock into place. Lastly, he reconnected the dainty chain lock.

The man turned back to them and put his hands on his hips. He was about average height—shorter than Aaron, but taller than Simon. He wore a blue and white gingham button-down shirt that was tucked into a crisp pair of khakis. Aaron's eyes fell to the man's feet, in leather sandals showing off navy-blue socks. Like the paltry chain lock in comparison to the heavy bolt locks, the sandals didn't fit the rest of the man's wardrobe or appearance.

Aaron ran a hand through his hair and rain droplets pattered to the blonde hardwood floor, which was already puddling with the water they'd tracked in. He looked up at their host, ready to apologize, but the man was waving a dismissive hand.

"Don't worry about the floor," he said. "You're lucky I was planning on cleaning it *tomorrow* and not today. In fact, you've given me even more motivation to do it! But hang on—wait there a sec while I fetch you some towels."

He turned and strode down a narrow hallway that ran adjacent to the central staircase and was gone from sight. A lemon scent hung in the air, reminding Aaron of the furniture polish Gram used for Sunday cleaning. He took in the home's interior, which wasn't what he'd expected from judging its outward appearance. The hardwood floors looked newer, as did much of the art deco furniture. To the left, a modest sitting room with an angular couch and a couple of small chairs surrounding a coffee table.

To the right, a large room with a baby grand piano at its center. Atop the piano stood several framed still-life photos of plants and flowers. Beyond the piano, at the far side of the room, stood a credenza topped by a coffee maker, some delicate-looking chinaware, and a candle, its guttering flame the likely source of the lemon scent. Aaron peeked around the corner of the entryway toward the front windows and saw a desk with a computer monitor and a printer. The desk, like the rest of the furniture, was made up of harsh angles.

Everything about the home felt angular, austere, and cold. But there was *some* warmth, he decided, as he ran a practiced eye over the foyer and its two adjoining rooms. Like the nature photos on the piano, there was comfort to be found in the paintings of natural scenery on the walls. A painting of a red covered bridge caught his attention. He walked over to it. Studying it closer, he turned to Simon to tell him he thought the painting might be depicting the old single-lane bridge south of the Sand Run Caves—which was now condemned—but paused. Simon's eyes were like murderous weapons, and they were trained on him.

"Well?" Simon said.

"Well, what?"

"You gonna finally tell us why you almost got us killed?" He folded his arms over his chest and made a show of looking in all directions. "Because it seems like we're in a pretty safe place now."

Aaron looked at Libby, who just shrugged. It was time to spill it. He was about to reply when the man reemerged into the foyer. He had two bath towels stuffed under one arm. Aaron didn't have time to wonder about a third because it was already fluttering at his face.

"Catch!" the man said. "You look like you got the worst of it. The *Weather Channel*'s predicting at least two inches today before it's all said and done, and you, my friend, look like you're wearing at least one of those inches."

The towel was warm, and Aaron happily buried his head in it. He hadn't realized how drenched he was and doubted one towel would be enough. After dabbing at his T-shirt and shorts, which were plastered to his skin, he glanced up to find the man studying him, his stubbled chin cupped in one hand.

"You know, I *might* have a shirt that fits you. What size are you?"

"Sir, we appreciate the towels and the clothing offer," Libby cut in, "but if we could use your phone first, that would be very helpful."

The man turned his attention to Libby, and he studied her for a long time. Something about the way he looked at her made Aaron's forehead grow hot.

"You're well built … maybe a medium?"

Libby flitted her eyes to Aaron and then Simon, unsure of how to reply.

"So, that was weird," Simon said.

The man glanced at Simon, a dark look passing over his features. It was gone in an instant. He shook his head. "I'm sorry. Where are my manners? By the way, name's Gil—Gil Stanford." He extended a hand to Libby.

She accepted it and introduced herself. Simon followed, mumbling his own salutation while ignoring the man's extended hand. When Aaron introduced himself, Gil paused and raised his eyebrows.

"Wait. Are you related to *Owen* Porter?"

Aaron nodded. "He's my older brother."

Gil's shoulders sagged. "I'm so sorry, Aaron. I read about the accident. Saw your name. My deepest condolences to you and your family."

Aaron waved this off, wanting to move off the topic of his brother, his family, his wreckage. "Thanks," he said, "but we have a more pressing issue."

Gil straightened. "Oh, yes—absolutely. What in god's name is going on? Because if there's trouble out here, I need to know about it. As I'm sure you're well aware, I don't have many neighbors round here save for the deer and raccoons."

Here it comes.

It was time to tell them. He could feel Libby's and Simon's eyes on him. The medallion was pasted to his chest, and he wasn't sure how much of it would be visible through his wet T-shirt but had to assume that Simon and Libby were starting to suspect he was wearing *something* given the cord around his neck, and after having watched him get strip searched by the woman.

"It's a long story," he blurted, wanting to seize control of this narrative, feeling that doing so would help soften the blow when it was time to fess up.

Gil gave an encouraging nod for him to continue.

"We nearly got killed at the Beaver Marsh by a woman who says I have something that belongs to her. She … killed a man who saw we were in trouble and tried to help." His voice felt feeble now, as if speaking of the officer's death had added weight to it.

"We all saw it. He was a cop from the Portage Falls PD, but he didn't give his name. But I *know* he was a cop, since I've seen him in uniform before. The man…" Aaron trailed off, his face growing hot, his gaze trained on the floor.

"He was just out for a jog," he continued, "and she killed him." He could feel a tear beginning to slide down his cheek but didn't bother swiping it away. There had been no opportunity to reflect on what had happened at the marsh, and now, the pent-up grief was going to escape one way or another. Libby was starting to sniffle.

He looked up at Gil through glassy eyes and could see the gravity of the situation playing out over the man's bookish features, his own eyes distant.

"She still out there?" he whispered.

Simon said, "Yeah, we think she is. And that bitch isn't alone. Someone shot arrows at us when we were getting away, and there's no way—*no fuckin' way*—it could've been her."

Aaron noticed Gil wince at Simon's language.

"I mean, arrows? Who the fuck shoots arrows nowadays?"

"Lots of people," Libby said as she dabbed at her cheeks with her towel. "But that's beside the point. We need to call the police."

Gil was nodding. "You kids have been through enough. Wait a second—what about your phones? Why haven't you called the police yourselves?"

"Because these idiots, for whatever reason, don't believe in bringing their phones with them into the remote-ass wilderness," said Simon.

"Whoa there, partner," Gil said. "What about *you*? If you're that smart, you surely must have your phone with you, right?"

Simon shook his head. "Lost it when we were running for our lives. Would've been nice had it not all depended on me."

"You mean to tell me that between three Gen Z kids, none of you has a phone, a tablet, a smartwatch—anything?"

Aaron shook his head. Simon started to say something, but Gil extended a palm. "Actually, never mind," he said. "Here's what I'm going to do. I'm good friends with Sheriff Fitzwater, and I'm going to call him right now. *But*, he'll probably want you to stick around so he can talk with you directly. That okay with you?"

They exchanged glances. None objected.

"He's a good man, believe me. I'm sure he won't be long getting here. In the meantime, I'm serious about getting you kids some dry clothes. I'll see what I can find after I call him." He paused and studied them again, as if sizing them up. His eyes lingered on Libby, her figure now more apparent under her wet T-shirt.

Aaron felt his forehead grow hot again.

"Okay," he mumbled to himself, "a couple mediums and maybe an XL, which might be too small." He brightened. "Oh, and by the way, there's a Keurig over there." He indicated the room to their right. "By all means, help yourself. I have all kinds of roasts. And for god's sake, take a load off."

***

Gil's voice echoed from somewhere deep inside the house.

"Hey, Bob ... no, that's not why I'm calling ... no, listen up. I have a few kids over here right now who say they were attacked over at the Beaver Marsh and that they witnessed a murder … yeah, serious as a heart attack…"

Aaron and Libby listened to the conversation from where they stood in the foyer while Simon remained in the sitting room, guzzling his second cup of coffee. Aaron peered around the corner of the staircase. Down the hallway and through another entryway—which he guessed led to the kitchen—he glimpsed Gil pacing back and forth, a cordless phone in the crook of his neck.

"Okay, thanks, Bob. I'm sure they'll be relieved to hear that."

Sensing the call was about to end, Aaron turned and padded on bare feet back to the sitting room. Libby followed. The three of them had decided it was best to take off their wet shoes and socks before entering the museum-like living space. The decision had been a good one, as the area rug felt soothing under Aaron's pruny feet.

He and Libby slumped back down onto the couch—which they'd covered with their towels—as Simon sat in a small wingback chair. Aaron, who wasn't usually much of a coffee drinker, had decided to help himself to a cup and was now enjoying the stimulating effects. Libby returned to nursing her cup of decaf as if it contained boiling acid that might incinerate her insides.

"I've never had coffee," she said sheepishly, as she caught him observing her dainty sips.

Aaron was about to rise and help himself to another cup when Libby abruptly set down her mug, curled her legs beneath her, and faced him.

"Aaron, you can tell us. I hope you know that. If you stole something, or did something you're not proud of, it's okay." She turned to Simon. "*Nothing* leaves this room."

Aaron looked at Simon, who had also set down his mug and was straightening in his chair.

Simon nodded.

Libby turned back to Aaron, and it seemed both her eyes were trained on him.

He forced himself to look into those hazel eyes, attentive eyes that in any other situation would have made him light-headed. He then nodded, sat forward, and steadied his elbows on his knees. After a while, he nodded toward Simon and said, "*You* know that one of my hobbies is garbage picking."

Simon nodded.

He glanced at Libby. "But you might not. And no, I'm not one of those weirdos who goes through people's personal belongings or things like that. It's just the obvious stuff that they set out on the tree lawn that they clearly don't want. You wouldn't *believe* some of the things people set out on junk night. I've found some cool stu—"

"Porter, you're stalling. Spit it out."

"Okay, okay. Anyway, I found ... something, last month in front of the Flores' house on Bernard."

He went on to describe the medallion but chose—for reasons he didn't altogether understand—to leave out the fact that there were two of them. But the rest of the details tumbled from his mouth before he could stop himself. He described the object's pull on him, and in doing so, felt as if a burden were lifting from his shoulders. When he got to recounting what had happened in the mine and how he'd *felt* like something was about to happen, a warm hand fell upon his forearm and gave it a gentle squeeze. He looked up to find Libby leaning toward him, nodding her encouragement. He glanced over to Simon, who was leaning forward too, but his eyes were narrowed.

Simon shook his head. "If that crazy bitch wants this damn thing so bad, then why the *hell* didn't you just give it to her at the marsh? I mean shit, Porter, it got someone *killed!*"

"Hey!" Libby barked.

Aaron said, "It's okay. I get—"

"No! It's not okay, Porter! And you *don't* get it!" Simon shot
to his feet. "I thought I was your best friend! But this whole
damn time, you've got this *thing*, and you don't even think to
tell me about it? I mean, shit, dude, you had this thing at *my
house*. Now, you've put us all in danger. How do I know she's
not on her way to my house right now? She sure as hell knows
where I li—"

"Good news!" Gil said, emerging into the room, toting a
stack of neatly pressed white T-shirts. "The sheriff is on his way
over here now. He's sending a patrolman down to the Beaver
Marsh to check it out ... is everything okay here?"

"Yes," Libby said, "Aaron was just telling us about some
things he's been going through."

"No," Simon said, shaking his head. "I think *my friend* needs
to show us what he's hiding. Am I right, Porter?"

Gil turned to Aaron. "Hiding?"

Aaron felt small, isolated. Libby now seemed further away
and Simon and Gil had somehow grown taller.

"I'd like to think I'm a pretty trustworthy guy," Gil said
evenly, "and I'm just trying to help, but I can't do that if you
don't tell me. This isn't drug related, is it? Because if it is, then
we have a problem." He paused, and with a growing edge in his
voice, said, "Actually, *I* have a problem. Especially with a law
enforcement official on his way to my house right now."

Aaron closed his eyes. He'd unburdened himself to Libby
and Simon, so what was the harm in including Gil? The man
had been nothing but helpful and had every right to demand
the truth—even demand that they leave his home. He had to
show it to them. Telling them wouldn't be enough, especially
not enough for Simon who had every right to hate him and
apparently already did. In fact, they all deserved the full truth
after all he'd dragged them into—including now Gil—who
could also be in harm's way if the police didn't find the woman.

Without so much as a glance toward anyone else, he reached into the neck opening of his shirt and grabbed the medallion.

I'm sorry.

What he was about to do felt no different from dropping his pants and exposing himself. No, it was worse. The medallion reached deep into some place he hadn't known existed. It was a place where he'd somehow found his brother, something he hadn't yet told the others and knew they would never understand. It was a portal, a doorway through which a slender thread of hope connected him to Owen. But it was weak, ready to be severed at the slightest disturbance. He could sense his lower lip trembling, his fingers shaking as he pulled his only lifeline to his brother up and out from under his shirt.

Libby gasped. From the corner of his eye, he saw her hand fly up to her mouth. He willed himself to look up to where Simon stood. His defiant expression was gone.

He looked over to where Gil stood framed in the entryway. The corners of his mouth were easing downward, his eyes glazing in quiet astonishment.

Aaron didn't remove his hand from the medallion—he couldn't. Instead, he encircled it with his fingers, allowing the others to take in its etchings, its swirling contours, its protruding glass chips, its central black *eye*. It caught the light of a table lamp and threw shimmering puddles over the walls and ceiling.

"My god, those have to be crystals," Gil whispered as he brought a hand to his chin and nearly missed.

Aaron tried to think of something to say, but couldn't. It was as if they were staring at his naked body, indulging every blemish. He hadn't before given any thought as to what it would be like to reveal the medallion to someone else, realizing he'd never intended to show it to anyone at all. He'd internalized a belief that he'd go his entire life with this enigmatic object as his ever-guarded secret. That he'd alone find his brother. That he'd rescue him from wherever and whenever he was being held.

He'd keep this secret *and* would somehow rescue his brother? The notion was insane.

Libby gasped again. Aaron looked at her. She was no longer looking at him or the medallion. Her eyes were on Gil. Aaron looked at the man. The stack of shirts Gil had been holding were now lying in a heap at his feet. Something had replaced them in his right hand, which was trembling. Aaron stared into the hole at the end of the black cylinder. Gil then spoke in a flat, measured tone despite the quaking gun.

"Aaron, I'm going to have to ask you to hand that over. *Now.*"

Chapter 19

Prisoners

The blood drained from Aaron's face as he stared into the gun's barrel.

"What the f-fuck is going on here?" Simon stammered.

"I'm only going to ask once," Gil said. "Take it off. Then place it on the coffee table and slide it toward me."

"Listen to him, Aaron!" Libby hissed. "Take it off!"

Aaron's fingers floated to where the cord hugged the sides of his neck. Slowly, hooking his thumbs under the cord, he raised the medallion up and over his head. It dangled in the air for what felt like an eternity as he lowered it to the table.

"Very good. Now, set it on the table and slide it toward me."

Aaron numbly set it down, feeling as if he'd just placed his soul on the table. He pushed it to the opposite end. In two quick steps, Gil came forward and snatched it up.

"Good," Gil said, dropping it into the front right pocket of his trousers. "Now, we're going to take a walk downstairs. On your feet—*all* of you."

"Fucking christ! You're gonna kill us?"

"Not if you listen to *everything* I say. Again, on your feet."

Aaron rose on unsteady legs. He and Libby side-stepped between the couch and coffee table until they were next to where Simon stood looking ready to faint.

"You," Gil said, pointing the gun at Simon. "Walk past the stairs and turn left down the hallway."

Simon did as he was told.

"I was wondering why you were so insistent on getting us fresh clothes," Libby said as she fell in behind Simon. "Guess it was an excuse to get your gun?"

"Keep moving!" Gil jerked the gun toward the kitchen.

Aaron shuffled in behind Libby as Gil faded further back.

"And that *phone call* to the *sheriff*," Libby said, forming air quotes with her fingers, "I'm guessing that was pure fiction too, huh?"

"Keep your hands down! No sudden movements!"

They entered the kitchen. With its large granite-topped island and stainless-steel appliances, it was far too modern-looking for the style and era of the home.

"Now, left through the doorway and then left again down the stairs."

They did as instructed, turning from the kitchen to another sitting room, which, in another era, might have been a formal dining room. Then they were turning into a basement stairwell.

The wooden steps were cold under Aaron's bare feet. A dank odor clung to the air and only intensified the further they descended. Then his feet were touching even colder cement. A narrow corridor stretched before them. A metal conduit ran the length of the ceiling, interrupted by naked lightbulbs every ten or so feet, which cast lonely pools of light onto a sterile gray floor. There were two rooms off the corridor, and they were both sealed with heavy-looking steel doors. One door stood just to their left, and the other was further down the hallway to their right, its metal pull-lever catching the light.

"Walk forward ten feet then stop."

Simon, sniffling and otherwise silent, was the first to walk down the hallway. Quiet as he was, his rancor was still present, and it was as if it had been transferred into Libby, who now said, "Far enough, asshole? Kinda forgot my measuring tape."

"Shut your mouth." A pause, and then he said, "Fine. Stop there."

They stopped. A jangling of metal sounded behind Aaron, followed by the *zip* of a key being plunged into a keyhole. The tumbler engaged, and a *click* sounded. The door groaned open.

"Turn around, *slowly*."

They obeyed, turning to face him, maintaining single file, Aaron now in the lead.

The man's eyes had a pained look in them. "Here's the deal," he said. "I'm not a killer, but don't give me reason to break character. In—*now*." He stepped back to the foot of the stairs and waved the gun toward the dark maw of the open doorway.

Aaron could feel it, knew this could be his only chance. He recalled an Internet article he'd read about what to do if ever under the threat of abduction. The resounding advice had been to *never* get into an abductor's car. But this wasn't exactly a car—it was a dark room in a basement—and a man was pointing a gun at him. He couldn't just run away. If he were to throw himself at Gil, he'd likely get shot but might be able to pin the man under his weight and give Simon and Libby a chance to escape. But before he could puzzle this out further, Gil was fading up the first couple of steps, the gun still trained on them. It was as if he'd read Aaron's thoughts and was putting himself out of reach.

"*In*. Last warning."

Aaron turned and walked into the pitch-black room. Libby and Simon followed like shackled prisoners. Seconds later the door banged shut behind them. Another *zip* and turn of the tumbler. They were being locked in from the outside.

"Why are you doing this?" Libby cried from somewhere behind Aaron.

Aaron didn't expect a reply, so was surprised when the man's muffled voice sounded on the other side of the door.

"Believe me," he said, in a voice now calm and almost paternal. "You'll be safer here."

"What the fuck does that even mean?" Simon called back.

No answer came, just footfalls fading up the steps. Then they were gone.

"Great, now what?" Simon said.

"I'm still trying to figure out what just happened," Aaron replied.

Simon and Libby grew quiet, and Aaron imagined they were also replaying the events that had landed them here. All he'd done was show Gil the medallion. Why had that earned him a gun aimed at his face? Being locked in a basement? He closed his eyes even though it was unnecessary in this perfect dark. His only lifeline to Owen had just marched up those steps and out of his life—probably forever.

"Well," Libby uttered from somewhere deeper in the room, "let's at least see if we can get some light in this place."

Aaron turned to the closed door, the useless sliver of light at its bottom not enough to make any sense of their new surroundings. But it was the only north star they had.

"There's got to be a switch around here somewhere," he said, groping the drywall to the left of the doorframe. Nothing met his touch. He tried just to the right of the door, moving his hand in a grid-like pattern up and down and across the wall's smooth surface. Nothing.

"Ow—*Jesus!*" Simon yelped from somewhere in the dark.

"What?" Libby said. "What happened?"

"Nothing—I think. My knee just bumped into something heavy. Hang on, feeling what it is. Feels like … like a cardboard box, and it's filled with books and binders and stuff."

"We're probably in a storage room," Aaron said. "And in judging from the lights in the hallway, I bet there are overhead bulbs in here too. I just don't know how to turn them on. Can't find a wall switch anywhere."

"Right," Libby said. "There has to be a string hanging down around here somewhere." A moment later, she said, "Found it!"

A *click*, and then the room lit up. Aaron winced and closed his eyes. He waited. A moment later, he eased them open, and his surroundings began to take shape. The single bulb lit a sea of cardboard boxes, plastic containers, and crates, many of which were stacked atop each other, a few of the stacks rising to eye level. Several of the individual cardboard boxes were either warped or decomposing, and some were literally bursting at their seams with overstuffed manilla folders, notebooks, and ringed binders.

They were quiet as they took in the paperwork monoliths.

Eventually, Simon said, "Christ, can you say pack rat?"

"Which is odd," Libby said. "I saw he has a computer. Must not believe in digital copies."

Aaron was only partially listening as his trained eyes went to work on the room from where he stood with his back to the door.

Sapere Verdere.

The adjoining cinder block wall to his left was about ten feet from the door, its white painted surface interrupted midway down by an opening the size of a large suitcase. It was a crawlspace, set at eye level, and it swallowed the light like a black hole, concealing inner dimensions and any hint of whatever may lie within.

On the opposing wall, a top-load washer and dryer stood next to a stationary tub with a rusty faucet. To the right of the tub, a large plastic laundry hamper, overflowing with the man's soiled clothing. The sleeve of a red button-down shirt hovered in the air just above the hamper. He ran his gaze up the sleeve to where it disappeared inside the mouth of a metal laundry chute jutting from the ceiling. The shirt was clearly snagged on something or it had been stuffed into the chute with too many other articles. He continued running his gaze along the same wall, ignoring the document skyscrapers in the foreground. Nothing else of interest.

The adjoining wall at the far end—which he guessed faced the front of the house—didn't reveal anything noteworthy either, but he decided he'd need to take a closer look as much of the wall's lower half was obscured from view. He turned to the wall at his back, which had been framed in and drywalled, but nothing met his eye save for a cobweb-covered fire extinguisher on the floor a few feet from the door.

He mentally inventoried the points of interest: a crawlspace, a laundry area with a stationary tub and a faucet—that might have running water—a laundry chute, and a fire extinguisher. The rest of the space was dominated by a lifetime of documents, which Aaron approached now wondering if anything useful might be buried among them.

"Knew I shouldn't have had that second cup," Simon muttered. "Gotta piss like a racehorse."

"Use the tub," Aaron offered. "Turn on the faucet. I wanna see if it works anyway." While he'd never admit as much in Libby's company, he'd often done the very same thing in Gram's basement when he'd been too lazy to trudge to the upstairs bathroom.

"Can't I just piss on this asshole's documents?" Simon said, as he walked over to the tub.

He arrived and opened the tap. The faucet groaned and vibrated before loosening a weak stream. He stood on tiptoes and moaned as he relieved himself.

"Just make sure you get it in the hole," Libby said as she scavenged through boxes. "I don't wanna smell it."

Aaron paused just as he was bending to a transparent Tupperware container. What had Libby just said? *"Get it in the hole?"*

He stood and picked his way to the wall with the crawlspace. The opening was actually about shoulder height, and he figured he might be able to wriggle his way up and into it. But that would be exhausting, and his left shoulder already ached enough. Another idea popped into his head. He turned to Simon.

"Hey, mind if I hoist you up?"

"Uh yeah," Simon said, zipping his fly, "I do mind, 'cause I'm not going into a fucking cave. What if there's a Brown Recluse in there?"

"Okay, so if there's something in there that can help us get outta here, you don't care? You're more worried about spiders?"

"Just do it, Simon," Libby muttered from somewhere amidst the clutter.

"What if he just comes back and lets us out?" Simon asked.

"Do you really think he's gonna do that?" she asked. "Seriously, he drew a gun on us and locked us down here. Nope, we have to get *ourselves* out and call the police."

"But he's still in the house. Even if we magically get ourselves out of his basement, he's still up there with a goddamned gun."

"I don't think he's staying," Aaron said absently.

"Why's that?" Libby asked.

"Just a feeling."

"Just a feeling, Porter?"

Aaron shrugged. "Yeah. He clearly knew about the medallion. How, I don't know."

"What d'ya think he's gonna do with it?" Libby asked. "Sell it on the black market?"

Aaron had ideas about this. The man had to know its significance and maybe even how to use it. But instead, he said, "Whatever his plans are, they won't help our present situation." He looked at Simon.

Simon rolled his eyes and let out an expansive sigh. "The shit I do for you, Porter."

"What you'll be doing for *all* of us," Aaron corrected as he lowered himself to one knee and interlaced his fingers. Simon pressed one bare foot onto the makeshift stirrup and Aaron hoisted him up—a little too fast. Simon gasped as his back crashed into the upper lip of the opening.

"Jesus! Take it easy!"

"Sorry. You okay?"

Simon nodded and massaged his right shoulder. He grumbled some more and then crawled forward into the space on hands and knees.

"Sure would be nice to have a flashlight right about now."

"I know," Aaron said, "but just try to feel out with your hands, okay? Anything?"

"Nothing so far." His voice sounded distant, the filthy bottoms of his feet having disappeared into darkness.

"It has to go pretty far back there," Libby said, appearing at Aaron's side. She leaned into the space. "Make sure you find the corners and all the walls."

She turned to Aaron, her eyebrows raised. "Maybe the drywall doesn't extend all the way. Think it's possible? There could be a cavity that leads underneath the staircase."

Aaron could only shrug.

Simon's distant voice now sounded to the left of the opening and was followed by a series of hollow knocks on what must have been the drywall.

"That's just me. Shit. Seems like the bottom of the staircase is walled in back here. There's nothing—it's closed off. I'm coming out. Enough of this shit."

Aaron exhaled. They couldn't climb their way out through the laundry chute. They couldn't break down the door, and they couldn't crawl their way—

"Hang on," Simon called out. "Wait, no—eh, it's nothing. Feels like there are some notebooks back here or something. That's it."

Aaron was about to tell him to forget it and to come out, but Libby cut in.

"Just grab them! You never know."

"Not sure what the hell more papers will do, but whatever."

He crawled back to the opening and tossed down a thin dust-covered notebook. It slapped to the concrete floor and Libby immediately padded over and scooped it up. Next, he threw down a photograph album binder.

Aaron extended his arms to help ease Simon to the floor, but Simon shook his head.

"Hell, no. Don't feel like breaking my back. I'll get myself down, thanks."

Aaron picked up the white photo binder, wiped dust from its unmarked cover, and began flicking through the plastic pages. The pockets of each page were stuffed with sepia tone photos, most creased with age. The setting for each photo was a large gathering space with benches and tables. He saw men with thick sideburns wearing suits and ties. He saw women with elaborate hairstyles wearing headbands, pearl necklaces, and shapeless dresses. The heads of a few people had been circled with red marker.

"Just old pictures," he said. He held up the binder so that Libby could see the photos of the people with circled heads.

She studied the photos, frowning. After a while, she shrugged.

Aaron flicked through more pages. "Not much else here," he mumbled. "Odd that it was hiding in a crawlspace. Wonder if there's anything useful in the other book?"

Libby was already wiping dust from the notebook's cover, which Aaron immediately recognized as the kind of notebook he'd used in school, its hectic black and white cover pattern like buzzing static. A white rectangle—now yellowing—at its center with a title reading: COMPOSITION BOOK. Below the title were a couple of lines for the author to write their name or some information about the work within. In this case, the lines were left blank.

"Shall we?" she said, flipping open the notebook's cover. Aaron approached and peered over her shoulder. The first few pages were stiff with age, but the paper slackened the further she thumbed through them. The first pages were filled with what appeared to be diary entries, some of which were dated back to the 1990s. Then pencil drawings of varying fidelity and detail were flicking past, almost all the illustrations depicting the same basic shape: a spiral.

"Stop there would you?" Aaron murmured.

Libby did and cocked her head as she rotated the notebook. She then looked at him, and Aaron knew she was thinking the same thing he was, *what are the odds?*

The illustration on this page wasn't just depicting a spiral. It was a rendering of the actual medallion itself. The circle was shaded in, and a spiral pattern had been erased out. An oval at the spiral's center was similarly erased out. Aaron's head felt like it was being filled with helium. How could this be? How could a notebook that they just so happened to find in a basement crawlspace of a strange turn-of-the-century home contain drawings of the very object that had essentially landed them here?

"I have no idea what's going on here," Libby said, before flipping through more pages. "I just can't believe any of this is some coincidence."

"Me neither," Aaron said.

Aaron puzzled it over. In a way, Gil's actions made more sense now, assuming he was the author of the entries and the artist of the drawings.

Simon was now looking over Libby's other shoulder as different kinds of drawings flicked past, which depicted stick figures, more circles, and nonsensical meandering lines. Libby paused on a page with a drawing depicting a map of some kind. Aaron saw trees and what looked to be caves sketched in careful detail in the page's upper-left-hand corner. A large S-shape extended down the center of the page, occupying the page's full height.

"The Cuyahoga," Aaron mumbled, noting the sketched train tracks running alongside the river in some spots.

"Yeah, and look," Simon added, "see that house toward the bottom?"

Aaron followed a line that ran straight down from the trees and caves. Near the center of the page it forked, another line branching off it, which angled down and bisected the river until it adjoined a rendering of a house in the bottom-right-hand corner of the page.

"What d'ya wanna bet it's this house?" he whispered.

"You're proba—" Libby stopped at the sound of harried footfalls above. Dust particles trickled from the exposed ceiling joists.

"The asshole must be in a hurry," Simon said.

"Shhhhh!" Libby hissed.

Then another set of footsteps, quieter and more measured, from somewhere further in the house—*higher* in the house. Gil wasn't alone.

Chapter 20

Visitors

Gil studied the unexpected windfall resting in his palm, its sharp crystals shimmering under the kitchen's overhead track lighting. With his other hand, he lifted his tumbler of Buffalo Trace bourbon, sipped it, and set it back down on the countertop. How much did these kids really know? Couldn't be much, or the Porter kid would never have worn it in public. And what the hell was he thinking anyway? He rotated the mysterious object in his hand, resisting the urge to run his tongue over it. The desire was urgent, primal, and somehow sexual. But it was stupid just the same.

You'll cut your tongue on the crystals, jackass.

Instead, he took another sip of his bourbon, a well-earned treat. A celebration was in order after all—he was about to take the biggest bugout of all time.

Sayonara, 2021, Gil's out. Mic drop.

He had already harvested the contents of his safe—$436,000 in cold hard cash—which was enough to live like a king in '72 ... while he righted the wrongs, of course. He just needed to get his bugout bag in order, a reality he'd never thought possible before the three teens came a-knock-knock-knocking on his door. But another thought nagged at him. The kids had been running from a woman. Had to be *her*, and she might be on her way right now. He couldn't linger.

He knocked back the rest of his drink. The route he'd secured to his destination had been a labor of love for the past four years. It was his back door, and it was time to use it. He'd figure out how to actually use the medallion once he got there.

He went to the pantry and shoveled into a plastic shopping bag an assortment of granola bars and trail mix packs, which would be far better fare than the stale ration bars he'd kept in storage all these years. Something else felt off, though, and it had nothing to do with the woman—or did it?

These kids had somehow found their way from the Beaver Marsh to a home that was separated by dense forest, marsh, and even a lake. It wasn't something a person just *happened upon*, especially if coming from that direction. The Towpath or the rail line would have been better paths to follow to get out of the valley and seek help. And, despite the home's brief history as a Cuyahoga Valley National Park visitor center, and more recently, a retreat destination for business types, it was now a private residence. Hell, it had been that way for the past five years. Not too many people knew about it.

His nostrils still abuzz with spirits, he fast-walked down the hallway and into the foyer. He was thinking about the clothing he'd need for his bag when he turned the corner to the stair landing, scaled the first step and … stopped.

Despite the gloomy conditions outside, the always-opened bathroom at the top of the stairs should have been aglow with daylight filtering through its frosted window. But that light was obscured by something large, dark, and man-shaped. The silhouette was either shirtless or wearing some kind of form-fitting attire. Their backlit head had something protruding from the crown.

A mohawk?

An unsettling noise met his ears then. It was the sound of something being stretched taut, a mounting tension. Something glimmered just in front of the silhouette.

Then Gil knew it at once. The gleaming shape in the foreground, which caught a sliver of light from the window, was an arrowhead.

A low moan escaped his mouth. His feet were cemented to the floor, his face feeling like it wore a cold mask. Then something odd happened. The arrow lowered, to the right, and—

The whistling force that slammed into his thigh knocked the wind from his lungs. Then he was bending and hobbling backward into the open air of the foyer.

***

Gil blinked at the three faces before him and then wished he hadn't, as the effort to focus his eyes sent barbs of pain into the base of his skull.

The memory of cracking his head against the front door took shape along with the three faces, which were now coalescing into one. It was the face of a ... woman.

"Hello, Mr Decker."

He winced at another sensation. There was a deep pressure in his right leg. He didn't want to look, but his eyes disobeyed him and fell upon the wooden shaft buried in his thigh. The fletching was almost at chin level. He ran his eyes down the shaft to where it disappeared into the folds of a blood-stained towel, which was crisscrossed tightly around his leg. His vision began to darken at the corners. His eyes were rolling back into his skull again, back to the safe place, and he was okay with that.

A cold hand struck his cheek. His eyes flew open.

The woman's face swam in front of him again, now more detailed. He saw a ruined eye, a grinning neck scar, and smeared makeup. She was bald. Her appearance was like that of a melted doll whose hair had been singed off. But it was her good eye he wished most to unsee. It was cold and calculating.

"Remember me?" she asked, her voice high and thin.

He was only partially listening, now realizing he was back in the kitchen. He again looked at the blood-soaked towel.

"No, you're not going to die just yet, Vaughn," she said. "He knew what he was doing and avoided your artery—at my instruction, of course. You're fortunate that he can shoot a squirrel dead in the eye from several feet away. But I left the arrow in, since taking it out *will* probably kill you. At your age—and with the pathetic shape you're in—it's doubtful I could remove it without you going into shock or dying on me. I need you coherent for a while. After all, today's your big day."

"How? How did you get in?"

She shook her head admonishingly. "Really need to trim those tree branches near the back of the house, Vaughn."

She rose from her squat and walked to the kitchen island.

He tried to move his arms and legs, but nothing happened. He attempted to peer over his shoulder, but his aching head protested at the movement. His hands were drawn behind the seat back of the chair he sat in and his wrists were bound together. He twisted his wrists, and the rope gave a little, but not enough to loosen. His ankles were crossed at the base of the chair and felt similarly bound. He looked down—ignoring the arrow for a moment—and saw more rope stretched taut against his sternum, binding him to the chair. He was also slouching oddly in the chair. The arrow in his thigh made it impossible for him to sit back and fully upright.

"I'm going to help you feel better, Vaughn." She returned with a tumbler half-filled with bourbon.

The glass held no ice, and he greedily swallowed the alcohol as she tipped the glass to his lips.

A shrill note floated in from the front room. Then, a series of experimental strikes on the baby grand piano's keys. He thought he knew who the player was.

"That a boy. Drink up."

He stopped and drew back.

"Drink, Vaughn, and drink now, for kings require it. Drink, for today is the day that you join my legion of redeemers."

He blinked at her and slowly sipped.

"That's it. Drink. For today we begin wiping clean the scourge that has been set upon this Earth."

She pulled the glass from his lips and a familiar object swung into view. It was the medallion, and it was dangling from her terrible neck, its central black eye staring back at him accusingly.

She tapped it with a forefinger. "Yes, this is what we're going to discuss."

He looked up at her. The spirits were starting to do their work, the pain becoming more manageable. Momentarily ignoring the eyes, the scar, and the bald head, he concentrated on the hard angles of her cheekbones and chin. The bridge of her nose, the thin lips, which he decided had once been … full. Kissable, youthful. *Too* youthful.

"Care Bear? You look…"

She snorted. "Knew you'd call me that. But that's in the past. I'm more concerned about our future, Vaughn."

A large serrated blade came into view. The girl he once knew rotated the Bowie knife as if she were showcasing a museum artifact, his red-rimmed eyes reflecting in its mirror-like steel.

"*This* is Care Bear, and she's going to help you tell the truth."

He drew back as far as the chair and restraints would allow. "How far back have you gone, Care Be—Caroline?"

The hilt of the blade came down on the side of his skull. He bit his tongue.

"Wrong again. *Caroline* was a naive little girl."

He spat blood. "Car—I mean—whoever you are now, I swear I didn't know what I was doing."

"Call me Mary."

"Okay…*Mary*…it was that place. Wasn't myself. It…changes you. Made me do things I would've never done."

Something occurred to him then: the man at the top of the stairs and the look of this woman, who had once been beautiful. "And you're *still* going back. Tell me, *Mary*, just how far down the rabbit hole have you gone?" He nodded at the arrow. "The man who did this to me … he's from *then,* isn't he? And he's out there in the parlor right now."

Her black eye didn't leave his. "I've gone back as far as necessary to save my little girl."

"*Our* little girl."

Another blow to his face, this time nearly tipping him and the chair over. Shimmering shapes danced across his eyes. A cold hand found his cheek and pushed his head back into position. Another pressed his opposing cheek, and together, they pulled him forward, the chair's rear legs coming off the floor. His cheeks were being squished together, causing his lower lip to bulge and blood to trickle down his chin.

"I don't think you understand, *Vaughn*. You don't get to call her that." She squeezed his cheeks until his eyes felt ready to pop from their sockets. She shoved his face, and he rocked back, the chair's front legs coming off the floor. She grabbed the arrow shaft and yanked him back.

He threw his head back and howled.

"I'm going to give you one chance, Vaughn. You're in a position for once in your pathetic life to do some good. You just need to tell me how it works. I know you've spent your whole pissant life researching it."

He shook his head and blinked back tears. The pain in his leg was electric. "I-I don't kn-know h-how it works!"

"*Focus*, Vaughn. Even back when you were dating—*fucking*—my whore-of-a-mother, I knew you were obsessed with this thing. And I'm willing to bet if I search this house, I'll find your lunatic diaries and sketches."

He spat and shook his head. "You're just gonna kill me anyway. Get on with it."

"I *am* going to kill you. But you decide how you go. I can slit your throat nice and clean and it will be over quick. Or..." She indicated his groin with the tip of the blade. "I can remove your training wheels for you." She drummed a finger on her lower lip. "Remember what you whispered in my ear that night by the cave when you *weren't yourself*? When I had to listen to you continually moan, *'C'mon, Care Bear, take the training wheels off'*? Is that what you tell all the young girls, Vaughn?" She chuckled. "You know, I actually thought you were cheating on my mother—who ended up deserving it by the way—and I was going to catch you red-handed." She twirled the knife between her fingers. "I suppose I did catch you red-handed, though, and later learned where you were going and why. How pathetic you were to think that was a worthy cause."

He shook his head. "You know nothing. Nor do you have any idea of the shitstorm that ordeal caused for my family."

"Oh, I know about shitstorms, Vaughn. Getting impregnated by your mother's boyfriend at sixteen kind of qualifies, don't you think?"

He fixed her with a hard stare. "You *still* think you can save her, don't you? But wake up Car—*Mary*—Hannah took her own life. That's right. I knew what happened. Hannah *took* her own life. Nothing you can do about it."

She slapped him.

He snapped his head back and narrowed his eyes, the arrow, the bindings, the pain forgotten. "Read about you in the paper, you know." He ran his tongue along his bottom front teeth, tasted blood and spat again. "In 2014, the story in the *Akron Beacon Journal* about the woman who paid a cabbie to drive her to an address in Portage Falls from the valley? How she'd instructed him to get her there *no matter what happened* to her?"

She didn't move or blink.

"But the woman didn't get there, because she started to come apart, bleed from every orifice. The cabbie was *a little* freaked by the Jane Doe who'd covered his back seat in vomit, shit, and blood, so he dumped her at Akron General. No ID, no relatives, no one to come and claim her. You think I didn't know it was you?"

"I did what I had to."

"Not how it works, *Mary*. *It* won't let you get close to her. Don't you think I tried to get close to my living grandfather? When that failed, and I nearly bled to death, don't you think I tried keeping my distance and calling him? You call, the phone rings, and the person answers. You talk, you plead, you scream, but they can't hear you. So, they hang up. Who knows what they actually hear on their end? And then you try to contact others close to them, which doesn't work either. I bet you tried Facebook with Hannah, didn't you? You try texting her? Tell me, Mary, what happened? Actually, never mind. All connections went bad, didn't they? The entire *network* goes down. Hell, everything on four legs starts to know you don't belong if you've gone far enough back and have overstayed your welcome. Then you're *forever* marked, and this whole fucking planet knows it. And how does that feel? Because I see it in you right now—a marked woman. You overstayed, Mary. You meddled. I see it."

She looked at him.

"And so, somewhere along the way, you learned of this medallion. And now you think it's your magical hall pass?"

"Yes. And you're going to tell me how to make it work."

"Don't know what good it's gonna do. There are no written records I could find, no petroglyphs in the caves—nothing that explains *how* to use it. Shit, several years back, I drove to upstate New York and into Seneca territory looking for answers. I sat down with descendants of the Iroquois Confederacy in Salamanca. Even the elders were at a loss. No oral histories, even though it probably predates them by hundreds if not thousands of years. Who knows who made it? Where and when it's from? The only history they could offer had to do with what they called the Demon Hole. Yes, Mary, there was a fissure on their land, and to them, it was demonic. Not to be fucked with. They spoke of the green man who came in the night and strangled two boys, after beating and sodomizing them. Later, the Senecas found him behind a grove of trees with another boy. Eight arrows and two blows to the head later—from war clubs no less—the man finally fell dead. He'd once been a normal and respected member of the tribe. The place breeds pure evil. *Is* evil. Wasn't *me*, Mary. And now, it's *you*. It's that place. That goddamned place." A thought occurred to him then. "Your pal out in the parlor. What is he? *When* is he?"

"Unimportant."

"He's a Mohawk, isn't he? They were supposedly ruthless. How is it he's doing your bidding?"

"I gave them a way to kill their would-be oppressors and reclaim what was rightfully theirs. Pretty simple."

"Them?"

"There are others."

"Others? And they're here, now?"

"Some."

"And they trusted you enough to come here? You know, they could be marked just like you if they overstay or help you change your past. And they should know better, especially if the stories from the Senecas are true."

"They are my blood and I theirs."

"*When* are they?"

"I gave them a chance. In return, they earned riches from land and sea they never could have imagined, no less keeping the land that was rightfully theirs."

"*Not* theirs," he said. "Not if you're referring to this land, this valley, which had belonged to the Whittleseys."

"No. My men were hunters. When their parties came west, they found the Cuyahoga Valley to be uninhabited. The Beaver Wars and the European diseases saw to that. This land was theirs for the taking. *They* were naturally selected. But I digress. It wasn't really their pasts that concerned me. It was their futures. I generally knew what *would* happen. I knew where the outposts were. I had an idea when and where the ships would come in.

In return, they just needed to help me get one thing. Our mutual desires had brought us together in time and place. We are one."

"You probably scared off all their four-legged prey too, so it seems you owed them more than they owed you."

She ignored this and rose to her feet.

"Did you not realize what you could have done?" he asked. "Imagine the repercussions. Didn't you think, just for one moment, that the actions you took might have somehow altered the course of American history?"

"And what makes *you* think that my part in this history wasn't ordained?" she asked. "That it all wasn't part of the big cycle, the elaborate dance, and that I wasn't supposed to be on the dance floor with them?" She glanced about the room. "Because as you can see, my actions didn't change history in any significant way, if at all. You're still a pile of shit."

He remained silent.

She twirled the blade. "Last chance."

He glared at her. "I've given you all I can."

She came at him in a blur. The knife was against his inner thigh. "You decide how you go."

"I-I think," he said, watching the knife's tip poking into his khakis, "you need to be in a trance."

The blade pushed further in. A soft tear, and cold metal was touching his flesh.

His words came fast now, "It has to be done inside the chamber itself—I *think*. You must gaze into its eye when you're in there. When you do that, it pairs with you somehow. Then you can travel unhindered, unmarked, and even make contact. I *swear*, that's all I know."

She watched him.

"I swear!"

She remained still.

He looked at her.

She pulled the blade away.

He gasped.

"Now, one last order of business. The kids who I sent here— where are they?"

"I let them go." The lie came easily.

"Then why are their shoes still in the foyer, Vaughn? And that book bag?"

"I let them dry off. Naturally, they took off their shoes since they were waterlogged. The same goes for the bag. It was soaked."

"And they just … ran off? My men would have spotted them. You know they can track them, and I will find out if you're lying."

He shook his head. "They were long gone before you arrived. I invited them in. They took off their shoes. I offered them towels, and then I immediately spotted *that.*" He nodded at the medallion.

"It was *under* the Porter kid's shirt," she said.

"Soaked shirt," he corrected. "Pretty visible. And the mouthy kid was sick of his friend keeping secrets that had nearly gotten them killed. Oh, and by the way, they mentioned the *woman* who attacked them in the park and killed a cop. So, if anything, *you* should be concerned since Brandywine isn't far from here."

"You lie."

"No. I ordered them out of here at gunpoint after taking it. I assume you found my Glock?"

Her dark eye remained on him.

"I am a lot of things," he said. "But I am *not* a killer."

"You're a coward."

"I don't know—"

She extended a palm. "Enough. You've been helpful, Vaughn. In fact, I'm going to give you a nice whirl down memory lane for all your troubles. Remember what you used to sing to me when you first started fucking my mother? You'd come in through the side door—your greedy eyes lingering all over my teenage body, of course—and you'd belt out Neil Diamond's finest. Remember that, Vaughn?"

He blinked. "What?"

"Oh, come now." She stepped to the island, set down the knife, and snatched up a plastic CD case. "You think I didn't know you'd still have a soft spot for Neil?"

She extended the CD case. A sepia tone photo of a young Neil Diamond stared back at him. "Neil Diamond's All-Time Greatest Hits," she said unnecessarily. "I've already checked, and it's track four."

Gil swallowed and shifted in his chair. "You said you'd make it quick."

She popped open the case and strode over to a small countertop near the fridge where his little CD player stood. The player hadn't been there before. Just this morning, it had been where it always was: on the floor next to his desk in the front parlor. She opened the CD player's lid and dropped the disk into place.

"Listen to that sound, Vaughn. I just placed a physical object into a machine to produce music. Quite a novel thing these days, don't you think?" She hit the Power button and then pressed the Forward Track button a few times, the player whirring in response. A familiar horn intro sauntered through the kitchen. She turned back to him. Cocking her head, she said, "You've been so helpful, Vaughn, I've decided that I'm going to help you."

"And how do you plan on doing that?" he mumbled, as Neil Diamond began to muse about where it all begin.

She shook her head, as if he were missing the obvious. "I'm going to remove your training wheels for you."

He started and squirmed. "You said you'd make it quick!" He lurched, but the chair lurched with him and scuttled across the tile. "You said you'd make it quick!" he screamed. He jerked and shrugged and twisted until the chair's front legs lifted off the floor. He rocked back.

"Thanks for the help," she said. She then came forward, pressed two fingers to his chest, and shoved.

His head hit cold tile. The overhead lights became a hazy yellow, dull pressure filling his ears, tears stinging his eyes. Through those tears he could see her leaning over him. A gust blew open the crotch of his pants. His boxer shorts were cut open next. Then the knife's cold tip gently lifted his scrotum.

A sob escaped his mouth.

"There we go," she whispered in his ear, "need to make sure I have plenty of room to operate."

His mouth went dry. The knife went to work.

The famous chorus, recalling how good times never seemed so good with that sweet Caroline, wailed through the kitchen and the entire house. But the man who called himself Gil Stanford could barely hear the chorus through his own screams. They blended with the song to create a new sound: an undulating shriek.

Chapter 21

Pockets and Hollows

Screams from above. When the voices had first sounded, they'd huddled themselves against the wall just a few feet from the laundry chute. From there, they'd heard everything, including Gil's bizarre lie about their whereabouts. Why had he done it?

Now, Aaron held his breath as he listened to the man's screams intermingle with the same Neil Diamond classic he'd spontaneously belted out while making drunken salt angels in the mine. Something squeezed his right hand. It was Libby's hand, and she was trembling. The shrieks were becoming inhuman, and they continued that way for another five minutes, long enough for *Sweet Caroline* to end and the next track to begin.

Then, silence. They waited and listened. A minute or so passed before more sounds drifted down. They were moans, and they were faint and feeble. The man was still alive.

The floorboards above began to creak. Someone who was either very light—or light on their feet—padded into the space directly over their heads. More whimpering. Then, a wet *rip*, like the peeling of an engorged grapefruit. A series of taps raced across the ceiling.

A small cry escaped Libby's mouth.

Aaron immediately squeezed her hand tighter, resisting the urge to cover her mouth with his other hand. "Shhhh," he whispered.

A dull thud rattled the joists. Silence fell again with the exception of Simon's breaths, which were growing increasingly ragged. It sounded like he might hyperventilate.

Aaron didn't give himself time to think about whether or not he should take his best friend's hand. Groping in the dark, he found Simon's forearm and felt down until he found cold fingers. He gave Simon's hand a firm squeeze and did the same for Libby with his other hand. They stayed that way for a long time, listening.

Then, more footfalls, fading toward the front of the house. The front door opened then slammed shut. Distant doors clicked open and closed before another faint sound: the starting of an engine.

They waited.

Eventually, Libby broke the silence. "Think they're gone?" she asked, her voice mouse-like.

"Yeah, think so," Aaron whispered. "Must've taken Gil's Jeep."

"But do ya think they're *all* gone?" Simon asked. "How do we know they really left?"

"We don't," Libby said.

"Let's be quiet for a little while longer," Aaron offered. "Say, five more minutes? Listen closely for anything?"

They murmured their agreement. Aaron closed his eyes, willing his ears to take over. Besides the rain outside, the only other sounds he heard were Simon's slowing breaths.

After a while, his own breathing relaxing, he said, "What d'ya think?"

"I think we're okay," Libby said. "And think about it, if someone stayed behind, then wouldn't they need a key to get in here?"

Aaron wondered if they could have found the key, which he guessed was still in Gil's trousers. And if so, did they even care? "I think they got what they came for," he said, finally. "We'll need to get outta here at some point."

"Oh, you think?" Simon quipped.

"Nice to have you back."

A *click* sounded, and the world was thrust back into blinding light.

"Christ! Coulda warned us!"

"Not sorry," Libby said.

Aaron squinted over to where Simon was half kneeling, his brow shielded with one arm. Everything about Simon was trembling, bent, and sallow.

He's in shock, thought Aaron. *Maybe I am, too?*

***

Ten minutes later, they were back at the center of the room after yet another exploration. Aaron turned in place, scanning the room again as if it would do any good. The locked metal door was impenetrable. There were no windows offering escape. The laundry chute was a no go. The floor drain below the stationary tub might allow a small rodent to slip through, but that was about it. There was nothing helpful hiding among the joists, pipes, vents, and electrical conduits above them. Nor was there anything in the crawlspace, according to Simon. It was empty save for a couple of books. *Empty.*

Aaron stopped mid-turn. Something he'd heard when Simon was exploring the crawlspace earlier had lodged into his brain like a foreign object. What was it? What had he heard?

Libby plopped to the floor and crisscrossed her legs as if preparing to meditate. She closed her eyes and began to massage her temples. "What are we gonna do?" she mumbled.

"Nothing," Simon said. "We're fucked. We're in a dead guy's basement with no phone. No food. No way out." He slumped soundlessly against the cinder block wall.

And then it hit Aaron. The cinder blocks don't make sound because they're solid. Simon had *knocked* on the wall when he'd explored the crawlspace, and those knocks had echoed.

Aaron turned to the drywall and rapped its surface with his knuckles. A shallow echo. "He might have insulation in here," he said, "but it's still mostly hollow."

"I get what you're saying, Aaron," Libby said from her place on the floor. "It's hollow, but we don't exactly have a sledgehammer to bust through it."

Aaron looked over his shoulder and smiled. "Yeah, we do."

Libby rose in one fluid motion and folded her arms over her chest. "Care to clue us in?"

In answer, Aaron walked over to where the fire extinguisher leaned against the wall. He bent to the big cylinder, which was much larger than the five-pound extinguisher Gram kept under her kitchen sink. "If Gil came back in," he said, "I was gonna use this to knock his head off."

He grabbed the extinguisher and lifted it, wincing as the pain rushed back into his shoulder. It had to weigh at least thirty pounds.

Libby, clearly noticing his discomfort, asked, "Aaron, why don't I do it?"

But he'd already brought up the extinguisher like a battering ram.

It's what Owen would do.

He reared back and heaved the bottom end of the extinguisher into the drywall. A *crack* sounded, a halo of thin creases forming around the impact site. But the wall didn't give. He drew back, a memory resurfacing of the time he'd helped Grandpa hang a mirror in the dining room.

"You gotta find the studs," the old man had said as he'd rapped his arthritic knuckles across the wall. "Hear that? It's more shallow here, at the stud. It isn't the same echo as *this.*" He demonstrated by knocking a few inches to the left, and sure enough, a deeper echo sounded. "Hear how hollow that sounds? Sixteen inches my good man. Sixteen inches *on center* from stud-to-stud if they built the house right."

Aaron took up the extinguisher. This time, he aimed several inches to the left of the impact site, reared back, and heaved. A deeper, more satisfying *crack*, and the wall buckled inward.

"There you go!" Libby cried.

"Welp," Simon said, "if anyone's still here, they sure as hell know we're here too."

There isn't, thought Aaron. He knew the medallion wasn't nearby. He could feel it. But it wasn't altogether gone. It was as if part of it was inside him. *Beneath* his chest. *Behind* his eyes. *In* his mind, from which a thin string extended back and ever downward, like a fishing line reaching to unknowable depths, trembling from gentle nudges and nibbles. It was part of him. A new sensory organ.

He ignored the shoulder pain, reared back again, and slammed the extinguisher into the crater with more force. The wall crumpled. He rammed again, and large pieces of drywall tumbled into the cavity beyond, exposing the flat foam board insulation. He reached into the cavity, yanked out the pieces of drywall, and pried loose the sections of foam board. Tossing the pieces of drywall aside, he drove his knee into the lower edge of the hole, the wall now cracking and buckling with ease. He set down the extinguisher, wedged his bulk into the gap, and worked at more loose pieces with his hands until he'd opened the hole as wide as the studs would allow and as high as what he could comfortably step through without having to crouch or hurdle.

Stepping back to catch his breath, it dawned on him that his shirt was soaked again.

"You good, Porter?" Simon asked, an uncharacteristic trace of concern in his voice. "I can take it the rest of the way."

Aaron shook his head. He felt an urgency now, a *need* to break through to the other side. He scooped up the extinguisher with fresh adrenaline and attacked the foam board, cleaving it in half with one strike, the entire wall shuddering. He ripped away the foam paneling with a free hand, prying loose the large staples that held in place, and exposed the opposing wall's brown interior. He reared back and slammed the cylinder through the outer wall in one strike.

"Holy shit!" Simon crowed.

Aaron turned and extended the extinguisher. Libby stepped forward, grabbed it, and gasped. "Jeez, that's frickin' heavy," she said as she lowered it to the ground where it clanked heavily. "That thing's got to be close to fifty pounds! Didn't know Aaron Porter was the hulk."

Heat crept into Aaron's cheeks, and it wasn't from his exertions. He wedged himself deeper into the tight space. He pushed, elbowed, and kneed his way through the punctured wall until he was staggering into the hallway in an avalanche of crumbled drywall and dust. Then he was on the floor, leaning against the hallway's opposing wall.

"Aaron!" Libby cried.

His shoulder howled, but he didn't mind. He staggered to his feet, dusted off his cargoes, and looked up to see that Libby had already joined him in the hallway. Simon was pulling himself through the hole.

"You okay, Aaron?"

He put his hands on his hips and exhaled. "Yeah, actually, I am."

An uncomfortable silence settled among them. They exchanged wary glances. Aaron knew they were both thinking the same thing as him. There was no way around it. They would have to pass through the kitchen, the place where the man had clearly been tortured and killed.

"Ready?" he whispered.

They both nodded.

Aaron led the way.

***

The steps went on forever. When at last they arrived at the top of the staircase, Aaron paused in the doorway. He inhaled and immediately regretted it. The smell of evacuated bowels was unmistakable.

There was something else, and it was just as sharp and pungent. It wasn't decay—*couldn't be* decay—because that type of thing didn't happen in less than an hour, did it? No, this was something far more sinister, the feeling that makes your pores seep, your palms clammy, your heart set to hurrying. *Fear.* And its long and ominous shadow lingered around the corner, beckoning them closer. Daring them to confront it.

He steeled himself and looked over his shoulder. "Guys, ready?"

Libby, pinching her nose between her fingers, could only nod.

Simon shrugged. "Do we have a goddamned choice?"

Aaron took a tentative step forward, his bare feet kissing cold tile. He turned the corner toward the kitchen. At first, nothing met his gaze besides the large island, on which rested a plastic CD case and a glass half-filled with whiskey. A CD player stood on a small countertop next to the fridge. There was something else, this new perspective from where he stood making visible a breakfast nook on the other side of the island. At its center stood a small wooden table, a curtained bay window just beyond it.

His eyes fell to the visible part of the floor just past the island. There he saw the black sole of a sandal, hovering in space about two feet off the floor.

"Well?" Simon whispered.

Aaron's shoulders relaxed a little. "You can't see much," he said. "His body is on the other side of the island." He looked down the hallway. Their shoes and Libby's backpack were lying near the foot of the closed front door. "And it looks like we'll get our stuff back."

Libby was now at his side, staring wide-eyed at the island and the dangling foot. "Should we check him? What if he's still breathing?"

"Are you kidding me?" Simon hissed. "Did you *hear* what happened to him? If that didn't kill him, then ... let's just get the hell outta here."

Aaron and Libby didn't protest. Averting their eyes and holding their noses, they exited the kitchen. At the front door they scooped up their belongings and began the uncomfortable process of pulling on soggy socks and shoes. When they'd all dressed, Libby's bag slung onto her back, they opened the door onto a bright, but overcast afternoon. The Jeep was gone. Aaron scanned the property and didn't see anything among the swaying trees and stretches of open grass.

"So, let me get this straight," Simon said, "those Indians—if we actually believe that they're here and that there are several of them—just got into a Jeep and drove away?"

"It could've just been her," Libby said, "and maybe they're going to meet her on foot, wherever it is they're going. I only heard one of them in the house, but I thought I heard multiple doors open and shut."

"Who gives a shit?" Simon said. "We need to get the hell outta here. Way I see it, we walk to Brandywine, call the cops and then call Gabe to come pick us up." He descended the stoop and started down the walkway as if the plan had already been decided.

"What if Gil has a cell phone though?" Libby asked. "I'm not even sure he *doesn't* have a working land line. Shouldn't we call someone, before fleeing the scene?"

"Uh, well you can count me right the fuck out then," Simon retorted, not turning or stopping. "I'm not spending another minute here. Let's go." He continued toward the parking lot, the sporadic rain dotting his T-shirt.

Aaron was barely listening, his mind still puzzling over something Libby had said, *Wherever it is they're going.* The place where he'd find Owen? He turned to the house. The notebook contained a sketch of a map showing several lines, one of which connected to a house. Had to be this house. What other house could it be? There were two doors in the basement, and why had Gil lied to the woman about where they were? Why had he said that they had *left*? Did he have something to hide? Did he not want to give them cause to explore his basement? Or was the lie some final kindness? Aaron didn't know, and he doubted he'd ever know the man's true intent. Before he knew what he was doing, he was walking back into the house.

"Aaron, explain," Libby said from where she stood on the stoop.

He paused in the foyer. "You guys go. Get help. Call the cops. Call your parents." He shook his head. "I should've never gotten you into this."

"Aaron, you need to start speaking English here," Libby said, her face screwed up in confusion. "What are you talking about?"

He ran a hand through his hair. There was no point withholding anything else. "Owen is alive," he said. "I saw him. It's a long story, but it has to do with the medallion, which she now has. I don't know where she's going with it, but this might be my only chance to find him. The opportunity might leave with her." He nodded toward the kitchen. "Libby, Gil was hiding something. I think this house has a path directly to that place—wherever it is. Remember how this house was under construction for all those years?"

"I'm not sure where you're going with this."

"That basement is like a fortress. Does it seem like a typical farmhouse to you? Or a corporate retreat? There's been no activity like that here for years. And why does Gil have all his documents locked away like that?"

"He's living off the grid," she said absently.

"Exactly. And you know what? That key he used to lock us in that room might still be in his pocket. I'll bet anything it unlocks both doors. Maybe that woman didn't find the key or care to find it."

"Caroline," Libby said in a detached voice. "Do you believe all of that stuff about her going back to save her daughter?"

"Hannah," Aaron said, nodding. He blinked. Something about saying her name made the world come into sharper focus. Hannah was as real to her mother as Owen was to him.

"Aaron?"

He shook his head. "You're gonna think I'm nuts," he said. "Actually, I'm sure you already do, so I'm just gonna tell you." He described what he saw in his vision: the flames that had names, the men waiting by the fire, and Owen, who was very much alive and sleeping in their encampment.

When he was finished, Libby, who was now pacing near the foot of the stoop, said, "And somehow, Caroline got linked up with those men—obviously, they're the ones who shot arrows at us."

"All I know," Aaron said, "is that tracking her down might be my only way of finding Owen. You guys need to get home. Your parents will start to worry. If you would, just tell my Gram that I needed some alone time. She'll believe that."

"Forget that," Libby said, "we're coming with you."

Simon flinched. "We?"

She turned and glared at him. "What else have you got to do? Sit on your ass, play video games?"

He extended two middle fingers. "Look into the camera, Libby."

She shook her head in disgust. "Your mom won't even know you're gone." She turned to Aaron. "You're not talking me outta this. You shouldn't do this alone. Plus..."

"What?"

"Nevermind."

"Well, what about the cop?" Simon asked. "If we both go with Porter, then who's going to report that murder? The guy's probably still face down in the marsh. And seriously, what the hell are three kids going to do *if* we catch up to a crazy murderer and her band of merry arrow-slinging men? I get you want to find your bro, Porter, but seriously? What if your dream or vision or whatever it was, was wrong? And what can we really do about it?"

Libby shook her head. "The longer we stand here, the greater the odds we miss our chance to find Owen."

"And *die*? You need to get your head checked, Libby. That woman winged a knife through that cop's neck as if she were playing a fucking game of darts. *This* isn't a game. We don't have weapons. We don't have anything."

"Then maybe when you go home and plop your feet up on the couch, you can trouble yourself to pick up the phone and call the police. Sound fair?"

"What is it with you? Why do you want so badly to kill yourself? I guess I get why Aaron thinks he should go, but you—"

"You wouldn't understand. There's something ... just go home."

Aaron extended a palm. "Stop it, both of you. Simon, I don't expect you to come." He turned to Libby. "I'm not expecting *you* to come either. For all I know, I might be wrong about what's in that house. And if so, then there's nothing we can do about it anyway. And Simon's right. We don't have weapons."

Libby didn't answer. Instead, she marched up the steps, shouldering her way past him and into the foyer. "I'm willing to bet Gil's gun is still in the house."

Aaron turned back to where Simon stood near the driveway with his arms folded. "Just watch your back, okay? Go straight to Brandywine."

Simon nodded but didn't move. He looked left and then right, and Aaron could tell that he was thinking about it, being alone in this rain, walking along a quiet rural road near a sprawling forest where they'd nearly been murdered. It was a stretch of nowhere, a place where someone could carry you off and kill you like a wolf could a lamb.

"Simon?"

Simon let out a theatrical sigh. "So, you're going to go check a dead man's pocket for a key that *might* take you to a secret passage, which *might* lead you to a crazy bitch and her army of warriors—who know where *we live*—and hope you can get there before she uses some weird object to travel back in time and stop her daughter's death, so that you can find your brother—who you dreamed was alive? Did I get all that right?" Without waiting for an answer, he shook his head and walked back to the house. "The shit I do for you Porter, the shit I do."

Chapter 22

A Key to...

Aaron caught up to Libby before she could enter the kitchen. "I'm doing this," he said. "You're not going in there."

Not waiting for a reply, he stepped past her through the entryway and turned toward the center island. Gil's torso was visible in profile through the narrow aisle made by the island and dishwasher, his arms tightly bound and pressed beneath an upended wooden chair. His lower half was concealed by the island, and his head was obscured by the casing of the entryway between the kitchen and breakfast nook.

Aaron took a couple of hesitant steps down the aisle, a mixed stench of fecal matter and blood invading his nose. He paused as Gil's khaki trousers came into view. They were cut to ribbons near his waist. He didn't want to look closer but knew he had to. He leaned over the island and the man's lower body came into view. An arrow shaft was buried midway through his right leg. A white towel stiff with blood and looking like some morbid flag of surrender dangled from his thigh where the arrow had penetrated it. Twine wrapped his ankles.

"What do you see?" Libby whispered.

He didn't answer. He wasn't sure he wanted to see what had become of Gil's upper half, but turned and looked anyway. What he saw made his world tilt.

The top of the man's head was gone, leaving behind only a glistening red slope. Tufts of hair poked from the puckered ridge that used to be his hairline. His ears had been cut away, leaving behind tortured holes from which blood had seeped and spread and dried on the floor, making it look as if his head had grown a pair of crimson wings.

Then Aaron's eyes caught on the mouth that had been stretched open and stuffed with...

The room completely turned on end. He staggered backward, struck the island, and fell to all fours. He vomited.

"Aaron!"

What little he'd had left in his stomach was now puddled on the narrow section of tile between the island and the dishwasher.

Simon's voice drifted in from somewhere nearby. "This is too much. I say we go. Enough of this shit."

Aaron heaved again, but nothing came out.

"Aaron, I can take it from here," Libby offered. "I'll just cover my eyes, and you can guide me to his pocket. Aaron?"

He shook his head and spat. "No. I've come this far. I didn't just look at that for nothing. You don't want to see it, believe me."

Standing and stepping over his puddle of vomit, he caught their questioning stares. He extended a palm to indicate he was fine even though he wasn't. He numbly rounded the island, trying to force his mind into that cold corner of objectivity. He lowered to a crouch as the chair's bottom came into view—a welcome barricade. Careful to avoid a drying puddle of blood, he squatted further and leaned around Gil's feet and the chair's jutting legs far enough to glimpse the right trouser pocket. The gaping hole in Gil's crotch dared him to look into it. The smell of feces was exquisite. He held his breath and refused to look.

Reaching two fingers up and into the folds of the pocket, he simultaneously pushed it open and slipped his hand further inside. Nothing met his touch. He kept his eyes on the floor and groped further upward. Something solid grazed his middle finger. He poked at it. It was there alright, but it didn't feel like the cool metal of a key. It was wadded fabric. His heart hastened nonetheless. It had to be the key, snagged in a fold. He worked his fingers at the wadded fabric until it loosened. Gravity did the rest, and the little key dropped into his palm.

"Got it!" he cried.

As he made his way back to where Libby and Simon stood wide-eyed in the doorway, something else caught his attention. It was a familiar object, resting on the countertop next to the CD player. It wasn't the medallion, but it might have been the next best thing.

The gun.

***

Aaron was the first to arrive at the far door in the basement. He held up the key and turned to Libby and Simon. "Well, here goes..." he trailed off as his gaze fell upon the grip of the gun poking from Libby's waistband, a sliver of her pale skin visible where her shirt had ridden up.

She caught his roving eye. "What, don't trust me with it?"

"It's just ... odd seeing it there, that's all."

"Well, maybe to you," she said, "but don't worry, the safety's on. There's a full mag in there, but there's no chance of it going off."

"I'm still trying to figure out why they didn't take the gun to begin with," Simon said.

"I get the feeling guns aren't their style," Aaron said. "Plus, why would they need one? There was nobody left to get in their way." He turned back to the door and slid the key into the lock. He turned the key, and a satisfying *click* sounded.

"Yes!" cried Libby.

He pulled the latch handle down and the door gave a little moan as it opened onto darkness. There was just enough light from the hallway to show a series of vertical metal rods in the foreground. Aaron stepped into the room and noted how dank the air was, a quality not present in the other room. A trickle of water sounded somewhere nearby, and it wasn't the rain outside—this sounded too close.

"I can't find a pull string anywhere," Libby said from somewhere deeper in the room. "Maybe there's a wall switch?" She approached the wall nearest the hallway. Aaron joined her and ran his palms over the drywall, feeling for anything jutting out.

"Found it," Libby said.

A series of fluorescent tubes flickered to life overhead, casting the space in a sterile light like that of a hospital room. Aaron blinked and took in the space, which was roughly the same size and dimensions as the other room, but instead of being crammed with paperwork containers, this room was neatly lined with wire shelving units, all of which were stuffed to their limits with enough dry goods to fill several grocery store aisles.

Libby gasped. Aaron looked at her then followed her gaze. She was looking at a large object set into the floor in the middle of the room.

"Holy shit," Simon whispered.

Aaron took in the hulking ring of stone, its pale mortar cracked and brittle with age. A small stepladder led up to its stone-capped ridge, a large pull-handle visible just beyond it.

"I get that this house is like a hundred years old," Libby said, "but I definitely wasn't expecting *that*."

"Damn," said Simon. "He wasn't just ready for an apocalyptic bugout. He had his own fucking well."

"I don't think this is a bugout room, guys," Aaron said. "And that well isn't for drinking water."

"The nut job was going down into it," Simon said.

Aaron nodded. "The map wasn't lying. This is how he got to that place. It's how we'll get there too."

***

Libby leaned over the edge of the well. "It isn't a well," she said, "it's a hatch."

Aaron saw a copper door set into the well about a foot down, its outer frame occupying the shaft's full diameter, the interior brick courses with which it was flush looking newer than the well's outer stone courses. The door had a U-shaped grab handle affixed to its top. A large hinge on the far side of the door suggested someone pull it up and push it back, away from the stepladder.

"Want to do the honors, Aaron?" Libby asked.

Aaron shrugged, leaned over the edge, and gripped the handle. He tensed, preparing for what he expected to be a laborious effort. He tugged the handle and was immediately staggering backward. The lid didn't just open. It *eased* open.

"Damn, Porter, you been juicing?"

Aaron knew it had nothing to do with strength. He came back and leaned over the well, watching the door complete its upward swing, the hydraulic mechanism within sighing as the door came fully perpendicular to the opening.

They stared into the dark maw below. Curved metal handrails were soldered into the sides of the shaft. Rushing water echoed up from somewhere deep. A sulfuric odor, like that of raw sewage, wafted up with it.

"There really is a tunnel system," Aaron said absently, "and, according to that map it—"

"Crap!" Libby cut in. "We need to go get that. I'll be right back." She bounded out of the room. In less than a minute, she was back, clutching the small notebook and gasping for air. "Got it," she said unnecessarily.

Simon caught Aaron's eye with an incredulous stare.

She flipped through the pages until she found the drawing of the map and slapped the notebook onto the ledge. Aaron and Simon crowded in behind her, and they studied the map for a second time. Aaron scrutinized each line and tried to guess the distances between the points of interest. He verified that the house drawn in the lower right-hand corner had only one line connecting to it and again followed the line's journey to where it intersected with the longer line, which traveled up the center of the page, eventually leading to the trees and caves.

"How far do you think these tunnels go?" he asked. "Because they *are* tunnels. Just look at where the one leading from the house goes under that bend in the Cuyahoga and meets up with the main artery ... which travels a similar path as the Towpath."

"I was thinking the same thing," Libby murmured.

"And, the only two destinations are the house and the cave area," Aaron said. "At least that's all Gil cared about anyway."

"Assuming he's the artist," Simon said.

"Is there really any doubt?" Libby countered.

An uncomfortable silence settled among them.

Libby broke it. "Well, if I had to guess the distance," she said, "I'd say we're about a mile west of the Towpath. But you know how crooked the Towpath is, especially where it runs adjacent to the river." She tapped the straighter of the two lines. "And from here, where the tunnels meet, it's anyone's guess as to how far it is to the caves."

Aaron thought about the Sand Run Caves, which were maybe a mile south of The Courts. Could the drawing be of them? He shrugged. "Well, that vertical line is about double the length of the diagonal line that connects to the house. So, even if none of this is drawn to scale, it still suggests that the real journey begins after the river."

"So, what are we talking?" Simon asked. "Four miles?"

Aaron massaged the corners of his eyes, as if doing so might prevent doubt from worming its way deeper into his head. It didn't.

"Guys, this is some serious shit," he said, "and if this map means what I think it does, then we're hiking for miles in darkness. I can't imagine there's a lighting system down there.

We'd obviously need flashlights and supplies. You don't need to do this. I honestly don't know what I'm gonna find down there, or even what I'm gonna do once I get there—wherever *there* is. I have no plan."

"Yeah, yeah," Libby said, "we've been through this." She leaned over the well. "I'm going."

"I don't understand, Libby. He's my brother. I *have* to go. You don't."

"There's something you need to know."

Aaron and Simon exchanged glances but remained silent.

She looked at Aaron. "The last day I ever saw my mom *alive*, she tried to tell me about someone she once saw—someone who didn't belong—while we were fishing at our special spot. She wanted, with all her heart, to tell me who it was, but she passed away before she could. You know how hard that is? I missed my mother's last words." Her eyes were welling now, her lower lip trembling. "She *labored* to tell me, but she couldn't get the words out." She wiped at her cheeks and straightened.

Through the corner of his eye, Aaron could see Simon fidgeting. He was pulling his hands in and out of his pockets as if trying to decide what to do with them. But Aaron knew what he wanted to do with his hands. He wanted to go to Libby now, take her, hold her, and draw her close. But hooking his thumbs into his pockets and staring down into the well seemed the easier and safer option.

Eventually finding his voice, he said, "I'm so sorry, Libby."

"It's okay," she said. "I know you've lost so much yourself. I don't even know why I'm burdening you with this." She wiped at her tears. "Just so you know, I'm doing this for me just as much as I am for you. I believe she saw someone from the past. I know *we* didn't see them directly, but it could very well be one of the people from today. She saw something that haunted her till the day she died. I think she thought she was crazy, which is why she'd kept it to herself all those years. But I need to know.

And I'm *not* gonna stop just because that fucking bitch crossed *our* path."

Aaron could feel a weight lifting from his shoulders. Libby would see this through with him and take the path wherever it led. They were in it together.

He gave her the most reassuring smile he could muster and then turned to Simon. "Last chance. There's no shame in turning back now if you don't want to come. You know I want you to, but—"

"Shut up, Porter. I'm not walking to Brandywine alone. Plus, my mom doesn't give a shit about where I am." He gave a humorless laugh. "I could sit in the basement for days, and she'd never come down there, just assume I was playing Xbox the whole time. Even when she does the laundry, she never so much as looks in to check on me."

Aaron couldn't argue this point after witnessing years of unintended neglect in the Kent household, despite how much he longed to be a part of it.

"With your mom not checking in," he said, "then Gram won't know I'm gone either." He turned to Libby. "Will your dad be expecting you?"

"At some point he'll start to worry. But I've come strolling into the house much later than this, even past dark."

"Okay, then. It's settled. Any thoughts on *how* we'll explore the underworld?"

"Yep," Simon said, pointing. "Check it out."

Aaron looked to where he was pointing: a shelf near the front of the room, on which rested a half dozen heavy-duty flashlights. Boxes of D batteries were stacked neatly next to the lights, and next to the batteries, a heap of elastic bands.

"Nice, he has headlamps too," Libby said.

They set to work, Libby dropping extra batteries into her backpack, and Simon and Aaron testing the flashlights, all of which were in working order.

"Say what you will about the nut job," Simon said, "but he was prepared."

"Yep, and we ought to take advantage of that," Aaron added, passing an eye over the other shelving units. "Let's stuff our pockets—and your bag, Libby—with as much water and food as we can bring."

"But not too much," she said. "Remember, one of us— probably *me*—has to lug this thing for miles."

Reconvening in the middle of the room, Libby held her bag open and Simon dropped in a handful of ration bars. Aaron added six water bottles and a couple of extra flashlights.

Aaron strapped on a headlamp. "There's one more headlamp. Who wants it?"

"Libby can have it," Simon said. "She's carrying the bag. Give me a flashlight."

They returned to the well. Aaron was first to climb the stepladder and lower himself into the hatch. He grabbed one of the curved handrails and used his other hand to switch on his headlamp before easing himself down onto the first rung. The ladder gave a little shudder but otherwise felt sturdy. He took a few steps down and looked up to see Libby lowering herself, Simon following close behind.

Chapter 23

A Descent into Darkness

Aaron had only to descend ten rungs before gooseflesh began to crawl up his bare calves. The air reeked of wet earth, sulfur, and decay. His echoing footfalls on the ladder were getting louder, as was the sound of rushing water. He aimed his headlamp into the claustrophobic dark below. A larger space yawned beneath him, and it was sliced in half by a glistening ribbon.

Water.

He continued his descent before finding himself in a tunnel. Reaching the last rung, he lowered a tentative foot to the earthen floor, careful to avoid the little stream, which was maybe a foot wide.

Aaron planted a foot on either side of the stream and looked up. "At the bottom!"

"Almost there," Libby called down. "I can see you."

He could stand at full height in this space with some room to spare. He looked into a darkness that greedily swallowed his light. The ceiling and walls were coarse rock, uniform in their brownish color, which could've been shale or sandstone for all he knew. He placed a hand on the wall nearest him, feeling its dampness. He turned and looked down the other direction of the tunnel. This time his light wasn't swallowed by darkness, it was instead met by a pile of rock. The little stream was flowing from beneath an oven-sized boulder at the bottom of the pile. The Kendall house really was the end of the line.

He warned Libby about the stream as she lowered to the last step.

She leaped outward, landing gracefully on the narrow bank between the stream and the far wall.

He repeated the warning to Simon, but Simon's short legs failed him midair and one of his feet splashed into the stream.

"Christ!"

Suppressing a chuckle, Aaron turned and adjusted his headlamp. "Okay, I guess I'll go first. Libby, how about you follow me, and then Simon at the rear."

"Works for me," Simon said. "I'll gladly die last."

***

Twenty minutes in, and the tunnel's ceiling abruptly dipped, the walls constricting. The floor was beginning to narrow and deepen into a V-shaped trough, forcing them to splay their legs and shuffle awkwardly along the bases of the walls. Simon grunted his displeasure at this latest development, but they otherwise shuffled in silence, their lights trained upon a stream that never rose above a trickle.

Soon a low hum enveloped the tunnel, and it grew louder as they walked. Then it was cacophonous and remained that way for a distance of at least fifty feet before diminishing.

"I think we just passed under the Cuyahoga," Libby said.

The space was opening up again, for which Aaron was grateful. His legs had begun to feel leaden, the arches of his feet strained. They walked on, and another sound began to echo somewhere ahead.

They soon found themselves at an intersecting tunnel, which was much larger than the one they'd just traversed.

"Oh wow," Libby whispered.

Like the small tunnel, this one had a stream—perhaps three feet wide—flowing down a trough at its center, to which the smaller stream adjoined as a tributary. But unlike the other tunnel, the elevated banks on either side of this stream were wide enough for a person to walk freely without having to straddle it.

There was something odd about the water, Aaron thought, but couldn't decide what it was. He stepped to the nearest bank, stretched, and massaged his shoulder.

"Well, that wasn't so bad," Libby said.

Aaron looked right and then left, his light revealing nothing but inky blackness in either direction. He glanced up, letting his light play across a ceiling abuzz with shimmering reflections. Pea-sized water droplets seeped from rock that had been grooved and gashed.

Chiseled?

"Who made this place?" he asked, more to himself than to the others.

Libby let out a small whistle as she combined her light with his on the ceiling, which was at least twelve feet off the tunnel floor.

"This was definitely not made by Mother Nature," she said. "How far down do you think we are?"

Aaron pursed his lips. "Thinking we climbed down forty, maybe fifty feet from Gil's basement."

He directed his light at the floor and paused. In a thin layer of dust and pebble, about five feet to his right, was a pattern.

Shoe treads.

He walked to the footprints, knelt, and inspected them. The prints were leading down the tunnel in the same direction they were about to go: south. He stood and turned, studying their path of origin. The person had come from the North. How far did this tunnel go? Did it extend as far as Lake Erie? *Underneath* Lake Erie? His heart hurrying now, he placed a foot next to one of the prints. About the same size.

Owen wears size eleven too.

He looked at Libby and pointed in the direction the prints were leading. "This is south, correct?"

Without answering, Libby wriggled off her bag, unzipped it and fished out her compass. She began to walk. "Yep, south," she said.

"Welp," Simon said, "given that's the general direction to our deaths, I think it's best not to die on empty stomachs. Food break?"

"Okay," Aaron said, "but I suggest you eat along the way."

***

They walked in silence up a gradual incline for the better part of an hour. Aaron scanned the ground for more footprints, his thoughts lingering on what had happened in the mines. Could Owen really have found his way out of the mines and into this tunnel system? He looked out along the tunnel and then stopped.

Libby scuffled to a stop behind him. "What's wrong?" she asked.

"Are you seeing what I'm seeing?"

"Not sure. I just see the stream and ... the other bank."

"Exactly," Aaron said. "You can *see* and it's not because of your headlamp. Let's try turning off our lights."

Aaron and Libby switched off their headlamps. Simon muttered something inaudible then turned off his flash light.

As Aaron's eyes adjusted, he could still see the planes and angles of the stream's banks. The stream itself sparkled with a dim and purplish light. He glanced further up the tunnel to locate its source. It took him a moment to realize that the section of tunnel ahead wasn't a straight thoroughfare, but a gentle bend to the right, with diffusive light glowing beyond.

His voice feeling detached, he said, "I think we've just arrived."

***

Aaron had heard stories about the other senses adjusting to compensate for limited vision, and he now understood why.

After having killed their flashlights, it didn't take long for the rushing stream to grow louder. And now something else was intermingling with that sound. It was a person, and they were wheezing, or perhaps dry-heaving.

The sound intensified as they approached. Then the familiar itch was at Aaron's chest, the skin and nerves beneath the absent medallion tingling as if in memory of some phantom limb. His mouth was on the verge of watering.

"You hear that?" Simon whispered. "Sounds like my dad after a night of getting shit-faced on Scotch."

Aaron noticed there was something else, a burning smell, and it was growing stronger with each step. It smelled of burnt plastic, reminding him of an overheated computer. They were close now.

An icy *click*.

He looked over his shoulder.

Libby's jaw was set, her eyes narrowed.

His gaze fell to the Glock in her right hand, its nose thankfully pointed to the floor.

"Need to be ready," she said, almost apologetically.

There was a sobriety in the cocking of the gun; a resoluteness of action; an unspoken finality. There would be no turning back now.

They rounded the bend and saw the mouth of another offshoot tunnel, from which the bizarre light spilled forth. Like the offshoot that originated from beneath Gil's basement, this one connected to the main tunnel from the right as well. The stream from the main tunnel made a sharp bend into the offshoot, despite the main tunnel continuing on indefinitely into darkness.

There was something else, and it had to do with the water again; that same feeling that had bothered Aaron when they'd first entered the large tunnel. In the improved lighting, he could see that the water was flowing in the same direction they were walking, which was gradually up and south, *up* the valley escarpment and *away* from the lake. How was water defying gravity and flowing *up*? It made no sense.

The wheezing was much louder now, just around the corner. He dropped to a squat next to the mouth of the offshoot and motioned for Libby and Simon to do the same.

They did so, pressing themselves against the wall next to him.

He had no plan. His desire to get to this place and his fixation on the footprints had occupied his thoughts until now. He hadn't decided on what he'd do once they'd arrived.

"Any ideas?" he whispered.

They both shook their heads. He turned back to the offshoot's mouth. The stream didn't flow into it, but *underneath* it, curving beneath a jutting lip of rock, the darkened cleft into which it flowed looking like a mail slot.

He glanced back at them and whispered, "I'm going to take a peek."

"Be … careful," Libby mouthed silently.

He got onto all fours and crawled along the wall until he was nearly on the rock shelf. At the edge of the offshoot mouth, he inhaled and leaned forward. What he saw around the corner was not another tunnel but a large natural recess set into the main tunnel. On the far wall of the recess stood a purple oval about the size of a man: the source of the light. The recess was bathed in that purple dusk, and a silhouetted figure was on the floor just in front of the oval. Like Aaron, the figure was on all fours, their back repeatedly arching and plunging. Gasping. Heaving. *Defenseless.*

It was her. The woman who called herself Mary Campbell was suffering, or recovering—from what, Aaron didn't know. Or care. The time was now. They wouldn't have a better chance. He turned to Libby and Simon. He froze.

They were no longer squatting next to him but standing. His mind tried to make sense of the scene before him. Libby's stance was staggered. Her arms extended in front of her. The gun pointed at Simon's face. Simon, whose eyes were like saucers, his mouth agape in silent terror.

Chapter 24

The Exchange

Aaron wanted to ask Libby what she was doing, but the words wouldn't come. He looked again at Simon, and then he understood. A rough-hewn blade was pressed against Simon's neck, the knife's wooden hilt held firmly by a dark hand. Libby wasn't aiming the gun at Simon. She was aiming it at the man hiding behind him.

Simon tried to speak, but was silenced as the blade pressed harder against his neck, forcing his chin up and away. Then he was being nudged forward, toward the recess.

Libby took several tentative steps back, keeping the gun trained in the direction of the man and Simon, but Aaron knew she didn't have a clear shot. From his vantage point, he could see that the man was lowered in a semi-squat as he edged forward behind Simon.

Aaron backed away too until he was bathed in that strange light, directly within the woman's sight line.

Through her slowing gasps, she said, "Nice of you to join us."

Aaron looked at the woman, who was now getting to her feet. She spat dryly and cleared her throat. Gone were the sunglasses and the neckerchief she wore at the park. The white of one blunted eye glowed like a pale moon and the deep scar upon her neck made it look as if her head might roll off if she were to look skyward. Another man was emerging from the oval behind her. The quilled headdress and painted face were familiar. It was the man from Aaron's vision who'd been smoking a pipe near the fire. He stood weaponless as he took in the scene he'd come upon. His eyes grew wide when they settled on Libby and the gun.

Aaron tried to think, but his brain was like mush. Their element of surprise, and probably any hope of finding his brother, were gone. Now, there were two men with this woman. All of them dangerous. He forced his mind to calm, tried to see the situation with new clarity.

Sapere Verdere.

He thought of the man's reaction when he saw the gun. *He's afraid.* These men followed the woman's lead, if everything she'd said in Gil's kitchen was true.

"Libby, Simon will be okay," he said. "Aim the gun at *her.*" He pointed at the woman, who'd now risen to her considerable height.

Libby gave him an incredulous look. *Are you crazy?*

"Just do it."

In one swift motion, Libby pivoted and pointed the gun at the woman's head.

Aaron watched the latest party guest.

The man reacted, his lips parting, his eyes darting from the gun to the woman and back to the gun again.

Aaron looked over to where the other man squatted behind Simon. The arm holding the knife faltered before stiffening again.

"How adorable," the woman said. "She has a gun. But does she know how to use it?"

"Been shooting since I was ten."

"You do look like you know how to handle that," the woman said. "You might make a great addition to my legion. We could use some diversity."

"Hands up," Libby said.

Aaron eyed the woman's right hip. The fingers of her right hand twitched, but she then raised both hands in the air.

Libby shifted uncomfortably, looked to Aaron, and raised her eyebrows. *Okay, now what?*

He returned his attention to the bulge at the woman's hip, where her hand would go if they weren't careful. Then he looked into those horrible eyes.

"You're going to bring me my brother," he said, "or Libby's going to shoot you."

The woman smiled.

"Return him now, and we'll leave and forget any of this ever happened."

She continued smiling.

He tried to think. What could he use? How could he scare her? His mind raced. Then, he had it. "I don't see why any of this is amusing," he said. "If Libby shoots you, you'll never see your daughter again."

The smile on the woman's face died instantly. "Don't you ever mention her," she said.

Fighting to keep his voice even, he said, "We have the gun. We'll dictate what happens here."

"So, you think? You cannot have your brother back unless I command it. You're only still alive because I've instructed them not to kill you. We don't kill just to kill. It's not our way. When we fell a tree, we use all of it. It becomes our spears, our arrows, and, if big enough, our canoes. When we slaughter a creature, we use its hide, its meat, and everything else. We don't waste the gifts that nature has bestowed upon us, and we don't take that which isn't needed. It's the reason why they didn't kill you in the forest. I only had use for what you carried. Do you think it was by accident that my men's arrows didn't find their targets?"

"Then what possible reason did you have for killing an innocent man at the marsh?" Libby asked. "Answer us that, bitch."

The woman's good eye shifted toward Libby. "He got in the way of the objective, and needed to be dealt with. As did

Vaughn, but for another reason—that greedy scourge of the Earth. I know you were in his house. My men sensed your presence, but I told them you'd be fools to follow us and to simply leave you be. But you've obviously proven me wrong. And clearly, you've found a way down here that I wasn't aware of. I suppose Vaughn, that filth, kept more secrets than I knew."

"That man you butchered," Aaron added.

"That man who deserved it," she countered. "As did Connor Littlefie—"

"You're the reason he's missing?"

She smirked. "Missing is a bit inaccurate. I know exactly where he is."

"What the hell have you done?" Libby asked.

The woman's smile held. "As with all things in nature, Littlefield was used to serve a higher purpose. And I used him well. *All* of him." She turned her attention to Aaron. "They tell me you paid your brother a visit. I must say, I'm learning so much about how this thing works." She pulled the medallion out from under her tank top and let it thump to her chest. Aaron's heart hurried at the sight of it. He licked his lips, but the nausea and the urge to quell it with the medallion wasn't as strong as it was before. He looked into its black eye, expecting to become entranced. Except ... *nothing.* Nor was there a strong desire to hold it.

She noticed him looking at the medallion and said, "Either Vaughn was lying to me—I wouldn't be surprised by that—or he thought he knew how to make it work and was wrong. I guess I wouldn't be surprised by that either. But *you* know how it works, Mr Porter, don't you?"

He pulled his gaze from the medallion and shook his head. "No, I don't," he said. In a sense, he didn't. He didn't know what really made it work. He just knew he'd had an overwhelming urge to put it in his mouth last night and he'd simply obeyed it.

"But you're connected to it somehow. Otherwise, how did you travel last night without actually making passage?"

He didn't understand the question or what passage meant, and he didn't care. "Beats me," he said. "You can keep it. I just want my brother back."

"And I want to get my daughter back, as you so accurately deduced. I need this object to make that happen. I just attempted to go back for her, and once again, was not permitted to do so. This was supposed to be the solution." She encircled the medallion with her long fingers. "So where does this leave us, Mr Porter? Tell me, because, as you said, you're calling the shots. But if you kill me, then your mouthy friend over there will get his throat slit, and you'll never see your brother again. They'll make sure of it."

Aaron knew she wasn't bluffing. He thought of the men from another time, before this country was heavily populated. Probably before colonization. Even if he tried to appeal to them individually, how would he communicate with them? How did *she* communicate with them for that matter? His mind went to work. What did this woman want more than anything? And, what did he want more than anything? What had compelled him to walk underneath the Cuyahoga Valley through a dark tunnel system to confront these people?

The answer was obvious. Before he could overthink it, weigh the pros and cons, consider Simon's and Libby's perspectives, he blurted, "My brother for your daughter then. As you said, you cannot get her. But I can."

"Aaron!" Libby cried.

He didn't take his eyes off the woman, who stared back at him, unblinking.

"I don't know how this all works," he continued, gesturing toward the purple oval, which he figured was some type of entryway or portal, "but I've bonded with the medallion ... somehow. It's part of me. I no longer need it and can go where you cannot." Whether or not this was completely true, he didn't know. But he *felt* it was true, and he needed to make her believe that it was.

The woman remained silent.

"Aaron, we're coming with you wherever you go," Libby said.

"She won't leave with you," said the woman.

"Why not?" he asked. "As you said, you cannot get her. And I assume you've thought of having your men go do it. Guess that didn't work out either?"

The woman remained still but turned her head toward the glowing oval, the light within ethereal and alive. She watched it as if she could see her daughter through it. After a lengthy pause, she said, "Hannah lets no one in."

Aaron didn't know what to do with that comment but wanted to keep her talking. "Tell me," he said.

She turned to him, cocked her head, and narrowed her horrible eyes, as if measuring his suitability for the task. "You'd be going back seven years from now. It's June. Hannah will be home. Of course, every door will be locked, every window latched and covered, everything shut. Holed up in her bedroom, probably reading one of her fantasy novels. She won't answer the door. She won't trust anyone. It's the afternoon—the rain will just have passed."

"Where does she live?"

"Well, you'll know the neighborhood, Mr Porter. She lives on Bernard Drive, at the end of the cul-de-sac. Seven seventy-eight."

Aaron inhaled sharply. Gram's neighborhood, his garbage-picking mecca, was the home of this murderer's daughter? He'd been down that street many times. Old Mr Kramer lived down that way, and Aaron had claimed dozens of random artifacts from the man's tree lawn over the years. An unsettling thought tugged at him. If this was Hannah's home, then it was *her* home too.

"So, where will … *you* be then?" he asked. "What happens if I run into the *other* you, if there is one? How does that work?"

"She won't be around."

"Aaron, you're not doing this alone," Libby said.

"I don't think you can go, Libby."

"So that means we have to stay here with *them*?"

He turned to see the pained look on Libby's face, the plea in her eyes. He thought it over. Could they go with him? They'd be going to Portage Falls, ground zero of their collective pasts, during a time in which they'd all be alive. He thought of the woman's conversation with Gil. How each of them had become sick and had nearly died when they'd come into close contact with their past lives. While Simon and Libby had always lived a couple miles from Sand Run Estates, might they come too close to theirs? Would they suffer and die? And would he himself even be protected by the medallion's power? He couldn't be sure, but this was his mess, not theirs. *No,* he concluded. They would be safest here, in their own time with the gun trained on the woman, not letting her leave their sights. It was the best he could do. Or … was it?

He looked at the woman. "Yes," he said finally, "but you're going to have Simon released."

The woman shook her head. "She has to lower the gun first."

"No."

Her dark eye bore into his, as if willing him to fracture. He stared back, holding his breath.

A moment later, the woman glanced at the Mohawk Man and gave a curt nod. The man lowered his knife and released his grip on Simon. With a shove, Simon was sent staggering over to where Aaron stood. He bent to catch his breath.

Libby gasped. Aaron followed her gaze, which was directed at the Mohawk Man, who was no longer obscured by Simon. Folded neatly beneath the leather string at his waist was what looked to be a dishrag. Except this dishrag was pallid gray and covered with thin hair, its edges ruddy and torn. Dangling over the man's bare chest were a pair of similarly gray ears, pierced through by a cord.

Aaron turned back to Libby to see the gun trembling in her hand.

"Hold it together, Libby," Simon wheezed, a tremor rising in his own voice.

Guilt completely seized Aaron then. He'd been the only one of them to truly encounter Gil's body back at the house. And now, he was going to leave his friends with people capable of this? Libby had been right. He couldn't leave them, even if they were armed.

He wheeled back on the woman. "Change of plans," he said. "I still get your daughter, but *they* go back to where they came from and send my brother back unharmed." He nodded toward the men. "I know he's in the past—*their* past. And they don't need to be here. They don't belong here, in this time."

The woman looked at him.

He stared back at her.

"No," she said. "They stay here. I'll bring your brother back."

No.

He couldn't let this cunning woman leave their sights. He also didn't want her anywhere near Owen. In making the others leave, he'd dwindle their numbers. Worry about one person instead of three.

The woman looked at Libby. "You might have a gun, but you'll never fire it. We're in a cave. You'll bring the ceiling down on all of us."

Libby's face darkened. "Let's put your bullshit theory to the test then. I have nothing to lose."

"You're a foolish girl."

Libby swiveled, aimed the gun, and fired. A flash. A deafening *POP*. The wall next to the woman's head exploded, rock shards spraying like shrapnel. Dust rained down.

Aaron reeled backward and nearly collided with Simon.

Then, silence. Aaron righted himself and immediately looked at the woman. She was lowered to one knee, her hands over her ears. The Mohawk Man was similarly hunched over. His knife lay on the ground, just a few feet away. The other man was trembling on all fours, groping about his shirtless torso.

Aaron didn't hesitate, stepping to the rudimentary blade and scooping it up. Couldn't hurt to have another weapon.

"You fucking *bitch*," the woman growled. "You have no idea the harm a firearm will do down here!"

Libby said, "I'd watch your mouth, *Care Bear*. There are plenty of rounds in this clip. The next bullet won't miss. Do as he said. Make them go back. *Now*. And keep your fucking hands up."

The woman's shoulders shook with rage. Her chest heaving, she gritted her awful teeth. "I shouldn't have listened to them. I shouldn't have left that fucking thing back at the house for you to find. Actually, I should have just had them seek each of you out and scalp you one by one."

Her hands still in the air, she flitted her fingers to beckon the Mohawk Man and the other man over to her.

The other man slowly rose and walked to her, his gaze not leaving the smoking gun. The Mohawk Man glared at Libby as he took his time approaching the woman. When he looked at Aaron, his eyes fell to the blade Aaron held at his side. He smiled before joining the other man next to the woman.

"Now," Libby said, "tell them."

The woman, who stood a good two inches taller than either man, cupped a hand over her mouth and began to whisper in the Mohawk Man's ear. The man was stoic as he listened to her instructions. A moment later, she pulled away, and the Mohawk Man glanced at his fellow warrior.

Together, the men strode to the opening and stepped through. They were soon gone from sight.

The woman turned back to Aaron. "I told them to bring your brother. But they have instructions *not* to release him until I have my daughter. The ball is in your court."

Something nagged at Aaron. While they'd shown her that they weren't going to back down, this entire transaction felt off, if not a little too easy. But he pushed the concern away, turned to Simon, and handed him the knife. "You might need this," he said.

Aaron was about to step toward the opening when the recess began to dim. The oval was shrinking. Seconds later, it was gone, and with it, all its light. He flicked on his headlamp and immediately found the woman. She looked on like a pale ghost in the lamp's cold light.

"What's happening?" he asked.

"This is normal," she said. "The portal will temporarily close when there are others inside making passage."

They stood, and they waited. Minutes later, without a sound, the darkness gradually pulled apart. Soon the opening was at the same scale and proportion as it had been before, the mechanics governing its size and ability to animate unknowable yet feeling as natural as an opening eye.

Aaron walked closer to the opening. Closer to the killer.

Libby said to the woman, "Step back and keep your hands up."

The woman did so, backing further into the left corner of the recess.

Aaron, still confused by what he just saw, drew nearer to the opening and paused. It was his doorway to Hannah. To *Owen*. He turned to the woman. "I have some ques—"

"I've already planned for them. You don't spend years trying to save your daughter's life without having contingency plans. I knew it might not be me retrieving her."

She looked at Libby. "I have written instructions in my left pocket. He'll need them."

Libby flitted her gaze to Aaron. "I don't trust her."

"Oh, hell no," blurted Simon. "You saw what happened the last time she reached for her hip. No, no, nope."

"Fine," the woman said. "But without them, he's lost. He won't be able to bring her back, and then he'll never see his brother again."

Aaron looked at the woman's right hip. Another hole in their plan, they should have disarmed her. But how could they have done so without forcing her to surrender the knife—which she could have thrown at any one of them in a split second—or have gotten close enough to her to forcibly take the knife without getting their throats slit?

"You can't just tell me?" he asked.

"No, not everything. You need to be precise. There are many details, and you cannot afford to slip up. I've been waiting for this moment a long time, and I'll be damned if I let you ruin it— assuming the medallion's power will even protect you, which I guess we'll find out soon enough. But you *will* do everything I've instructed."

Aaron exchanged a look with Libby and then Simon, who just shrugged.

"Okay," he said. "Reach into your pocket, *slowly*, with your left hand only. Keep your right hand up, where we can see it. Libby, if she moves too fast, put a bullet in her leg."

The woman kept her right hand raised and her eyes trained on Libby. She slowly lowered her left hand to the pocket of her jean shorts, slipped two fingers in, and pulled out a thin flat object, which was pale yellow. She extended it to Aaron. "Take it.

It explains how to make passage. But you must read it as soon as you enter, because things will be confusing, especially the deeper you go in. There's also a message on the back intended for Hannah. She must read it."

Aaron plucked the paper from the woman's hand and immediately stepped back.

"There are some things that haven't been written down," she said, "but are no less important. Are you listening?"

Aaron nodded.

"Empty your pockets. If you have a smartphone, leave it, or you will incur its anger. Also, possessing something such as a coin with a future date may cause complications if someone were to discover it on you. You don't need questions. You don't need to welcome opportunities that would cause indefinite delay—or worse, get you trapped indefinitely in another time. Lastly, when you emerge into the light of the past, your skin color will look different. It'll return to normal quickly, but make sure you are *not* seen before it does. I want this done cleanly and efficiently. Do you understand?"

Aaron nodded. He couldn't help but think of airport security. A phone was no problem because he didn't bring one. He didn't carry a wallet. He felt inside his hip pockets for change. Nothing. He stuffed his hands into his cargo pockets, rooting around for anything hard, and came back with nothing but some pea-sized balls of lint.

"I'm good."

"Your light," she said. "Leave it too."

He tugged it off and dropped it to the ground.

"Wait," he said, "will it get dark in there?"

"No. The light source is interminable."

Aaron didn't know what that meant but nodded and said, "I think I'm good."

"For your sake and *mine*, I would hope so."

He stepped to the opening but paused, the concern of leaving his friends alone with this killer resurfacing. Turning back to the woman, he asked, "How long does it all take?"

"If you go in and out properly, without lingering, less than half an hour *for us*. Once you're in 2014, that's time we don't experience. But don't linger, no matter what you see. Precipitation activates the portals. But they'll close if you delay too long after the rain. Once they close all bets are off. You're on your own, and must wait for the next steady rain."

Aaron could only nod. He thought about the time interval. Simon and Libby wouldn't perceive him as being gone very long. That is, if he didn't screw up and get stuck in 2014. But he decided it was welcome news.

His head feeling light, he stepped toward the opening, its edges smooth and curved, like parted lips at odds with the coarseness of the surrounding rock. The quiet light pouring out seemed to reach for him. Through this opening, he would have to find a girl he didn't know and somehow persuade her to follow him back to this place in 2014.

He paused and looked back at his friends. Simon held the knife. Libby stood in a shooter's stance, her gun trained on the woman. These two people, who didn't particularly like one another, united in this moment to hold a killer at bay, sacrificing their own safety so he could rescue his brother. No matter what happened next, whether he succeeded or failed, whether he lived beyond this day or died, he would never forget this sight.

It had been a strange twenty-four hours, and things were about to get even stranger. He turned back to the opening, raised one foot, and stepped through. His world changed just as soon as he lowered his foot on the other side.

Chapter 25

Into the Complex

Once inside, he felt as if he'd been submerged in water. The soles of his shoes were slow to make contact on a purple-gray floor that was neither rock, nor concrete. *Metal?* Whatever the surface was, it was smooth, clean, and uniform. He was in a world of perpetual twilight. The air felt charged, and it was abuzz with tiny swirling motes. He brought his left foot up and then down onto the floor. The tap was barely audible and stirred no echo.

He glanced over his shoulder, through the opening. The earthen chamber from which he'd arrived sounded distant, the rush of the subterranean stream muffled. Libby and Simon looked like hazy figures painted in watercolor.

He turned back into the murk. The burning smell was stronger here, making him feel as if he might sneeze. A part of him *wanted* to sneeze, if for nothing else, then to see what would happen to the droplets that erupted from his nose. He thought they might float.

He was in some kind of tunnel, which bent gently to the left and was maybe thirty feet high and just as wide, circular in diameter, like a massive tube laying on end. All was curved except for the floor, which ran flat in every direction before bending imperceptibly to form the walls, which themselves bent to become the ceiling. He saw no seams that would provide any hint of construction.

He remembered what the woman had given him. He pulled the folded-up sheet of paper from his pocket, unfolded it, and read her words through the swirling particles. She wanted him to follow the spiraling path, no matter how small it became, until he arrived at "the central chamber." Once there, he was to walk to his right, around a black pool. He folded it back up and stuffed it into his pocket.

He walked on, each buoyant step making him feel as if he were walking on the moon. The inner structure of this place was beginning to feel familiar, as if it had been programmed inside him like a line of code. That code was running now, and he picked up his pace like a migrant bird, his internal magnetite propelling him through a coiling thoroughfare. He was walking through a nautilus, the medallion's engraved pattern its perfect miniature replica. To his right, fist-sized crystals jutted from the wall at eye level every few feet. And as he continued on, the tunnel's walls became narrower, its ceiling lower, the spiral tightening proportionally like that of a mollusk shell, its precise dimensional sequence as certain as the universe itself.

The tunnel contracted further, shrinking to perhaps fifteen feet in diameter. Then, ten. That's where the debris began. Pale pieces of what looked to be crushed terra-cotta and stone covered the floor like some menacing carpet, making him glad he wore shoes. He saw pieces of stone inscribed with petroglyphs. Many were covered with smaller fragments, including what looked to be human teeth.

Do not linger.

He continued on, crunching over the debris.

Further in, the smashed ruins became denser, a tapestry of bone, stone, and clay. Soon he had to crouch as the tunnel contracted further still, that electric burning smell growing stronger. Then, the walls and ceiling were on him, his right shoulder nearly catching on one of the crystals jutting from the outer wall. He rounded another claustrophobic bend and stopped.

What should have been a confined space in the heart of the ever-contracting spiral was instead a large one. He was in some kind of an antechamber, about ten feet high and just as wide, its curved walls and ceiling as smooth and as uniform as the spiral tunnel. He stood to his full height and stretched. Set into the far wall of the antechamber was another oval-shaped opening. But it was what awaited on the other side of that opening that stole his attention altogether.

He saw a cluster of flames capering above a black pool. He saw a series of shimmering spikes suspended above the fire, looking like massive stalactites and throwing purple mote rivers in all directions. Except they weren't stalactites. They were massive crystals. He didn't have the medallion to study for comparison, but he didn't need it. Its visage was burned into his memory. These were the same crystals but much larger.

He made to step through the portal but paused. There was something different about this opening. Carved in relief on either side of it were a pair of tall humanoid figures, their slender bodies conveying no sex. Nor were there hints of clothing or armor; their bodies smooth and monolithic. He studied the statue to his right, running his gaze up the torso, to the delicate neck, to the ... there was no face. Hasty-looking gouges where the mouth and eyes should have been. A crater for a nose. He looked to the left figure's face. It had been obliterated, its smooth jawline all that remained. It looked as if someone had mutilated their faces in a bout of rage.

Do not linger.

He stepped over the lip of the opening and into the space beyond.

His foot fell heavily into a large domelike room, its entire surface smooth save for the crystals that hung from its crest like a chandelier. The bones in his hands felt magnetic, his shoulders weighted. The gravity hadn't just returned, it was insistent. He looked down upon a narrow bank that ran along the edge of the pool and sloped imperceptibly down into it. He followed its journey with his eyes, around the diameter of the pool, out to where it passed behind the field of flames, eventually arriving back to where he stood.

According to the woman's instructions, he needed to walk counterclockwise around the pool. "Stay near the wall," she'd written. "Look straight ahead, and keep walking no matter WHAT you see or feel." He turned right and took one laborious step forward. He took another, staying near the outer wall.

He was about a fourth of the way around the pool's diameter when his world lit up. It was as if a bolt of lightning had been thrown upon his head. Warmth began to spread about his forehead, expanding and then contracting into a single shape, narrow and austere. It traced up to the crown of his head like a finger. Then, down to the base of his skull. His arms and legs were trembling, his teeth chattering. He put a steadying hand on the curved wall to keep himself from collapsing. Had to keep walking. He felt no pain, just numbing, disorienting heat.

The finger was tracing his arms now. Then his legs. Soon it was back up again, climbing his torso, *through* his neck, *behind* his eyes. *Inside* his head. Then a voice spoke to him. It spoke into his mind without words. It was the same voice he'd heard when he'd gazed into the medallion's black eye that night in the rain. Its language was phonetically impossible but understandable.

"Mine boy who rides Shelby," said the voice, "may your bones be in process."

His thoughts were stiff with fear. He felt he shouldn't speak—couldn't speak—but he thought, *Are you God?*

No answer.

I don't understand. I—

"We are the Superposition."

Then, *silence*. He lifted his gaze from the floor, blinked, and looked to the center of the room. The crystals were there, just as they had been before, suspended and lifeless. The flames quietly flickering. He returned his attention to his remaining journey and realized that there was none. He'd circumvented the pool.

He surveyed his arms, his legs, the backs of his hands—expecting them to be raw and red—but there was no sign of injury or irritation. Exhaling, he pulled out the paper and skimmed the woman's instructions again. He needed to backtrack the way he'd come, through the tunnel. He folded up the paper, stuffed it into his pocket, and turned toward the opening where the mutilated statues would be waiting on the other side. He stepped through.

It didn't take long for him to see that this journey through the spiral would be much different from the last. Around the first curve stood an opening that hadn't been there before. The crystal that had been there was gone. A thin membrane of organic-looking material was stretched taut across the opening like calloused tissue, puckered at its edges where it met the wall's smooth surface. The membrane was translucent enough for him to glimpse a jumble of shapes beyond it.

He squinted through it. There was something large and cylindrical inside. On the object's surface were weathered-looking hieroglyphs, more rudimentary than what he'd seen earlier on the broken pieces of stone. He brought a tentative hand to the membrane and grazed its surface with his fingers. It was bone-hard, like scabbed-over skin to protect ... what? He stood back and looked at the large object on the other side a bit longer. Something about its placement looked deliberate, as if it were intended to cover the opening.

Do not linger.

He pressed on, crunching over the smashed ruins, more scabbed-over openings passing to his left, the tunnel expanding and the ruins on the floor thinning until there were none to walk over at all. He came upon an opening that wasn't calloused. It was open, inviting him into a dark and dry-looking space. It couldn't be his destination—which was the third opening from the last according to the instructions—because he'd traveled maybe halfway through the spiral. Yet he couldn't help looking through. The earthen floor wasn't the same rocky aggregate from under the Cuyahoga Valley. This floor was coated with a fine powder, piled in areas like snags in carpet.

Sand.

His breath caught. Just beyond a mini sand dune, partially clipped at the sharp edge of darkness, were shapes he hadn't expected to see: letterforms. He studied them, figuring that someone must have either used a finger, tree branch, or some other narrow instrument to write a message in the sand. They spelled out a phrase: STALL 4 TIME. SV.

The message felt presented, intended for whomever would glimpse it from inside the coiling complex. *Stall 4 time? SV?* He wondered exactly who the message was intended for, and why. Why would someone want to stall for time in here?

Do not linger.

Picking up his pace, he passed several more openings, all of which *were* open, but the purple light wasn't bright enough to determine what lay within. He rounded another curve and stopped. The end of the line, one opening remaining on his left. Straight ahead, at eye level where the tunnel made a sharp curve before rounding back onto itself, like the cul-de-sacs of Sand Run Estates, jutted a single crystal. His way home, back to 2021, and it was shut.

Panic overtook him, but only for a moment. He remembered that the woman's instructions had told him to expect this. By making passage, he would convert the crystals into *portals*. But the inverse was true for the portal through which he initiated his passage.

He turned and backtracked, until he came to the third opening from the last, which was darkened. An unsettling feeling hit him, and it had to do with that last crystal. Why were there no openings beyond it? Why did the spiral complex end there? If the portal he was about to enter led to 2014, then that meant there were only three more created in the intervening years, including—and *ending with*—his present. If he could travel from *his* native time to a place in the past, then why couldn't someone from the future do the same and travel into his present and beyond? Why weren't there more?

He thought more on this and then quit thinking altogether. The paradox of time travel was too big for him. Hannah was his first objective, then Owen. He went to the opening that led to 2014 and stepped through.

Chapter 26

2014

Empty. No Libby. No Simon. No woman.

Aaron brought his other foot down, fully stepping out from the complex. A wall of sound swept over him like a gale. He winced and covered his ears. The noise was raw and urgent. His instinct was to stand and wait, and so he did. After a while, the sound becoming more manageable, he lowered his hands from his ears and walked to the edge of the rock shelf that jutted over the stream. The stream was still there but now a mere trickle.

He turned back to the small recess, which was identical to the space he'd been in ten minutes ago, and began to scan the dust-coated floor. A single set of footprints led out of the portal, through the recess, and turned south down the main tunnel— the direction he was supposed to go. He thought they belonged to the woman. He *had* time-traveled, because if he hadn't, then there would be more footprints. He looked for the spot on the wall that should have been cratered by the gunshot. No evidence of a disturbance of any kind. It was as if all he'd just experienced in this little alcove had been airbrushed from existence, like an elaborate prank. He turned back to the stream and looked right and then left. No footprints were visible to the left, the direction from which they'd arrived ... seven years from now.

He turned right and began to follow the prints, letting them guide him through the tunnel. After a while, the portal's light source now far behind him, he began to wonder why he could still see the prints so well. He looked up. Straight ahead, a pale shaft abuzz with tiny dust motes reached down into the tunnel like a ghostly finger. It was daylight.

He continued on, the grade of the tunnel rising gently, his feet making squishing noises as they sank into soft clay. He soon found himself at the base of a large rock pile. Between a pair of large boulders, a tiny footpath crawled up and into the rocks. He made his way up the path, through spots equally bathed in light and shadow. The path was maybe a foot wide and was steep, making it difficult for his feet to find purchase. Over the course of twenty-odd minutes he fruitlessly grasped at slick rocks, tripped over his own feet, and nearly rolled an ankle. At one point, he stumbled forward and banged his knee against an outcropping, which he knew would leave a bruise.

By and by, the light source drew closer. He found his way to the summit a short time later. At the top, he slumped against a large rock resting at the edge of the descent. His chest heaving, his shirt clinging to him like Spandex, he stared down into the abyss from which he'd just emerged. The grade looked much steeper from here. How he'd get a girl he didn't know—who was apparently already mistrustful—to follow him into this treacherous hellhole was something he'd have to figure out. He thought about the paper in his pocket. The woman had written a note directly addressed to Hannah on its other side. Would it be enough?

Pushing himself from the rock, he found he could stand in this place. He peered up at a sandstone ceiling that was maybe eight feet high. He glanced about the small chamber, which was about the size of his dormer bedroom. The source of the light was to his right, a long, jagged crease, about chest high. He could hear chirping birds through it.

He looked past the opening, toward a dark corner where the chamber's ceiling angled downward. Something caught his eye: a sliver of pale green fabric, tucked deep into a crevasse, just visible beyond the shaft of light. The crevasse through which the object showed was smaller than the one leading outside. He took a step forward, but his body blocked the light from the outer opening, shrouding the crevasse in perfect dark. He stepped back to let the light back in, and there it was again.

He considered the color of that fabric, and then he recalled the letterforms in the sand.

Sapere Verdere.

But getting into that crevasse to investigate would require effort he couldn't afford to expend right now. He had to move on, and so he did.

He went to the crevasse that led outside, hoisted himself up, and wriggled through. Then he was sliding down a sandy rock face into an outer cave awash in pale light. He landed hard. Dust filled his nose, his eyes, his mouth. He spat dirt, stood to dust himself off, and almost hit his head on the low ceiling. He crouched and glanced up. The opening was nearly invisible from his position. He dropped to one knee and looked at the broad ceiling of this outer cave, which had its own severe downward slope, sharp and concave where it met the wall before abruptly jutting up in its back-right corner—where he now kneeled.

The elevated crevasse would look like a subtle crease between the wall and ceiling or even a strip of shadow to the casual observer. Then again, there were no longer any casual observers of this place, which, according to the instructions, would be the Sand Run Cave system, long condemned for the public. How many people knew of this hole's existence? And if they did, would they be motivated enough to scale a wall higher than the average man could reach to enter it? The crevasse had to be at least eight feet off the ground from here. He thought about getting back up to it, because he would have to with Hannah in tow. The woman had written that there would be hand and foot hold divots set into the rock face, but he didn't see any.

He drew nearer to the wall and stood, the only place in the back corner where he could on account of the ceiling's suddenly jutting upward. He ran his palms over the rough sandstone, feeling for any indentations. Nothing met his touch. Bending, he continued, running his hands in a grid-like pattern, from bottom to top, from left to right, and then from right to left. Then, a shallow divot, about two feet from the floor and to his right. He rose, continuing his sweep, and found another divot about chest high and to his left. He stood back as far as he could in the tight space and tried to imagine using the divots to hoist himself up and over the edge of the opening. He decided he could do it. He relaxed. He didn't need another major obstacle for retrieving this girl and was grateful that this wasn't going to be one of them. He ducked, turned, and walked out of the outer cave.

He found himself standing beneath a bright pale sky, high above the place where the Cuyahoga sliced deep into the earth. He squinted out over the gorge, the steepest and most treacherous place in the valley. The cave from which he'd emerged was about halfway up the cliffside, putting him at eye level with the tree canopy. A light gust was rippling through the trees now, enough to stir their leaves into a chorus, but not enough to impress their stoic bows.

He turned back to the cave, observing the horizontal bands of sedimentary rock that stretched across its sunken face in various shades of yellow and orange. They were historical records in their own right, and he wondered what these records could tell him if they could speak. How long had humans known about the cave's secrets? And for that matter, at what point in the history of this valley had someone chosen to dig the large tunnel? Who had created it, and where had they put all the excavated rock? It was as if someone had directed a laser under the river plane and had simply zapped the large tunnel into existence. It wasn't as if there was some massive rock field lying around in the park. But maybe it wasn't a field. Perhaps a pile or many piles? He'd learned of the mound-building people in history class and wondered if there were enough mounds dotting the valley and the surrounding area to account for that much debris.

He made to turn and locate a path for descending to the valley floor, but his eye caught on a worn-out bronze placard to the right of the cave's mouth. He approached it. The engraving read:

IN MEMORY OF MARY CAMPBELL

Who in 1759 at the age of twelve years was kidnapped from her home in Western Pennsylvania by Delaware Indians. In the same year these Indians were forced to migrate to this section where they erected their village at the big falls of the Cuyahoga. As a result, Mary Campbell was the first white child on the Western Reserve and this tablet marks the cave where she and the Indian women temporarily lived. Later, in 1764, she was returned to her home.

Erected by the Mary Campbell Society

Children of the American Revolution of Portage Falls

Maybe not the first white woman.

He stepped back and reappraised Mary Campbell's cave, imagining how someone might have taken shelter in it. It was deep enough to provide respite from rain and snow, but certainly not enough to shield from the cold or even the wind. The real Mary Campbell had lived here among Indians, and it was plain to see where the killer had drawn inspiration for her alias. But from what he'd overheard her tell Gil back at the Kendall House, her situation wasn't one of kidnapping; it was one of chosen assimilation. All for a medallion.

His mind lingering on the medallion, he turned from the cave, found a small dirt trail, and followed it down to the valley floor. Gil and the woman believed that the medallion was some kind of skeleton key, a physical talisman with the ability to unlock one's access to the past. But Aaron didn't believe there was anything physical about it. Nor did he believe that the unlocking needed to happen anywhere within or near the underground complex. No, whatever had been unlocked had happened when he'd placed it in his mouth. It didn't unlock a place or time. It unlocked you.

He was no more than half a mile from Gram and Grandpa's house. The medallion was back with the woman, but he felt fine. No nausea, weakness, or headache. Then, panic rose inside him. *Do I look fine?* He looked down at his arms and legs. They were green.

***

He looked about the forest for anyone who might see him. There was no one about. He walked on, deciding that if someone happened to see him and questioned him about his appearance, he'd explain he'd fallen into one of the stagnant pools covered with green scum down by the Towpath—of which there were many.

But fifteen minutes later, his skin was back to its ghostly pallor. In a sense, he was a ghost, from another time, haunting a stretch of forbidden forest. The trail was his alone, and it soon flattened to a narrow floodplain caked with black mud along the eastern riverbank. After weaving back and forth on the trail—occasionally wandering into the wet brush to avoid the muddiest spots altogether—he arrived at a closed gate blockading the small trail from the Towpath. A sign nearby forbidding entrance.

He wiped his shoes on a patch of stiff grass, rounded the gate, and walked up and onto the crushed limestone of the Towpath, the adjacent river sounding and looking no different than it would in seven years, its rushing current pushing forth fragrant air that felt charged, as if the river itself were a byproduct of some voltaic machine.

The afternoon sun was in its slow swing down the western sky by the time he arrived at the obscure footpath leading from the Towpath up to The Courts. He began his ascent up the steep incline, grasping slender beech tree trunks along the way. Soon his chest burned, his breathing ragged. For not the first time in his life, he wished for Owen's physique, fortified by years of weightlifting and intense football drills. Despite rarely ever going down into the valley, Owen would have scaled this incline in no time.

Yet up Aaron climbed, pausing occasionally to quell a stitch marching up his left side. Eventually, the grade leveled out, stubborn as an unclenching fist. At the top, he picked his way through overgrowth denser than what he remembered in 2021 and was soon at the northwest corner of The Courts. Winded, he plopped onto a fallen tree branch and swept his gaze across the field, noting there was more growth here as well and the grass coverage was more uniform than it had been in 2021. But, despite Mr Ipser's efforts—which Aaron knew extended as far back as 2014 and even earlier—there were still plenty of dandelions and mangy weeds poking up. It was a surface that hadn't yet experienced the beating it would take when the Porters would move into the neighborhood two years hence, initiating impromptu football games with other abusers who were all too happy to trample the little patch of earth.

But some things hadn't changed. A smattering of the usual suspects lay about nearby: crumpled beer cans, used condoms, spent cigarette butts, and a half-eaten Egg McMuffin crawling with flies. He didn't know what day it was, but knew that Mr Ipser was as predictable as the sunrise itself, and if litter were lying about, it was only here because the man hadn't yet gotten to it.

Breathing easier, he labored to his feet and walked out of The Courts and up the footpath leading to the Maplewood cul-de-sac. He thought of Grandpa and Gram as he stepped onto dark-gray asphalt that was destined to turn sun-bleached white. Would they be home?

Ribbons of lingering storm water were trickling into the sewers near the intersection of Maplewood and Sunset as he approached it. His forehead felt just as wet, the temperature up here much hotter than it had been in the gloom of the valley, the asphalt feverish despite his wet shoes. A few houses up Sunset, an elderly couple sat creaking on their porch swing, sipping iced tea. They gave a cursory glance his way but were otherwise unconcerned about the sweaty teenager walking down the middle of Maplewood. He didn't recognize them, and they must not have recognized him. He wondered if they were still alive in 2021.

Further up Sunset a young girl was being dragged by her yellow lab. The dog's nose was on the air, its big body jerking and pulling a leash to which the girl clung two fingers precariously as she stepped hard after the dog up the sidewalk. The dog didn't so much as glance back in Aaron's direction.

The animals had been fleeing the park when the woman came after them. It was as if she'd been marked. Gil certainly thought she was.

Has the medallion's power masked my scent?

He considered other aspects of traveling back in time and whether or not they would affect him, and he them. He thought of intervention then. He thought of rescue. He thought of the boy. Across town was a lonely seven-year-old who'd likely be huddled under his bed covers, lost in a comic book and munching on potato chips. But Aaron knew it wasn't reading or eating the boy was engaged in. He was escaping. Escaping a world that had ripped his dad from his life. Escaping a home that was no longer truly his, a home routinely invaded by strange men who would disappear into the bedroom Mom used to share with Dad. Escaping the aftermath of such visitations, which usually ended with Mom sobbing on the living room floor in her half-opened bathrobe, surrounded by syringes and little rubber tubes.

A lump was forming in his throat as he approached Bernard Avenue. He wanted to run to that little boy right now, take him in his arms, and tell him it would be okay. He wanted to squeeze that frightened child and whisper to him that Grandpa and Gram *will* rescue him from his hellhole, that things would get better. But would that be true? Had things turned out better? Would he tell his former self that Grandpa would pass away only two years after taking custody of him? That his brother would go missing in a freak accident? And, that he would find a strange object that would send a cold-blooded killer chasing after him?

Lost in thought, he didn't realize he'd already walked past the Bernard intersection, his inner autopilot directing him one street over to Juneville. *Home.* He stopped at the Juneville intersection.

Turn left, and you're home.

It wasn't just a place. It was afternoons tinkering with Shelby in the garage. It was Gram watching him ride his new bicycle up and down the street and clapping her hands as if she were urging on a toddler's first steps. It was nights sitting on the front stoop and listening to the tree frogs, sipping a Dr Pepper while Grandpa nursed an ale after tinkering with his Mustang in the garage. It was *home,* and it beckoned him forward.

He looked over his shoulder toward Bernard. Just up that street, at the end of its cul-de-sac, was a girl who needed returning to her mother; a girl who was dead in 2021. The goosebumps came stalking back. He knew he should go now and not belabor visitation to a past that didn't really want him. But he remained still. Maybe just one peek down Juneville? He wouldn't approach the house. One look and that's all. He approached the edge of the intersection and paused just a few feet from where he'd be able to get a line of sight.

The woman's words came back to him. She'd warned him not to invite suspicion. Not to create a scenario that could inhibit his return. What if Grandpa was sitting on the front stoop? Gram bent to her flowers in the front bed? Even if they didn't see him, how would *he* feel if he saw them? Did he trust himself?

Trust himself to have the strength to not abandon this bizarre errand and go to them? And how would he explain his suddenly advanced age?

No, he decided, looking would be like torturing himself. What good could come from it? He might do more harm than good. Grandpa's heart attack might happen much sooner if he were to suddenly see his seven-year-old grandson at fourteen. He turned and walked away.

Chapter 27

The Dead Girl

There were two types of homes in Sand Run Estates, brick ranches and aluminum-sided bungalows, their arrangements as random as a flip of a coin. Seven seventy-eight was a ranch, and by the looks of it, it had seen better days.

The shingles on its weather-beaten roof were peeled and cracked, making the house look as if it were in the process of going bald. The shutters were a puke yellow, which Aaron guessed were white at one time. The salmon-colored paint on the front door—which might have once been red—was bubbled and water-stained. He ran an eye over a pathetic lawn. Instead of a carpet of Kentucky Blue, a patch of crabgrass glistened proudly in the pale light.

The same grass sprouted through cracks in the single-car driveway which he now walked up, trying to remember what this home would look like in seven years. He thought he recalled a freshly paved driveway and the house having black or dark brown shutters. The roof and the door must have been replaced at some point, or else he'd have remembered the mess he was seeing right now.

He ascended crumbling steps to the front door. The windows on either side were curtained by thick and stiff-looking drapes. He tried to compose himself, but it was no good.

No pressure, just get this girl to come with you or you'll never see your brother again.

He pulled the sheet of paper now damp with sweat from his pocket and unfolded it. Turning the paper to the side with the hand-written note, he read silently:

Sunshine,

I need you to trust this person. You may think I'm away at one of my training sessions right now, but I am actually somewhere else. I will explain all to you when you arrive. This person will take you to me. Where they take you may seem strange, but I need you to trust me — and them.

Some people are worth melting for.

Let the storm rage on.

Mom

PS — leave your phone behind.

Aaron didn't know what the lines about melting for someone and the storm meant, but he guessed they represented some code only mother and daughter shared. Not seeing a doorbell button, he lifted a trembling hand to the door and knocked.

He waited. Nothing.

He knocked again, this time a little harder. He waited. The windows were too far apart for him to see any potential disturbances behind the curtains. He stepped down from the stoop and into the grass thinking that the angle from inside the house might be just as bad, and that it would be best to let her see him out in the open. Less of a threat.

Still nothing.

A *bang* behind him, followed by the cough of an engine. He whirled. *Great,* he thought. Maybe whoever was pulling out of their driveway would see the teen stalking their neighbor's house. He watched the Honda Civic back out of the driveway, click into drive, and accelerate down the street. He turned back to the house and stiffened. The door was cracked open, a pale face staring back at him.

***

Aaron hadn't known what to expect of Hannah's appearance. What he saw was a teenaged girl wearing eyeliner as black as her shoulder-length hair, which was streaked with violet highlights. The soft curve of her pale cheeks was unlike her mother's copper-pipe cheekbones. Her heavily lip-sticked lips were velvety where her mother's were thin and cracked, and her eyes were placid blue where her mother's one good eye was black, and pierced you like an arrow.

But Hannah did have one thing in common with her mother: a murderous stare. It bore into him now.

Aaron tried to speak, but her words cut the air first.

"The fuck you want?"

"I—"

"Kenny Lipscombe put you up to this?"

"No, I—"

"Seriously, I don't know who the hell you are, but I'm gettin' tired of this fuckin' shit." She shook her head. "I seriously can't believe that fucker can't just leave me alone."

"No, I don't know who that—"

"Oh sure."

She slammed the door shut.

Aaron stood slack-jawed in the crabgrass. She hadn't given him a chance to utter a word, much less allow him to convince her that she needed to follow him into a dark cave beneath the valley.

The thought of that journey seemed like a pipe dream now; a delusion of a naive teen who'd made a stupid promise. The woman had hesitated when he'd proposed the trade, but she'd gone along with it anyway. Why? Had she known something he hadn't? Either way, she was wrong. He wasn't going to get this girl to do anything. The whole thing was a mistake.

He would just have to figure out another way to get his brother. He thought over the possibilities. He could go back to the cave and try on his own to locate the portal leading to the time and place where they were keeping Owen. Except he had neither weapon nor backup of any kind. He thought of Gil's harvested corpse. The men he'd seen in his vision would be there and would happily relieve him of his scalp or worse. It was suicide.

He thought about the other side of town, where the boy and his older brother were living. Could he warn them? Could he make a change now that would alter the course of events to follow? He considered what might happen if he warned his past self about all that would happen in the intervening years leading up until now. Would his past self remember the warning? What about Owen? Would he remember? He considered it further, and decided that if Owen were to see a future version of his younger brother, it might just make things worse. The same for his past self. How would the younger Aaron reconcile it all? *No,* he decided, showing up in person was out. Could he leave them a note? Send an email somehow? Even at nine or ten, Owen wouldn't read anything that didn't involve sports. And there was no guarantee that the younger Aaron would know what to do with the information other than to retreat further into his shell. There was no good answer.

Even if he were to somehow succeed in altering the past and the course of events to follow, it might result in changes that could make things worse. For all he knew, he may do something that could result in his *own* death. He tried to imagine what would happen if his past self died.

None of these questions would help him determine what he could do *now* to get Owen back. He massaged his temples. His best option would be to persist with this girl. Fix it right here, right now. He didn't know why he assumed any of this would be easy. She was on guard and skeptical, this girl who would take her own life. Damaged and jaded, she wouldn't be fooled by anything or anyone.

He marched back up the steps and rapped on the door again. Not waiting for a reply, he yelled into the door's scarred surface,

"Hannah, your mom gave me a note to deliver to you. You need to read it. I wouldn't be here if it wasn't important."

He waited for a reply. Nothing. But the faint creak of wood on the other side of the door told him she might be listening. He pressed on.

"I'm going to read it to—"

"Not funny, asshole!"

"It's not a joke. I swear, I really don't want to be here, either."

"Hang on," she said in a hushed voice that sounded closer to the door. "Don't tell me she's bangin' your mom?"

"What?"

"I knew it! Your mom's one of her whore clients, isn't she? Let me guess, she goes to self-defense *training* at a little studio down on Main?"

"Um, no," he said, "I don't know what you're talking about." His mom had done a lot of things, but taking a self-defense class wasn't one of them.

"Well, answer me this, is your mom a petite blonde with perky tits? If so, I've got some news for you and your poor daddy. She's having an affair with my dyke-of-a-mother. And let me tell you, she's not the only one getting *trained* by butch Caroline."

Aaron couldn't keep up with where this discussion was going. He also hadn't thought anyone could have a dirtier mouth than Simon, but he'd been wrong. This girl's words were calculated, cutting into dark places he couldn't fathom.

Except he *could* fathom them. He'd walked in darkness at a young age. He'd lost his dad after never knowing his true father. He'd stepped past used needles and past his equally used mother. He'd lost his grandfather. And now this mouthy girl stood in his way of getting his brother back. Something heated inside him then. It had been lingering deep, smoldering but growing amidst the hellish journey he'd suffered through to arrive at this very place, this very moment.

Anger.

It now licked at his stomach like an indignant flame. The words tumbled through his clenched teeth before he could filter them. "You listen to me, *goddamn it*. I don't give a *damn* about your mommy issues. I don't give a *damn* about which coward is bullying you. I don't give a *damn* about your jaded outlook on life. The only reason I give a shit about *any* of this, is because I don't get my brother back unless you come with me."

His forehead was hot. His words felt as if they'd come from another person but somehow necessary, cathartic even; a detonation of ordnance that needed to go off. The only thing that *could* happen after sidestepping it your entire life. He was done sidestepping. He was done letting things happen to him. Maybe this girl's attitude — her language, her disposition — had opened inside him an unexpressed frustration that had lain dormant, unexploded.

He continued, his voice holding its edge but now more measured, "Here's what I'm going to do. I'm going to leave this note from your mom at your doorstep. When you're ready to listen to what I have to tell you, I'll be down at the stop sign. Because honestly, I have my own problems and I'm not in the mood for your shit right now."

He pulled out the sheet of paper, set it at the foot of the door, turned, and stalked off. He didn't look back.

Chapter 28

Ties That Bind

Aaron sat on the curb at the corner of Maplewood and Bernard, still within agonizing reach of home. He massaged his neck and closed his eyes. Maybe he'd been too direct with the girl, insensitive to what the world had done—*was doing*—to her.

Five minutes passed. No Hannah. He watched a lazy rivulet of rainwater run behind his heels along the curb before it surrendered to the darkness of a nearby storm drain.

Movement, at his periphery. He looked up. There she was, walking his way, her eyes downcast, her hair pulled back in a ponytail. *She was coming.* He tried to remain surreptitious as he took measure of her. She was shorter than her mother, and fuller figured. With her full lips and soft features, he decided she was pretty and wondered why she'd been subjected to such bullying. The bottom of her black tunic fluttered above her equally black jeans in the gentle breeze and her small black purse swung from her shoulder in rhythm with the clacking of her heavy-soled black boots on the sidewalk. His bitterness dissipated the closer she got, leaving room for an unsettling thought to take its place. *This girl will take her own life.* He again considered the paradox of time. What if all of this had already happened? But this thought didn't have time to germinate.

"Let me make two things clear," she said. "First, I don't owe you anything, especially my trust. I don't trust anyone. Second, I have pepper spray in my purse and won't hesitate to use it on you. Oh, and I don't give a shit what that note from my *mom* says. I'm bringing my phone. I have no fuckin' clue where I'm supposed to go, and I don't know you from a goddamned hole in the ground. End of debate."

Aaron struggled to field her words, which felt hurled instead of spoken. He knew she couldn't take her phone, but he'd cross that bridge later. Better to not give her even the slightest reason to hesitate since the moment was already fragile enough. He figured his best move would be to act as disarming as possible, which wasn't much of an act at all for him.

"That's fine," he said, rising and wiping his hands on the back of his filthy shorts. "Name's Aaron Porter by the way." He extended a hand.

She folded her arms and narrowed her eyes. But something flickered in those eyes, like a dawning recognition. It vanished just as fast as it appeared. "Yeah, and what's this I heard you say about your brother? Why the hell are you here then if he's missing?"

It was a good question and one he didn't want to answer—yet. But he knew he had to give her something. He had a feeling that telling her, "It's a long story," might get him an eyeful of pepper spray. But he also couldn't tell her *everything*, including the awful truth about her fate. He had to tread carefully.

He studied his feet a moment, then looked up at her, willing himself to meet those piercing blue eyes … eyes like her father's.

"What I'm gonna tell you will sound insane."

"Well, it's a good thing I like insane."

"The mom who wrote that note to you isn't the same mom who's at her training session right now. She's the same person, but she's—"

"From another time."

His mouth fell open. "What?"

"I know who you are, Aaron Porter."

He blinked and shook his head. "How?"

"You've been in my dreams. Didn't know it was you till you said your name. But in my dreams, you … don't look like a person."

"I don't?"

"No, you're more of a feeling. I never hear your name spoken audibly. I just know it. And you wanna know why I like insane? Because I've been having the same *insane* fuckin' dream over and over again, especially lately." She pursed her lips. "Though it might be a recurring astral projection—I can do that too." She added this as casually as someone might say they can speak French.

Aaron had no idea what an astral projection was. He was more concerned about how she knew him. "So, have you been expecting me?"

It was her turn to look at the sidewalk. "In the dream I'm stuck over a black lake, surrounded by spirits or angels. Hell, maybe they're demons. But they're all sad. None of them speak to me or each other, and it's actually pretty damned lonely." Her voice caught, and she cleared her throat. "Everyone is together but alone. It's like being in Hell. But then you arrive, and suddenly I'm not alone. I feel … known. And every time you show up, I wake up and have no idea what happens after that. Sometimes the dreams include my mom too. God knows why. I tell her strange things about a mine, and something about Cleveland, but I don't know why I'm saying those things." She lifted her eyes to him. "You have to think I'm insane now."

"No, I don't. I've had that same, *similar*…" He trailed off, his own vision coming back to him. One of the tiny flames over the water had been named Hannah. She'd been on the verge of guttering out.

To his relief, she didn't prompt him to elaborate. Instead, she muttered, "I need a cigarette." She dug into her purse, pulled out a pack of Marlboros, shook out a cigarette, and popped it between her lips with practiced efficiency. A Zippo lighter seemed to materialize from out of nowhere in her right hand. She brought the lighter up and paused. "Want one?" she asked around the dangling cigarette.

"No thanks," he said, wondering when the stigmatization of cigarettes kicked in over the past few years. It either hadn't been as taboo in 2014 or Hannah didn't care. Probably both.

She lit up, indulged a deep drag, and jetted twin streams of smoke through her nostrils. A moment later, she said, "Well, let's get this over with. Where's this mystery place? The instructions she wrote on the other side of the page might as well be the directions to Diagon Alley."

In response he stood back and ran an eye over her clothing.

She leaned back. "Um, care to take a picture?"

"Sorry, just wondering if you might want to change your shoes. We have to go down into the valley. Trust me, it's not the most pleasant trip. There's plenty of mud and dark caves involved." He thought about asking her if she was hot, because her clothes were more suited for a crisp October day than an eighty-degree June. But he decided to not press it further.

Mirth glistened in her eyes as she took another drag on her cigarette. She pulled it from her lips and blew more smoke through her nose. "Oh, Aaron Porter, you sure know how to treat a lady. You had me at dark and dirty."

***

They found the switchback trail off the southwest corner of The Courts and began their descent. Given he now had a companion, Aaron figured this gentler path would be more appropriate than the footpath he'd taken on his way up. But to his surprise, Hannah chose to take self-imposed detours anyway, occasionally pulling herself up into tangles of branches before hopping back down onto the trail again. At one point, she strayed off to walk a felled tree like a balance beam, all of this with a cigarette dangling from her lips. They rounded a bend and came upon a hollowed-out tree stump on the side of the path where the land fell away.

Hannah hopped onto it. "Had no idea this path was here," she said sheepishly.

"Not many people know of it," he said. "They still don't in…"

"Still don't know in, what?" she asked, jumping down from the stump. "You're from the future, aren't you? Otherwise, why'd my future mother send you?"

He cursed himself inwardly. As much as she seemed to be warming to him, he didn't want the conversation steering toward his real time. The less questions, the better, since too many questions right now might sow the seeds of doubt in a girl who already had sensitive bullshit detectors. But here she was now, stopped dead in her tracks. He had to be honest, or she wasn't going anywhere.

"Dude, it's okay," she said, apparently noticing the conflict advertising itself on his face. "You can tell me. I'm probably the least skeptical person when it comes to crazy shit like that. So, what year are you from?"

He traced a withered vine's journey up the trunk of a tree with his eyes to where it encircled one of the tree's bows. It made him think of a child tugging its mother's arm. "I—"

"Forget it," she said. "Don't answer that. Just … tell me what it's like, where—when—you come from."

He considered this for a long time. He thought of mass shootings. He thought of civil unrest, and fractured families. He thought of how Gram—already widowed and estranged from her daughter—would break into tears on a nightly basis, her usual glass of cream sherry becoming three or more. He thought of one terrible thing after the next. Finally, he said, "Pot is legal in several states. Electric cars are popular and are getting more affordable. Oh, and the Browns are competitive, and the Cavaliers have even won a championship."

He looked at her to find her watching him, her eyes narrowed. "So, you're telling me that Cleveland, aka *The Mistake on the lake*, actually won something? And where *the hell* will I be able to buy pot legally? Please tell me in Ohio?" She then shook her head. "Actually, forget that. I'll be long fuckin' gone from Ohio."

Yes, long gone, he thought.

"What ... what is it?" she asked. "You puttin' me on?"

"No, no, I'm serious." But even as he said this, he could see her mouth slowly curling into a smile. She crinkled her nose, and in that moment, she went from precocious teen to a naive girl, pure and innocent.

The innocence was gone in the next instant. "You asshole," she said. "You had me going there."

He noted a trace of disappointment in her voice. He was about to say, "No, it's true," but caught himself just as she began to walk, which was what he wanted.

They rounded another sharp turn, the temperature gradually falling the further they descended. The thought of the temperature jarred something loose in his head, something he'd almost forgotten.

"In that note from your mom," he said, "it mentions something about melting for someone. What's that mean?"

"It's just something stupid we'd jokingly say to each other, during the brief time when she actually tried. It's from the movie *Frozen,* in case you didn't know."

"Oh, that's that Disney movie, right?"

She chuckled. "Yeah, I know what you're thinking. It came out just last year, and I was the fourteen-year-old who went and saw it with her mommy at the theater. Feel free to laugh."

"No, that's cool," he blurted, not wanting her to sense any hesitation on his part. In truth, it resonated with him, as he had few precious memories of doing anything with his own parents.

The memory came back to him then, the one that would add weight to his heart if he lingered on it too long. He'd been in kindergarten at the time, Owen in second grade. It had been the best day of his life. Dad, who'd been gone on tour for months, had shown up at school wearing his military fatigues. After the surprise, he took them to McDonald's for lunch where they'd scarfed down Happy Meals and played for an hour on the germ-infested indoor playground equipment. Afterward, Dad *and* Mom took them to see Grandpa and Gram. Eventually, father and sons found their way down to The Courts, where they played Eye Spy and hide-and-seek until the shadows were long and the sun was an orange sliver between the trees.

When Aaron had found Dad hiding behind a large oak at the tree line, Dad pulled him in for a tickle session until Aaron cried. It was then that Dad had said it, had told Aaron that he and Owen would always find him. That he would never be far from them, no matter the distance. Martin had become Dad that day. Aaron had cried, and it wasn't because of the tickling.

"Penny for your thoughts?"

He blinked back to the present and realized they were at the bottom of the switchback.

"Just ... remembering something from when I was little," he said.

They walked the flattening trail to where it intersected the Towpath. He nodded south. "Need to go that way."

His thoughts returned to what Hannah had said about her mom. He struggled to visualize the cold-blooded killer watching an animated princess movie, let alone with Hannah, who was fifteen going on thirty-five. After a while, he said, "I'll admit, I'm struggling to see you and your mom going to a princess movie together."

She gave a soft chuckle as they headed down the Towpath, its coarse limestone surface alive with moving shadows.

"It was her last-ditch effort. Her motherly role had been in its death throes for a while—still is. So, in her own twisted way, she thought it made sense to take a break from training lonely mommies all over Portage Falls and take her teenaged daughter to a movie better suited for a nine-year-old. She's always tried to reduce my age like that, in total denial that I have tits and actually like boys—which she clearly doesn't. Hell, to this day, I don't know how I was born. I'm convinced she'll go to her grave before she'll tell me who my dad is. But in a way, I don't wanna know."

If only you did know, he thought, the guilt sinking into his gut like a spike. But he also felt relief. It was less of a burden knowing that she didn't want to know about Gil. Had she expressed any desire to learn the truth, he wasn't sure he trusted himself to remain silent.

"But you wanna know something nuts?"

He looked at her.

"The day she took me to the movie was the best day of my life. We went to Swensons afterward and got burgers. Well, *I* got a burger, and she watched in silence as I ate it."

He snickered despite himself.

This made her laugh.

They walked on. After a while he could sense her eyes on him. He looked at her to find her watching him, her eyebrows raised, as if to say, "Well?"

"What?"

"You think I'm nuts, don't you?"

"No," he said. "Nothing you've told me is nuts at all." He considered her memory of her mother and then thought of his memory of his dad. Either the memories were eerily similar, or he was imagining they were. He decided he'd tell her about his own memory, thinking he could do so without giving away any details that might reveal too much about his native time and provoke more questions, which could get out of hand. She was coming with him and had given something of herself, something personal and vulnerable, and he didn't think it was fair to remain coy. He would give himself to her too.

He looked at her. "My dad isn't my real dad. Like you, I don't know who my real dad is. When I was very little, my mom married another man, and we took his last name. A Black man, which is pretty rare in Portage Falls, right?"

"Uh, yeah, you could say that. Definitely rare in *Porcelain Falls*."

He chuckled. "Exactly. Well, my best memories of him were the times he'd take us to The Courts. Even when I was little, I knew his goal was to kill time by taking us down here. It was a win-win for him: more time with us—since he was always away on deployment anyway—and more time *away* from my grandparents. My grandpa was never comfortable with his daughter marrying a Black man, and even though it was never said—at least around me or Owen—I could tell that my dad *felt* it and that it bothered him. So, whenever we'd visit my grandparents, Dad would wink at me and Owen, like this." He demonstrated by winking at her. "By then, we knew his meaning."

She tucked a strand of hair behind her ear. "Well, what was his meaning exactly?"

"Let's stall for time together. It was our…" He stopped, the memory of the letterforms he'd seen in the complex coming back to him. *STALL 4 TIME. SV.*

"What's the matter?"

He shook his head. "Nothing—just thought of something, that's all."

"Was it about something your dad said?"

He began to walk, deciding he wasn't ready to explain what he'd seen in the complex. He couldn't even explain it to himself.

She fell in next to him, her gaze still on him.

Finally, he said, "Dad liked telling us that stalling was sometimes the best strategy. The best plan when you didn't have a plan at all. It was all about being patient, dragging things out if need be. A solution might emerge, a problem might correct itself, an intervening circumstance might change things, or the uncomfortable moment might simply pass you by if you waited it out long enough. Time can be your friend, and sometimes conditions on the ground change."

As they walked the Towpath, he recounted his memory of the day Martin became Dad. He recited every detail and every emotion, right down to how he'd reacted when Dad had told him he'd never be far. His voice was trembling by the time they arrived at the sign forbidding entrance to the Sand Run Caves.

***

The journey up the cliffside to Mary Campbell's cave was uneventful, if not peaceful. As they entered the cave and walked to the camouflaged handholds and footholds, it felt as if something inside him had come unstuck, unbound. He felt cleansed, and could sense he and Hannah had become closer. There was now an unspoken trust.

He scaled the wall, his shoulder howling. He bit his lip as he forced himself up and into the crevasse. Swinging both legs inside, he thumped to the floor. He extended a hand to Hannah, who'd placed a foot on the foothold and a hand on the handhold. As she reached up to take his hand, her tunic sleeve slid down to reveal pale skin covered with red slashes. He pretended not to see the cuts as he took her hand and pulled her up and into the crevasse. She was quiet as she went horizontal on her belly and swung one leg over. She shifted until both her legs dangled inside and glanced hesitantly over her shoulder.

Aaron *didn't* hesitate, stepping forward and putting his hands on her waist. He guided her down.

"Don't get any ideas," she said.

There was a nervous edge in her voice as she said this, and Aaron wondered if she'd ever been with a boy, or at the very least been touched by one; if this was as uncharted a territory for her as it was for him.

Then the haunting reality of her future hit him again as his fingers pressed into the cotton fabric of her tunic, her soft body giving under his touch. There was a gentleness here, under this hardened exterior. At her core, she was just a girl who wanted a mother and a father; a girl as deserving of love as anyone else. In that moment, he willed his hands to transfer to her all of his love, his warmth, his empathy. He wanted to let this girl who'd languished in a life of abandonment, subjected to the cruelty of her peers, *feel* that she wasn't alone. For he thought if he could still feel love after all he'd been through in his own life, even after a day like today, then maybe he could channel it into her. Because if he did, then maybe he could change the future—*her* future.

He couldn't tell what she was feeling as her boots clunked softly to the cave floor. She was silent. But as he went to remove his hands from her waist, she gripped his fingers and held them fast, pressing them to her before giving them a gentle squeeze and allowing him to remove them.

"Thank you," she whispered.

"You're welcome," he whispered back.

He turned to the darkness, a mixed stench of rotting vegetation and dank earth wafting up from below. It was more pronounced now after his journey into the open air of the past. The pile of rubble lay ahead. He told Hannah what to expect as they waited for their eyes to acclimate. He was tempted to look into the dark crevasse where he'd seen the green fabric before but decided it was best to leave it for another time. Because down a pile of rock, through a subterranean tunnel, and on the other side of a mysterious complex, his brother and friends awaited him. He had his end of the bargain, and now, she was about to walk this ponderous path with him. By his side.

Chapter 29

On the Clock

Twenty minutes later, they were standing in the recess off the main tunnel. He turned to her. She was ghost white and hugging her shoulders.

She nodded at the portal. "What's in there, Aaron? Is she really in there?"

"She's *through* there. We have to go through it to get to—"

"When, Aaron? *When* the hell is she? I'm serious. We're *really* going to travel through time?"

He knew there was no point withholding anything anymore. She was here, on the threshold of a waiting aberration.

"I'm going to go forward through time," he said. "Back to where I belong. You need to follow me till we get to the portal leading to 2021. There, you wait."

"Just wait? That's it? Where will she be coming from?"

"Where I'll be going, 2021. The exact place is … here. And it's strange, because your mom is standing in this very place seven years from now. Two of my friends are there too."

"Why can't I go, too?"

He shifted, considering his next words. "There are rules," he said, finally. "I don't know how it all works, but I think if you travel to a time and place that's closely tied to your past or future, you could become sick and even die, especially if you get near any family members or relatives at that destination. Some kind of safeguard I guess."

She shook her head. "That makes no sense. What if I wanted to change something else that didn't involve my family? What if I wanted to go undo some assassination or something?"

"Not sure," he admitted. He thought of the flame field, those incessant murmurs that grew to a deafening pitch. It was as if they'd been left behind, awaiting salvation that would never come. Who else to rescue them but someone who loved them? Or their own blood? He considered the safeguards, if that's what they truly were. Maybe they weren't in place to prevent someone from altering the course of history, but instead, to prevent someone from resurrecting the dead. And the dead had to stay that way.

"I still don't understand."

He breathed deep and exhaled. "I'm not going to bullshit you. I don't know how this all works. I agreed to come get you during a tense moment. Your mom has friends that don't exactly fit in with our time, and they're helping her. But long story short, those *others* have my brother, and if I don't deliver you, then I'll never see him again. I might not anyway." He shoved his hands into his pockets and looked away.

"What in Christ's name has she done? You talk as if she's some kind of kidnapper. I mean, I know she's a goddamned weirdo..."

He bit his lip and weighed his next words. After a while, he said, "Hannah, I'll just say that the woman will do anything—*anything*—to get you back."

He looked at her to see her frowning, her eyes flitting over the strange light pouring from the portal, as if some answer might materialize from it.

"Get me back?" she whispered. "Back from where?"

The question was weak, lacking any edge or conviction. He could see it in her roving eyes that she knew.

"Hannah, I—"

"No," she interrupted. "I know. I've always known. In one of my dreams I come into a place like this but never come out. I read somewhere that it's impossible to die in your dreams." She turned to him. "But I died, Aaron. In that vision, that projection, that dream—I'm dead."

He had no words and knew he shouldn't.

"This is some heavy shit, Aaron." She uncrossed her arms and let them fall to her sides.

"I know," he whispered, taking one of her trembling hands, "but I'll be with you every step of the way."

"Do you know how it happened?"

He didn't have to guess what *it* was. He looked into her pleading eyes, which sought an answer he couldn't give. "I don't know exactly how, but I know that—"

"Oh, for fuck's sake, say it, Aaron!"

He swallowed and dropped his gaze. "You did it."

She was silent for a long time. Then she barked a harsh laugh, which sent a jolt through his shoulders. Her next words spilled from her mouth. "Of course, I did. So weak. Weak little *bitch*. Such a weak little b-bit..."

Then she was crying. She didn't so much as lean into him as she crumpled into him, her head crashing into his chest, her hands clutching at his shirt sleeves.

He wrapped awkward arms around her and held her there for a long time, swaying in the light of the portal.

***

Just as Aaron had been cleansed by his tears after recounting the memory of his father, so too had Hannah been cleansed by hers—or so it seemed. When she pulled away from him, her cheeks were streaked with eyeliner, her eyes wet, but something shimmered in those eyes now. Was it determination? Or resignation? Whatever it was, it was sober and present. She turned back to the portal, its light seeming to pulsate under her renewed attention.

"Ready?" he asked.

She shrugged.

He walked forward, stepped through the portal and into the light. She followed. They were in, and it wasn't any less weird for Aaron this time around. He glanced back to where Hannah stood just inside the opening. Her lips were parted, her eyes roving the strangeness of the space.

It was a different experience being here with someone else. Before, he hadn't had the presence of mind to closely study his own hands, arms, or feet. He'd been too absorbed with the surroundings. But as he watched her now, it seemed as if she were only partially there, as if spat out by a printer that was low on ink. Her form was made up of thousands if not millions of tiny buzzing particles that shifted and parted to allow equally tiny purple particles to pass through. He held up his own hands and watched them. His skin was dithering, rippling, moving.

"Okay, so this is weird," Hannah said, her voice coming from everywhere and nowhere.

She was standing three or so feet away, but it was as if her voice had intermingled with the swirling particles to create the ultimate surround sound. It emanated from behind him, before him, above him, below him, *through* him.

"Holy crap, your voice is everywhere," he said.

Hannah's eyes grew, and her mouth fell open. She then smiled. "Aaron, your voice just penetrated me. I mean, we just met and all. I'd prefer a couple dates, maybe dinner first."

They both burst into the kind of laughter reserved for the carefree and honest. They hooted and hollered, watching their pixelated forms shift and distort at the sound waves passing through them. It was another quirk of this place he couldn't have observed when he'd been here alone. But now he wasn't alone. He hadn't imagined any of it, because now she was here. She provided testimony to this place. It was real.

After a while, their laughter subsided. It had been good to see her laugh. But this made Aaron think of Simon and Libby. According to Hannah's mother, time would again become relative once back inside this complex. He was on the clock now and shouldn't delay. He looked at her. "Time to follow me through the funhouse."

Eventually, they came upon the debris field.

"I've seen this in my dreams," she said, looking down at the crushed remains as she gingerly stepped over them.

"Your voice," he said, "it's sounding normal again."

"Huh. Yours does too."

She paused at a spot in the debris field as thin as one could find, yet still coated with ground-up remains as fine as talcum powder. She began to rock back and forth on her heels. "Feel heavier too," she said. "If not heavier than normal."

He nodded, noting he felt the same. He looked more closely at her. "And you're looking normal again."

"Same with you." She looked down at the debris again and pointed. "Holy shit, is that a jawbone?" She was indicating a jumble of bleach-white bones to their left, intermingled with pieces of what looked to be a broken statuette and some pottery shards.

Aaron stifled a gasp when she suddenly bent, grabbed the jawbone, shook it loose of debris, studied it a moment, and cast it aside.

"Place just keeps getting darker," she murmured. "I love it. How did it all get here?" Without waiting for an answer, she lifted a crumbling humanoid torso from the pile. "This stuff had to be pretty high value. I mean, look at this thing." She turned the limbless statue over, its painted surface long faded. "Can't tell if this is Asian, Egyptian, or what, but it would have to be worth a shitload of money now. Think about it, Aaron. We could literally be standing on a goldmine. They sure as hell won't miss it." She nodded toward the nest of bones, rose to her feet, and tossed the statue back onto the floor.

Then it hit Aaron. This is where Gil could have gotten the money to buy and then renovate his turn-of-the-century home, stock a bugout supply in his basement worthy of a doomsday prepper, and retrofit an old well with his very own space-aged hatch. Did he *pay* to dig out the connecting tunnel too?

They walked on. Soon they were passing the innermost portals, and Aaron found himself having to deflect Hannah's questions just to keep her moving. Finally, they slipped through the last claustrophobic bend and into the antechamber.

Hannah gasped when the decimated statues came into view. She hastened over to them, completely ignoring the opening revealing the inner chamber. She drew close to each figure then stepped back, cocked her head, and folded her arms like a museum visitor admiring a fresco. "How morbidly beautiful," she said. She then glanced over to where he stood fidgeting and sighed. "Okay, fine. This is only the darkest, most beauteous place ever. I could spend hours down here. But if you insist."

Aaron was the first into the large space, his feet coming down hard and fast on the floor. "Keep away from the black stuff," he warned as she stepped in to join him. "It's as if it has its own gravitational pull. Stay near the wall."

She got her bearings and silently took in the field of flames.

He himself was no less mesmerized his second time here. He wondered if the little flame that represented Hannah was still in that conflagration. She answered the question for him.

"I'm out there," she said.

He looked at her sidelong, the orange firelight flickering over the dried tracks of mascara on her cheeks making it look as if she had tiger stripes.

"How do you know you're still there?" he asked. "How can that be if you're *here*, too?"

"I can feel it, Aaron. It's like some other sense I don't understand or can explain. I'm here, but I'm there." She pointed an unsteady finger toward some place in the flames he couldn't discern. "Out there. Alone."

She didn't need to explain. He decided it was true. He had to believe it was true. If the day's events had taught him anything, it was that he didn't understand how anything worked. As much as he wanted to move things along, he knew better than to rush her here. It wasn't every day you learned the places of your dreams—or nightmares—were real. It also wasn't every day you learned you were destined to take your own life. How she'd held up as well as she had to this point, he had no idea. Then again, she knew all these things already. She knew of this place, her fate, and even him.

After a while, she broke the silence. "So, am I supposed to sing it a song or something?" She nodded at the crystal structure. "What does it want me to do?"

"We need to walk around it, one at a time, according to your mom's instructions. Go left and stay to the outer edge. I'm not sure if it matters who goes first, but I think you should. Either way, it needs to…"

"Needs to what?"

He wasn't sure what it had done to him the first time.

He shook his head and said, "I really can't compare it to anything. But just to warn you, it might feel weird. But no matter what you feel or hear, you have to keep walking."

"Well, it's a good thing I like weird," she said.

Before he could say anymore, she was walking. A dawning realization washed over him. The purse, dangling from her left shoulder.

No phones.

She had told him earlier she was bringing her phone. He didn't know what would happen, but he opened his mouth to call her back, to tell her to leave her purse in the outer chamber. But the words caught.

At his periphery, he could sense the crystal structure growing brighter. *Hotter.* Blinding white now. The light was seeping into the bases of the suspended crystals. Then down into their tips. At the end of each tip, the restless light dripped and swirled and coalesced to form an orb. Each orb then shot forth a piercing ray.

All the rays combined a short distance from the furthest crystal to form a single column. He shielded his eyes with his forearm as the soundless column lit Hannah like an X-ray. She was a darkened skeleton, her clothing rendered filmy and translucent.

Then, a red sliver curving down the walls. He lowered his arm. The base of the crystal structure had turned red too. The color began to drain into the tips of the crystals, eventually spilling into the white orbs like blood clouding into water. The slender rays emitting from them were next to be infected. Then, the column turned red, like a geyser of arterial blood. Hannah stopped walking. Stopped moving altogether. The entire process had been silent, but there was a sound now: her screams.

Chapter 30

Judgment

Aaron wanted to run to her, but his legs were leaden. Something was sloshing about. He followed the sound to the black pool, which was beginning to churn and toss like a violent sea. Then it was dense, viscous, congealing at its edges. It didn't move like any liquid he'd ever seen. A globular mass rose a few feet from where Hannah stood paralyzed at the end of the red lightning bolt. It unfurled into a series of tentacles. They whipped about and began to slither up the smooth lip of the bank. They were reaching. Probing. Searching. The largest of the tentacles shot up and slapped onto Hannah's back. The appendage grew taut and began to tug her. Another tentacle leaped and latched onto her purse.

The purse.

He made to run but his right foot slipped from underneath him. He crashed to the floor and bit his lip. Then he was sliding toward the pool. He flipped onto his backside and planted his palms onto the smooth surface. His toes were within inches of the roiling substance.

Hannah's wails echoed louder.

He ignored the taste of blood, turned onto all fours, and clamored to his feet. Hannah was tensing her legs and leaning away from the pool, but it was only a matter of time before the thing dragged her in. He didn't so much as run but fall forward, crashing into her.

The large tentacle released from her back and latched onto her purse. She didn't move from the blow.

He shouted, "Let go of your purse! It wants your phone!"

"I can't! It's pulling too hard. It's gonna rip my fuckin' arm off!"

He squinted in the red light, which was now consuming him too. He tried to hook a thumb under the purse strap where it dug into her collar bone. It was no good. The tentacles had pulled the strap too taut for him to wedge his fingers beneath it.

Hannah's shoes were now squeaking across the floor. He grabbed her about her torso to keep her steady.

"Aaron!"

"Hang on!"

Reaching his left arm full around her torso, he grabbed one end of the purse strap at its base and gripped the other with his opposite hand.

He screamed and yanked upward. Nothing. If anything, the tentacles seemed to strengthen. He looked down. The two tentacles had braided together to form a single appendage, thick as his forearm. There were other smaller tentacles whipping about near the base of the mass. He thought if they all combined it would be over.

He drew a deep breath and gathered himself. He shouted, "On three, dip your shoulder while I lift! Got it?"

She nodded.

He squeezed the bases of the straps, his hands nearly coming into contact with the tarry substance.

"One. Two. *Thre—*"

He heaved with all his might and screamed. Hannah's scream joined his. Then she was no longer standing in front of him. It was just him now, stuck in a tug-of-war with this thing. The edges of the leather straps cut into his palms. But it was the easiest game of tug-of-war he would ever play. He wanted to lose. And so he did. He released the purse, and it was yanked down into the whipping tentacles. They greedily enwrapped it. His heart pounded as they wrapped and wrapped, covering the purse until it was no longer visible.

Then, silence. He put his hands on his knees and gasped for air, knowing it could have been Hannah entangled and dragged under.

Hannah.

He glanced up to find she was still next to him, paralyzed in a half-leaning position, her head against the wall as the silent red geyser continued holding her fast.

"Aaron, what's happening? I can't see!"

"It took your purse. I think it got what it wanted."

He looked back down into the blackness below. The tentacled monster had submerged, leaving behind only concentric ripples. The pool was turning to liquid again, the transformation reversing just as fast as it had started. Then, it was still as glass.

The reddish hue was dissipating around them. He looked up to see that the red pigment was being replaced by the same stinging white light as before. It spilled from the bases of the crystals and into their tips before entering the fiery orbs beneath them. The blinding white light was upon them again.

Hannah crashed to the floor.

Aaron knelt into the harsh spotlight, gripped her from under her armpits, and guided her onto wobbly feet. She was a skeleton again, her black bones quivering.

When satisfied she could stand on her own, he released his grip, noticing his hands had turned skeletal too.

"You okay?" he asked.

"Yeah, but my shoulder hurts like a bitch. And..."

"What is it?"

"It feels like something is inside me right now. What do I do?"

"You need to keep walking—alone."

She shook her head. "I have no idea why I agreed to do any of this."

She walked. From near the chamber's entrance, Aaron watched a black skeleton in filmy clothing pass beyond the field of flames, as if walking through them, like some fire-borne demon to which the flames owed their very existence. Minutes later, she completed the circle, and the light extinguished as she came to a stop in front of him. The temperature plummeting despite the flames, the crystalline chandelier again the silent sentinel suspended over its dominion of fire.

Her eyes were wide, her lips parted.

"You okay?"

She nodded without looking at him.

"Did you hear a voice?"

She shook her head.

***

Then it was Aaron's turn to walk. Eventually, after having been doused with the blinding light, his every body part feeling as if it were being examined, he arrived back at the chamber entrance next to Hannah. There had been no voice this time.

She was watching him. "Good?" she asked.

He nodded.

They stepped through the portal and into the small antechamber with the statues. When they entered the spiral tunnel and rounded the first curve, Hannah pointed at a crystal jutting from the wall. "That was supposed to happen, right?"

"As far as I know," Aaron said. "When I first entered this place, this is exactly how it looked."

"And, so, the entryway to 2021 will be the only one open now?"

He hesitated but said, "Yes," hearing the lack of conviction in his own voice. He wasn't sure if the portal would be open at all. He had to trust that it would.

She turned her attention back to the curving passage. "I guess I can understand why it would make 2021 the only open entryway for *you*. But what about me? Is the way back to 2014 still gonna be open for me?"

Aaron turned this over in his head, which took some effort. How did that thing reconcile who belonged where and which portals to change to crystals and back again? How did it decide what to unlock when two travelers from different times and places made passage together in close succession? For all he knew, he'd overwritten the 2014 entrance by being the second traveler to make passage. He had no idea.

He shrugged. "Guess we'll find out soon enough."

Before long they were crunching over the pulverized remains. As the tunnel grew ever wider and higher, the curves more gradual, both his and Hannah's bodies started to lose their fidelity, the lightness in their steps returning. They were getting close.

He paused and turned to her. "You don't happen to have those instructions, do you?"

"Nope," she said, her voice issuing from everywhere and nowhere now. "It was in my purse, which got eaten by the creature from the black lagoon."

He nodded. "I remember most of it anyway, and I don't think there's anything left for you to do besides wait."

"Okay," she said, "but then how's this all supposed to work if I can't go meet my mom in her time? And she in my time? Why do any of this? Clearly, she couldn't come back to 2014, which is why *you* were sent."

It was a problem, he knew. The woman couldn't go back to get Hannah without getting herself sick, and Hannah couldn't go forward in time without getting sick either. Where did that leave them?

"I don't know what her plan is," he said finally. "I just know you need to wait inside this tunnel, which is apparently some kind of safe zone. Maybe she plans on meeting you in here and then going somewhere else. Maybe to some place where neither of you have ties to your past." He willed himself to meet her eyes. "But just so you know, whatever happens, I—"

"Save it. I know what you're gonna say, and you don't need to. Whatever I was planning on doing, I'm *not* gonna let it happen. Just worry about getting your brother."

They walked on. Soon, they were at the last opening, where the complex reached its full size and the passage swung back onto itself. The way back to 2021 stood yawning like some toothless mouth.

He recalled how Simon and Libby had been standing on the other side of that opening, along with the woman, who had been backed against the wall. But the space without was dark and nondescript. How long would Libby and Simon have perceived his absence? What had happened back at the pool would certainly have tacked on several more minutes.

Something occurred to him then. 2021 really *was* the only opening. 2014 had been sealed like the rest of them, or else they would have seen it by now. He looked at Hannah. She was watching him.

"I know you're bothered by something," she said. "What is it?"

"Nothing," he said. He gave a weak smile. "I just hope we see each other again."

"Sappy words aren't my style," she said. "But I like you, Aaron Porter. You're one of the few good ones."

Without warning, she grabbed his hand and squeezed it. She looked into his eyes and he into hers, that underlying message they'd shared in Mary Campbell's Cave now passing from her into him. That torrid signal. The husks of words burning away, leaving behind only smoldering cores of meaning, pure and true. The first and only language. All that is, and forever deemed permissible, now alight inside this silent plane of knowing.

His heart pounded, and his cheeks grew hot. No matter what happened to this girl, whether or not she would overcome a destiny of which neither of them would ever speak of again, he felt known by her. Seen. Understood. And he knew her, this quiet little flame. *You will never be alone,* he thought, as he squeezed back.

She gave a weak smile of her own and let go of his hand. "Go get your brother. I'll deal with my mom soon enough."

He smiled, turned to the portal, lifted his foot, and stepped through.

***

As he leaned through the portal, his first instinct was to look slightly to his right to locate Libby and Simon. What he saw made the blood drain from his face. Simon and Libby were no longer standing. They were bound and gagged, lying on the ground in the southwest corner of the recess, where the woman—who was nowhere to be seen—had been previously standing. Simon's eyes were closed, his mouth stretched open with a cloth. But Libby's eyes were wide and were trained on him.

She shook her head rapidly and darted her eyes over to the opposite side of the recess—his blind spot. A sinking realization took hold of him then. She was warning him. He slowly turned his head, but didn't get a chance to react as powerful arms gripped him and pulled him through.

Chapter 31

Owen

Voices drifted toward him.

"I don't know why the hell any of this was necessary!" shouted a distant voice.

"Of course, you don't," came a calmer, colder voice, which sounded much closer. "But we have much to talk about. I can explain."

"I think you'd better start then."

A soft chuckle, which only seemed to agitate the more distant voice—*Hannah's voice*.

"And look at you! You're a goddamned dumpster fire. Forget your hair, what happened to your eye? Your neck?"

"Redemption is messy, Sunshine. And now I'll have it. All that matters is that you're here. Believe me, I'll explain all to you."

"Well, I'm not exactly *here*, am I? I'm stuck in this place which is neither 2014 nor what, 2021?"

"You'll see soon enough. I have big plans for us. Well, for *everyone*. I'll be joining you in there shortly."

Saliva was building in the back of Aaron's throat, his ability to swallow restrained by the cloth holding his mouth open. He attempted a couple unsatisfying swallows, but the gag just seemed to tighten.

"He didn't do anything to you. Neither did his friends from what I can tell. I don't know why you did that. And who the hell are *they*?"

Aaron knew who she was referring to. He didn't have to look about to confirm their presence. The smells of rawhide, pipe smoke, and dried blood were enough, as was the manner in which he'd been efficiently manhandled to the ground facedown, hog-tied, and gagged. He never saw them but knew it couldn't have been the woman's work alone.

How had this happened? When he'd left for 2014, he'd watched the Mohawk Man and the other warrior enter the portal, presumably to retrieve Owen. Libby and Simon were left with the woman, but they'd been armed. Libby wasn't afraid to shoot.

He looked at the dark figure standing in front of the purple oval. The woman looked like an evil queen gazing into some enchanted mirror. But she wasn't lost in soliloquy, she was speaking to Hannah, who stood framed on the opposite side.

"You can't stop me from coming through," Hannah said. "All this talk about getting sick? I call bullshit."

All calm fled from the woman's voice. "Don't you *dare*. You want to know about my eye? My scars? Let me tell you, Sunshine. I sold my soul to bring you here. I had my hair yanked back, my throat slit, and nearly bled out. I fell into a ravine, slammed my head onto rocks, and lost nearly all sight in my eye. I killed men. I plundered their camps. I sent sailors and impostors to the bottom of Lake Erie. I eviscerated all who stood in my way, and nearly died each and every time I tried to come back for you. If you think I'm going to let you come through that opening, you had better think again. Your body cannot handle it. Now, I have just one more order of business. You *will* wait, and then we'll be going somewhere together."

"And where will that be? I can't come there, and you can't come to 2014."

"A world where cowards don't exist, where silence is sovereign." She lowered her voice to a whisper. "I'm taking you away from all the hate, all the fickle vanity, all the misery."

"What if I don't want that? What if I don't want to leave? What if I don't believe you?"

"You have to believe me. You won't *want* to come back to this place."

The arguing continued, and Aaron took a moment to reassess his situation. He was facing onto the open recess from the same corner in which he'd previously seen Libby and Simon bound and gagged. They were lying behind him, along the southern wall.

He ran his gaze along the wall that held the portal, past the woman's looming figure, and to the corner opposite him. There, on the floor, stood three metal canisters. They hadn't been there when he'd made his journey to 2014. Next to the canisters, a clear plastic bag with something dark inside. Beyond these objects, a beige duffel bag, resting against the cave wall.

He shifted his head on the floor and ran his gaze past the objects in the corner and along the mottled rock surface opposite him. There were three men there, all sitting on the floor with their backs against the wall. The new man was busying himself with an arrow, running a flat rock up and down its black arrowhead. The other warrior who had previously gone back to retrieve Owen was sitting with his head lolled against the wall, his eyes closed, his hands dangling listlessly over his knees.

But it was the third man who made Aaron's skin crawl. *Him.* The Mohawk man's eyes were trained on him, a hint of a smile on his lips. He absently twirled a knife between two fingers, the same knife the woman had used to kill the police officer—and probably Gil. The Glock was lying on the ground near his feet. Libby's book bag was nowhere to be seen. Nor was Owen.

Owen.

Trying to ignore the Mohawk Man's watchful eyes, he lifted his head off the floor and looked over his shoulder. He could only see Libby's ponytail. He was tempted to make a sound to get her attention but decided he wasn't ready to draw more attention to himself. He wondered if he could signal her with his hands. But what would he even communicate?

He lowered his head to the floor, the muscles in his neck grateful for relief, and could soon hear the steady hum of the subterranean stream. But something was off—the hum was now the *only* sound he heard. He returned his attention to the portal. The woman and Hannah had stopped arguing; had stopped talking altogether. They were both staring at him.

In the next instant the woman was in front of him and lowered to her haunches. "You're invited to our conversation."

He could only blink.

"I know this is uncomfortable." She reached long fingers to the back of his neck, her cold touch prickling his skin. The gag fell loose.

He gasped.

"There, better?"

He coughed and drew deep breaths through his mouth, his stomach juices roiling from the built-up saliva that had slid down his throat. Something else slid down with it: shame. Simon and Libby were still gagged, and for how long he didn't know. He'd been traipsing through 2014, oblivious to their suffering, and now he was being given a reprieve, and they weren't.

"Please," he wheezed, "take their gags out too."

In answer, he received a playful slap on his cheek, which wasn't playful at all. "How sweet," she said.

"Leave him alone!" shouted a distant voice.

Aaron didn't know what she wanted with him. She'd gotten what she wanted—Hannah. He had no recourse. No plan. Nothing. Then the words came back—Dad's words. His husky voice was in his ear again, *"Sometimes it's the best plan when you don't have a plan."* Those endless games of hide-and-seek and Eye Spy at The Courts. All to waste time. All to ... *stall* for time. He considered again the writing in the sand: STALL 4 TIME. SV.

Stall for time. SV. Could it really be? *Sapere Verdere?* No, ghosts aren't real. *But could it be? Or maybe it's me? Maybe my future self wrote that message?* He didn't know who the author was, but there was no other plan. He needed to stall for time, and keeping her talking might be his only strategy left.

His voice feeling raw and thick, he said, "I thought we had an agreement. You said you'd make them go back." He nodded toward the men against the wall. At this gesture, the woman's attention was drawn to her men, and Aaron used the opportunity to look over at the portal. Hannah wasn't looking in the same direction as her mother, she was looking at him.

He held her eyes and then winked. He watched her.

Her nod was almost imperceptible, but it was there. Without taking her eyes off him, she said, "What have you done with his brother?"

The woman turned back to her daughter.

"He's fine. Better than ever, in fact. Mr Porter will be glad to know that I'm a woman of my word. He's fulfilled his end of the deal, and I'm nothing if not fair. After all, fairness is the reason I've gone to all of this trouble. So, now, I'll return his brother just as I said I would."

Aaron's pulse quickened. *Owen.*

"And, Mr Porter will be glad to know that I didn't harm a hair on his brother's head. Well, he doesn't exactly have hair anymore." She swept a hand over her own stubbled scalp. "It's quite liberating to part with one's hair. My men of course chose to incite the white man's anger by showing off their scalps, but my reasons for going bald were more pragmatic." She turned to Aaron. "Maybe you can ask your brother about his."

She rose and looked to the man closest to the portal who'd been sharpening the arrowhead. Without hesitation he set down his weapon, got to his feet, and approached the portal. Hannah took a few hesitant steps back as the man stepped through to join her in limbo.

"Don't worry, Sunshine. He won't bite."

Aaron watched the man stride past Hannah and into the swirling dusk. The woman turned back to him. "It won't take long," she said.

After a time, total darkness. The portal was gone, taking with it all its light. Aaron thought about Hannah. She would be alone and probably confused as she stared at nothing but a stoic crystal on the other side. Then the light increased again, and through the growing portal he could see Hannah staring back at him, concern etched on her face. She glanced over her shoulder and stepped aside. This time, she hadn't done so to allow a warrior to pass. She'd done so to let Owen pass.

***

The first thing Aaron noticed about his brother wasn't his bald scalp, which would have been startling had he not known to expect it. It was his eyes. Even in the low light, he could see Owen's eyes were dark and vacant, not the once bright and lively eyes always on the lookout for mischief. Owen's eyes were locked on a different kind of mischief now: the woman's own anemic eyes, which seemed to be summoning him forward.

Owen strode forward shirtless, his bare chest covered with zig-zagging black lines extending from armpit to armpit. The same pattern was visible on his forearms, reaching from wrist to elbow, making it look as if a pair of bear traps had been snapped shut over his arms, leaving behind darkened rumors of their machine-sharpened teeth.

He wore his Portage Falls athletic shorts, and his feet were covered by leathered moccasins, which barely made a sound on the cave floor. What Aaron saw in his brother was a chimeric mashup of the past and the present; a life once sanguine dressed in a dour costume; a cold and sudden transformation that felt no need to reveal its process or reason. His brother had gone somewhere, far away—for many weeks—and had returned as something else entirely.

Nevertheless, his heart pounding, Aaron found his voice. "Owen!"

The person who had once been his brother stiffened. He turned his head in that same slow mechanical manner as the woman. It was a gesture of mild curiosity, as if in response to the sound of a mouse scurrying behind a wall.

"Owen!" Aaron called again, his voice cracking. "Owen, it's Aaron! I knew you were alive!"

Owen turned, walked over to where he lay, and squatted to his haunches.

In response, Aaron labored to lift his head off the floor, his neck raw with pain, and strained to implore his brother with his eyes. "We have to tell Gram," he said. "She's a wreck right now. We have to—"

Owen flung his hands out.

Aaron flinched.

But Owen didn't strike him, he did something far worse. In silent dismay, Aaron could only watch as his older brother and protector reached to the base of his neck, grabbed the sodden cloth, and slid it back over his mouth. Then Owen reached to the back of his neck and tied the gag even tighter than it was before.

Aaron's mouth would have hung open in any case, but now it was stuck that way.

Owen rose to his feet and turned back to the woman.

Through his gag, Aaron screamed anything he could to wake Owen from his trance. And he wasn't the only one shouting. Libby's grunts of frustration were just as fruitless.

Owen stood still as a statue as the woman whispered instructions in his ear. When Libby's grunts died down, Aaron thought he heard the woman say something about keys in a bag and an ID. He then forced himself to concentrate on every word that came next, knowing any bit of information might be valuable, but he could only make out fragments because the woman had lowered her voice to match the growing silence.

He instead decided to focus on her moving lips, watching for the formation of words and phrases. He thought he saw, *The phone in the bag. Don't touch the screen. The clothes will be big. Parked at the edge of The Courts. Hopkins. Boarding pass saved as the background image. Infect check-in kiosks and then the security scanner.* And finally, *Board flight to Atlanta.*

Owen abruptly strode over to the far corner and scooped up the duffel and plastic bag. Inside the bag was an iPhone. Owen placed the plastic bag inside the duffel and slung the duffel over his shoulder. Then, without a glance or a word to anyone, he walked out of the recess and into the dark tunnel.

Chapter 32

Redemption

Aaron's head lay on the floor. All energy gone from his body.

Maybe this is my destiny.

Everyone around him went away. Maybe the universe was trying to end him all along, but was simply misfiring. He thought about Hannah, who he could now barely see through his welling eyes. If he were to die instead of her, then maybe the force that pulled all the strings would simply call things even and spare everyone else. He thought about Simon and Libby. They were now a part of his life's wreckage, too, weren't they? Why hadn't he talked Owen out of going to the mines that night? Why had he found the medallion at all? Why had some instinct directed him down Bernard Drive, under a gathering storm to find an object coveted by a killer? Why had any of this happened to *him*?

Yes, this is my destiny, and it has been all along.

And with any luck, his impending death would be a quick one — for he was surely about to die — along with his two friends. She would kill them, or maybe one of her men would do the honor.

As if in answer to these thoughts, the woman accepted the knife from the Mohawk Man and strode back over to Aaron. She squatted, and for the second time, untied his gag.

"Your brother may be done with you, but I'm not," she said, her thin lips twitching at their corners to stifle a smile. She studied him, twirling the knife between two fingers, as someone might twiddle a pencil while contemplating difficult arithmetic. "I need you to help me with my insurance policy. You're going to show me how this works." With her opposite hand, she pulled the medallion out from under her tank top. "I suggest you give the information freely, unless you'd like me to motivate you." She nodded in Libby and Simon's direction. "It's the only reason they're still alive. I'll let you decide who goes first."

Aaron just looked at her. He was done. All anger, all fear, all hope had left him. He was a shell. He looked at Hannah, as if she might be able to offer any semblance of help.

Hannah was watching him, despair making its way over her features. But then, something else began to surface. It was a look of growing determination, like what he'd seen before they'd made their journey into the complex.

She looked at her mother. "Why, Mom?" she asked. "Why the hell are you doing this? There has to be a reason, and it had better be a good one."

The woman stopped twirling the blade and turned toward the portal. She said, "I don't harm others without reason or cause. Mr Porter has an opportunity to not be harmed or *give* me cause. All he has to do is explain something."

"Explain what?" asked Hannah.

The woman ignored this and turned to Aaron. "I *do* know that you know how it works. In fact, you're probably the only one *alive* who does."

Aaron watched the woman. If he gave her the information, then there would be no reason for her to keep him or his friends alive. He knew she wouldn't let them live, despite her words to Hannah.

Stall for time.

He had to keep her talking and hope for a break. Finally, he asked, "What's Owen about to do?"

The woman shifted on her haunches.

"Mom, you'd better answer him," Hannah said.

Without taking her gaze off Aaron, the woman said, "Something heroic. A realignment of natural selection. He's a redeemer now."

Libby made a series of grunts that to Aaron sounded like, *"Is she insane?"*

The woman cast an eye toward Libby. "That's exactly what's wrong with this world. We reject that which we cannot understand. If we cannot like it, retweet it, or *cancel* it, then it doesn't matter. It's not real to us. But what Mr Porter's brother is about to do is very real."

"What exactly is he doing?" asked Aaron. "And what did you do to him?"

"I just told you. Now, you'll do the explaining."

"You'd better explain, Mom," Hannah said. "Or else I'm not going anywhere with you."

The woman dropped her gaze to the cave floor and began to carve shapes in the dust with the tip of the blade. "It's incredible that he crossed my path at all," she said absently. "And even stranger, is that his brother possessed the very object I sought to help retrieve my own daughter."

She looked up at Aaron. "Do you believe in fate, Mr Porter? Confluence? Because I don't. *It* knows all. *It* pulls the strings. And *It* pulled your brother to me."

She looked at Hannah. "When I returned to the quiet time to visit my men, I learned they had quite the surprise waiting for me: a young man. My men had told me that a white man had been spared by the underwater panther and had wandered south through the tunnel. You see, the name *Erie* comes from the word *Erielhonan*, meaning *long tail*, which the Erie tribes associated with the eastern cougar or panther. The Eries, who'd settled along the shores of Lake Erie, were known as the cat people, and even though my men's tribes had dominated them as they'd traveled west beyond the Western Door, they still couldn't help but become influenced by local lore and legend. Assimilation, you see, is a two-way street."

"But I knew better, especially after learning about the mine incident. There was a collapse during a night of irresponsible teenaged depravity—am I right, Mr Porter? It must have opened a hidden pocket near the shoreline once the aquifer drained into the mine. He somehow found an opening beyond the collapsed vein with just enough oxygen sifting out from the mines. It led to this very tunnel."

"He groped his way through darkness for miles before arriving here. And when he did, where do you think he chose to go? The blast happened at night. Had it been daytime, maybe he would have seen a faint light coming in from Mary Campbell's cave just a few hundred feet from where we are now. But he didn't. One of my men just so happened to be near the portal when he saw someone stagger past him on the other side. Mr Porter's brother had found his way inside the complex, the only source of light, and appeared to be exhausted, disoriented, and injured. He had a nasty gash on his shoulder but miraculously, nothing else."

"Seeing his physique, his apparent grit, and believing that he had the spirit of the underwater panther inside him, my men chose to take him in. They helped him make passage and took him back to the quiet time. They nursed him back to health. Mr Porter, you should be thanking them."

"But the best part of it is what happened to your brother when he traveled back. Yes, Mr Porter, you know what I speak of. It changed him, didn't it? It changes all of us. The further you go back and the longer you stay, the better you get. You see the truth in all things. The cellular structure of the world is revealed to you: its beauties, its intricacies, its mysteries. But so too are its flaws, particularly when you return to this modern shithole after a lengthy visit. I had been gone for years, living among the hearty ones and doing what I could to improve their odds against their oppressors. But when I came back, all I saw — and still continue to see—is a cesspool of human-shaped shit."

Hannah shook her head. "You've gone insane, Mom. I don't know what happened to you."

"Not insane. Enlightened. And speaking of enlightenment, it's time Mr Porter shows me how this works." She turned to him and extended the medallion. "And who knows, if you're helpful, I might just let you come with us. As for *her*, I can't make the same promise." She shifted and nodded in Libby's direction.

When she did this, Aaron caught a glimpse of Hannah. She was leaning closer to the portal, her brow furrowed.

He decided he had nothing to lose. Even if he had no idea what would be gained by drawing things out further, he had to try. The woman wanted Hannah to go with her, but Hannah was already doubtful. He had to drive that wedge between them deeper. He had to fully expose the woman. Show Hannah what she'd done. Turn daughter against mother. Hannah wouldn't back down to her mother. He saw that now. Maybe he could get Hannah angry enough to turn and leave. Return to 2014. She knew how to make passage now, and it would truly wreck the woman's plan. It was *his* only plan.

Stall for time.

"But, *Hannah* doesn't deserve this," he said, emphasizing her name. "*Hannah* didn't ask for this."

The woman's mouth twitched.

"You're a killer," he continued. "*Hannah's* mother is a tainted killer. No animal will come near you. I witnessed that myself just hours ago. Everything on four legs hightailed it out of the valley when you arrived. And why should *they* even continue to trust you?" He nodded toward the men. "You're tainted. Worse, you're a hypocrite. You say you don't harm others without cause. Bullshit. That cop at the marsh. Innocent. Didn't have to die. Gil and Connor? Didn't have to die either." He narrowed his eyes at her. "*Hannah's* mother is a hypocritical, tainted killer who harms innocent people. Innocent people like *Hannah*."

The blow to his right cheek forced his head to the ground. A gray fog began to spill into the corner of his right eye, as if the blow had released poisonous gas into his head. Then she was yanking the gag back up and over his mouth, cinching it tight at the back of his neck.

Her breath was heavy and ragged. "You've clearly made your choice. I tried. I really did. I don't prefer to harm others without cause—especially in front of my daughter—but now you've given me one."

Through the pain and the tears, he watched her slip the medallion back under her shirt. "I'll find another way." She then drew close to him, and in a whisper said, "In the meantime, I'm going to carve off that bitch's ears one at a time. And when I'm done with her, I'll cut the tongue out of that mouthy little shit over there. But first, I'm going to unzip that belly of yours."

She brought the knife up. This was the end. She was going to kill them all. He'd failed, and the person who was once Owen was going to do something awful to innocent people.

Then, movement in his periphery. From the portal.

Chapter 33

Strangers and Impostors

Aaron's muffled screams and widening eyes must have looked perfectly natural given his current predicament, because the woman didn't turn to follow his gaze and watch Hannah step through the portal and into 2021. Instead, she was pressing the tip of the blade into his abdomen, muttering words through gritted teeth he couldn't understand.

Hannah now stood a few feet from the portal, swaying on her feet and hugging her shoulders as if she'd swallowed a bottle of pills and was bracing for their inevitable effects.

The warriors had gotten up, clearly aware of what was happening.

That's when Hannah doubled over and fell to the floor.

"Hannah!" Aaron screamed through the gag.

The woman didn't respond.

He bore his eyes into hers. "Hannah!" he screamed again and darted his eyes over to where she was writhing on the ground.

The man who'd been sharpening the arrowhead was now kneeling beside her. He slid over to the top of her head, gripped her from under her armpits, and nodded to the other men. The pipe-smoking man from Aaron's vision came over and took her ankles. Together, the men hoisted her off the ground.

The woman didn't register any of this. It wasn't until the Mohawk Man approached her from behind and jostled her shoulder that she was wrested from her trance.

She whirled and then gasped. Seconds later she was with the two men who were fighting to control Hannah's contorting body.

Blood was spilling from Hannah's nose, her ears, and the corners of her eyes, which were rolled back in their sockets.

"Get her through!" The woman shrieked.

The men hoisted her higher, and together they hauled Hannah spasming and face down to the portal.

Something red and fibrous dropped from her mouth and splatted to the cave floor. Then another glob dropped. Then another.

The woman screamed something incoherent as the men awkwardly angled Hannah through the opening. Then she was on the floor on the other side, obscured from view.

The Mohawk Man, still standing in the recess, peered through the opening, seemingly unsure of what to do next.

Then Aaron heard something else. It sounded like a person wheezing. It was coming from the outer tunnel. Getting closer. Soon, a series of shuffles. Getting closer. Was it Owen? Was he coming back? Maybe the effects had worn off faster than the woman had expected. The wheezing grew louder still, as did the shuffling.

He returned his attention to the portal. The Mohawk Man either didn't hear the sound or didn't think it merited attention.

Then the figure was in the recess, the shuffling growing quieter, the wheezing shallower and more controlled.

Aaron tucked his chin to see if he could catch a glimpse of the figure, but the figure remained outside his periphery.

Then they were immediately behind him, causing the hairs on the back of his neck to stir. Ragged wheezing in his ear. A mixture of earth, blood, and vomit filling his nose. But there was something else in this person's scent—something vaguely familiar. The person didn't say anything, but Aaron could feel his bindings being loosened by shaky hands. He didn't make a sound, not wanting the Mohawk Man to turn from the portal and notice what was happening.

The hands became clumsier as they fumbled with the bindings. But sensation eventually began to creep back into Aaron's wrists. The person let go of the bindings, apparently deciding they were loose enough. What happened next was something Aaron wouldn't understand until much later. Trembling fingers found his left hand and pressed something smooth and rubbery into his palm. He closed his fingers around the tube-like object, feeling it squish in his grip.

The scuffling steps sounded again, louder now. The person had stood and was now crossing to the middle of the recess, their labored breathing increasing. It was as if they were less concerned about being heard.

The Mohawk Man slowly turned to face the stranger.

Another sound cut the air. It was a cold sound that Aaron had become all too familiar with in the span of just a few hours: the cocking of a gun.

***

Unable to see the figure, Aaron had to settle for the reaction of the Mohawk Man, who was raising his hands and backing into the opposite corner. He opened his mouth as if to speak, but then seemed to think better of it and closed it.

Aaron twisted his wrists against the bindings, testing their firmness. They were looser, but he guessed it would still take him several minutes to free himself. He looked over at the portal. The woman was hunched over Hannah's unseen body. Only one of the other men could be seen through the opening. His shoulders were slumped, and he was looking away.

Hannah, no. Please don't be dead.

The woman glanced up, through the portal, apparently having noticed something had changed on the other side.

Aaron's heart skipped a beat when those dead eyes found his.

She gritted her teeth and rocketed to her feet. In the next instant, she was through the portal, the knife's hilt clenched so tight in her hand that the flesh around it was whitening.

"You did this," she snarled.

The crack of the gunshot reverberated in the small space. Aaron's head jerked at the report. Sharp dust particles entered his eyes, which he'd squeezed shut a little too late. The dust stinging. The flash rendering a whitewash behind his eyelids. But he couldn't keep his eyes closed. He had to locate the monster with the knife.

He didn't have to look far. Through the retreating dust cloud, there she was, lying a couple feet from the portal, her left leg bent at an awkward angle, blood darkening the floor beneath her. The Mohawk Man was still in the corner, his shoulders tensed, his face angled away.

The woman lifted herself to her elbows, twisted, and craned her neck to inspect the wound. She looked like a snake that had been caught by its tail. Her face was impassive as she calculated the damage.

Easing her good leg underneath her, she rose to one knee until she was nearly on all fours. She looked out at her attacker and studied them behind that same mask of indifference.

"You don't have much time," she said. "Look at you. You're dead on your feet."

No reply, only more strained breathing.

Then, recognition surfaced on the woman's face. "I know you," she said. "The Le Griffon. That's it. Yes, it was *you* in the passageway. But I watched you die. Saw the blood. Nobody could've survived that throw." She then cocked her head. "Unless ... you're a hell of an actor. Which I suppose you are. You were after it too, weren't you? Did our little boarding party ruin your plans? Were you not ready to break cover and take it from that little bitch? How you made it off the boat before that last wave hit had to have been a miracle." She flashed a crooked grin. "Well, you'll be glad to know I'm wearing the prize you so clearly failed to retrieve. Want to see it?"

Aaron's attention went to her right hand, which was hovering above the ground, not supporting her weight, but giving the illusion of doing so.

No.

He looked past her hand to her right knee, which he also knew wasn't just supporting her body; it was obscuring what lay beyond it. *The knife.* It had to be on the other side of her because it was nowhere else to be seen.

He'd gone silent on the bridge when she'd thrown the knife at the police officer. He wouldn't make the same mistake now.

"Knife!" he screamed, but it came out muffled.

The woman turned her attention to him, her smile growing, stirring awful movements all over her face. The fingers of her right hand twitched.

Without taking her eyes off him, she shot her hand to her knee, grabbed the knife, and—

Crack. The gunshot's report shook Aaron's insides. More dust. But he'd kept his eyes open—he couldn't lose sight of her.

She was right where she'd been kneeling moments prior, but lying on her side. Her dead eyes were truly dead now, open and looking out to some unknowable place. The scar on her neck had been torn open at its center, the gaping hole singed at its edges from the heat of the bullet. Dark blood pouring out. Her right hand was outstretched on the ground as if groping for a light switch in the dark. The knife lay just inches from her fingers.

He exhaled deeply.

The figure came forward in the recess but stopped again— still out of view.

Then another movement, this time in the opposite corner. The Mohawk Man was turning from the corner to face the stranger. He looked at the figure, then at the portal, then back at the figure. He shook his head, brought a hand to his temple, and formed the shape of a gun with his forefinger and thumb. And when he opened his mouth this time, words came out.

"Just fuckin' do it, man," he said.

Aaron wasn't sure if he was hearing things or simply delirious from the day's events. But the foreboding figure from his vision, the man who wore another man's scalp under his belt like some used dishrag, continued in perfect Midwestern English, "What are you waiting for? Pull the fuckin' trigger, man."

No reply.

The Mohawk Man shook his head, his eyes pleading. "I'm telling you, man. I'm done with this shit. There ain't nowhere else to go. Do it!"

The gunshot made the Mohawk Man's head snap back. Brain matter, bone and blood, all looking the same color in the twilight, rocketed from the back of his head and onto the cave wall. The matter began to slide down the wall, and with it, the Mohawk Man's lifeless body, which sat down and tipped over. Then he was lying on the ground to the right of the portal much in the same manner as the woman to its left.

The sight of the bodies made Aaron think of the two mutilated statues within the complex. Now there were two broken figures framing its outer entrance.

He looked to the portal to find the other men within. They were hazy shadows now, retreating into the murk. Leaving. Silence enveloped the recess, the only sound the person's ragged wheezing. Then, the space went dark. There came a soft rustling of fabric. Aaron guessed that the figure was making some kind of adjustment to their attire, but couldn't be sure. He flashed on the woman's words, *"You don't have much time."*

After a couple minutes, the portal opened again. The figure came scuffling into view: a slouching shape, lost inside an oversized gray trench coat with its collar upturned. The figure's head was covered by a hoodie sweatshirt they wore underneath their coat, and their face was angled away.

The figure stepped to the base of the portal, hesitated, and lifted a heavy boot over the portal's lower lip. Halfway through the opening, the figure paused, lowered their gloved right hand, and let Gil's gun clunk gently to the floor. Then, the figure didn't just step through the opening, they fell through, crashing to all fours on the opposite side. There, they remained for a long time, their body rising and falling in rhythm with Aaron's pounding heart.

Are they looking at Hannah's body? Aaron wondered. *Is she truly dead?*

The figure rose to their feet and staggered forward into the purple dusk. But to Aaron, it looked as if their movements had become less labored once inside. Then they were gone from sight.

Chapter 34

In Pursuit

Then it was just the three of them, bound on the floor a few feet from the corpses of killers. Releasing the object that had been pressed into his hand, Aaron began to furiously pull at the loosened bindings about his wrists.

He dug into the ropes with his fingertips. Moments later, the bindings fell loose. Rolling onto his side, he pulled his hands free, yanked the gag from his mouth, and shouted, "Hang on!" He army-crawled over to Libby, not bothering to undo his ankles. He unknotted her gag and pulled it from her mouth. "You okay?"

She coughed in response.

He then wriggled over to Simon, whose hair was plastered to his forehead in sweaty ringlets. He undid his gag.

Simon gasped and wheezed. "The shit ... you got us into ... Porter."

Libby coughed and cleared her throat. "Aaron, there might still be time to stop Owen. But we gotta go, now."

He knew she was right. But stop him from *what*? And *how*? They had no phones. There wasn't anywhere nearby where they could use someone else's phone or even get help. They didn't have a car or transportation of any kind and the only way out of the cave and the valley was on foot. He crawled back to Libby and started tugging at her bindings. The thought of transportation nagged at him.

"She said something about Hopkins airport," he said. "How's Owen getting there?"

"Gil's Jeep," she said. "I saw what she said to Owen too. Read her lips. Said it'd be parked at the edge of The Courts. Plus, think about it. How'd she and her men get here so fast?

They drove to The Courts and parked there, Aaron. The Sand Run Caves parking lot has been gated off for years. That leaves your Gram's neighborhood, which has the closest streets for someone to park their car and hike to the caves."

He nodded. If that was the case, then Owen would be within spitting distance of The Courts by now—if he ran. Aaron hoped that his brother, who ran like a gazelle, didn't run. He might be at the Jeep already. But why would Owen run? Maybe to make a tight boarding time?

"How much time do you think we have?" he asked.

"If he's going to do something *heroic* before boarding his flight," Libby said, "then I doubt the bitch would've cut things really close. But who knows? Either way, we've gotta move."

"How's he going to *infect* kiosks and a scanner?" Aaron asked as he continued working on Libby's restraints. "You heard— saw—that too, right? I don't understand."

"Yes, I saw it. And I don't know, but I think it has to do with that phone she gave him. The phone was sealed inside one of those thick plastic freezer bags. She also told him to not touch the screen. No idea what that means, but tampering with public machines like that ... think about how many people come and go through that airport."

"And he's going to Atlanta," Aaron said absently.

Libby nodded. "One of the biggest travel hubs in the world."

Aaron considered what other possible motives Owen would have to hasten things. Anyone who could've stopped him was already tied up and not a threat. Or was there a threat? He thought of the stranger who'd just prevented their deaths and left them the gun. Could this person have encountered Owen? Stopped him even?

Then there was the object that had been pressed into Aaron's hand. He looked at the spot on the floor where he'd set it down. It looked how it felt: a section of black rubber tubing, about three inches long and an inch thick. He had no idea what it was, no less its significance.

He returned his attention to Libby's restraints and gave them another sharp tug. He wasn't getting anywhere with them—at least not fast enough. The stranger must have been strong to loosen these bindings, sick as they were.

They were sick.

"The knife," Libby said.

He looked over at the dead woman, half expecting her to be standing and ready to sling the knife at him. But she was as dead as before. He crawled on raw elbows over to where the knife lay. Ignoring her unseeing eyes, he grabbed the knife and turned away. The knife felt heavy in his hand as he rolled to a seated position. He used it to saw the bindings at his ankles.

When they fell away, he rose to his feet, wincing from his cramping legs, and crossed the space to Libby. He knelt and began to saw the ropes at her wrists. When they splintered away, he moved on to her ankles and repeated.

He went to Simon but paused.

"Aaron, please explain," Libby said, laboring to her feet.

Simon added, "Porter, I get I'm a pain in the ass…"

"No, that's not it," Aaron said, turning to Libby. "Here, cut him loose. I need to—"

"Oh, hell no, you're not. You're not going in there, Aaron. You won't like what you see. *Please* don't. We have to leave!"

"It'll just take a second," he said. "Just work on Simon."

Libby sighed and accepted the knife.

Feeling light-headed, he slowly walked to the portal. Two feet from the opening, he paused. Hannah's outstretched arm was visible on the other side. Like her mother, she was reaching out to some unseen person or place. But her arm wasn't solid; it looked like footage from an old grainy film. As he watched, the buzzing particles grew more disorganized, and he wondered if Hannah would dissolve entirely. He didn't want to see more but felt he had too. He had to see her face, or what was left of it.

He took a tentative step forward. A hand gripped his shoulder.

"Aaron, please," Libby whispered.

He glanced over his shoulder. "I owe her that much, Libby."

"Aaron, there's gonna be a whole lot of people who get hurt or worse if we don't stop Owen—*including* Owen."

Aaron looked down, his shoulder sagging under her grip.

"Let me look instead," she said.

Before he could protest, she was past him and peering through the opening. Her body tensed. When she turned back to him her skin was ashen, her eyes downcast. "She's gone, Aaron. I'm sorry."

He knew it was true even before she looked. He stuffed his hands into his pockets. He'd given Hannah something he didn't think he had to give. And she'd given back. She'd opened herself up to him. This jaded girl who'd erected walls around herself had opened a window for him to peer through. And through that window, he'd glimpsed something beautiful. Something fragile. And now she was dead. He'd brought her to this end. That little flame had been extinguished, and he'd been the one to do it.

The heat rushed into his cheeks and into his eyes. Then the tears came. He didn't fight them. He was too exhausted and overwhelmed to care anymore. Libby was on him, murmuring in his ear. He hugged her back. Then he was sobbing into the crook of her neck. She didn't rush him but just held him there, letting his grief have its way.

When his hitching breaths slowed after what might have been thirty seconds or five minutes, she whispered into his ear, "It's not your fault, Aaron. She knew what she was doing." Then, with a tinge of guilt in her voice, she added, "Simon messed up his ankle. He's in rough shape. We need to get going."

Aaron rubbed at his eyes and turned to see Simon leaning against the cave wall, all of his weight resting on his left foot, his arms folded over his chest.

"Looks like you're not finished carrying me, Porter."

Aaron blew out a hot breath and looked back once more.

I'm so sorry, Hannah. If I could undo it—

He frowned. Could he undo it somehow?

As if reading his thoughts, Libby said, "Aaron, she's gone. I don't know how any of this voodoo works down here, but you *can't* bring her back. Dead is dead. Maybe she was meant to die all along. Maybe the past doesn't want to be changed. And maybe she knew that."

Aaron nodded weakly. The word *voodoo* gave clarity to a thought that had been caught in a fog in his brain. "Fine," he murmured as he swiped another tear from his cheek, "but she's still wearing the medallion." He nodded at Hannah's dead mother, who was separated from her daughter by a mere five feet—but still a world away. "She doesn't get to keep it."

In answer, Libby strode over to the dead woman, hooked her fingers under the string at the back of her neck, and gave it a vicious yank. The woman's head bobbed.

Aaron reflexively retreated a step.

The medallion came loose, and Libby tossed it to Aaron as someone might lob a set of car keys. "I'd say you have enough pocket room. Ready?"

Aaron went over to Simon. "Let's do piggyback this time. I don't think my shoulder can handle another fireman carry."

"Oh, forgot," Libby said, trotting over to the portal. She bent and grabbed the Glock.

A moment later, they were in the darkness of the outer tunnel.

"Damn, forgot how dark it was in here," Libby said. "Would've been nice of them to leave us our flashlights. And I should've checked how many rounds we have left. Can't be many. How long till we get outta here, Aaron? Aaron? Why are you looking at me like that?"

"Sorry. Just wondering what happened when I was gone. You had the gun on her. How?"

Libby exhaled. "I know. That third man was out here in the tunnel, apparently, some kind of lookout. Never saw him coming."

Aaron shook his head. "I'm sorry. I really didn't—"

"Save it. We're fine. Now, what's next?"

Aaron nodded in the direction they were walking. "Dead ahead. See the daylight coming in from above?"

Simon squirmed on his back. "You're kidding me, Porter, right? How the hell are we gonna get up that rock pile, no less catch up to your suddenly bat-shit crazy brother?"

Aaron knew he was right. Assuming the pile hadn't changed over the past few years, it would be slow going—even without Simon on his back. He made a decision then, one he hoped he wouldn't regret. He didn't want to put his friends in any more danger than he already had, but there was no way around it. Libby had been right. If what the woman said about Owen's mission was true, then many more people would soon be in danger.

"Libby, you gotta go after him," he said. "You're the fastest. You know how to..." he trailed off, not wanting to say, "use a gun," not wanting to acknowledge that it might come to her having to shoot his only brother; not wanting to consider any of it after Owen had just miraculously resurfaced in his life ... like some cruel joke.

Libby didn't reply right away. Her shoulders were tensed. Fear was making its mad dash through her body. Finally, she said: "Aaron, I don't know that I—"

"You said it yourself. Hannah didn't deserve to die. But if you don't catch up to him, *many more* could. By the time we get to my Gram's house and call the police it might be too late. Plus,

I don't know how we'd explain any of this in time to stop him. And, even if the police intervene, Owen might fight back, and they'll kill him anyway. He didn't deserve any of this either. He's not himself."

Libby's stride was becoming more confident, more resolute. "Okay," she said, "but where exactly are we? How do I get to The Courts?"

He explained what she'd encounter above and what he figured would be the fastest way to the Towpath. He described the hidden trail that led up to The Courts, which could be a difference-maker if Owen walked instead of ran and chose to use the switchback. Aaron thought he would.

Libby nodded as they squished through a stretch of black mire near the base of the rock pile. "Okay, anything else?" she asked.

He didn't answer right away, his attention on the finger of light illuminating the rock pile; the dark trace crawling through it. The footpath was still there.

"No," he said, "but if you do catch him, keep your distance. Don't let him touch you."

Libby was picking her way between the rocks before he could say more. He and Simon watched as she slipped in and out of craggy shapes. Then she was gone from sight for at least five minutes before emerging again at the top of the pile as a silhouette. A moment later, she was gone, stealing into the pale light.

"Think she'll catch him?" Simon asked.

"I honestly don't know," Aaron said. Part of him wasn't sure he wanted her to. He'd be lying to himself if he didn't fear for Libby more than he did for Owen, who might react like a cornered animal. There was no telling what he might do.

Aaron and Simon labored up the path, which hadn't changed since 2014. It was a victory in that he knew which parts to avoid—especially the jutting rock on which he'd banged his knee before—but a small victory at that. The climb was long and arduous, and Simon began to use a free hand to help them gain purchase on the slick rock surfaces.

Halfway up, the space around them brightening with barbs of daylight, Aaron began to smell something he didn't recall smelling in 2014. It smelled of ripe decay, and it was growing stronger with each step. They continued, pausing every few minutes so he could gather his breath and wipe the sweat from his forehead. The stench grew stronger still. When they arrived within ten feet of the summit, something caught his eye. What he saw made his mouth go dry.

A few feet to his left, just below eye level and partially visible inside a hollow among the massive rocks, was the red rubber sole of a shoe. It was a Lebron James basketball sneaker, lolled to the side, making visible the Nike swoosh near its heel, and Aaron knew only one person who wore that exact same style. From within the shoe extended a white ankle sock and a stretch of pale skin, which ended abruptly in a tormented stump, raw and dark at its edges. The severed ankle was leaning against a thicket of hair, the tops of its curls kissed by the partial light.

Aaron had seen his fair share of trash. And what lay hacked apart and stuffed into the hole looked like someone's idea of it. The flies buzzing in and out of Connor Littlefield's remains were all too happy to agree.

Aaron coughed as bile rose into his throat.

"Dude, you okay?" Simon asked, his view of the hole obscured by Aaron's head and the way in which Aaron had instinctively angled himself in the other direction.

Aaron coughed again and wondered if Libby had glimpsed this horror on her way up or if she'd been going too fast to notice. He hoped for the latter and decided that no one else should see this, including Simon.

"Yeah, just need a breather," he replied.

"Same here," Simon said, "but for another reason. It smells like something died down here."

Aaron pointed up to the light, hoping to draw Simon's attention elsewhere. "Check it out," he said, dully, "almost there."

"'Bout damned time."

He averted his eyes to the hollow and side-stepped past it, ensuring Simon's view remained obstructed until they were safely away. They summited the rock pile five minutes later, and, from within the small chamber, he hoisted Simon up and through the crevasse. He followed, skidding down the sloped sandstone wall—now more practiced—and came to rest next to Simon in Mary Campbell's cave. Simon stood gingerly and dusted himself off. He tried putting weight on his ankle and found he could, but still winced after taking a couple tentative steps.

"Hang on," Aaron said. He trotted out of the cave and into the dusk of 2021. It didn't take him long to find a sturdy branch near the base of a large oak. Soon, Simon was hobbling at his side with his makeshift cane down the steep trail and into the failing light of the present.

Chapter 35

Creature

Chest pounding, Libby raced up the Towpath. Trees whisked past, their trunks blotted with lichen, making them look as if they'd been sickened by the day's rain. When she'd first emerged from Mary Campbell's cave and onto the cliffside trace overlooking the gorge, she'd half-expected it to be night—she'd been underground for so long. But to her surprise and relief, a sliver of sun still peeked above the horizon.

Now, she'd have to use every last bit of it. And so she ran, eating up as much distance as her long strides would allow, the Glock bouncing at her waist. She'd double-checked that the gun's safety was on before setting out, but her strides were still tentative. She couldn't afford tentative, so she slowed, yanked the gun from her waist, and accelerated onward, gun in hand.

Aaron had explained how the two paths leading up to The Courts would be about thirty minutes north on foot, but she figured he'd be thinking in terms of walking, not all-out sprinting. Ten minutes into her run, she cut her pace and began scanning the hillside to her right. She'd never descended into the valley from The Courts, and so had no frame of reference aside from Aaron's descriptions. She was to first look for a zig-zagging path up the hillside, which would be smooth and wide enough for a person to walk a bicycle. And a few hundred feet after that, she was to locate a smaller and more overgrown footpath. That would be the one to take.

But she saw nothing but reed-filled gullies along the path. She pushed on at a little more than a jog, scanning, searching. At one point, she stopped, thinking she'd found it, but it was just a shadow cast by a large maple on the other side of the Towpath.

She ran on, the gullies becoming more barren, stretches of swaying reeds and foxtail giving way to beds of stony aggregate. Then, a small section of raised earth extending from the Towpath to the eastern hillside. It looked like a manmade land bridge. A curved metal lip poked from beneath the landfill, creating a tiny culvert for storm water to pass through. She'd found the first trail.

She trotted past the path, noting how much it matched Aaron's description; how it cut its way up the hillside in a series of tight switchbacks. She went on, surveying a slope crowded with trees, dense brush, leaves, and long shadows. A tiny footpath would be like a needle in a haystack. She decided to focus her attention on the draw to her right, which was becoming shallower and less rocky, as if consigning itself back to nature. Then, a thin slip of uninterrupted dirt, just visible beyond a cluster of goldenrod. The overgrown trail dipped from the Towpath and faded into the brush. She could see why the trail wasn't well known. She'd have missed it walking—no less running—had she not known to look for it. She quit the Towpath and took the tiny trail into the brush.

The trail steepened in a hurry, and she stuffed the Glock back into her waistband to free up her hands. She groped for branches and jutting roots as she climbed, pausing every few minutes to listen. Nothing but the gentle rustling of leaves in response to the western wind. The silence felt heavy and pregnant, as if the trees were holding their breath. She was in a place where chittering birds and scurrying rodents should be joining with the leaves to create a bustling evening chorus. Except nothing was bustling save for her heart.

Then, a gentle *thunk*, barely audible, but loud enough to make her drop into a squat. She flung her arms around a tree trunk to avoid a hillside tumble.

A distant *clang*.

She waited, her pulse hurrying. Nothing. Drawing a deep breath, she willed her heart to slow. She crept up the trail in a bear crawl now, hoping the crinkling leaves beneath her palms and feet weren't as noisy as she feared they were; telling herself she'd grab the gun once the trail leveled out near the top. But the black Jeep's bumper came into view before that would happen. The vehicle was backed up to the edge of the ravine about thirty feet up and just as far to the right.

He *was* here. But the question was for how long. Conventional wisdom suggested she confront him while she still had the element of surprise, but the thought of it made her chest heavy. She wasn't afraid to stand up for herself—never had been—but that still didn't make this any easier. She'd seen the emptiness in Owen's eyes when he'd stepped through the portal before re-gagging his only brother. His face had been a closed door, his bearing animalistic. She'd have to play this right.

She crept higher up the path and squatted again. The Jeep was now visible in profile, its front grill slightly angled toward her. The hood was propped up, and there he was, wearing an oversized navy button-down shirt and wrinkled khakis. His back was to her, and he was bent over the engine block.

She remained in a squat, watching through gaps in the trees while he busied himself with something under the hood. After a moment of rummaging, he stood.

She gasped. His head and neck were pale green. He hadn't looked that way when they'd been underground, bathed in that odd purple light. He was lifting a softball-sized hunk of metal from the engine block. She thought it was the alternator. He scrutinized it before tossing it aside. He bent again, and this time came up with a handful of loose cables and hoses. He inspected them with an air of detachment and let them drop to the ground.

Someone had sabotaged the Jeep. Libby didn't have to guess who it was. While she hadn't gotten a good look at the person who'd intervened on their behalf outside the portal, she'd seen the section of hose they'd given to Aaron. She hadn't known what it was then, but she knew what it was now. A message. *You are not alone.*

Buoyed by this thought, she rose and pulled the gun. Owen had been expecting the Jeep to be his vehicle, and now he'd have to devise a Plan B. She'd stop him before he ever got the chance.

***

Staying low, she slipped from tree to tree, keeping the Jeep at her right. Movement caught her eye. She flattened herself behind the trunk of a narrow beech tree. She looked.

Owen was stepping away from the vehicle. He paused and put his hands on his hips and cocked his head. He stayed in that position for at least two minutes, didn't so much as move a muscle. It was as if he'd been petrified.

She remained just as still.

Then, without warning, he stepped forward, pulled down the metal rod that had been propping up the hood and let the hood clang shut.

She leaned back behind the tree trunk, swiped a bead of sweat from her forehead. She took a breath, realizing she'd been holding it.

What the hell was that? What the hell was ... he?

She peered around the trunk again.

He was now at the rear passenger door nearest her. He flung the door open, bent, and grabbed something. A moment later, he rose with the duffel the woman had given him and slung it over his shoulder. Something else was in his hand: the plastic bag with the phone. He held the bag to his face. A small smile creased his lips as he studied the phone in the bag. It was as if he were admiring one of his football trophies.

He then closed the door and went around the rear of the Jeep and began to shuffle sideways along the vehicle's back bumper at the edge of the ravine. The decision was a bizarre one. Why not go around the front of the vehicle where there was more room? Arriving on the other side, he opened the opposite rear passenger door. Through the window, she saw him bend to retrieve something unseen in the footwell. This was also odd. Why hadn't he gotten whatever it was when he'd been leaning into the backseat from the other side? Maybe it was a heavy object and he needed better leverage to lift it?

She decided it was fruitless to try to understand his actions. The Jeep was between her and him now. This was her chance. She drew the gun, and, watching her step, hurried in a circuitous route until she was at the edge of the clearing, the outfield of The Courts. This was what she wanted. There were less leaves and twigs to crunch over here, and she was in front of the Jeep now with her back to the open field, barring Owen's escape into the neighborhood. *Into civilization.*

From here, she could see the right rear passenger door hanging ajar. His brown loafers, the bottoms of his khakis, and the duffel bag were visible from underneath the door. But the feet weren't moving. What was he doing? Had he gone still again?

She decided it didn't matter. He would be vulnerable while facing into the vehicle and there wouldn't be a better chance. She thought about calling out to him but then thought better of it, deciding that it would only forewarn someone who could run like a deer and would have plenty of forest to disappear into.

She rounded the Jeep in a wide arc, gun trained on the open door. The field at her back. Her heart thundered with each soft step. She prayed a twig wouldn't pop under foot. Still no movement. No swishing of fabric. No shuffling of feet. Something pinged her insides like a chiming bell, but it was faint. She knew her subconscious was having second thoughts. *Go to hell*, she imagined herself telling it. The opening into the backseat was almost in full view now. She steeled herself. *Here we go.* She exploded forward, arms rigid, gun pointed.

Her breath caught. *No one.* No one was there. It was as if he'd vanished. Her mind raced, wanting to reject the scene in front of her. But it couldn't. The khakis were there, draped over the edge of the backseat. She ran her eyes down the slacks, pushing down panic but failing, seeing how the bottoms of the leg openings had been carefully fitted overtop the shoes. Her legs buckled. She swallowed and slowly turned her head, not wanting to see who she knew was behind her; not wanting to see who had waited for her to make a foolish mistake—which she now had.

He stood at an angle a few paces away, his untucked shirt falling to mid-thigh, his bare legs a sickly green. But she was only dimly aware of his clothing—or lack thereof. In his right hand, pinched between two fingers, was the plastic bag with the infected phone. Yet, as alarming as that was, it was his other hand that stole her focus. His left arm was cocked back, and in his left hand, the alternator. He was gripping it like a football.

Paralysis overtook her. Her head was turned in his direction, but everything else—including the gun—was pointed toward the Jeep. If she were to whirl and point the gun and fire, it would be too late. At five or so feet, he couldn't miss. The large chunk of metal could strike her in the head or the chest—it didn't matter. The only thing that mattered was that he'd get to her first and then would get away.

Oh, god, Aaron, where are you?

There would be no help, at least not in time to make a difference. She willed herself to focus. He could have already thrown the alternator but hadn't. Maybe he was struggling? Maybe there was a war being fought inside his head? Maybe she could use that to stall him? In a small, trembling voice, she said, "Owen, I know you're not a killer. You haven't hurt anybody. You can stop this now."

He didn't reply. Instead, he cocked his head, the abrupt movement more feline than human. The pupils of his green eyes were dilated and unfocused. It was as if he were neither looking at her nor away from her. He was looking *through* her. But he still hadn't thrown the alternator.

She forged ahead. "Owen, just set it down. That's all you have to—"

"They taught me how to walk," he said, his voice both quiet and hoarse.

What?

But she didn't have time to consider his words further because his arm jerked back. In the next instant, the alternator was growing in her field of vision.

Reflex took over. She twisted and brought the gun around. The gun was almost pointed at him when the chunk of metal slammed into her shoulder, the impact rattling her teeth and every bone in her body. She fired, cutting the air with a sharp CRACK.

Then she was reeling backward. Searing pain was racing through her, the gun floating from her hand. She couldn't watch where it would fall into the brush because she was staggering now, giving ground. In her periphery, she could see him coming forward to claim it.

Then she was on her back. The world was spinning, her shoulder feeling as if it was the only thing existing. Tears stung her eyes. She had missed him with her shot, because here he was now, standing over her. She blinked away the tears and tried to scream, but all that came out was a cracking moan.

He then left her field of vision, which was now growing fuzzy at its edges, and returned a moment later, holding that same hulking metal object in one hand. He dropped to his knees beside her, clasped the object in both hands, and brought it over his head.

In that moment her eyes found his vacated pupils. There was nothing there. A perfect void, a barren waste from which nothing could escape. He was going to bash her skull in.

She tried to scream again, and this time her voice seemed to work. But the guttural howl that leaped from her mouth was all wrong. It seemed to come from somewhere else—from someone else. In her daze, she didn't realize it wasn't her scream at all.

Then Owen was no longer kneeling next to her. There came a thud, followed by a grunt, and a sharp intake of air. Then a series of more thuds. Her head lulled to the side, toward the direction of the open field and the commotion, registering two forms grappling on the ground.

Chapter 36

Brothers

The trip up the Towpath had gone quicker than Aaron had expected, Simon having found his hobble-walking rhythm on his makeshift crutch. Now, just a few feet up the switchback trail—the only option for Simon to scale the hillside—Aaron wished he had a zipper for his friend's mouth. He thought he'd heard the sound of a distant car door banging shut but couldn't be sure because Simon's second wind was issuing from his mouth.

"Shhhh," he hissed, and raised a finger to his lips.

Simon gave an annoyed look but grew quiet.

Another sound echoed down the hill. This time, it sounded more like a dull *pop*. In his mind's eye, Aaron imagined a door handle being engaged, its inner mechanisms popping out of place to allow the door to swing open.

"Sounds like a car door," Simon whispered.

Aaron nodded and ran his gaze up the hillside and back down to where Simon stood supporting himself with the stick. It would take forever to scale the hill.

Simon, apparently noticing the concern on his face, said, "Just go, Porter. Stop dickin' around with me. I'll be fine."

A distant *clang* sounded. Aaron didn't pause this time to listen further. He ran.

***

Ten minutes later, he slowed and bent, his chest heaving. The number of steps it took to ascend the switchback had to at least double that of the small footpath. But it couldn't be helped now. Or could it? He put his hands on his hips and lifted his gaze up the hillside, ignoring for the moment the zig-zagging trail that sliced it at intervals ranging from ten feet to forty feet depending on the trail's slope and direction. The vegetation was dark and dense in the untamed spaces between the passes, but not impenetrable. He would have to scale the small but steep embankments along the path where it cut into the hillside, but there were plenty of trees and roots to grab onto.

He backed up to get a running start and exploded forward, leaping up the first of what he knew would be several embankments. He grabbed a gnarled root and hoisted himself up and into the scrub. Chest hammering, he scrambled up the section of forest in a bear crawl, branches whipping his shoulders and back, matted leaves crackling under his hands, until he reached the next section of trail. There, he repeated the same run-and-jump maneuver and was up and into the next untamed section.

He repeated three more times. When he burst onto the trail again, he paused, noticing that something was different here. The faint light above—modest as it was—wasn't right. It was interrupted somehow, as if a gnat had been caught in his eye and was blotting out a small but noticeable part of his vision.

To his left. He looked. The Jeep was backed up near the edge of the ravine and set at an angle. The door to the rear passenger-side seat facing him hung open, but he couldn't see into the vehicle from where he stood.

There came a crunching of leaves. Footfalls, urgent, coming from somewhere beyond the vehicle. Then abrupt silence. What he heard next made his heart skip a beat. A voice, quiet but unmistakable, uttered something about learning to walk.

Owen.

A gunshot ripped the air.

Aaron's body was in chaotic motion then. He no longer had the presence of mind to calculate his next steps—where they took him, the scene he'd stumble into, the danger he'd find. His mind was an empty shell as his body propelled itself up the remaining hill. He wasn't just bear crawling. He *was* the bear, ignoring the scrapes accumulating on his arms and legs from the thorny bushes and whipping branches, impervious to the decomposed vegetation and soil giving under his palms and toes as he repeatedly dug in and launched himself upward.

As he burst over the crest of the hill and into the woods at the western edge of The Courts, his clouded mind processed two things, Libby was lying on her back, and Owen was kneeling beside her with something large and silver in his hands.

The object was over Owen's head now. Aaron didn't need to be fully lucid to understand what his brother was about to do. A deafening roar sounded. It was coming from him, and now the world was rushing past in a smear of browns and greens. A moment later, he was sending every bit of his two-hundred-and-thirty pounds into his brother's back.

The collision sent little zig-zagging sparks of light darting through his eyes. The world was somersaulting now. Light becoming dark, dark becoming light, as he rolled with his brother in a snarl of limbs. Only when he emerged on top of Owen could he see the vacuous eyes. Owen wasn't there. Under his grip was a green animal of some kind. And now that animal thrashed its sinewy body. In a flurry of movement, Aaron's arms were pushed apart, and he was twisted to the ground and onto his back, the twilit sky spinning into view.

The creature snarled, reached back, formed an anvil with its fists, and brought them down. An explosion of pain erupted in Aaron's left cheek. Another blow pulverized his nose, sending blood-flavored tears down his throat. Another struck the side of his jaw, seeming to rattle loose all his teeth. More blows rained down, threatening to cave his head in. They found the other side of his face. His eyes. His chin. His neck. The world began to fade. Darkness was inviting him, urging him forward with open arms. The distant recess in his brain that still had some semblance of lucidity was stepping away.

Then, purple circles. They interlocked like chain links. They drifted past him, vanishing into darkness. Or was he the one drifting? Eventually, their speed—or his—increased, accelerating until the individual links began to blur together to form a single, trembling line. He was being ushered into the black expanse, and he knew exactly where he was going, his internal navigation true and confident. It was the place where the first seed germinated before it became the trunk that extended ever outward and upward through billions of years, sprouting branch upon branch as it grew to impossible heights. He knew he would be too small, too simple to comprehend its grandeur, its superposition. But it wanted him to come. His summons was here. It was his time to go; to wrap himself inside its crushing cloak of darkness and let it consume him forever.

But something happened before he could see it. The darkness was flaking away. It was no longer welcoming him. The pain behind his eyes, his nose, and inside his mouth grew. Pain and now rude light were conspiring to strip away this serene darkness, peeling it and casting it off like curled paint chips.

And then a voice, just as rude, peeled back the darkness altogether. "C'mon, dipshit, stay with me."

He had a vague awareness of being jostled. Some force was pushing his body, a body which seemed to exist below him, as if tethered. The force continued pressing against that body's left shoulder. Why couldn't it just leave him alone? Why couldn't it let him go to sleep inside the dark place? Remove all burden?

But the rude force just kept shaking the body below him. Then he was falling closer to that body, which he knew was broken in some way. Something had happened to it, but he couldn't remember what.

"Seriously, Porter, don't you pass out."

The shaking increased. And then a sliver of pale light showed through the slits where his eyes used to be—still were. It was growing larger, and—

"Finally! Now stay awake, asshole. Help is coming."

A vague shape hovered over him. Aaron blinked several times, this abrasive world coming into focus. The shape grew in definition. It was Simon's face, and his eyes and mouth were narrowed in their customary annoyance.

Simon's mouth opened and exhaled a pungent gust smelling vaguely of Pringles and Mountain Dew.

It took Aaron a moment to realize that it was a gasp of relief. He blinked again and watched Simon roll onto his backside and put his forearms on his knees, his chest heaving, his dark hair spilling over his eyes.

"Christ, Porter, you scared the shit out of me."

Then sickness overtook Aaron. It raced from his gut and into his throat. He turned his head and vomited. Only phlegm came out. He spat some more, and the world started to clear. He blinked, finding that his right eye was the only one he could open all the way. His left eye was a shrinking tunnel. Then he noticed the body lying face down a few feet away, just past Simon. A tree branch was in two pieces near the figure's pale green head, and the figure's wrists were tied behind him with a length of black hose. His ankles were similarly bound.

Aaron tried to rise to his elbows and ask what had happened, but nausea overtook him again.

"That walking stick is pretty fucking hard," Simon said. "Busted it over the back of his head. But don't worry, he's still breathing. And, Porter, you look like shit. Lucky I got here before he killed you."

Aaron tried to rise onto his elbows again.

"Better not do that. Just relax. Help's coming."

"Where's Libby?" Aaron croaked more than spoke. The effort of talking nearly making him vomit again.

"She's pretty dazed but was able to get up. We both made sure your bro was out of it and tied up before she went over to that old guy's house to use his phone. You know, the guy who takes care of this dump."

"Mr Ipser?"

"Yeah, I guess. Oh—there they are now." Simon staggered to his feet and winced. He waved at someone Aaron couldn't see, beckoning them over. He then looked down at Aaron and shook his head. "The shit I do for you, Porter. The shit I do."

Chapter 37

Secrets, Scars, and Lost Things

The air was crisp and the stars were faint in their slow scroll across the dawn sky. The wet earth was forgiving under his Skechers as he descended into the mist-filled valley. The gentle switchback was a welcome warmup this morning, as he knew there would be plenty of rugged terrain to navigate ahead that would surely make his swollen face throb and his shoulder ache. He'd need any reprieve he could get. He was alone, which is what he wanted.

As he descended, he watched a pair of turkey vultures dip and bank over the tree canopy, the invisible vectors on which they drifted only known to them and known in their blood for eons. He considered what he now knew in his blood, those unsettling truths he'd carry with him into an unknown future, and probably to his grave. Those secrets he'd decided to keep. Those secrets that had to *remain* secrets.

Five days ago, after being released from the hospital and having been questioned by Detective Monsato of the Portage Falls Police Department, Aaron immediately called Simon and asked him if the detective had stopped by to ask any questions. Simon said he hadn't and proceeded to curse his way through *Fortnite*. Aaron reminded Simon of what to say to the man if he followed up with more questions, but only received a grunt in reply. He'd decided in that moment he wouldn't ask any more of Simon and that it was best to leave him to the little pond that was his basement. There was something else he'd realized during that one-sided phone call. He didn't want *anyone's* help, including Libby's, who'd prove trickier to shake.

The day he'd been released, Libby had called *him* before he had a chance to formulate his thoughts on what he'd say to her.

She'd recounted her and Simon's actions following the incident and asked if the detective had spoken with him. He'd told her that the man had, and that the detective's questions were easy enough to navigate—for now. He knew that didn't mean there wouldn't be more, tougher questions ahead.

With those questions about the detective and other questions about his health out of the way, Libby launched into her own dissertation about what they'd experienced, how it worked, and why they needed to remain silent about it ... forever. According to Libby, if the greater public were to learn of the subterranean complex, it could spell disaster. She theorized that private investors would find a way to buy the land surrounding the cave system—despite it being a national park—and put it to commercial use.

"Think about it, Aaron," she said, "imagine purchasing a ticket to your past, or some other distant past, like you might an airline or amusement park."

Aaron thought the complexities of the place would make this type of scenario unlikely. There was no normalizing it. Nor had Libby actually experienced what it was like. She'd pumped him for answers, and he'd given them to her honestly and with as much accuracy as possible. But what she said next during that conversation gave him pause.

"But more likely, Aaron, the government will find out. In fact, I shouldn't even be talking about *it* over the phone right now. No one should find that substance. Imagine what might happen if someone actually *did* weaponize it. We're not talking global pandemic. We're talking global annihilation."

It was then he decided he needed to shut the way. But he couldn't do anything about that now. Nor had he any idea how he'd even go about it. The people from the past had found ways to block the other portals. In time, he would too. Just not yet.

Then Libby asked him the question—the question he didn't want her to ask. She wanted to search out the answer to that question with him, to make the journey together. And a part of him desperately wanted her to come with him, to walk by his side into the darkness. He imagined holding her hand as they confronted it. But he knew he had to go alone, his resolve on this matter deepening over the course of their conversation. So, he'd made a lame excuse about needing more time to recover both physically and mentally. He knew she wasn't buying any of this. He didn't either and heard the lack of conviction in his own voice. But in the end, it had gotten her off the topic ... for a time. The conversation had moved on to other things: how school would be starting soon, what everyone would think of Owen now that he'd miraculously resurfaced, and what would happen next.

Aaron thought he knew what she meant by *next*. It was another topic that made him squirm, but for another reason, which wasn't altogether unpleasant. What had happened that day in the valley hadn't just rekindled an old friendship, it had ignited something else. He felt it and he thought she did too.

There were many things left unspoken during the remainder of that phone conversation, but that didn't mean they weren't communicated. Before the call ended, they made a tentative plan to go bike riding on three conditions: he would have Shelby again, his face would have *mostly* healed, and they would stick to mundane neighborhood streets—no valley and *no* Towpath. After a brief pause, Libby added another consideration, which made the blood rush to his swollen face.

"I guess I can ride my own bike," she said, "but are you sure you don't want to double up on Shelby again?"

***

The trail began to flatten, but the earth at the bottom of the switchback was made of hardened ruts where countless bicycles had dug deep into the soil during wet times. His head aching with each jarring step, his thoughts returned to the cause of the pain. After the beating he'd received courtesy of his brother, he'd been partially aware of Mr Ipser and Libby telling him to stay on the ground until the ambulance arrived. By then, Mr Ipser had called Gram, and through the slit of one eye, Aaron had watched her run up from the Maplewood cul-de-sac and into The Courts in the only way a grandmother can, a tottering tiptoe, arms pasted at her sides and her palms flattened to the earth, making it look as if she were petting a pair of imaginary dogs. Her brow was furrowed as she crossed the baseball diamond to the outfield. Her hand flew to her chest and her mouth fell open when she saw Aaron. When her eyes found Owen—his skin having faded to its normal color by then—she fell to one knee and began to hyperventilate.

The ground was becoming smoother now where it rose to meet the Towpath. The pain subsiding, he crossed the small land bridge spanning the gully and stepped up and onto the bleached limestone of the Towpath. But he wouldn't go south— not yet. A lost friend needed his help.

He turned north and walked on, his thoughts lingering on Gram's reaction to Owen, who'd been handcuffed by first-responding patrol officers that night, despite the hoses already binding his wrists and ankles. According to Libby, the officers had arrived just minutes after Gram and shortly before the ambulances and had managed to pull their cruisers through the narrow hedge path and into The Courts as far as the field would allow. Anyone in Sand Run Estates who hadn't known something was going on surely knew it by then.

The officers had quickly assessed the scene, and after a brief exchange with Simon and Libby, established Owen as the perpetrator and read him his Miranda rights despite him being a semiconscious minor. Libby would go on to tell Aaron that Gram had become incensed by this development, and for the second time, fell to the ground and hyperventilated. The first of the ambulances had arrived by that time, and Aaron had been fitted with a neck brace, placed onto a stretcher, and taken to Akron Children's Hospital. Libby had used the opportunity to discuss with Simon what they would tell the officers, knowing that difficult questions would follow.

They had agreed not to mention Gil, as doing so would likely lead authorities to discover the hatch in his basement, which might lead them to find the underground tunnel. From there, it would only be a matter of time before they located the portal. As much as they knew Gil would eventually be found dead in his kitchen, and as much as they didn't want to disavow any knowledge of the man, they'd decided it was best to make his death look like a separate incident. After all, there was nothing to place them in his home. There were no witnesses nearby that could've seen them enter and then exit the home before deciding to go back in. They'd taken all their clothing and Libby's bag. And if the police later dusted for finger prints, then they'd deal with that issue when it arose.

Libby had told Aaron it was a good thing she and Simon had discussed a plan because the two officers had immediately separated them after it had been determined Owen was no longer a threat and that the medical teams were prepared to provide aid and transport. Libby had stuck with the plan, and she claimed Simon had too. They'd told the officers about the woman who'd pursued them through the park. They'd described the scene on the Beaver Marsh bridge and the police officer she'd killed, which according to Libby, made the officer questioning her pause and walk away, taking several minutes to gather himself.

The dead officer's name was Randall Tolliver, a twelve-year veteran on the police force. He was leaving behind a wife and a three-year-old daughter. According to the officer, Tolliver's body had been found by a jogger. Libby's voice had trembled when she recounted those details to Aaron, and then tears were in her voice as she'd described the rest.

They'd left out any detail of arrows and warriors as it would have done no good. Who would've believed them? Instead, they'd claimed that the woman must have kidnapped Owen and then brainwashed him. When Tolliver intervened, they ran away, but Owen caught up to them. There were no signs of the woman thereafter, and the officers didn't seem to believe that there was any woman at all. But that would all change with the news of Connor Littlefield's disappearance, which would come later.

He walked on, his excitement building for this upcoming reunion, which wouldn't be as tumultuous as his reunion with his brother—or so he hoped. The extent of his injuries looked worse than Owen's, but in reality, Owen's ailments were worse. No paramedic, no matter how skilled, could have discerned what was afflicting him. Nor could any of it explain the sabotaged Jeep and the physical confrontation that had left two brothers battered and their female companion with a mild concussion. Monsato's questions about the attack, their injuries, and how they'd just so happened to come upon Owen after his being missing for six weeks would come later, as would the media coverage.

Gram had gone to Portage Falls City Hospital for observation and was released the following day. But instead of going home, she'd chosen to spend the next several nights in the waiting room where Owen was staying. When she'd been admitted, her skin had been clammy and she'd been dizzy, but her health was otherwise remarkable according to doctors. Just a mild case of shock, which was understandable after seeing her presumed dead grandson alive again. The attending doctor had told Mr Ipser—who'd checked on Gram and had later relayed the news to Aaron—that it was a miracle Gram hadn't fainted. But Aaron suspected it was because she'd never given up on Owen. She'd always believed.

He walked on. Thirty minutes later, a familiar recess in the foliage appeared to his left: the entrance to the bridle trail. He approached it and turned toward it, but his gaze remained up the Towpath, half expecting to see her again, bearing down on those skates, the glimmering knife in hand. But she wasn't there. No one was, save for a tiny chipmunk, which skittered across the Towpath a few feet from where he stood.

He descended the trail, his fingers absently rising up and under his shirt to where the medallion hung about his chest, feeling its contours, its new energy, which had been growing over the past several days. His energy had returned too, but now his head was aching again with each hard step down the rutted path, his left cheek growing hot where Owen had done the most damage. He knew he was lucky it hadn't been broken or fractured. His nose, on the other hand, *had* been broken and the splint jutting from between his blackened eyes was all too happy to advertise it. His jaw and left eye were still a little swollen, but he was otherwise recovering faster than he'd expected. Still, the thought of being seen in public gave him enough anxiety to leave the house at a quarter past six that morning, early enough to avoid most joggers and bicyclists. So far, only the chittering birds and skittering rodents were accompanying him on this jaunt. They were welcome company.

The clearing and the railroad tracks came into view fifteen minutes later. He stood and glanced about, trying to gauge where he'd been the last time he was here. The dense bushes were just as thorny and unforgiving as he recalled, and when he reached into a small arbor, he winced and yanked his arm back. A white perforation appeared on his forearm. He cursed and searched the ground for a fallen tree branch. The white line was beginning to redden when he finally found a stick suitable for the task. He rubbed at his arm and used the stick to part the bramble where he could, estimating he needed to see about five or so feet into the underbrush to find his quarry. *Nothing.*

He worked his way further down the path, pausing every four or five feet to part the vegetation. Still nothing. Then, about ten feet from the tracks, he noticed a section of undergrowth that had been matted like a flattened head of hair.

He forgot about the now bubbling crease on his arm. An angel was looking back at him. Her lustrous red coat glimmered through the branches as a ray of sunlight cut the mist from the east and kissed her top tube, illuminating her name: Shelby.

He shoved his way through the bushes, thorns be damned. Then he was gripping her handle bars, feeling their familiar contours. He yanked her upright and backed his way through the narrow gap he'd bulldozed. As the branches bent and snapped around his shoulders and back, something else glimmered in the corner of his eye—to his right. It was Simon's bicycle, which didn't so much as get a mention when Aaron last talked to his friend. Knowing Simon would never bother to retrieve it, he made a quick mental note of the surrounding vegetation but figured the path he'd cleared would make this a nonissue, assuming he didn't wait too long to come back for it.

Minutes later, the stubborn forest relinquished its grip on Shelby. He leaned her against a tree at the edge of the trail and examined every inch of her: frame, tires, chain, and gears. He came away mostly satisfied. Her handlebars were misaligned with her vertical head tube, and her back tire was deflated to its rim. Both things could be remedied now.

He braced her front tire between his thighs and gave her handle bars a sharp jerk to the left, shifting them back into alignment. For the tire, his solution lay tucked away inside his left cargo pocket. He pulled out the canister and knelt to Shelby's back tire. When Gram had asked him if there was anything she could do for him while he was resting at home, his only request had been for her to purchase a small can of Fix-A-Flat foam.

Eventually deciding it was best to just let him choose what he wanted, Gram had let him purchase the product on his own, using her account on what she called "The Amazon." It arrived just yesterday morning.

His thoughts drifted back to his conversations with Gram as he filled Shelby's back tire with the sealing foam. Gram hadn't had many questions about where they'd been that day or what had happened to Owen. She only wanted to know two things, where they'd found Owen, and why Aaron and Owen had come to blows, which was what she'd found most troubling of all. As it happened, Aaron didn't need to make up a story. The doctors attending to Owen had done that for him. According to their diagnosis, Owen was suffering from acute post-traumatic stress, which was common for someone who'd survived a near-death experience and had been missing for weeks, cut off from all loved ones, and possibly traumatized by a head injury.

Even after multiple MRI scans had turned up no definitive proof of neurological damage, they'd chalked up Owen's aggressive behavior to a combination of stress, delirium, and short-term memory loss. They concluded it all might have triggered psychosis, which could explain his attacks on Libby and his only brother.

According to therapists, Owen volunteered little to no useful information. He told them he'd traveled to the quiet place, where the quiet ones had taught him how to walk. Anyone who asked Owen about his whereabouts—including Gram—would receive this same reply.

Aaron recalled the previous afternoon, when he'd accompanied Gram on a visit to Owen at the hospital. Owen had been busying himself with a fidget spinner given to him by one of the therapists. When Aaron had entered the room, Owen had paused and cocked his head. And what he'd whispered next sent a chill down Aaron's spine.

"Mine boy who rides Shelby."

He'd then returned his attention to the whirling object pinched between his fingers. The remainder of the visit had been uneventful. The police officer who'd accompanied them to Owen's room caught Gram's eye and tapped his watch after fifteen minutes of them watching Owen stare intensely at his spinner. It was time to go. Despite Gram's initial protests, the cop's presence had been a mandatory precaution given Owen was still considered a danger to himself and others. But, according to his attending doctor, Owen was making progress. Aaron learned from Gram just last night that Owen had mumbled "Thanks" after she'd brought him his favorite meal for dinner: a container of steaming meat lasagna and two slices of garlic bread.

Owen would recover. But not everyone had—or wanted to. As he walked Shelby up the path to the comforting soundtrack of chirping birds, his thoughts drifted to the woman and the Mohawk Man. He thought about the Mohawk Man for a long time. How long had the man been living in the past? What had compelled him to become a vicious killer capable of scalping and mutilating people? Did he possess the presence of mind to know who he was and what he was doing all along? The woman clearly knew what she was doing, and Aaron wondered if Owen knew what he was doing that night at The Courts ... including the horror he would have unleashed had he been given the chance.

These thoughts settled inside him like heavy stones as he straddled Shelby's saddle. Twenty minutes later, he was gliding south down the Towpath.

Chapter 38

Sapere Verdere

He spotted a fallen tree about twenty feet off the path that led up to the caves and wheeled Shelby around it and laid her in a swale on its other side. She'd be safe there. The hike up to Mary Campbell's cave was exhausting, his splinted nose not doing him any favors. When finally he strode into the cave, the objects in his right cargo pocket were beginning to feel heavy. Arriving at the back corner, he grabbed the headlamp that had been strapped around his neck and pulled it up and onto his forehead. He switched it on, found the subtle hand and foot holds, and climbed the sloped wall to the narrow crevasse at the ceiling. A moment later, he was inside the small chamber.

The cold light from the lamp cast an ominous glow inside the confined space, giving it a much different feel this time. He remembered the last time he'd come into this chamber from the outside. Hannah had been with him. He stood there for a long time. Then his face began to grow hot, and it wasn't because of his injuries. The tears came moments later.

He slumped to the floor and leaned against the outer wall. He switched off the lamp. He'd cry for her in the dark, which seemed the only appropriate thing to do. He thought he'd cried for her all he could, but he'd been wrong. If anything, being in this place made it worse. They'd barely known each other, but they'd shared something sacred here. That unspoken knowing.

When the tears dried up, he remained sitting there a while, listening to his thin breaths whistle in and out of his splint. He reached up and flicked the light back on, sending angry shadows racing over the walls and ceiling. His final tasks awaited, and he would need all his strength to complete them. He stood and dusted himself off. His quarry lay inside a small crevasse to his right—at least it had in 2014. Unless its owner had relocated it, he felt certain it would be there. He walked to the jumble of rocks framing the hole. Aiming his light inside, he saw it, tucked further back into the space than it had been in 2014, but there, nonetheless.

The drab, olive-green duffel bag looked maybe half full, its lower half bulging and its upper half blanketing an upturned rock. Leaning into the opening, he angled his body so that his right arm could reach further into the space but in doing so, obscured his view of the bag. He groped in the dark until his fingers found canvas. He had to be careful not to pull the bag from the bottom and risk spilling all its contents into the dark. Walking his fingers up the bag, he found its top lip and was relieved nothing skittered up his arm in the process. He grabbed and gently pulled, the contents shifting as he brought the bag forward. There seemed a mix of large and small objects judging from the sounds within.

He pulled the bag up as far as he could until it caught on the opening. Rotating the bag, he gave it a gentle shake and felt its contents shift again. With another pull, it came free, and its lower half swung forth and banged his shins. He yelped, turned, and hobbled in a circle.

When finally the pain became bearable, he returned to the dusty bag, which looked like it could have been purchased at an Army surplus store. He bent, grabbed the top of the bag, and opened it. He peered inside.

The first thing he noticed was the large pair of scuba flippers. Nestled next to them was a diving mask, a black flashlight, a wadded-up bundle of clothing, and a garment that reminded him of the musketeer-styled hat the Cleveland Cavaliers' mascot wore, with the exception that the sides and back of this hat were pinned up to form three triangles. He studied it closer and decided it looked more like something a soldier might have worn during the American Revolution. There was also a dark object just under the flippers, which was probably what had smacked his shins. He ignored it for the moment, reached down, and grabbed the wad of clothing. As he did, a few items spilled out: two small black cylinders with red letters on them that said "STAGE BLOOD" and a piece of drab yellow paper folded tightly into quarters.

He unfurled the clothing to see if any other surprises would fall out, but none did. Then he found he was holding two pieces of clothing instead of one: a pair of dark woolen trousers and a flowing white shirt or gown that reminded him of the oversized smocks he used to wear in art class. A large red stain was smeared a few inches below its drooping collar, and there was a tear in the fabric at the center of the stain. He set down the clothes and grabbed the piece of paper and unfolded a printed news article. He rotated the paper so it was right side up and read the large title at the top, "Shipwreck in Lake Erie Could be 300 Years Old."

He skimmed the article, which had been published in December of 2012. The majority of the wreckage had been located less than a mile offshore—just west of downtown Cleveland—and could have belonged to any number of vessels. He skimmed the names of the possible ships. One caught his eye, *Le Griffon,* which had been underlined in pencil. It would have stood out without the underline though. The woman's words to the stranger played back in his head. He hadn't understood what those words had meant then, but they were making sense now.

The remainder of the article lamented the poor condition of the wreckage and the lack of public interest and support in salvaging something of historical significance. It was a short article, which left enough space at the bottom of the page for something else, a crude pencil sketch of the boat, presumably the *Le Griffon*. The artist had drawn a double-masted vessel in profile with large sails. Its relatively flat hull was scribbled in with additional details, suggesting a set of stairs, which descended on a short passageway leading to a large room at the boat's rear. The words "THEY'LL BE HERE" were scrawled next to the boat with a hasty arrow pointing to the room. Written just below those words was a date: 1679.

He stared at the sheet of paper for a long time, no longer seeing its contents. His mind was elsewhere, trying to snap disparate pieces of information together into something comprehensible. His thumb found the medallion and grazed its crystal-studded surface. This person had been there with the woman on the boat. She'd thought she'd killed them, and they'd planned an elaborate trick to make it look as if she had. To make her *see* what this person had wanted her to see. *Sapere Verdere.* Then the person came forward in time, somehow found this boat's wreckage, and dove down to it using this equipment. So far, the hypothesis held up, in addition to the artist's use of *they*, instead of *it*, when describing what was in the room.

He remembered the heavy object in the bottom of the bag. Leaving the clothes, the fake blood, and the printout near his feet, he bent and lifted the lip of the bag and pushed aside the flippers and scuba mask. Grabbing the last object, he pulled it out. As expected, it *was* heavy—maybe thirty pounds or so—and he let it clunk to the floor rather than attempt to hold it out in front of him and further aggravate his shoulder. He knelt and let his light play over the object's pockets, fasteners, heavy-duty zippers, and adjustable straps. It was a vest, and in judging by the hard plates inserted into its external pockets, it wasn't intended to protect its wearer from a winter chill, it was intended to protect them from something much worse: bullets. Or, perhaps a flying Bowie knife.

He ran a finger over the nylon-covered chest and paused at a ripped section of fabric. It was tiny, but it was there. He mentally overlaid the bloodied smock on the vest, and it wasn't hard to imagine the two tears aligning. But how this person had taken a knife to the chest, despite having body armor, and managed to coat the area with fake blood and make their death look convincing was another matter altogether. There were many unanswered questions. But if his next task was successful, then maybe he'd get those answers sooner than he expected.

He piled the items back into the duffel and peeked into the opening to get a sense of how to best lay the bag to keep its contents from spilling. He paused. He'd previously thought that the bag had been resting atop an upturned rock but had been wrong. It was instead a gray oxygen tank, speckled with rust.

Minutes later he was descending the rocky path to the tunnel floor. It was drawing near, the smell of rotting flesh growing stronger with each step. He paused and gathered himself for what he knew would be the hardest part of the journey. The corpse had been here for at least five days now, if not longer. As he approached the place where Connor Littlefield's dismembered body was stuffed into a hole, he faced away from the rocks so he wouldn't have to see it. But he *felt* it nonetheless. It was death, and it was all around, surrounding him like tendrils of fog. Those wan fingers reached out from between the crevasses in the rocks and grazed his back, giving rise to gooseflesh on his arms and legs. The temperature seemed to drop as it coiled about him. Then it was in his ears.

Don't turn away, Portly, the nasally voice insisted. *I'm right here. That's right, you fat fuck. Come and see. Come and see what you and your brother have done. It's all your fault, and you're the only one who knows what really happened.*

He knew that the chill and the voice weren't real. But they still felt that way. He hadn't told anyone about what he knew of Connor's fate. Connor was still considered missing by his family and the general public and had last been seen by Carrie Mattingly at the Portage Falls *Rockin' on the River* festival. According to the police report, Carrie had seen him leave with a tall unidentified woman, who was wearing sunglasses and had been previously coasting through the crowd on Rollerblades. A sketch of her had been shown on the evening news just last night, and she was also considered a suspect in the death of Officer Randall Tolliver. There had been no mention of Gil.

Just look at the shitshow you've started, Portly, said the voice. *And now, you're withholding evidence. They still think I'm in the fucking river.*

The news had reported Connor's Audi being found in the Cuyahoga, just a mile upstream from the town's namesake waterfall, where the river was deepest. It was assumed Connor's body was still hidden in the murk of the river and would eventually wash ashore if it hadn't already. In response to this growing concern, authorities had restricted access to various waterfront attractions, and residents were all too happy to comply out of fear of seeing a bloated body wash up near any number of the establishments lining the river where it bisected downtown.

But Aaron wouldn't come forward. He'd known it the moment he'd first laid eyes on these remains.

I'm not doing this for you, you callous bastard, he thought. *I'm doing this for your family and everyone else in the community.*

The voice drifted back. *That's just like you, Portly. Fucking coward. Tuck your tail and walk away.*

He did walk away, the memory of the mines resurfacing as he negotiated a narrow stretch of path. Connor had been aware of the unstable tunnel. Aaron knew that now and suspected he'd always known it. Connor had egged Owen onto the loader, and it was by sheer luck that the tunnel's collapse hadn't killed him.

As he descended, he cleared his throat and addressed the darkness, "You tried to kill my brother, asshole. But you failed. Rot in peace."

The voice grew silent as he made his way down.

***

They were gone. Both the woman's and the man's bodies had been dragged through the opening, which was now a little over half its former size. Subtle drag marks were visible in the thin layer of dust coating the floor. They led to the base of the portal through which the light now showed dimmer than before. He guessed that the shrinking would continue over the next few days, and maybe the portal would vanish altogether, not to open again until the next major storm—if the woman's words were to be believed.

A troubling thought occurred to him then. The woman had died here in 2021. But what about the 2014 version of her that would have been very much alive? Hannah would have likely been declared missing in 2014 instead of being found dead by her mother. He stood rooted in place. Had something changed? What about the woman? What would that version of her be doing now, assuming she was still alive? He should have searched for her online before this little escapade, but that couldn't be helped now because he'd left his phone behind.

But while the woman who'd sought vengeance for her deceased daughter had died, the version of her from 2014 had *still* lost her daughter—albeit not from a drug-overdose suicide. Had that distinction been enough? Would it have given her nowhere to direct her hate? Would she still be living on Bernard Drive given Hannah's death had occurred differently? Had he somehow altered the future, sprouting a new branch of reality, where the woman wouldn't get the motivation to go back in time, seek an object capable of allowing unobstructed time travel, band with warriors from the past, and become a killer? Even if he'd made some changes for the better, had he made other things worse?

Hannah had still died, despite his efforts and the lunatic actions of her mother. Was Hannah meant to die all along? And was Owen meant to live? The accident in the mine could have—maybe should have—killed him, but it hadn't. What were the odds of that, in addition to Owen finding his way out and into an ancient tunnel that ran the length of the Cuyahoga Valley? Was it all just chance? Aaron didn't meditate often on the existential, and could only conclude that the presence inside the portal—which referred to itself as *the Superposition*—had some kind of grand design that only it knew. In a way, it was comforting, because it was far too big for him to understand.

His thoughts returned to his remaining task. It was time. The objects still stood in the corner of the recess. He walked over to them. Kneeling, he gingerly stacked the canisters on top of each other, lifted them to his chest, stood, and walked to the shrunken portal. Stepping higher this time, he entered the world of low gravity and buzzing particles. Hannah's body was gone as he thought it would be. And the outer portal wasn't the only thing to shrink in size. As he walked, he noticed the crystals along the curving wall had shrunken, too, like melting snowballs, including the one marking his final destination. He would return to it in a few minutes if all went as planned.

He continued on, crunching over the remains as he neared the disproportionally large central chamber. He thought about the people who'd once journeyed through this place. They'd known something. They'd known of the power that lay buried beneath their feet, whenever and wherever their feet may have once stood. This place. This intelligence. This *presence*. This seamstress who sewed together disparate worlds, pinching together the fabric of time and passing through it a needle and thread to cinch it all together. Orchestrating shortcuts along that great trunk, that main line that extended ever onward, where all other branches diverged yet eventually converged in time into its main thoroughfare. Never ceasing. Always to be reconciled, whether it took seconds, minutes, hours, years, or eons. Maybe these shortcuts had once been for the good of man, as evidenced by the pottery, the art, and the presumed sharing of culture. But when had it all gone wrong? When had those people of the past decided that enough was enough and that they were better off shutting the way?

The inner portal flanked by the mutilated statues stood before him now, the flames within making the opening look like a sideways eye that was sickened with anger. *It* was in there, alive within that massive crystal structure. He figured he could make his delivery from the other side of the opening and didn't think he'd need to open the canisters to let the fluid out. After seeing what that substance could do, he had no doubt it would find a way to reclaim its belongings — *itself.* He lobbed the first canister into the pool. It barely made a ripple. He repeated with the second, wondering why the woman had thought three containers were needed at all if the fluid could be transferred through screens and initiated by a single contaminated phone. She must have wanted enough on hand to ensure that the world would truly go hurtling into some stone-aged utopia. But now she'd never get the chance. He cast the last one in.

From his right cargo pocket, he pulled out the plastic bag containing the contaminated phone. Libby had told him where he'd find it this morning. Despite being knocked into a daze by Owen the night of the fight, she'd still had the presence of mind to grab the bag and Gil's gun and bury both next to a tree near the edge of the clearing before she'd gone to Mr Ipser's house to call 911. Aaron didn't think he could have liked her any more than he already did but was wrong. His heart sped up as he again thought about their upcoming bike ride.

He wrapped the loose part of the bag around the phone until it was taut, guessing the payload would sink faster this way. He didn't think this phone would provoke the same chaotic response as Hannah's phone since the fluid had already penetrated it, essentially claiming it. But he couldn't be sure. Remaining where he stood, he tossed it in.

He stood waiting for a long time. When finally it seemed nothing would happen, he stepped through the inner portal and made his journey around the pool. It was the same as before, but the light that washed over him wasn't as intense. The force that probed him felt weaker. There was no voice. He completed his journey and stepped out and into the small antechamber.

One last task remained. He retraced his steps, passing the portal that was blockaded by stone monoliths. He passed others, these calloused entryways like mildewed mirrors reflecting the vague intentions of the ghosts who'd sealed them. But that wasn't entirely true. He had a decent working theory as to why those people felt they were better off without this junction which allowed those from other times and perhaps places to come into their midst. It was messy. Those of ill intent wanting to abuse its power, seeking a way to hot-wire the vehicle without ever learning to use its key.

He reached for the medallion and let his fingers graze its surface. It had looked deep inside him the night he'd stared into its central eye, which now felt so long ago. The medallion had gauged his desires, his intentions, his true place along that impossible trunk. But the medallion was really *It* the entire time. He knew that now. Whatever it was, the object that dangled from his neck was a part of it made portable. It had judged him that night and had later given him a vision of what he'd desired most: his brother. That which would have been forbidden him had he not paired with the medallion. Paired with It.

Had the woman, Caroline, not been so blinded by her own rage, maybe she would have found the humility to understand its nature and learned to use it. Well, at least *this* medallion. There was another, stuffed inside a small envelope, and he reached for it now, pulling it from the same pocket he'd used to store the infected phone. The other medallion had been right where he'd left it several weeks ago, inside the section of attic accessible from his tiny dormer bedroom.

When he'd discovered the two objects that June night, he'd immediately taken them upstairs into the attic space—his usual cache for garbage pickings he didn't want Gram to find—and slipped them above a section of exposed ceiling joist. He'd claimed the medallion he wore now for himself but hadn't been sure about what to do with the other medallion, thinking maybe he'd give it to someone close to him—maybe Owen. Certain events had ended that possibility.

Until now. There was someone else who could benefit from it. It was the person who'd come to his rescue outside the portal. The person who'd sabotaged Owen's getaway vehicle. The person who'd somehow been on the Le Griffon hundreds of years ago, narrowly avoided death, and had later dived down to the ship's wreckage. And he now knew that it was the same person he'd seen the night he'd found the medallion; the person who'd been staggering toward The Courts wearing a large overcoat. It hadn't been Mr Ipser, it was this guardian angel, delivering the tools needed to prevent something terrible from happening. Something they knew would happen. Something they'd glimpsed. Something they couldn't have prevented themselves for perhaps they didn't know how. But they'd thought Aaron would know; that he'd find these tools, that he'd *see* them for what they were.

He held the envelope in his hand, still unsure of his guardian's native time and place. When had they found this path? Had it been shortly after their platoon was ambushed? Were they on the same branch of time as his, or had they found another? Whenever and however it had happened, this person had set off the chain of events that had guided Aaron to this very moment. They'd bided their time. They'd laid the path. The envelope shook in his hand as he gazed into the portal where a fresh set of footprints led through the sand and into darkness. This person had come from a world of sand, which many would call the cradle of man. But it was now a place of modern turmoil, a place from which many people didn't return. A place of war. A place of desperation.

He thought of desperation. He thought of the wheezing, the shuffling footfalls. He thought of how much this person must have suffered to get close enough to plant the medallions. How much they'd been suffering when they'd intervened outside the portal. But Aaron wouldn't step into this world now. As much as he thought the medallion might protect him, he didn't want to risk putting this person in jeopardy. This fellow traveler. But he hoped, for not the first time, that he'd have a chance to meet his guardian and ask them how they'd known all along what needed to be done. They'd somehow learned of the power of the medallions. They'd learned they could put things right. They'd *seen* the way forward. And the final piece of the solution now rested in this envelope along with some written instructions.

The portals were getting smaller, and Aaron didn't know how much longer it would be before they closed altogether, and a part of him felt guilty about not being able to make it down here sooner. He'd walked in the past, but the future was a shadowed hallway, a darkened vein off a main tunnel, an overgrown offshoot from a forested path. When another chance would come, he didn't know. He thought of his mother, wherever she may be. Maybe certain relationships could be mended. Maybe damaged people could change. Maybe there was still *time*.

He extended the envelope into the opening and let it fall into the sand. It landed face up, as he hoped it would. He lingered there for a moment, gazing into the darkness beyond, and then began to turn away. But before he did, he spoke aloud the words he'd written on the front of the envelope, "*Sapere Verdere.*"

A short time later, after making passage again, he reopened his time and emerged into the brightness of his world. Where he belonged.

***

Get Free Bonus Materials for *The Towpath* at:
www.thetowpathbook.com

About Jonathan Walter

By day, Jon is a senior User Experience (UX) design professional and leader with more than 20 years of experience in his field. His career has included roles at US-based Fortune 500 companies in insurance and industrial automation. Additionally, Jon has earned 17 patents focused on industrial software applications and has worked for small startups in the commercial security and real estate technology industries.

Jon often spends his "down time" writing on User Experience and related topics. His thought leadership has been on display in *UXmatters*, *UX Collective*, and *The Startup* digital magazines. Jon has been a contributing columnist for *UXmatters* since 2017. As a fiction writer, Jon's short fiction has been featured in GHOSTLIGHT, THE MAGAZINE OF TERROR (SPRING 2019), DARK DOSSIER #32: THE MAGAZINE OF GHOSTS, MONSTERS, AND KILLERS, and THE DEVIL'S DOORBELL: AN ANTHOLOGY OF DARKEST ROMANCE.

Jon resides in the Cleveland, Ohio area in the US with his wife and two sons. He gets by just fine with the help of hoppy beer and strong coffee and enjoys hiking and biking on the Ohio & Erie Canal Towpath Trail in the Cuyahoga Valley National Park where much of *The Towpath* is set.

Connect with Jon at:

www.jondwalter.com

www.twitter.com/jondwalter

A Message from Jon

My dear reader, I sincerely thank you for reading *The Towpath*. I hope that you enjoyed the story as much as I enjoyed writing it. To be candid, I didn't know much about what I was doing when I first set down the path of writing a novel — I'd never done it before, and just knew that I had a story brewing in me and that it wanted to come out. In the early stages, the writing process felt like I was pushing a boulder up hill. There were many false starts, and frankly, many crappy pages and chapters to boot. I had to start over and brutally rework the first few chapters several times before I felt the story was worthy of progressing. But as time went by, something interesting happened: that boulder started rolling more easily — it felt like things were beginning to level out.

Then, at some point, the boulder was rolling downhill. That was when I gave up deciding on what Aaron, Libby, Simon, or even The Redeemer would do and let them make those choices for themselves. They would take the story where it needed to go, and I simply needed to keep up with them and capture it the best I could. I wish I could bottle up that weird mixture of clarity, momentum and willful acquiescence and sell it — I might be independently wealthy if I did! It's a wonderful feeling as a writer, and perhaps you've had the fortune of having a similar experience yourself, whatever your profession or calling may be.

That's how *I* felt as a *writer*. Now, more importantly, I want to know how *you* felt as a *reader* of *The Towpath*. I've often found that the most compelling stories continue in the reader's head and heart long after they've read the last page, closed the book, and set it back upon their bookshelf. I hope that I've given you even just a hint of that experience, or at least sparked enough of your interest to continue this journey with me, down *The*

Towpath, at www.thetowpathbook.com. There, I will be sharing bonus materials and providing deeper dives into the lore and backstory that set *The Towpath* in motion. And who knows, there may be more of this story to come. Was the portal ever shut? Furthermore, if you have a few moments to add a short review on your favorite online bookstore site, I would be very grateful. Reviews are very important feedback for authors, and I truly appreciate each one I receive.

Finally, a note to my fellow Northeast Ohioans, with apologies. Parts of this story required that I make some changes to the geography of the region and take other liberties—including altering location names and embellishing some historical facts and landmarks—that allowed the story to unfold in the way that it did. I'm looking at you, Cuyahoga Falls residents, as your town (where I lived for 15 of the most formative years of my life) was a blatant inspiration for Portage Falls. However, despite these liberties, I hope that I've adequately captured within the pages of this novel the spirit of the community and the beauty and splendor that is our Cuyahoga Valley National Park.

Acknowledgments

First and foremost, I must sincerely thank John Fadden, owner and founder of the Six Nations Iroquois Cultural Center, in Onchiota, New York. John was instrumental in helping me accurately depict the indigenous characters from the distant past, with sensitivity, and with having imparted many lessons along the way. I learned a great deal about the Six Nations of the Iroquois Confederacy: the people, their customs, and even the ways in which they named themselves and others. As a white male, I understand that I'm in no position to depict underrepresented groups without having taken the time to solicit expertise and feedback from people in those groups. Thank you, John, for your time, effort, and willingness to support my work.

A special thanks also goes to Michelle Krueger, for providing me timely, quality copy-editing support. Michelle also has expertise in American history, which was an additional bonus and another reason I chose to partner with her. If you're ever in need of a solid fiction editor, I highly recommend reaching out to Michelle at www.reedsy.com/michelle-krueger.

Finally, *The Towpath* wouldn't have been possible without the following supporters and contributors:

- Brooke De Lira
- Mark Ferguson
- Elliot Jackman
- Jennifer Ortiz
- Rod Raglin
- Scott Rhine
- Dee Walter

- Judd Walter
- Rebecca Walter

Sapere Verdere.

ROUNDFIRE
BOOKS

FICTION

Put simply, we publish great stories. Whether it's literary or
popular, a gentle tale or a pulsating thriller, the connecting theme
in all Roundfire fiction titles is that once you pick them up you
won't want to put them down.
If you have enjoyed this book, why not tell other readers by
posting a review on your preferred book site.

Recent bestsellers from Roundfire are:

The Bookseller's Sonnets
Andi Rosenthal

The Bookseller's Sonnets intertwines three love stories
with a tale of religious identity and mystery spanning
five hundred years and three countries.
Paperback: 978-1-84694-342-3 ebook: 978-184694-626-4

Birds of the Nile
An Egyptian Adventure
N.E. David

Ex-diplomat Michael Blake wanted a quiet birding trip
up the Nile – he wasn't expecting a revolution.
Paperback: 978-1-78279-158-4 ebook: 978-1-78279-157-7

Blood Profit$
The Lithium Conspiracy
J. Victor Tomaszek, James N. Patrick, Sr.

The blood of the many for the profits of the few… *Blood Profit$*
will take you into the cigar-smoke-filled room where American
policy and laws are really made.
Paperback: 978-1-78279-483-7 ebook: 978-1-78279-277-2

The Burden
A Family Saga
N.E. David

Frank will do anything to keep his mother and father
apart. But he's carrying baggage – and it might
just weigh him down …
Paperback: 978-1-78279-936-8 ebook: 978-1-78279-937-5

The Cause
Roderick Vincent
The second American Revolution will be a
fire lit from an internal spark.

Paperback: 978-1-78279-763-0 ebook: 978-1-78279-762-3

Don't Drink and Fly
The Story of Bernice O'Hanlon: Part One
Cathie Devitt
Bernice is a witch living in Glasgow. She loses her way
in her life and wanders off the beaten track looking for the
garden of enlightenment.

Paperback: 978-1-78279-016-7 ebook: 978-1-78279-015-0

Gag
Melissa Unger
One rainy afternoon in a Brooklyn diner, Peter Howland
punctures an egg with his fork. Repulsed, Peter pushes
the plate away and never eats again.

Paperback: 978-1-78279-564-3 ebook: 978-1-78279-563-6

The Master Yeshua
The Undiscovered Gospel of Joseph
Joyce Luck
Jesus is not who you think he is. The year is 75 CE. Joseph
ben Jude is frail and ailing, but he has a prophecy to fulfil ...

Paperback: 978-1-78279-974-0 ebook: 978-1-78279-975-7

On the Far Side, There's a Boy
Paula Coston
Martine Haslett, a thirty-something 1980s woman, plays hard on the fringes of the London drag club scene until one night which prompts her to sign up to a charity. She writes to a young Sri Lankan boy, with consequences far and long.
Paperback: 978-1-78279-574-2 ebook: 978-1-78279-573-5

Tuareg
Alberto Vazquez-Figueroa
With over 5 million copies sold worldwide, *Tuareg* is a classic adventure story from best-selling author Alberto Vazquez-Figueroa, about honour, revenge and a clash of cultures.
Paperback: 978-1-84694-192-4

Readers of ebooks can buy or view any of these bestsellers by clicking on the live link in the title. Most titles are published in paperback and as an ebook. Paperbacks are available in traditional bookshops. Both print and ebook formats are available online.

Find more titles and sign up to our readers' newsletter at www.collectiveinkbooks.com/fiction